Little white rectangles fill the reflection of their irises. They're all plugged in. All of them are unaware of what's going on around them or who is in front of them, collectively yearning for acceptance from their phones.

brazen

Praise for *Girl Crush*:

'Dark, funny and wild'
CHLOE ASHBY, AUTHOR OF *WET PAINT*

'As ballsy as you'd hope'
GRAZIA

'The words just sizzle off the page'
GLAMOUR

'Another triumph for feminism'
RED

'A thrilling, bisexual romcom that doubles
as a smart skewering of social media'
EVENING STANDARD

'... the voice of her generation'
THE TIMES MAGAZINE

'It's Carrie Bradshaw's columns in *Sex and the City* on steroids'
THE TIMES

'It's a kind of rags-to-unexpected-riches-to-devastating-realisation-back-to-older-wiser-rags type tale, almost 18th century in progression, except set in a thoroughly modern, even slightly futuristic world where life online is even more all-consuming than we know it now.'

SUNDAY INDEPENDENT

'A hot debut novel with a dash of relatable existential dread'

COSMOPOLITAN

'*Girl Crush* is a funny, filthy and furious exploration of sexuality, identity and the expectations on us all. It's a rare combination – a page turner with a message.'

DAISY BUCHANAN

'It feels like a ball of energy coming right for you. I loved this debut.'

EMMA GANNON

Previous books by Florence Given:

Women Don't Owe You Pretty (June 2020)

Women Don't Owe You Pretty: The Small Edition (September 2021)

GIRL CRUSH

A HOT, DARK STORY

FLORENCE GIVEN

brazen

June 2023

2

First published in Great Britain in 2022 by Brazen, an imprint of
Octopus Publishing Group Ltd
Carmelite House
50 Victoria Embankment
London EC4Y 0DZ
www.octopusbooks.co.uk

An Hachette UK Company
www.hachette.co.uk

This edition published in 2023

Distributed in the US by Hachette Book Group
1290 Avenue of the Americas
4th and 5th Floors
New York, NY 10104

Distributed in Canada by Canadian Manda Group
664 Annette St.
Toronto, Ontario, Canada M6S 2C8

ISBN 978-1-91424-057-7

A CIP catalogue record for this book is available from the British Library.

Printed and bound in the UK

1 3 5 7 9 10 8 6 4 2

This FSC® label means that materials used for the product have been responsibly sourced

To all the women
who live within us

September 2030

Hi, Wonderland.

It's Eartha on a burner account.

The 'real' Eartha.

I am here to tell you all that I'm not insane. That I'm not a liar. But that I have been abused by the powerful. And that I want to raze Wonderland to the ground.

How am I going to do that? you must be asking yourself. With the only shred of power I have left: the truth.

CHAPTER 1

PREVENTATIVE HAND JOBS

Wonderland followers: 1,303

I have an unshakeable sense that I was meant for something bigger than the life I'm currently inhabiting. What's a girl to do when she wants to have sex, just not with her own boyfriend? Is this normal? Horny, but not for *him*. Craving something more, but not from *him*. I'm convinced that my relationship with Matt is not only draining my zest for life but that it's also majorly contributing to the climate crisis. As an excuse to get away from him and the flat I've found myself taking the bins out when they're barely half full. There are only so many cigarette breaks a girl can take before even the most naïve men start to notice you're avoiding them. My vibrator is always plugged into the wall, recharging and spiking my electricity usage. I guiltily contemplate my water waste as I've also started to take extra-long showers before bed just to avoid having sex with him. If I'm lucky, by the time I get out of the shower he's fast asleep. And if he's still awake when I get out, I tell him I'm too tired. A simple 'no' is far too frightening, especially if he's been drinking, which is almost always.

I've started hiding the bottles of booze we have in the flat. I put them away in a cupboard that I've told him is full of cleaning products. Unsurprisingly, he's never once opened it. If he asks where they went I just say he drank them all. If we don't have sex he'll ignore me the next morning, or storm out without saying goodbye. Sometimes I give him a preventative hand job just to avoid any ugly scenes. I wonder how many other women have given their boyfriends preventative hand jobs to 'keep him happy'?

My grandma used to say those very words with a forced smile on her face as she served us spoonful after spoonful of roast potatoes when I asked where Grandpa was during Sunday dinner. He'd invariably come back later from the pub pissed out of his face, and she'd immediately prepare a plate for him. The words '*Silly me!*' were always on the tip of her tongue, ready to apologise or assume the blame for anything he wasn't happy with. Apologies fell out of that woman's mouth far more frequently than laughter. Women in my family are well trained to act as PR representatives for the men in our lives who've let us down. We lie on behalf of them, we lie about where they are, to ourselves and even to the people we care for the most, to preserve and protect our reputation. To protect *him.*

This afternoon I've cocooned myself in my best friend Rose's flat in an attempt to stay away from my own. It's an ex-council flat turned cosy jungle with plants on every surface, whitewashed floors and a bunch of furniture Rose found on the side of streets and put back together themself. Recently I've felt so separate from myself. I've started to watch myself on auto-pilot, witnessing my body act incongruently to what I think, feel and desire. I'm living instead to please *him* – absorbing any uncomfortable emotions so that he doesn't have to feel them or face the pain of self-reflection. I do all of the emotional work and reasoning for him, like a mother bird regurgitating its food before it gives it to its young. *Matt's not done any chores for a few days?* Well, he is busy and I have a spare half-hour. *He shouted at me when he was drunk?* Well, I guess he was tired and I can be sensitive. I wear this life and my relationship like an ill-fitting sweater you used to love but that's since shrunk in the wash. It no longer fits and is abrasive on my skin, but I can't give it up. It's as if I'm almost attached to this uncomfortable way of life. I fear I'd be allergic to the sensations of something, or someone, new.

Even his touch has begun to feel like a stranger's. When I roll over at night, feeling his hand on my shoulder or his cock pressing against my back, my entire body closes up at his touch, like an anemone. I feel like I'm living a double life: one as an assertive feminist and another as a shell of a woman, playing the role of both mother and girlfriend to a failing DJ with no hygiene routine, who once confidently called himself '*The Tracey Emin of Techno*'. He jerks his head to the beat during his sets at such a horrendous speed I think it might fall off one of these days. I want to blame romantic movies as the reasons I've chosen to stick by this embarrassment of a man – but it's the women in my family who remain my blueprint for how and who to love.

It feels like I'm splitting when I'm with him, as I shrink and hold myself back. It's only with friends like Rose that I feel I really get to be *Eartha*. Maybe these days they're the only person I can be myself with. It's Rose who disrupts me from my thoughts now to ask me if we should keep watching whatever we are watching. I just nod. *Please*, keep it going all bloody night just so I can stay away from the man that I chose to live with. I wonder how much longer I can drown out my reality.

'These girls should all just start shagging each other!' Rose says in their charming Irish chatter, shaking their head and sweeping the few black strands of hair from their eyes as they watch TV from the huge sofa that takes over the tiny sitting room.

'If you want?' I say, realising I haven't been listening to them, but heard enough to register they expect a response.

'What do you mean, *if you want?* Have you not been paying attention?'

They scoff and pause the show with the remote.

'Right, these girls ...' They point with a beer bottle in their tattooed hand at the screen. Their fingers are covered in silver rings, mostly collected from women they've slept with; one simply says *Dad*. A single silver hoop sits in their left ear and a ribbed white tank top cups their perky boobs tenderly. Rose has refused to wear a bra or shave ever since I've known them because they want to 'let nature take its course'. I have to remind them occasionally that deodorant is still important. Everything Rose does has intention, even now as they angrily explain the show to me with a dribble of beer running down their chin …

'They're all competing with each other to win a date with this …' gesticulating at the suited man. 'The most boring, ugly man. It makes me so fucking sad. The girls are so mean to each other to get his attention. It's so primal. They collectively sniff out the one girl who's the threat and slowly wear her down, bit by bit, to reduce her chances.'

It's rare to see Rose, an old soul, get so passionate about something they'd usually describe as 'hideously modern' and 'frighteningly heterosexual'. I'd point out the irony to them but they'll only make some quip about my relationship. I hold it in.

'She's so fake. Who does she think she is? She thinks she all that,'

Rose says, impersonating the girls on the screen. 'What does "all that" even mean, anyway? And then BAM,' they smack their hand onto the crate pallet coffee table, their rings clanging, 'they decide to get rid of her, spread rumours about her, stop inviting her to things. It reminds me of school.' They swirl the bottom of the beer in their hand; a sad expression falls across their face before they swig it again.

Rose and I met in school, when they joined as the new pupil who'd moved from Ireland to England to live with their dad, who 'was living in sin'. I'd always been friends with the girls that laughed at people like Rose. Sitting with these girls in class afforded me the protection I didn't have at home. Until one day, for no good reason, I too became one of their victims. That's when Rose and I decided to pair up. They are one of the toughest people I know. They never even had to come out as gay or non-binary – the way they would recline into chairs with their legs wide open did that for them. They couldn't give a fuck what people thought of them. The girls at our school avoided them like the plague as though being queer was contagious, but they didn't care what anyone thought.

Rose soon became impossible for me to stay away from. Everything about them drew me in. I still kick myself to this day thinking of the years I wasted trying to fit in with anyone else when the real deal was right in front of me. Well, behind me: the queer misfit at the back of class who didn't give two shits about anyone's reaction to their choice to wear the boys' blazer-and-tie combo instead of the cardigan and skirt for uniform. I was, and remain to this very day, mesmerised by them. And I have never told them – or anyone – the other reason for our delayed friendship: I also distanced myself from Rose because I couldn't admit the secret crush I had on them. I'm still unsure of what this meant, I never had long to think about it. I've only ever been with Matt since I was nineteen.

Rose hits the play button and continues their commentary. 'Why are they being so mean to each other? I just don't get it!' they say as two girls on the show whisper in the corner of a party about another girl.

I watch the screen fill with women and my eyes glaze over. I zoom out and look at the cracked glass console the TV is sitting on and the white walls of the room.

'Well, what would happen if the producers actually encouraged the girls to work together? The girls would soon figure everything out, wouldn't they? The whole *point* is that they're taught to compete because women aren't as exploitable when they form bonds together. They'd figure out that male attention is not only worthless, but abundant. The girls would realise that, actually, the man isn't that great, women aren't so terrible, and that yeah, they'd be better off turning each other *on,* than turning on each other,' I reply, surprising myself.

'We're still talking about the show, right?' Rose says, suggestively raising their eyebrows. I redirect the conversation.

'So what then, you really can't see why women compete? You're really saying you've *never* felt in competition with another person?' I ask them.

'If I'm being *honest* ... no.'

They run their fingers through their short dark hair, rest their arm above their head and turn to look at me. I call this Rose's 'pose', it's dangerously hot. It radiates levels of charisma so potent that it has melted the toughest of women into smooth pools of butter.

'I think I'm too gay to compete. I don't see the point in passive-aggressive fights with a girl, when I'd rather just, you know, kiss her.' They shrug their shoulders with the moral authority of someone who has never dated men. I break eye contact and look down at the neck of my beer, caressing my fingers around its edge.

'I think you've not felt in competition with anyone before because you're the one people compete *for*. You're this guy!' I say, reaching over to grab the remote and pause the TV. 'You get to have your pick of the bunch, so you can always just relax. The women come to you because you're ... well, you're Rose!'

They smirk, absorbing the compliment and filing it alongside the thousands they receive a year, then snatch the remote from me to press play.

'Right!' I exclaim as I stand up readying myself to leave, when I'm cut off by a loud thud, followed by a deep, prolonged wailing noise coming from Rose's flatmate's bedroom.

'What's that?'

I turn around, looking over my shoulder suspiciously into the corridor with both of the bedroom doors on.

'Shhh!' Rose says, silencing me with a finger and turning up the TV. The noise becomes louder, deeper and more consistent. Realising that the wailing sounds are bursts of sexual pleasure, I politely sit back down.

'Did Billy bring someone home? I didn't see anyone come in.'

I scrunch up my face. Rose doesn't reply and gives the TV programme they proclaim to hate undivided attention. I turn back to look into the corridor and Rose tilts their head at me, raising their eyebrows.

'Oh,' I say as it finally clicks. 'That reminds me, I need to whack my vibrator on charge when I get home.'

I pat the cream cotton sofa with my hand, looking for my phone to add a memo to my notes.

'How come? What about the penis you keep attached to a body? Is that not doing it for ya?' Rose says with a smirk.

'My "penis" is playing a set later,' I say, taking a sip of the warm, bitter dregs of my beer.

'How is ... everything? I wanted to ask earlier but ... you know,' Rose says in the way a friend does when they know you don't want to talk about something. *Tepidly. Very tepidly.*

'Good. It's good. Everything's a bit different, though, since we moved in together, but we're doing okay,' I say, nodding my head at a speed that must look like I'm trying to convince even myself that my answer is affirmative.

Rose half smiles and returns to watch the TV. I can feel the silence between us, when finally Billy's moaning from the bedroom stops. The bedroom door swings open behind us. Out comes Billy, wrapped inside her duvet with the button-side dragging on the floor behind her, like ancient lesbian royalty. She walks towards us on the sofa.

'Hey, Earthy-wurthy!' She reaches down with the hand she just used to pleasure herself in her bedroom to scruff my hair, leaving it messy over my face.

'Roooose, you got any spare batteries?' Billy says in a whiney voice.

Rose turns around and says, 'No, and I'm watching this show now, so *shhh*!' Then turns to continue watching the TV.

'All right, stroppy,' Billy mutters and then she whispers to me with a wink, 'Eartha, pass us the remote, will ya, love?'

Billy is still clutching her duvet, joining it in the middle with her hands to just about protect her modesty.

'Oh, sure,' I say and reach over Rose's lap to get the remote. Rose swats it away from me.

'She's going to take out the batteries,' Rose says, turning to glare at Billy.

'BILLY!' I say, staring up at her with a look of disapproval.

'A girl's got to finish!' she replies with a casual shrug.

'What? You didn't finish?! Just get one of them rechargeable dildos like Eartha's,' Rose says snarkily.

'Whatever, I'll just go analogue,' Billy mumbles. She turns around, shunning Rose and me with the back of the duvet that's formed over her head like a giant white traffic cone with her tight afro curls popping out at the top as she retreats back into her sweaty lair of pleasure, pouting her lips melodramatically.

'Wait,' Rose says resentfully.

The cone stops shuffling.

'You can have them. But! You MUST bring them back.' Rose removes the batteries from the remote. Billy turns to collect them.

'Yes, I will, don't worry.' She nods obediently.

'And don't think I haven't noticed you've been nicking them out of the clocks.' Rose points to an orange alarm clock turned on its side on the pallet table with its battery seal open.

'I don't know how you two do it,' I say as Billy disappears off, getting her duvet stuck in the door before managing to shut it behind her.

I'm struck by the comfortable and easy interaction I just witnessed between two people I once watched finger the shit out of each other on the edge of a pool table.

'Do what? It's called a compromise, Eartha.' Rose's tone suggests that's something I know nothing about.

'No, living with your ex! You make it seem like an easier living arrangement than what I have with my actual boyfriend.'

'That's because you live with a man, Eartha. A *man*. A fucking man! You have nothing in common with him.'

'I do; we like the same music,' I say, looking down and burying my face from view.

'No, not stuff like that. I mean, how cis men are, it's completely different. Different communication skills, different expectations about what they're supposed to do around the house, different—'

'Okay, I get it! Anyway, speaking of men I should get home.'

'Why? I thought your "penis" was out playing tonight.'

The word penis seems so funny coming from Rose's mouth, probably because one never has.

'Yeah, he is later, but he's been working in his mate's studio all day, so he'll want some food when he gets in.' I stand to leave for the second time, collecting my bags.

'Food for when he gets ... Sorry, since *when* did you have a child?' I shrug and start off down the hall to the front door. 'Have fun with your man baby!' Rose shouts down the hallway after me.

Billy's muffled moaning starts up from her bedroom again. 'Speaking of odd living arrangements, have fun listening to your ex fuck herself!' I reply.

I set off back to my flat to look after my 'penis'.

CHAPTER 2

WONKY WOMEN

Wonderland followers: 1,302

I take a deep breath before turning the key in the lock and slap on a smile as I push the door open.

'Hello,' I say as I enter.

No answer. Relief washes over me. I check the digital clock on the oven: 7.38 p.m. I'm a bit late. He was supposed to be home from work by now too. I throw my tote bag onto one of the two chairs at the kitchen table and walk over to the sink to fix myself a glass of water. I spot a bottle of red wine without a cap on the kitchen surface and hold it up to the light. Another empty. I drop it into the swivel-top bin. *How did he find it?*

Our place is tiny. He moved in a couple of months ago because Mr Dahku put up my rent and Matt suggested it would be cheaper and easier to live together. But all it did was put our existing problems into a pressure cooker. The price for rent has just moved out of my bank balance and into my headspace.

We cohabit a studio flat but the kitchen and bedroom are separated by a flimsy nothing of a wall, so it's technically a one-bed. Which of course is exactly what I tell people so they think

I'm doing exceptionally well for myself. *My boyfriend and I share a balcony one-bed in central Olympia! He's a DJ, I'm an artist!* I leave out our lived reality from this marketing pitch – that Matt is yet to be paid for a set. The fact that our central heating is so dodgy that turning on the oven full blast and opening it up is our most reliable source of heat, or that the 'balcony' is actually the roof of the building below, and we share it with the couple next door who have a routine of arguing, then blasting 'Tainted Love' by Soft Cell as a precursor to aggressive make-up sex.

I walk into the bedroom and turn on my fringed bedside lamp. It's hard to do any feng shui in a tight studio flat but I've still managed to fit in a nightstand on each side of my bed to balance out the shifty energy of cooking in practically the same room that we shag in. Well, used to shag in. Our bed's smothered in Mongolian fur and velvet pinwheel cushions, and the crumbs that keep appearing from my no-boundaries approach to working from home. At the foot of the bed stands a floor-length mirror: it leans against the wall and has a neon-pink flyer I designed for one of Matt's free sets tucked into the side of the frame. I pull out the pink velvet chair from my desk that sits adjacent to the bed and gaze up at my collages, all tacked to the wall with a strip of Sellotape, gently pressed, so as not to aggravate my landlord. Some of the collages are completed, some are half-finished, but they all feature women. I've tried to make little adjustments to the décor since he moved in, but he hasn't complained much. Though he has on occasion 'accidentally' left his laptop screen open on his 'futuristic Berlin interiors' Pinterest board before his bar shift.

My hand starts to draw a line on the page in pencil, connecting the link between the curve of a woman's hip and her thigh on a multimedia piece I started this morning. I look over at the paints, magazine scraps, glitter, fabric swatches and typefaces on my desk. I want this one to become a moving video made up of layers of texture, but first I need to draw this woman before giving her flesh and bones. I hear the clash of keys in the front door and the line I'm drawing swerves. I quickly erase my mistake on the page, brushing away the rubber scraps. The front door slams and I shudder. He's home. Shit. I've completely forgotten to prepare the pasta and sauce I bought on my way back.

'Hey, babe, you're back late,' I shout, leaning my body to project my voice through the doorway.

'Hey,' he says.

This is followed by the dull thud of his bag on the floor. I roll my eyes. Another thing that I will have to put away later. *There's a coat rack for a fucking reason.*

'I'm just in here . . .' I shout from the bedroom.

I begin to reconnect the line between the hip and thigh on the paper in front of me. No response. I hear the sound of cupboards slamming and opening, followed by passive-aggressive grunts and moans at the sight of ingredients that he'll have to prepare for himself. I curl my toes in my shoes. *Don't bite, Eartha,* I tell myself. I refuse to ask, 'What's wrong?' and continue drawing. If he wants to say something, he can come and tell me.

Buzz

Buzz

My phone is vibrating somewhere. I pat my pockets to find it. My face lights up from the glare of the phone.

Text message from Rose to Eartha

20.01

Hey love, I'm sorry for being harsh about Matt earlier.

I know he's a great guy really. I just want what's best for ya, so I'm always gonna be honest with how I feel. Love you.

20.01

Also, two of the girls in *The Bachelor* kissed!!

I smile at my phone and start to type.

Text message from Eartha to Rose

20.02

Hey babe, don't worry about it. Matt's great to me, it's ...

My typing is interrupted by something that flashes past me, landing on the floor by my feet. I glance down to inspect the missile and discover a pair of faded black holey boxers. I hear the screech of the shower knob, followed by the hiss of water that gets louder as its pressure slowly builds. Mine threatens to overtake it as his entire outfit is flung like cannonballs of garments through the door.

Belt.

Clunk.

Jeans.

Thud.

Shoes.

Thud. Thud.

Loose change.

Clatter.

I delete the last sentence to Rose.

Text message from Eartha to Rose

20.02

Hey babe, don't worry about it. I know you'll have my back always. Also, send me a pic of those girls...

20.04

... so I can use it for one of my collages!

I continue with my drawing while he's in the shower and feel happy about where I've got to with it. I hold it out in front of my face and squint, using my eyes as a spirit level to see where it should hang among the sea of collages and pieces of coloured paper, spewed with words and faces on them. This one deserves to be front and centre. Just as I'm about to press it on to the wall, a large wet hand reaches out and snatches it from me. I turn to face it.

'Excuse me?' I say sarcastically.

He leans into the door frame, which his head almost touches, with a white towel wrapped around his hips, his hair jet black and wet from the shower. He tousles it with his free hand, revealing his little dangly cross earring. He looks down at the drawing. I wait for his feedback.

'She's a bit wonky, isn't she?' he says, passing it back to me without looking at my face.

The drawing is crumpled and wet from his hands. It has large wet fingerprints imprinted on its side. I shake my head at his entitlement and wonder if it would be more effective to articulate my anger into my next collage.

'Well, she's supposed to look that way, because that's how I drew her. Women deserve to be viewed through a wonky non-sexual lens!' I say a bit too defensively.

Don't let him know he's got to you, Eartha.

'Looks pretty sexual to me,' he retorts.

I want to remind him that boobs aren't sexual. That there are actual life-giving uses for them other than tit wanks. But I swallow my real thoughts back down.

'How was work?' I ask, as he opens the wardrobe with his back to me. I cringe at the irony of the yin and yang symbol etched permanently into the shoulder of a man who's never shown balance in his life – but once wrote a terrible poem about it.

'It was good … What have you been up to?' he replies dispassionately.

'Posted a few birthday collage commissions, then just got back from hanging out at Rose's.'

'Cool, cool …' he says, nodding his head. 'So, uh … no dinner?'

'I just got back myself, not even five minutes before you did.'

I fold my arms.

'But I've been working all day.'

'So have I,' I say, death staring the wall.

'Riiiiight.' He turns around to look at the wall above my desk. 'You've been doing your little collages or whatever.' He rolls his eyes.

He turns back round to continue inspecting the contents of the wardrobe we share. We've split it into two sections on one rack. My clothes on the left, his on the right.

'Right … and I suppose you've been doing your silly little mixes, *or whatever*,' I say as I hoist myself up to sit on top of the desk with my legs dangling off.

He ignores me but pushes the clothes slightly harder back on the rack. I can't stand the blatant resentment brewing between the two of us so I walk over to stand behind him.

'At least I actually have an audience,' I joke, trying to employ some playful sarcasm to break the tension.

I place my hands on his hips and kiss his back with a small peck. He turns around to face me and grabs my head, kissing the top of it.

'Well, I actually have a set to get ready for tonight, so you're not the only one,' he says.

'It was a joke. Where is it again?' I ask as I sit at the end of my bed, watching his hand flick the garments to the right and his fingers creeping closer to my side of the wardrobe.

'Sam got this one sorted for me just from chatting up one of the bartenders. Think she wants to fuck him, so she got me a set at her pub in South Olympia to impress him.'

'Oh, are they dating?'

He shakes his head and chuckles.

'Nah, Sam's just gonna keep letting her think they will.'

'Well, don't you think that's a bit fucking awful?' I laugh, in disbelief.

'Not really, no.'

He relaxes his shoulders and lets out a big exhale, turning around to crouch down to my height.

'Look, babes, I know it's a man's world and all that, yeah. Come on, I'm a feminist! But like, she's a barmaid and she makes more money than I do, so technically ...who *really* has more power here?'

An interesting thought from the man who thinks it's 'odd' that my mum wants to get a better-paid job rather taking stipends from my dad. He gives me his smouldering eyes and then raises an eyebrow. In this moment I am sure that I have never been so repulsed by anyone as I am by him.

'Matt, you're both in hospitality. You probably make the same money as her; that has nothing to do with the power dynamic. Shut up.'

'You wouldn't get it. You're not in the music industry, you have to do these things every now and then ...' he says through strained vocal chords as he stands up, stretches his arms up to the ceiling and returns to the wardrobe.

I mock him behind his back, mouthing the words 'you're not in the music industry' over and over while I screw up my face like a piece of paper. He's flicking through my clothes now. I watch each top and dress get disregarded until he lands on something he wants. He pulls one of my T-shirts from its hanger.

'Woah, can I borrow this?' He yells this, even though I'm sitting right behind him. He positions himself in front of our mirror at the end of the bed and yanks it over him. The rest of his tattoos peek out of the caps of the black sleeves.

'Wait, which one is it? I can't see.'

'This Fleetwood Mac one,' he says, turning his head from side to side, as he checks himself out in it from every angle. He turns his body around to face me and I see the T-shirt.

'Ugh, that one's my favourite!' I sigh and wrinkle my nose.

I screen-printed this T-shirt in college for an art project. I made up the venue: *Fleetwood Mac, live at The Titty Twister.* It's one of my favourites because it reminds me of Mum. She always imitated Stevie Nicks when I was growing up. In the mirror, singing in the car, cooking dinner and floating around in a shawl when she had guests over for dinner. She's always prided herself on being the perfect host. Parties were the only time when Dad let her shine. He was often wiped out with his ME and would then turn to the bottle even more, causing a downwards spiral. Mum loves to get out the fancy glassware that she saved up for months to buy, the fringed shawls passed on to her from Grandma to cover the table tops and a patchouli-scented candle lit in every corner. *None of that cheap vanilla-scented crap you like, it smells sickly!* she'd yell. My mum, like me, lives to please. If everyone else is happy, she can be too. She can't rest if there is something that feels a fraction 'off' about the energy in the room. I'd be mad at her for it, growing up, but after getting older and consuming my fair share of psychology, I realised she probably learned to be aware of everything around her because she had to be. Grandpa was a drunk. She would go on to marry, divorce and (semi) reconcile with one, too.

Matt brushes the loose strands of hair behind my ears. He thinks he's being romantic. I shake my face to remove his hand.

'Pleeease let me borrow it. I promise I'll bring it back in one piece.'

I look at his stupid little dangly earring waggling around while he talks, as though just like me it aches to be free of him, hanging on reluctantly by a thread.

'Fine. But that T-shirt is one of a kind. Be careful with it.'

He leans further into my body and smiles.

'I promise,' he says as he kisses me on the top of my head and I close my eyes.

Hopefully this generosity will bank me some points ... though I'm not entirely sure what I can expect from a man with holes in his boxers, sixty quid into his overdraft and one weekly pub gig contingent on the romantic manipulation of a bartender.

I walk over to sit back at my desk while he stands in front of the wardrobe choosing his trousers and I begin to upload my latest collage on to Wonderland. I take a picture of it with the wet fingerprints indented into the side and type in the caption Matt inspired:

> The fingerprints are a metaphor for men whose CaReLeSs WoRds leave marks on women and their art, ruining their self-perception forever. *Why must men leave their mark on everything?*

I play around with the image and hashtags, pretty sure that he won't bother to check my Wonderland page. There's already a comment from one of my followers.

@*VeronicaEscher* so cool! ☺

I started my profile on Wonderland around a year ago and used it as a portfolio to share the collages that stores told me were too 'feminist' to put on their shelves. It's seen some engagement – I have 1,300-odd followers and if I imagine all of those people in a room it's quite frightening. I'm not as plugged in as everyone else, though. Rose uses it to flirt with girls and save vegan recipes, hoping to open their own café one day; Matt uses it to promote his mixes on Noisecloud and upload squinted-eye selfies of him and his dangly earring; Mum uses it to escape her real life and pretend that she and Dad are happy and well despite the divorce, uploading pictures of her smiling next to him, sat in a chair, drunk and miserable. I don't know how the big influencers on Wonderland do it, talking to all their followers and sharing their information with billions of people. I don't really use Wonderland for that. I have one selfie on there, you know, to humanise it a bit. But no pictures of Matt. I don't think my boyfriend would be good for my feminist 'brand'.

'Ooo OOoooo, girl power!' Matt shouts condescendingly, forming his hand into a fist and pumping it up and down as he looks over my shoulder at my phone. I decide to go and sit on the loo until he leaves. As I walk past the bed, he gives me a pat on the bum. My arsehole clenches.

'See you later.'

I turn to look accusingly at him – he does look very handsome. He might be the worst man I've ever met, but he's the first I've ever loved. We met when I was hanging out in the town centre after college on a summer evening, downing an enormous bottle of corner-shop cider with Rose. He was wearing a Portishead T-shirt, so obviously, he was *the one* and I kissed him immediately. We've been together six years. That's got to count for something. There must be *something* keeping me here, right?

'What time will you be home tonight?' I ask.

'Around midnight, I reckon.'

'Okay, love you!' I say, out of habit. Not intention.

'Love you too!' he replies as he shuts the door, and I reach for my phone to text Rose.

Text message from Eartha to Rose

21.53

My penis has finally left.

21.53

Did Billy return the batteries for hers, in the end?

Text message from Rose to Eartha

21.55

Nope. The girl's been playing a game of operation with every device she can find.

21.55

(image of Billy scaling the kitchen counter to remove the batteries from the smoke alarm)

21.56

If I die in a fire, you know who to blame ...

I laugh into my phone remembering Billy's little waddle to her bedroom in her duvet.

Ping

Someone has messaged me on Wonderland. My face lights up and my heartbeat quickens.

@sallylovesthesea Hi Eartha, just got the birthday card

for my friend in the post today. OB-SESSED! She's going to love the dolphin coming out of the vagina! (Thanks for not asking any questions, it's an inside joke ...) I'll ask her to tag you if she posts! Your shit deserves to be seen by EVERYONE.

I reply with lots of lip motifs, thank her and plug my phone in to charge on top of the bedside table. I notice my nails are looking a little chipped and reach into the drawer of my nightstand, rustling my fingers through an assortment of hairbands, outdated vibrators and nail varnish to find a shade I like. I pull out two small bottles. *Liquorice Black* and *Bubblegum Pink*. I can't decide which I prefer. I flex my hand in front of my face, envisioning each colour on the tips of my fingers.

Why should I have to compromise when I like both? I decide to paint each hand a different colour.

CHAPTER 3

PHAEDRA

Wonderland followers: 1,298

My mind is exhausted by my body and my body by my mind. They want to lie between these sheets for the rest of their days. I can't find it in me to move, knowing that he didn't come home last night. Should being awake be this hard? Would iron supplements help? Or perhaps I should start eating actual oranges instead of the effervescent tablets I dissolve once a week after a hangover.

I turn to look at the perfectly plumped not-slept-on pillow beside me and something in me aches. Where is he? I catch a glimpse of myself, slumped over in the mirror at the edge of the bed. When does this become my fault? When do I have to start taking responsibility for the part I have played in allowing this man to break me down? I chose this man. What does that say about me? I check my phone: it's empty.

Text message from Eartha to Matt

23.29

Hey, shall I wait up for you?

00.02

Just checking you're okay?

02.07

Matt, are you alive?

I roll over to bury my face into his pillow, my mind filling itself with all kinds of worst-case scenarios about where he is and why he hasn't replied. Maybe he shagged the bartender he was talking about, maybe he ended up at an orgy and some groupies came by to suck him off. Or maybe I'm giving him too much credit. He probably did one too many lines and ended up back at Sam's after the set. Sam lives in South Olympia and the set was in South. That sounds about right. 'That's probably what happened,' I find myself saying aloud.

With this explanation installed in my mind I muster enough energy to complete the two-stride stretch from my bedroom to the kitchen to fix myself a drinkable dose of vitamin C. I'm exhausted from being the live-in maid. None of this aligns with calling myself a 'feminist'. *What's that quote?* I scramble around my mind as I punch out a powdery tablet into the glass of water. *That one about modern feminism being a trick where women are now expected to bring home the bacon as well as cook it?* I am so tired of spinning all the plates and lying to people about it. What would the 'truth' sound like anyway?

Hi guys, so nice of you to ask about Matt and me, yeah I now share a literal pigeon hole with a broke man-child that I cook for and clean up after. But it's okay! I love him! I promise I am dead happy, in control of my life and a really good feminist! Would you like an orange?

There's a lot that I feel is missing from my life. Something's not clicking. It's as though I've fallen out of step with my own existence. Where did my fire go?

Waiting for the tablet to dissolve, I turn to face my stretch of land on this earth. I squint and measure the distance between the bed and the kitchen counter with my eyes. If I really wanted to, with lots of practice, I reckon I'd be able to brush my teeth and spit into the sink from the comfort of my own bed. I reach for my phone. Still no word from him. I check his Wonderland and it's unusually silent. No interactions. No one has plugged him into any posts either. He is nowhere to be seen ...

In among the dirty sheets of my disappointment I find a sense of relief because, as of today, I no longer have to feel guilty for questioning whether this relationship is what I want for myself. Today, I have an actual reason to be angry at him. It's nice to have something or someone to point to and blame. Your boyfriend, the government, whichever moon is orbiting Pluto. It absolves you of the responsibility for your own life. It's not me, it's very much *him*.

I decide I need to get my head down to distract myself from Matt's radio silence. This feels so tragic. Waiting for a text back from my boyfriend, who I don't even like as a *person*. I need to wipe him from my mind for a few hours. So I start work on a commission for a new vegan, ethical deodorant company that I was put it touch with through Billy. The couple who launched it want entirely different social media graphics and, rather than just saying upfront they would need two very different videos to meet both their briefs, I have been trying to find some sort of common ground in their double visions, just like the child of divorced parents that I am. The woman wants something sensuous and botanical, whereas the guy wants something postmodernist and playful. They both nodded as the other was describing their 'shared' vision and then countered it with their own diametrically opposed vision. I guess that's one way of resolving conflict: mutual denial.

My desk sits by my bed but the sunlight hits the wall that I tape all my picture boards to so they become a little faded as a result. It's beginning to look like a collage of those menus you see in the window of a kebab shop, all sun-bleached doner and falafel.

I've been going steady for a few hours, immersing myself in the world of orchids and their female counterparts, figuring this is both sensuous and postmodernist, when I see my phone screen light up and my attention snaps.

Caller ID: Mum

Still no Matt.

I pick up despondently. 'Hi, Mum.'

'Hi, love, all good with you? How's Matt?' she says, already sensing something in my tone.

I do a quick cost–benefit analysis in my mind about whether or not to tell her how I actually feel. That he didn't come home last night. That he's the biggest let-down of a boyfriend. That I have no idea where he is and I don't know if I am still in love with him after the years of shit he's put me through. But I don't want to get into it. And besides, knowing Mum, if I give her a scrap she'll ask for the whole therapy session.

'He's good! He played his first set at that pub—'

Before I finish she butts in.

'Oooo yes, I saw on Sam's Wonderland last night! I was plugged in for the whole set. Looked like a great gig. The venue's a bit dodgy looking, though?'

I don't know what she's talking about. I didn't plug into Sam's Wonderland last night and I've not even seen this video of my own boyfriend: why didn't I think to look at his page when I knew Matt was out with him? Or has Sam hidden it from me? I resist the urge to hang up the call and check for updates.

'Matt says the owner of the venue's picked him up a few regular slots, though; I think he's gonna work really well with them.'

I make this all up on the spot. *I am pathetic.*

'Did I see that he was wearing one of your T-shirt designs, love? That's so supportive of him. Honestly, you two make me so jealous!'

I laugh it off.

'I love how he is always sharing interesting female-focused articles, not like men my age – I can't get your dad to bloody read anything I send him…' she continues. I don't tell her that these are the very same articles that I force him to read after he's called me a bitch for asking him to put the toilet seat down.

Something sticky hangs between us at the mention of her underdeveloped love life, which centres on never leaving my father. We code switch to my asking about her job applications for local shops down where she lives and then we reach a dead end of things to talk about that don't step too close to our mutual source of discomfort: her ex-husband, my dad. Before she goes, she asks me to send Matt her love. I promise I will through gritted teeth and go back to work.

Just as the sun hides herself behind a cloud and the room darkens, I flick my glance at the top right-hand side of my laptop screen: 13.14. The vegan deodorant brand has already sent three emails this morning asking me to tweak this collage for their social media graphic. I decide to send them exactly the same PDF I tweaked the third time and pretend I've made the changes they asked.

> We both love it, but think we need to sit with it today. Can we let you know EOD tomorrow?

I shut my laptop and pull out a tote from under my desk. Earlier today I sent a Matt SOS message to Rose, who asked me to come down and join them on their lunch break in the café-cum-workspace where they have worked their way up the chain. A recent review in a local newspaper even cited them as 'Rosey', praising them as the soul of the place. I make a mental note to tease Rose about this more.

I walk up the steps from the canal and, as I approach the café, I see a couple of tech dudes shuffling over to the table where I usually sit outside. They're about to place their laptops down when, out of nowhere, Rose runs out of the café, pulls the towel from an apron pocket and whips it down onto the table before they can stake their claim.

The sun's in their face and they place their hand against their forehead to shield it from their eyes, turning to look out for me. As I watch them, I realise in that moment that I will never tire of Rose. How to describe this love? Somewhere between romantic and platonic, affectionate, all-consuming, impenetrable bond that unites us and secures us both. I run over to them grinning and they scoop me up, lifting me into the air in a tight hug.

'Babe, what's going on? This one's on me, what you havin'?' Rose asks with their arm around me.

'Same as always,' I reply. Rose streaks off into the café – moving faster than any other human on the planet.

I sit down and look out onto the view of colourful bookshops, cafés and independent businesses that run parallel to this street. I turn to see if Rose wants a hand inside, but they've passed my order to a new girl working the coffee machine and now stand in front of the bar, brushing their fingers through their hair to slick it back and resting their arm above their head. Rose is so lean and fluid. Seduction comes as effortlessly to them as breathing. They put their foot up on the back of a chair seat … Oh no, they're doing *the pose*. Someone's going to have an aneurysm.

They walk back outside with a foldable chair under their arm and a baccy pouch in their hand to join me in the sun. 'You always balance out the freak show when you're here, I love not being the only one people stare at!' Rose mumbles, an unlit rollie waggling between their lips.

'Rose, stop throwing a pity party, you're not a freak show. People stare at you because they think they've just seen Leonardo DiCaprio in his heartthrob era. Plus, you constantly eye-fuck everyone you meet,' I groan.

Rose lights the rollie and takes a toke, leaning their head back against the café's sun-soaked window. They side-eye me and go to put their arm around my shoulder, but halfway through get distracted by a couple of girls walking past, checking them out. Both the girls turn their heads back to look at Rose.

'Okay … yeah, maybe that is why,' they say, messily blowing out smoke and laughing. 'Anyway, enough about me and my flirting, thank you very much. What's the *penis* done now? How was last night? I see you're an expert at deflecting questions today …?'

'He didn't come home last night,' I say matter-of-factly.

'Shit. I'm sorry,' Rose says, pulling themself back.

'Don't look at me like that. Don't you dare say, "I told you so." Don't you dare.' I point my finger in their face.

'When have I ever? You know I've just always had an overall distrust of men, and it's yet to be proven wrong. It's not *my* fault that I'm a wise old soul!' Rose protests to dispel the tension.

I feel like everyone's looking at me: that bloke over there

walking his huge dog, the woman unlocking her fold-up bike, the man wiping the windows of his bookstore with a J-cloth. Even the guy's dog is locking eyes with me. I feel as though the whole street knows that I'm hurting. That I'm a wannabe feminist with a shit boyfriend who can't admit that she lets him walk all over her.

'Well, I'm sure he'll text you when he can. Maybe he lost his phone!' Rose making excuses for a *man*? This is tragic. They must really feel sorry for me.

'You don't have to bullshit me. Come on. *Lost his phone?*' I say the last part with air quotes.

I pull out my phone and quickly plug into Wonderland. The pub's been posting their night all over again and Matt commented on the post one hour ago with a fire extinguisher emoji. For fuck's sake. He hasn't lost his phone. I shake my head and lock my phone to look away from Rose's concerned stares.

As a tray and our drinks crash onto our metal-topped table, I see a flash of fuchsia ahead on the street, and my gaze falls onto a girl with pink hair. She stops at the doorway of the chemist, a stone's throw away from our table. I've always thought that people with coloured hair were begging for attention, like a walking human highlighter demanding to be seen more prominently than the rest. But there is something magnetic about this girl. She's wearing an oversized T-shirt with knee-high socks and tall, chunky pink platforms made from patent leather. Her look is quite the statement for a trip to the chemist; in fact, they look like last night's shoes. Maybe they are? *Good for her.* I don't think I've ever seen such a—

'Eartha!' Rose hollers.

I'm wrenched out of the little narrative I was creating in my head. Rose looks at the chemist to see what's distracting me and smirks.

'What?' I snap defensively.

'She's fit, isn't she?' Rose retorts.

'I like her hair,' I reply, looking down at my lap.

Rose shrugs and pushes my iced latte on its coaster towards me.

'Maisie brought this out for ya but you missed her, you were looking at that other girl.'

We sit drinking in our coffee and the scene, until my attention falls back onto the girl with pink hair – she's leaving the chemist now, adjusting her headphones, swaying her head to the music, like the world belongs to her. She turns and faces us as she walks away with a paper bag in one hand, clicking her fingers to the music with the other.

Wait ... Is that ...?

Is she wearing—

It can't be?

Nofuckingway.

How on the bloody earth ...?

'Eartha, what's wrong?' Rose places a hand on my shoulder.

'That girl is wearing the T-shirt I made; Matt was wearing it last night,' I reply.

I gave it to Matt last night ...

And it's the only one in existence.

'FUUUUCK!' I yell.

Rose reaches a hand over to my thigh now and tightens their grip to comfort me.

Fuck this.

I'm not having this.

I swat their hand off me. It can't be. Someone must have

printed the T-shirt, or stolen the design. I leap out of my chair. My body's overpowered by a confusing cocktail of intrigue, desire and rage about the hateful nature of this …vivacious … woman. God! I run over to confront her. I can see she's about to cross the road and I start to chase after her.

'EXCUSE ME!' I shout.

She turns around and looks at me with eyes full of fear. She has olive skin and her eyes are a deep reddish brown. She still has on last night's liner that's now smudged around them. How does she wear a hangover so well? She removes her headphones and pauses the music on her phone.

'Hi, I didn't mean to startle you. My friend and I were just admiring your, umm … T-shirt. Where did you get it?' I say, playing for time.

'Oh, uhh …' she says looking me up and down, assessing the crazy woman who has just run across the street to talk to her.

'It's actually not mine. It belongs to some guy I shagged last night.' She laughs. 'I didn't get his number after I left his mate's house. It was one of those nights … He said I could keep it, though. It's cool, isn't it?'

I note the post-sex, inside-out glow radiating from her pearlescent pores.

'Did he—' my words catch in my mouth. I can't get them out.

'By any chance … did he have a little dangly earring?' I manage to finish, squinting my eyes from the sun.

'Let me think …' she says as she looks into the distance, trying to picture what I am starting to believe is my boyfriend. 'I think so! A little cross or something? Or maybe it was a sparrow? I dunno. He was the DJ! I went to his gig with my friends. Do you know him?' she replies curiously.

Eartha.

Do not cry right now.

Do not fucking cry.

'Yeah, I do know him, the-guy-you-fucked-is-my-boyfriend-and-that's-my-T-shirt,' I say, not pausing to breathe in case I crack.

A look of terror washes over her face. Her lips part and then close again. She looks ashen.

'I'm … I'm so shocked … I didn't know he had a girlfriend. I'm so sorry,' she says quietly.

A relief.

'If you didn't know, then it's not your fault. We've been together for six years so it's not something he can exactly forget to mention. *I'm* sorry that you had sex with a lying, cheating prick.'

'I'm sorry that your *boyfriend* is a lying, cheating prick!'

Even when she swears her words are lyrical, like the sound of little birds waking up outside your window. The girl's a real-life siren. Maybe that's how she lured Matt out of monogamy? Who am I kidding? *He's obviously done this before.* I wonder then why I don't feel hurt. This should be crushing me from the inside out. I should be bent over, hands on my knees howling and crying at the sky. *Right?* But maybe every time he has let me down over the last six years has slowly been leading me up to this moment, preparing me for the ultimate betrayal. Being cheated on with a girl so mesmerising that even I was distracted by her beauty. I don't feel sick at all. In fact, the anxiety I felt about him not coming home has washed itself away. Because now I know where he was last night. I feel *free*. I look at the bag clutched in her hands from the chemist. I realise it's probably a morning-after pill.

'Is that …?' I point to the bag.

She hides it out of shame.

'Just to be safe.'

'He can't even cheat on me respectfully! What if he gave me something?'

'Oh, he used a condom! But ... I don't trust these guys. Some yank them off before they cum and don't tell you.'

A look of panic crosses her face as she realises she's talking about my boyfriend.

'I'm so embarrassed. I should've known there was something off about him. He was telling me he makes art about how women have the right to be "viewed through a non-sexual lens".'

'ARGHHHHFFFFFUCCCCCKKKAAAA.'

I place my hand over my mouth, shocked at the sound that came out. He's pretended to be me ... to get laid?

She continues, 'At first, I thought it seemed believable. Most art-bros say that shit nowadays. But I should've realised he was making it all up when he said he hosts some therapy club for guys who want to be better men and discuss women's issues "without making women uncomfortable" ...'

Matt's been using feminist clickbait to get laid?

'Imagine! A man doing something selfless ... with a bunch of *other* men?' I say.

We stare into the distance, imagining what Matt's feminist circle would look like.

I begin to laugh weakly at first and then violently, all the tension from the last twenty-four hours flooding out of my body. Envisioning my boyfriend crying in a room full of men, whining about how they need to 'stop sexism' while they toss each other off about what good feminists they are. Maybe the sadness will visit me later or maybe this is what I've wanted all along. Did I manifest this into existence somehow? I wonder how many other poor women he's fed his feminist-porn lines to.

'I should have listened to my gut,' she says, pulling me out of my hysteria. 'Honestly, it sounds laughable saying it out loud now. But I was drunk and horny and the girl I had my eye on had her eyes on someone else, so ...'

The people and the scene around her slow down. There's suddenly a shift in the air between us, any shred of anger I felt towards her now burnt to ash and alchemised into desire. *She likes girls.*

'There might be a way we can fuck him over,' I say.

'Oh ... I don't wanna hurt anyone or anything like that,' she says, shaking her head.

'No, of course not. But I have a plan,' I say, pointing at the T-shirt I'm wearing.

'I designed this T-shirt, too,' I say, pinching the tee into tents to showcase the wording 'Venus in Furs' in red lettering, with a two-tone screen-printed image of a stripper heel and a whip.

'Wanna swap?' I ask.

'Sure! But why?' she says, wrinkling her brow, trying to figure out what it is I'm suggesting. It finally clicks. 'OHHHH. That's kind of brilliant.'

The sadistic glee of *schadenfreude* seeps into the marrow of my bones as I imagine the look on Matt's face when I get home later. She starts taking off her shirt. As she lifts it above her head, I look around to see if anyone's watching. I can see her nipples peeking through the red mesh bra she's wearing. They're pierced. They're perfect. They're unforgettable. As her shirt comes further over her head, I quickly remove mine so it doesn't look like I'm staring at her tits. I cup my tits with my hands while I wait for her.

She finally lifts the shirt off her body and her mouth opens. She's surprised to see that I'm not wearing a bra.

'Your tits are out!' she exclaims, looking around self-consciously.

'I never wear bras; in fact I don't own any, well, sometimes, unless it's a—'

'Noooo, come back here! Those men are staring at you,' she says, pointing at the tech dudes who have taken up residence with their laptops in a shady greasy spoon.

She grips the small of my waist and yanks me out of sight, protecting me from becoming a nude public spectacle. We're in the alleyway next to the chemist.

'Oh, shit, there's someone about to walk in.'

She says and pulls me further out of view by my waist until we find ourselves leaning against the staff exit of the building with her back against the wall. Our chests are still exposed in the sun-dappled alley, T-shirts scrunched in our hands, just us. Her hand is still on my body and we're both looking out to see if anyone's coming and if the techies have stopped with their slack-jaw gaze. I laugh and turn my head to look at her. We lock eyes. Our faces are inches away from one another and she starts laughing. Face to face with the woman I should hate above all others, I discover instead that the sound of her laughter ripples over my body. I can see now that she has a few freckles emerging out of last night's foundation. I want to know how many freckles she has on her face. I want to know her hair colour beneath the pink. I want to know who her friends are, what songs have saved her life, what makes her life worth waking up for every morning, I want to spend hours cooking her dinner. I want to buy books about things she's interested in so we can talk about them. I want to be close to her and talk for hours about our lives until we drift off to sleep. I want to touch her fingertips. I want to feel the warmth of her breath. I want to breathe in her breath.

She paralyses me.

And it's then that I remind myself: she has just shagged my boyfriend. No matter how delightful the warmth of her breath, *there's bits of him in her mouth.* I break eye contact.

'Let's change these shirts, then,' I say swiftly.

Have I just ruined a very beautiful moment? Did I want to kiss her or was it all adrenalin? Maybe this is just a way of me getting back at Matt. Maybe I just really want her to be my friend? She hands me the Fleetwood Mac shirt and I hand her mine.

'Here you go.'

We're both putting them over our heads but I'm taking a little longer, buying myself some time as I think of an excuse to see her again.

'Okay, I've got to head back home, get ready to kick this arsehole out,' I grimace.

'Shit, you live with each other …' she replies anxiously.

'Unfortunately. Who knows, maybe I'll get home and he's already there hosting one of his little *man circles.*'

We both laugh but silently this time.

There's a pause.

This is it.

This energy.

It locks us up.

It makes me aware of every part of her.

How close we are.

How far apart we are.

I feel like the doors of opportunity are slowly sliding closed in front of my face.

I need to do something.

Say something.

'So, I'm going this way …'

I gesture with my hand to the right, slowly starting to walk away. *Nice one. You fucking bottled it. Obviously.*

She must have felt it too. She must. There was a moment.

You're going to regret this for the rest of your life, aren't you? It's too late now. Here you are, walking away, with nothing but your weak internal monologue screaming at you to do something. Your mind and body working in opposition.

'Wait! Let me give you my number,' she shouts from behind me. 'I'd love to know how it goes down with your boyfriend.'

'My *ex*,' I correct her.

'Ha, sure, *your ex*.' She winks.

I take my phone out of my pocket and hand it to her.

'Pop it in here.'

She punches in the numbers. 'Here you go.'

She hands it back to me and I peer down at the contact page on my screen, realising I never got her name.

'*Ph-deree*.'

'It's pronounced *faye-drah*,' she corrects me. 'And you are?'

'Eartha.'

'*Eartha* … I think those names sound quite nice together, don't you?' she says walking backwards, before turning to walk off.

I wait for her to disappear out of sight before running over to Rose, still at the table.

'Matt slept with her last night!' I exclaim with both my hands catching on the café's tabletop.

I breathe out. It turns into a six-year-long, protracted, painful, heavy sigh.

'He's a piece of shit,' I say, holding my hands up. 'You knew it, I knew it. Everyone knew it.'

'I had no clue you actually … *knew*?' Rose says, standing up to put an arm around me.

'Oh of course I knew, I just needed to get there myself.'

'So, what are you gonna do?' Rose asks.

'I'm going home, now. And I'm going to dump him.' I realise I am shaking.

'Fucking hell, mate, you're doing it!' Rose says, holding both of my shoulders to face them.

'Right …' I grab my tote bag from under the table. 'I'm off.'

Rose plants a kiss on my forehead. 'I'm proud of you, and I am here. Always.'

I head home, with the taste for revenge in my mouth. I feel like there are little bolts of power surging around my body, charging each step I take closer to our flat. *Our flat.*

Not for much longer.

CHAPTER 4

THE TRACEY EMIN OF TECHNO

Wonderland followers: 1,297

I hear the jangling of keys from behind the door, followed by a thick hawking of phlegm which sends a wave of neat, undistilled resentment through my body, manifesting itself in a singular truth – that Matt will always love drugs and booze more than he loves me.

I stop mixing the ingredients for my dinner on the kitchen counter and run to the speaker. If he won't listen to me, perhaps he'll listen to Robert Plant.

I whisper, 'Hey, Athena …'

The light comes on, ready for my song command.

'Play "Babe I'm Gonna Leave You" by Led Zeppelin.'

I've never been great at confrontation but I've always had a flare for the dramatic. Trying to cut my tether to the deadweight of a 6'2" man who's holding me back from everything I want to be and become in this world isn't going to be *easy*. What happens in the next few minutes is loaded with the possibility of either launching me into the next chapter of my life or ricocheting into my heart. But I'm finally willing to take that chance, because life has *got* to be better than this. There absolutely must be more to life than a relationship with a man who you have to beg to clean his own cock so you don't contract a UTI. I wonder if he really doesn't know how to look after himself or if he performs this incompetence, knowing I will always be there to pick up the pieces he so carelessly drops all around him. He's looking for a mother in a girlfriend. And a sex doll. And a carer. I wonder what his favourite – *Freud* – would make of that …

I also wonder if he's done this before. I wonder if he fucked her any better than he bothers to fuck me. I need to get myself tested. Maybe that's why I'm always getting thrush? I grab my phone, open up the notes app and type 'VISIT SEX CLIJIC'. I stare at the typo for a split second, contemplating whether or not to correct 'clinic'. Not enough time.

I think of all the things he scoffs at and feels superior to: the female rap music I love, the incense sticks I burn. I think of the parts of myself I'll recover when he's gone. He hates my *joy*. He has squandered all the things I love, belittled them, made them seem worthless, not because they inherently are, but because I, Eartha, take such joy in them. Joy he wants to control, leaving me with only *him*.

I'm trying to focus on the mantras 'the future is bright' and 'everything's going to be okay if I just choose myself', like all the women's self-help books proclaim. But what none of them talk about is how it's your own fear that acts as the weighty obstacle between you and the life you desire. And how safe the room you are in feels in comparison, even if it hurts, even if the person in it repulses you. The new place I'm going towards is frightening. It's empty. It's dark. I've never made a decision as big as this in my life. I don't think any of the women in my family have.

The unoiled door signals his arrival and neat resentment returns, coursing up through my body to my gullet.

Change is coming.

Spatula in hand.

I am on the cusp of everything.

Or, Eartha, are you about to destroy the world you have built for yourself?

Are you actually on the precipice of death?

Shut up shut up shut up.

He strides into the kitchen, puts the keys he will soon have to return on the side counter and inhales deeply.

'*Finally*, food when I come home from work.'

And just like that, the wave of nausea I have been surfing for the past few minutes is replaced with a resolute reassurance that I am, in fact, making entirely the right decision. *What an entitled, lying piece of shit.*

'What's that you're cooking, then? Smells delicious.'

'It does smell delicious, doesn't it?' I say, turning off the hob and focusing on the next task at hand.

I sway myself to the music as I move. I think of Phaedra dancing with her headphones.

He hawks back again and spits his cokey phlegm into the sink. I'm staggered at the sheer audacity of this man. How dare he walk in here ... how dare he even fucking stand near me after everything he's done? How dare he breathe the same fucking *air* as me?

'You're vile,' I say, looking at the glob of phlegm he's not bothered to wash down the sink.

'You love me really.'

No, I don't, actually. I reach over to turn on the tap to flush a part of him down the sink. He's stood behind me and instinctively I know he's about to place his hands on my hips, pulling himself into a hug from behind. The sensation of his cock against the small of my back once turned me on. *All the way on.* I'd have moved myself up and down on my tiptoes, teasing it. I'd have unzipped my trousers, yanked them down, bent over submissively and taken it right there over the counter while I was cooking. His girlfriend: the live-in maid and pleasure hole.

But now the mere thought of intimate physical contact with him is enough to revive my nausea. If my clitoris could shrivel up like a flaccid penis right now, it would. I find myself so repulsed that my stomach feels like a cement mixer, its contents getting thicker and tighter by the second.

I hope he's beginning to sense the mood shift in the flat. I think the lack of arse grinding and bending over has finally made him notice the abrasive atmosphere. The girlfriend who's usually so submissive is suddenly acting out of line. He sits at the table and begins to unbutton his shirt, sighing deeply. I look over my shoulder to watch him and feel the misandry coursing through my veins.

Led Zeppelin's playing in the background and I know the intense guitar is about to kick in. Right. This is it. Carpe fucking diem. I'm going to seize my moment.

I turn around to face him with my full plate in my hands. He's looking down at the floor, yanking off his pointy boots and throwing them behind him into the bedroom. They land on the bed I made. Fucking arsehole. I can't believe he's even in my flat sitting on my chair. And then I suddenly make the connection. This casual disrespect and entitlement are all too familiar. This man is my father. I don't want to keep dating alcoholic wastemen just because Grandma did, then because Mum did. I don't want to live out the ancestral nightmare. We don't all have to live the same story. I feel they're in the room with me now, calling for me to step in a new direction.

I sit at the table and he finally turns around to face me. His expression freezes. He looks down at my chest to read the words 'Fleetwood Mac' on the T-shirt I'm wearing. I look up from my plate with a golden piece of halloumi pronged onto the tines of my fork.

'I'm fucking leaving you.'

I eat a mouthful. Robert Plant echoes my sentiment in the background.

'Mmm, salty and delicious!' I say. 'Now *this* is how cum should taste!' I'm quaking inside, but I don't think from reading his expression that he can tell. I'm not sure what's about to happen. Electricity shocks through my wrists. He hasn't said a word.

'Where did you ...? How...?' he stammers. 'Where did you get that T-shirt from? What the fuck is going on?!'

The panic in his voice is rising and it crescendos at the end. I'm finding sadistic joy in watching him struggle to gain an upper – or frankly any – hand. His eyes shoot from side to side, avoiding me and my T-shirt at all costs as he frantically sifts through his filing cabinet of excuses.

'Y'know the girl with the pink hair you shagged last night? She's very fit, by the way. Excellent tits.'

Excellent tits?!

'WAIT! What girl? What are you on about? What if this was some poor random girl you stole a shirt off, Eartha? She probably has the same shirt! Are you just going round stealing people's things? You're fucking crazy.'

He's still not looked me in the eyes. Instead, his gaze is darting around the room, scrambling for a foothold. He pays so little attention to my life that he has no clue I designed it and that it's physically impossible for there to be another. I pinch my T-shirt, pointing to the fictional venue.

'This concert literally didn't even happen. I made it up.'

He looks down at my finger, pointing to the venue on the shirt that reads, *Live at the Titty Twister.*

'I—I—' he says, while shaking his head. The stupid dangly earring is swinging along for the ride of its life.

'What are you shaking your head for?' I do an exaggerated impression of him, aggressively shaking my head side to side like one of those wobbly toys people put in the front of their cars.

'Is this how you come up with your excuses? Are you SHUFFLING around trying to see which one to land on?'

Silence.

'Come on then,' I add.

'Okay, yes, I met her last night at the gig, but she borrowed my shirt—'

'*My* shirt.'

'Okay she borrowed *your* shirt . . . because she was with one of the other guys! She's just a fucking groupie and she ended back at Sam's, our clothes all got mixed up. That's why I'm wearing this shirt! Why do you always jump to the worst conclusions? All I do is love you and try to make enough money for rent so we can have this place together and it's never enough ... It's so unfair. I work so hard because I love you, Eartha.'

He's inviting me on a guilt trip, I decline to join.

'Matt, what does that have to do with any part of this discussion? You've lost it, mate. Give it up. It's over.'

'EARTHA! I'm telling you. She was with Sam. Go on, you can even ring him up if you don't believe me,' he goes on.

Even now, a chamber of my battered heart still wants to believe him.

'Oh, so one of your boys can back you? You know what …'

I reach for my phone from the kitchen counter.

'Phaedra and I actually exchanged numbers. I'll text her now!'

'*Who?*' he asks, scrunching his face with genuine confusion.

'You can't even remember her—'

I cut myself off, raising my palm to him and shaking my head. I don't have time to start. I text her.

> *Text message from Eartha to Phaedra*
> 18.30
> Hi, gorgeous. It's Eartha, the girl from earlier. You know, the one with the cheating dickhead for a boyfriend … He's denying everything. Don't wanna be a pain in the arse, but do u have any info u can give for me to shut this down?

I press send, lock my phone and place it face down. There's silence.

'You're crazy. You're actually crazy, Eartha,' he says.

Ping

She's speedy! I'm surprisingly giddy to see her name on my screen. I read the text out in my head.

Oh, fucking hell.

> *Text message from Phaedra to Eartha*
> 18.31
> Hi girl from earlier ;) don't worry about it! Speaking of arses (… sorry), he asked for a pinky up his! I don't know if that helps.

'What does it say? Eartha? What does it say?'

Phaedra. *Phaaaaaedra.* I flip her name around in my head and try not to smile. I don't know if I *should* feel happy about this text, but I turn the phone around to show him with half a smirk anyway.

'DOES SAM LIKE A CHEEKY PINKY UP THE BUM BEFORE BED TOO?'

He's cornered, up against the wall, with his balls in the palm of *my* hand. His expression is furious. He says nothing and pushes the table forward.

'I'm not doing this with you, Eartha.'

'Did you ask her to stick a *likkle-pinky* up your bum? Little cheeky pinky before bedtime like you do with me?'

I feel a worrying amount of pleasure tormenting him about this.

'STOP KINK SHAMING ME!'

'OHHHHHH! NOT THE KINK SHAME CARD!'

'Sam must have asked her to do it. Eartha, you can keep telling yourself this shit, that I "cheated on you", but it's not true.'

He flicks his head.

'This is just you telling yourself whatever you need to so you can get out of admitting that you're actually gay.'

Well, I didn't see that coming.

'You've gone quiet. Maybe you got her number because *you* want to be with Petra.'

'PHAEDRA!'

'See.'

'Matt, remembering the names of people you've slept with is the base respect you can give them.'

He thinks he's got leverage.

'Am I wrong?' He's smirking as he says this. The wider his

mouth gets, the more nauseous I feel. There it is again, that churning feeling inside me.

'If you love this girl's "excellent tits" so fucking much, why don't you go shag her?'

'Matt – stop it. You don't know what you're talking about. I am not gay.'

'Sounds like something a gay person would say, if you ask me.'

'I'M NOT FUCKING GAY!'

'Wooooow, you're losing it right now! You're flying off the fucking rails again.'

He raises his palms to the air as though to surrender, resting his case. The dangly earring shakes again, and I lose it.

'Pull that STUPID cross out of your ear. YOU'RE-NOT-EVEN-FUCKING-RELIGIOUUUUUUSSSSSSS!'

He places his hand to his ear self-consciously.

'Kink shaming. Pfft. Stop shaming *me*! YOU. CHEATED. ON. ME. YOU. SLEPT. WITH. SOMEONE. ELSE. LAST. NIGHT. HOW. COULD. YOU?'

I finally explode. He's stopped talking and takes a deep breath. He lowers his head into his hands and starts shaking it again.

The top of his head is so ugly.

Wait.

What's happening?

Oh shit, is he?

Oh God.

'I'm so sorry, Eartha.'

He's crying. For fuck's sake.

'Please, you can't leave me,' he whines. And carries on, trying to find emotional purchase.

'Come on, we make such a good team. I'm so sorry, it was one mistake. Please. She was a fucking groupie begging for it, she means nothing to me … I – I don't know what I'd do without you. I don't know what the point would be in anything if I didn't have you. When I become successful, when other people start to *finally* recognise me as the Tracey Emin of t—'

'LITERALLY NO ONE THINKS YOU'RE THE "TRACEY EMIN OF TECHNO". WHAT DOES THAT EVEN MEAN?!' I yell.

'You're just saying that because you're mad. It will all be meaningless without you, when I've made it. Don't throw all that we have away.'

He lifts his water-filled eyes to meet mine and it's the first time he's made sustained eye contact all evening.

'You're the only one I've ever wanted to be with. It's only you. Always has been …'

He's literally never said that to me before.

This is the first time I've ever seen him cry. This is the first time he's showed even a grain of genuine feeling. Maybe he does regret what he's done. He reaches his hand out across the table and I remember all the incredible times we've had together. It's like he's live-streaming a highlight reel of all our best moments directly into my brain. He *does* feel like home. Forgiving him *would* make the gnawing pain in my stomach stop.

'Matt …'

I extend my hand to meet his in the middle of the table.

'You don't just slip your arsehole onto a girl's finger by accident.'

I push his hand away.

'You have to forgive me.'

He's stropping so much I expected that sentence to end with 'Mummy'.

'I'm done forgiving you for being such a shit excuse for a boyfriend.'

He looks around the room, as though he's just caught a whiff of some bad smell and he's trying to figure out where it's coming from.

'Are you …are you playing Led Zeppelin right now? It's so fucking *you* to do this to me. So DRAMATIC. One honest mistake and you're letting us go.'

He's crying again, scrunching up his face, appearing as ugly to me as he is on the inside. But still my instincts to nurture and comfort subsume me. I want to hold him and tell him I will forgive him, that I love him and everything will be okay. I have to physically restrain myself from caving in on whatever crumb remains of my self-worth.

Then, something cold and calculating presents itself across his face, as if he is trying to find a way to reach into the kindness dam within me. He wipes his tears with his shirt and pushes his chair away from the table. He stands up and wipes his face with his wrist.

'If I can't have you, then what's the point in being here? I might as well just go.'

'That's what I'm saying, Matt. It's over. You need to move out.'

He looks into the distance.

'No, you don't understand what I'm saying. I don't want to be here, on this *earth,* without *Earth-a.*'

'Don't you dare start with that. Who do you think you are? You're not Kurt Cobain. You're not Ian Curtis.'

I'm certain this is all theatrics, a desperate grasp at something to break down my barriers. A pattern that's been too ugly for me to ever confront starts to present itself in front of me. He's threatened to take his own life before. Once when he saw that I'd walked home with a photographer from my old studio. We argued for hours about it and just when I said I'd had enough of him telling me what to do, he threatened to kill himself if I left him. He told me that it would be my fault and I'd have to live with that guilt. He convinced me it was romantic, a sign of how unbearable life would be without me. So I left the studio and I never spoke to my friend ever again. He did it another time, too, when I was getting dressed up for a night out with Rose. We got into an argument about my outfit; he tried to tell me to change. Through our entire relationship, the underlying threat of his mental health being my responsibility has tethered me to him.

'Matt, stop it, don't be ridiculous. You're trying to make me feel awful. It's not going to work this time,' I say firmly, knowing that I'll likely start throwing up with guilt if he continues begging me for forgiveness.

He walks over to the hob, placing his hands on either side. He sighs loudly. His shoulders drop and his whole body deflates. He's being so dramatic, demanding all eyes are on him.

Click click click click click.

I can hear the gas starting up on the hob behind me. Is he gonna light the thing or what?

'Matt, light the fucking thing or turn it off.'

Click click click click click.

'Matt, stop fucking about,' I say with my back still turned to him, sat at the table.

Click click click click click.

'I don't want to be here without you, Eartha. *I might as well go …*'

I turn around to see him with his head lowered into the hob

and his jaw hinged wide open over the gas. Calmly, I walk over to turn it off.

'Matt,' I say, as his mouth still hovers over the ring on the hob, 'your mouth's not even *close* enough for that to kill you nor is there enough gas for you to die from it.'

He pulls his head away from the hob angrily.

'You know that. I know that. Please stop.'

His eyes now dart to the drawer to the left of the oven. He grabs the handle to open it, his eyes searching the contents. I sense he's getting desperate.

'What you looking for, mate? A butter knife to stick in the toaster?'

He's probably never seen the inside of this drawer in his life. I watch as his eyes flit between all of the things in my 'things' drawer. Paracetamol. Tealights. Hairbands. Coppers. Elastic bands. Birthday candles. Medicine boxes. Berocca tubes. He pulls out the first thing with a nozzle he can find, opens his mouth wider than I've *ever* seen him do to give me head and frantically sprays it into the back of his throat.

Psst

Psst

Psst

Psst

Psst

I stare him dead in the eyes, cross my arms and let him continue.

He's still squirting.

Psst

Psst

Psst

Psst

Psst

'EARTHA, DON'T YOU CARE?! I'LL FUCKING DO IT!'

'Matt,' I say as calmly as I can find strength to, 'you do realise you're trying to "kill yourself" with tonsil spray.'

He looks at the bottle as I yank it from his hand and turn it around to show him the label. I slam it back onto the counter. The room wreaks of methane now. I feel like the worst is over. I've almost done it. I've almost got him out the door.

'Thanks for the show, Matt. Dinner *and* a movie! This is the best date we've had in years.'

He screams at this.

'I ALWAYS KNEW YOU'D DO THIS TO US!'

And then, he turns from the kitchen and walks through to the bedroom. I don't respond or follow him. He wants me to be hurt.

Don't let him see your pain, Eartha.

'You're one of the worst artists I've ever seen in my life!' he shouts from the bedroom. I bite my tongue, refusing to lower myself to his final blows. This is just our relationship's death rattle.

'You're going to be posting your PATHETIC collages on Wonderland for the rest of your life and when I make it ... you'll regret ever leaving me. All the merch and posters you could have designed ...'

He starts pacing the room, shaking his head like he's in some Jacobian revenge drama.

'... that's the best your life could ever get with your talent! I look forward to receiving your fan mail one day, begging to take me back when you hear one of my mixes on the radio and realise you've made the biggest mistake of your life. I'll write a song about you, I'll call it ... *The hag that loved to nag and never wanted a shag.*'

'Bold of you to assume I'd want to have my art associated with a man who looks and sounds like a malnourished, even whinier Morrissey,' I say as I stick my head around the door frame and look into the room.

'Don't you dare even say his name. You know how I feel about The Smiths,' he says, flicking his head and sulking, lifting up a silk scarf that I'm hoping he's about to pack into a bag.

I realise everything I once loved and even revered about Matt – his fashion sense, his ability to float in and out of gender roles – are now the things I detest the most. Because they were the things that drew me to him, that lured me into a false sense of security in his femininity, an energy that I felt safe and comfortable in. The illusion of it all. These 'symbols of safety' adorned by men like him to ensnare girls like me. How easy it is to mistake the man with the painted fingernails for your soulmate.

I try to hold my voice, even and slow.

'Please leave.'

'Fine, I'm leaving *you.* You're making me do this!'

He's pulling shirts off the hangers, socks out the drawers and records from the shelves.

THIS IS IT.

IT'S HAPPENING.

I can hear my heartbeat in my temples.

I stand in the doorway to watch him in case he steals any of my things. He looks up at me from the floor where he's shoving and scrunching his belongings into an IKEA bag. It's painful to watch hours of *my* ironing go to waste.

'You're going to regret this,' he says, struggling to wedge a signed copy of *Fleetwood Mac – Future Games* on vinyl into his bag.

'Give me the keys,' I say, holding out my hand with a look on my face designed to instil terror.

The more he looks into my eyes the more attractive he is becoming again. My resolve not to cave in and forgive him wavers, too. My desires are starting to scare me. This is the man who has formed and created so much of my life up to this point.

I can't show any sign of weakness.

'Go!' I shout.

'After six years together? No kiss goodbye? Just like that?' He says 'just like that' as though I haven't already tried to leave him and forgiven him several times.

He brushes his fingers through his hair, placing his right hand above my head and leaning on the door frame. He moves his body closer into me. He drops the IKEA bag and with his left hand reaches over to my face to brush my fringe out of my eyes, tucking it behind my ear. I shake it back into place.

'*Just like that,*' I say, shunning him with my profile.

His hand is still above my head. I'm not sure if he's going to hurt me or try to fuck me. Our faces are inches away from each other.

'Come on, baby, one last ride, before I go?' he says, brushing my face.

'I know you want it,' he says as he begins to trace his finger down my stomach.

I grab his hand so hard that it smacks as I take it.

I open the door and push him outside.

'You don't get to fucking touch me any more, you don't get to fucking THINK about me, and you don't even get to say *my* name. Good luck out there. I'm sure you're going to make the next girl INTENSELY fucking miserable.'

I throw the IKEA bag full of his belongings out the door and with that he says, 'You're frigid. Frigid as a fucking fridge! My next girlfriend's gonna be more successful, hotter and better in bed than you.'

'Great! *So's mine.*'

CHAPTER 5

LANDSLIDE

Wonderland followers: 1,298

I'm pacing up and down the narrow stretch of worn carpet between my bed and my desk, scrunching its pile tightly between my toes as I wait. My fingertips attached to my phone are shaking uncontrollably. My teeth are gnawing at the fingernails on my other hand, blood is starting to push itself out from around the nail. My eyes are struggling to contain the overflowing reservoir.

Brr-brr

If she doesn't pick up, I'll run out of my front door right now, chase him down the road and tell him to come back. If she doesn't pick up, there's still time to override my decision and tell him that we can work through this, that we are meant for one another. I can feel my need for him rising up inside of me, trying to take hold of the steering wheel in what feels like a car chase of my own self-worth.

Ping

I remove the phone from my cheek and look down at my screen.

Text message from Matt to Eartha
19.45
I don't know who I am without you.

This break-up still remains a non-permanent decision. This pain could just be temporary. It doesn't have to be like this, I don't have to be strong, I can be weak. It's my choice. *I could take him back.* I never realised until right now how much my softness and desire to forgive people could be a threat to my own safety.

'*Pick-up-pick-up-pick-up-pick-up,*' I mutter through my teeth.

With each ring, the tension between what I want and what's right for me heightens.

'EARTHAAA? Is that youuuuu?'

'Mum, of course it's me, you've got caller ID.'

'Oh yes, of course, what's goin—'

'Mum ...'

I tense my jaw as I try not to cry.

'Eartha,' she says, her tone serious, 'what's wrong?'

'I've broken up with Matt.'

As soon as the words are out, the dam breaks, and my sadness gushes in every direction. I can't contain it, it's taken on an energy all of its own.

'Oh, baby! No! No-no-no-no!'

'Y-yeah, j-just, just now, I-I-I—'

'Eartha, take a deeeeeeep breath, it's okay.'

'Phewwwwwww.'

'That's it. Now ... listen to me ...'

My face is puffy from my salted tears and my lips already feel gluey from saliva curdling at their corners.

'Are you safe?'

I start to choke on my sobs.

'Eartha, love, I don't know what's happened, but—'

'HE CHEATED ON ME. MUM. HE SLEPT WITH ANOTHER WOMAN AND DIDN'T COME HOME!'

I scream uncontrollably through my tears and my bottom lip and hands shake with anger rather than panic. Six years of betrayal sink in. I can hardly see myself in my mirror's reflection: a blurry half-formed woman bursting at the seams, flushing the old Eartha out.

'Have you tried lying down?'

I lie down on my bed, looking up at the paint-chipped ceiling.

'Now, what I was going to say was … I don't know what's happened …'

She pauses for a second.

'But … I'm proud of you.'

'Y-you're what?'

'I'm proud of you. You're gonna do it on your own, but … wait … hold on, let me get some privacy.'

I take a few more deep breaths while I wait for her to speak again. I hear the latch of a door close on her end of the phone.

'I'm on the porch. Listen … I never had the courage to do what you've done. *Actually* leaving him once and for all.'

She lets out a deep, mournful sigh. Exhaling the many lives she could have lived if she'd left Dad.

'Oh, Mum, that's not tr—'

'No. Enough of that. It is true. I knew your fella wasn't good news. But I knew you wouldn't listen to me either. Because, well, I married your father!'

'Yes, but you *did* divorce him, Mum …'

'Well, that didn't stop me from falling right back into it again, did it?' she continues. 'Who am I to tell you who to be with, when

…' She lowers her voice to whisper. '… *when I have put up with all of his shit, for all these years?*'

Mum and I have been having hushed conversations on the front porch for years. The earliest memory I have is when I was five years old. Dad threw a china plate at the wall in the kitchen and just missed her in the heat of an argument about why my mum had fed me supper first. Then he grew even more explosive because he missed. Instead of turning to protect herself, she calmly walked me over to the front door, placed my arms into a fleece coat, telling me a story about the game we were going to play outside, all while he yelled. The porch became our safe place from then on; he'd never follow us out there because we shared a front garden with our neighbours. Dad might have had an uncontrollable temper, but he was still calculated and calm enough to know that a single slip in front of the wrong person could ruin the image he'd been crafting – and my mother protecting – for years. My poor wonderful mother, a bird that's made peace with her cage.

'Mum, if you knew that …that Matt was no good, like Dad, why didn't you just say?'

'You've never listened to me and you certainly wouldn't start if I told you to sack off your *boyfriend,* now would you?'

I purse my lips. She's right.

'So, why did you leave him?'

'WHAT DO YOU MEAN?! I just told you he cheated on me.'

'No, why now? I know this can't be the first time you've tried …'

'I-I-I, I don't know.'

I soothe myself with a few deep breaths and return to the conversation.

'I've been feeling really confused. I–I can't explain it. He's been so horrible to me, Mum. For all of these years. I haven't told *anyone*. I felt like I had to … like I had to …'

'Protect him.'

'Yes. How did you know?'

'Pffffffff,' she sighs. 'I know we don't always see eye to eye on things, you've got your opinions on the world – all your feminist stuff and whatnot. Honestly, I've always been a bit worried you thought less of me as a woman … because of your father … what I've put up with. You asked me how I "know"; well, love, I've been protecting him for years. I know what it looks like … at least he's got his AA meetings to give me a fucking break a few times a week …'

'Mum, you know he's probably going to the *pub*, right?' I say, laughing through my tears as I drag my face along my pillow to try to wipe them up. Dad attending meetings …? I don't believe it for a second.

'As long as he's out of the house, I don't care.'

But I know that's not true because I know she still loves him. I know how much she wishes he *would* go to those meetings. Just like I know Mum probably doesn't feel she's worth much if she doesn't have him to look after. They divorced when I was in school, but they still live together. Mum's essentially his carer. Addict and enabler. They each get something from a relationship that destroys them both in the process. Though I'm sure Mum is some form of addict too, the way she keeps going back to him. Even with all the programmes and resources I've offered up to her, the hardest lesson I've learned is that you can't save your mum from herself.

'Mum, what you said earlier, I've … I've …'

The words won't escape my mouth.

'I've never thought less of you.'

'My life, Eartha ... I just don't want it for you. I did what you've done, with the divorce, but only halfway. I went back. It doesn't have to be this way for you. It's not going to be you. I just want you to know that even though you've got this ... life, away from home, your mum's still here if you need her. I'm sorry you don't have sisters or brothers, but you do have me.'

'Did I do the right thing giving up on Matt?'

'I think if you have needed this for longer than tonight, then yes, of course. It will hurt. It will hurt like hell. Stay strong ... Now, I don't mean to make you feel worse, I want you to know how much strength you have shown tonight, but we should think practically, too. Are you going to be able cover the rent without him paying half, on top of bills? Can I help?'

'I'll figure it out. I think my birthday-card commissions can help pay for my rent, although I probably won't have much left over. I'll just have dinner at Rose's! I'll bike everywhere. I'll charity-shop clothes. I just ... I just feel that there's more for me ...'

I look up at the chipped paint in the corner of the ceiling.

'But I have to believe it's going to be better than this. I want to do something that matters. I want to find out who I am. It's got to be better than this ... And, Mum ... he had sex with someone else while I waited for him in our bed and ... it was with this beautiful girl. I feel so confused about it.'

'Oh, Eartha. I'm so sorry. I'll never forgive him for it. Are you really okay, love?'

'It's just that since I found out today, I can't stop scrolling and scrolling through *her* life and comparing it to my own, and her body to my body, and then I wonder *why* I am so maniacally obsessed with this woman. It wasn't her fault, she didn't know he had a girlfriend. But I feel so enmeshed in her; I can't stop thinking about them together. I'm going to be single, alone, in a damp flat, confused, begging for food from my mates ...'

'Eartha, come on now, that doesn't sound totally realistic and I'm not sure that's what you'll be doing in the next ten years. But you know what?'

'What?'

'It's still better than being with *him*, isn't it?'

I take a deep breath and pinch the top of my nose. I nod.

'Yes.'

'Even if that's the worst it can get, being single is better than being with him, *isn't it*? And the universe, god, goddess, whatever you want to call it ... it rewards women like you. Women who jump into the unknown.'

'*Mum* ...'

'Sorry. But ... You're brave, that's what I'm trying to say!'

'I built my whole existence around him and when I looked around at the view, there wasn't a single thing I was happy with.'

'You know, love, there's a perfect song for that ...'

'Oh yeah, who's that one by, then?'

I playfully roll my eyes and mouth the words, *Fleetwood Mac.*

'Fleetwood Mac!'

I smile, suddenly the sound of her humming is at the end of the phone and I close my eyes.

'Can you hear that? Eartha?'

'Yes.'

'Listen to the lyrics ...'

She starts to sing the song on the other end of the phone.

'Well I've been afraaaid of chaaaaaanging cause I've built my liiife around youuuuu …'

We sing the song together. I pause occasionally as the sobs rise in my throat, allowing them to flow out of me.

As I sing, I think about how hard it is to leave someone you've created your entire sense of self around. You can't just get up and go. It's frightening because it feels like they get to keep a part of you, and you are left with nothing but the shell of a person you've become in giving yourself to them. But the fact I asked him to leave must mean there is a shred of self-love or at least self-preservation coursing through me, out of sight right now, but not out of mind.

My phone remains wedged between my ear and the duvet and I can hear my mum still singing out to me miles and miles away, sitting on the porch outside our house.

I curl up obediently on the right side of my mattress, realising that the usually warm side of the bed next to me is now completely cold.

CHAPTER 6

FUCKBOYS KNOW NO GENDER

Wonderland followers: 1,324

Eight days later.

Flushing Matt out of my system has been an ongoing process of hyper-real visualisations, disorientating nightmares and lacerating regret. The first morning I wake up without him I feel severed in half. I didn't realise how much purpose he gave me, even if that purpose was constantly begging a man to love me. Getting rid of him is like an ongoing exorcism of the possession he had over my life. Everything he has left behind haunts me. I open the fridge and see beers that he had bought to drink in the flat and I feel a wave of urgent loss because I no longer need to hide them. The first time I get into the shower I find his '*body gel FOR MEN*' in its hyper-masculine black packaging. I open the lid, lather it all over myself and the smell makes me cry. I find strands of hair still curled inside the bed and leave them to lie beside me. I discover a stash of poems he'd written for me, scrunched up in the back of my nightstand; one is titled 'The Yin to my Yang'. He wrote it as an apology for not texting me back for a week. I realise if I hadn't broken up with him that night, our argument would have become just another terrible poem stashed in the back of my drawer – a collection of all the times I tried to leave but caved in and forgave him instead. I decide to rip up each one. (Recycling them, of course. I have to do *something* to counteract the impact of all those long showers I took.)

My future without him seems so out of focus. I can only see small flashes of what I could do or who I could become next. Tiny openings of a new life reveal themselves through texts from Phaedra. Phaedra – who course-corrected the train of my life, which had been heading in the wrong direction for years, by shagging my boyfriend – has been checking in on me. At first I assume it's guilt, then I start to think she wants to be in contact with me because she felt something between us, too. I wait for her texts every day and they throw flashes of rose-coloured light into the darkness that has been filling my mind since.

> *Text message from Phaedra to Eartha*
> 00.16
> Uh-oh Matt's progressive women ensnaring begins ... I wonder if he'll put a call out for one of his *man-circles* ... *(Wonderland link attached)*
> *@MattSounds* Hi, I just wanted to come on here quickly to shed some light on issues which have been profoundly shocking for me to realise. I cannot believe women get paid less than men in most industries. We need to get it together, boys. Come join me for my set this Friday at The Shipley Arms where all women get in for free, all night. You don't even have to PAY! I'll absorb the cost for you girls. It's the least I can do. Just doing my bit #AllyToWomen

When I'm not thinking of Matt, I've found myself thinking

about her. I see her pink hair in flashes of colour on the street. I feel for my phone in the hope she will have sent something to me, or updated her Wonderland page with a new selfie. I comb my hair thinking of hers. I remember her nipple piercing when cutting naked women from magazines for my collages. I replay the words we exchanged. My body remembers the charge that coursed between us and tries to recreate the sensation by staring at her face on my screen.

At first, I assume that my obsession with Phaedra is born from the fact she shagged Matt, as the woman who 'ruined my relationship'. But I've tried to hate her and I can't. I don't feel an ounce of resentment towards her. These emotions are coming from a place so deep within me. Phaedra was the catalyst, but it's something I have always known. A truth I've needed to fish out of myself for such a long time that when I finally ensnare it and reel it out, it lies still and whole on the bank of my new life. A truth I have always known would surface.

I like women.

Possibly as much as I like men.

Possibly more.

These feelings have been living inside me for years and as they've been growing so has my discomfort with hiding them. So much has been resurfacing in the time I've spent alone and untethered to Matt. Without him to cater to there's no more distraction and the void within me has opened up, exposing the naked, fleshy and vulnerable truth of who I am and the things I've been avoiding. And it's not just the realisation that I have burgeoning romantic feelings for women, but the pain I've endured at the hands of men who were supposed to love and protect me – the many things I've put up with over the years now refuse to be smothered; instead they're rising up and pouring out of me, the generations of hurt and shame felt by the women in my family that were passed down to me, keeping me prisoner to their ways of living and loving for so long. It feels as though I'm the first in a long line of women to free myself from a life of passive resentment.

I've been so consumed by this messy discovery of myself that I've ghosted everyone I love this week while I've tried to make sense of it all. I think I'm bisexual. I still fancy men, but ... there's a whole other part of myself that loves women just as much. It needs exploring. It needs air. It needs to be watered, fed, tended to and nurtured, so that it can blossom into the beautiful garden I so desperately need it to grow into. The thought of actually being able to act on the thoughts and fantasies I've had over the years frightens me and turns me on at the same time. I don't think I've ever felt so liberated.

Now I've given myself permission to feel this way about women, my mind is consumed by them. Girls girls girls. Everywhere. Girls walking arm in arm together on the street no longer appear as friends to me, but potential lovers. I see girls even when they're not there. The way I look at the world has become a colourful frequency. Women smiling at me are no longer just being polite, they could be a lover. I feel less inclined to judge other girls and more inclined to kiss them. In all the confusion and pain of my break-up, a fantasy floats around my brain that gives me hope this will not last ...

Phaedra.

*

During this awakening, I sent Rose one voice note.

Voice note from Eartha to Rose (23 seconds)
22.09

Rose, I did it. I fucking dumped Matt, babe. I wish someone had TOLD me he was such an arsehole all these years! My head is in tatters, though ...The girl, the beautiful one with pink hair who you said was fit ... her name's Phaedra, she's making me feel ... a bit weird. I'm a bit obsessed with her, babe, I'm checking her profile all the time. Anyway, she helped me put the nail in the coffin with Matt. You should have seen his face ...

I hoped Rose would pull on the tangled thread I presented about my confusion for Phaedra and unravel it for me, ask me what I was confused about, tease a confession out so I didn't have to do the work. But they didn't. They told me they'd bake me an enormous vegan brownie to commemorate the loss of that 'absolute toenail of a man'.

I've been speaking to Mum and she's been more than supportive in my awkward confessionals to her over the phone. I've not properly 'come out' to her, but I received a pair of knickers with a little rainbow on them in the post yesterday. I think that's her way of letting me know she knows. But I've decided Rose needs to be the person I tell first because Rose knows me better than anyone on this planet. They are bringing their super-sized brownie over tonight and I've been running around my flat like a panicked nutter spraying a knock-off can of Febreze that I grabbed from the corner shop, cleaning the mirrors, picking up the crispy leaves that have fallen from another indoor ivy plant that I've failed to keep alive. I have lit a candle and chosen the right album; I feel like the budget version of my perfect hostess mum.

I'm not normally one to get the flat ready for people, especially Rose, who on many occasions just lets themself in – but this is different. Besides, I'm a ball of anxiety and cleaning up has really helped take the edge off.

I stand in front of my floor-length mirror with my hands in my back pocket, trying to emulate the same energy as Rose.

Just tell them you like girls, be casual, be COOL!

There's a knock at my door.

Shit, shit, shit.

'It's open, babe, come in!'

They push the door open slowly, as though they aren't sure what to find inside my flat. My invite was pretty ambiguous now I think about it; I just said I had something exciting to share and to bring drinks. Rose probably thinks this is a break-up pity party.

'Helloooo ...' I see a bottle of wine clutched in their right hand as instructed, along with a white cardboard box. 'My love, come here and give us a big hug! Here is a vegan brownie made in *your* honour by *yours truly*.' Rose places the box and the bottle down onto the kitchen table, opens their arms wide and walks towards me. I embrace them. They smell of Rose: a leathered strength underneath more amber notes. I breathe them in and realise I have needed this for eight long days. The rough texture of their black biker jacket feels like home.

'How have you been, kid?' Rose asks affectionately.

They pull back to look at my face, brushing my fringe out of the way with a look of sisterly concern. Then their face drops. They wrinkle their nose.

'Have you been spraying Febreze?'

'No, actually, it's *Befreze*!'

I'm rattling and grab the bottle of wine from the table, about to take it to the kitchen counter, but as they walk further into the room, I catch the glare of my laptop screen: 'How to Give Away you are Queer with Your Body Language' is still playing on mute. I sprint out of the kitchen and slam the computer shut. I sit myself at the end of my bed in the room where I do pretty much everything – eat, sleep, shag, work, cry, masturbate. They follow me through and stand above me in front of the mirror.

'I'm so sorry I went ghost. I've been all over the place. There's so much I've needed to figure out.'

'I can't imagine how you've been feeling. But next time, I'm here, you know? I'm just a bit confused why you've not reached out to me this time? What's going on? What's it been like without Matt here, living alone again? Are you really doing okay?'

'Well, there are less dishes to do …'

'Come on, is there any new work stuff? What collages have you been working on?'

'Well, I was talking to Mum the other day and—'

'SUSE! My girl! Tell her I said hello, will ya?'

'I will. She was proper worried about me … I was telling her I'm so sick of creating things for other people, you know? I want to be a proper artist, in my own right. I think I'm going to have to upload more stuff onto Wonderland even though it feels awkward. I want to get to that level where brands want to work with me for my collages, I want that status …'

As I'm talking, they fetch the red wine and a wooden spoon and bring them back into the bedroom with a kitchen chair latched onto their other arm. I'm still telling Rose about my ideas when they place the chair down and sit on it, spreading their legs open to reveal the top of their boxers. They maintain eye contact as they wordlessly stab the spoon handle into the bottle, forcing the cork to *pop* into the liquid within. Listening intently to me, they seamlessly hand me a very full glass of wine. *How is it possible for a person to move so smoothly?*

I reach my arm out to cheers their glass.

'WAIT! What are we cheers-ing to? Why am I here again? You've still not explained. Are we cheers-ing to your break-up with he who shall no longer be named?' Rose asks, topping up their drink with another dribble of wine.

I clear my throat. 'Well, that's why I invited you over, I've been working some things through in my mind this week and I want to tell you that ...' I cough and clear my throat. 'I like boys ... and girls.'

Rose chokes and spits out a mouthful of wine, spraying it across the room.

'Jesus, Rose!'

'EARTHA! I always knew you were a little fruity, but I didn't know you had *this* in you. You wanna go for the girl that shagged Matt? I'm impressed ... Cheers to fucking THAT!'

'Wait, no! What? What do you mean you always knew?' I shake my head, confused by the anticlimax. I feel stupid for being perceived as queer before I even knew it myself. Even though it's Rose, it feels like a violation to be seen in this way.

'I always knew.' They fold their arms, all matter-of-fact.

'How did you *know*?' I ask, confused.

I blow upwards to shift my fringe, which is blocking my eyes. Rose looks above my head at my wall and bursts out laughing.

'What's funny?!' I ask petulantly.

They put down their wine, reach out to tuck my fringe away for me and spin me around on my desk chair so that I'm facing my wall.

'How did you *not* know?' They nod their head towards my collages. I absorb the sea of imagery, all of them of women with their tits out ripped from vintage copies of *Playboy*. There's one of a woman in suspenders, an unbuttoned white shirt revealing her tits while another woman lies spread out on a chaise longue looking flustered.

'You stole my thunder.' I fold my arms and go on, 'Let me have my dramatic, coming-out moment, won't you?!'

Rose takes a big gulp of their wine, puts their glass back down and places their hand on my lap. 'I've always known and don't worry, I know you had a crush on me way back when, too.'

'Piss off.'

'I'm sorry. I don't mean to tease you. I mean ... I've just ... been there. My first crush was on my best friend Louise in primary school. We used to show each other how to dry hump teddies at sleepovers and her mum used to give me the evils. Fancying your friend ... it's a queer rite of passage, baby!'

I look back up at my wall of women.

'Trust me. The girls are gonna *love* you. My God, we've got to do your first gay night out soon. Just don't fuck any of my exes, okay?' Rose says, laughing.

That's a lot of people.

'And we can set you up a dating profile! Anything you want to know about sex with women, come to me ... there's so much to learn. The sex is gonna last a hell of a lot longer, too. You'll wear yourself out. You blink and BAM! It's like 6 a.m., the sun's rising and you've got to leave for work in two hours.'

I stare at them, wide-eyed, completely overwhelmed by all that I don't yet know.

'Sorry, only if you're ready. I know everything's fresh with

Matt. I just feel like I've finally gained an actual purpose for all of my years of dating girls.' Rose laughs into their glass of wine.

'No, please, keep going. Your dating life always makes me feel better about mine,' I say, smiling now.

As Rose keeps talking, I see that they are going to fill a role in my life that I need: my *glorious gay guide*. They spend another ten minutes reeling through all the lesbians I might encounter at Slinky's, a lesbian bar they frequent and plan to take me to.

'Eve: works behind the bar, you'll love her, she's never fucked anyone in the scene because she's married. Sammy, avoid. Short butch daddy, long brunette hair with a leather waistcoat and a little cherry tattoo on her neck.'

'*Avoid?* She sounds hot,' I say.

'Sure, she's hot. But she's *such* a Shane. Everyone has a story about her. I mean, go for her if you want, obviously, she's not a bad person, but everyone's been with her and it's totally a "thing" that she likes to be the first to sleep with newly out queers. It's consensual but still a bit fucking weird to want to be "the first".'

I can't help but feel the reason they dislike Sammy so much is that Sammy reminds Rose a little of themself.

'What's a Shane?'

They roll their eyes. 'Oh dear GOD, I need to show you *The L Word*.'

They insist that *The L Word* is the best and worst thing, and tell me that 'Shane' was the character on the show that everyone fancied, but who was emotionally unavailable and caused chaos wherever she went. 'Fuckboys know no gender, Eartha.' They nod at me with concern.

I have been warned. For the next hour, almost entirely uninterrupted, they give me recommendations and tips for spotting a queer woman in the wild. 'If you wanna keep it casual, babe, don't do all the cute stuff. Don't take her for breakfast or spend the night ... trust me. You'll break a girl's heart. Although if we're being honest, you're more likely to be the one getting your heart broken. My poor little baby queer.'

I nudge them away with my shoulder. Although, finding people who couldn't provide me the emotional nourishment I deserve is *clearly* my forte. Rose is pouring out so much information it's becoming overwhelming. I grab my phone and open up my Notes app. I wonder when I'll get to put their tips on eating pussy into practice. This is the first time since the break-up that my dreams have started to feel attainable. I think of Phaedra and those big, reddish-brown eyes ...

Eartha's Notes app

- Sammy, ~~hot!~~ Avoid.
- Dates with women last a long time. Try to keep boundaries and keep dates to one-night stays maximum.
- Women can and will hurt you. Don't assume they won't because they're not men.
- 'Scissoring' is not a thing??? Was made up by men in porn? Girls do it sometimes, but not really.
- If you want to keep things casual don't give the girlfriend treatment. Don't make her playlists, have sleepovers or spend too much time with her or it's a recipe for heartbreak.
- Don't fall for straight girls.

After almost another hour of sex tips and getting to grips with the who's who of Olympia, Rose is finally exhausted and goes for a piss. They leave the door wide open, zoned out, forearms resting on their thighs and a piece of tissue folded in their hands.

They look beautiful, even now. My favourite thing about Rose is their hands. Covered in tattoos that mean absolutely nothing to them and masses of rings, some of which were sequentially gifted over a series of weeks by a silversmith they were shagging. They dated her a few years ago and they still wear the rings like they're nothing. Whereas sentimental value is one of the greatest forces in my life, Rose has this wild ability to not attach meaning to anything. Their hands tell a story about who they are as a lover. Looking down at mine now, both painted a different colour, I suppose mine do too.

'How are you really feeling about Matt? He's just like ... fucking gone, mate. What the hell?' Rose hollers from the loo. They don't know I can see them in my mirror, an expression of deep thought on their face.

'Honestly, I knew for a while it needed to happen. I just felt so guilty. I was waiting for him to fuck up so I didn't have to be the one to do it. I thought about girls while I was having sex with him and thought that was totally normal. I thought all girls did that.'

Did I just say that out loud?

'Do you fancy a cocktail?' I shout through to the loo, noticing the wine is almost empty.

'Go on, then. We're going to need one or two more if we're going to be talking about HIM.'

I have some coconut cream left over from a curry I made earlier in the week and decide to fix us pina coladas with a twist – the twist being vodka as I don't have any rum. I find a bottle I stashed away from Matt in the 'cleaning' cupboard under the sink and make up the drink while Rose finishes in the bathroom. I pour us two glasses, leaving the rest in a pitcher, bringing them back into the bedroom and onto the floor at the end of the bed, where they sit smiling up at me, waiting patiently.

'I see he's still left some of his shite here ...' they say, taking the drink from my hand as I sit next to them on the floor.

I've always loved the way they say shite – their Irish accent makes it irresistible. They point to a small pile of records in the corner of my room.

'Oh no, I told him I'm keeping those.'

Rose laughs. 'So ... *did ya tell him*?' they ask, moving their eyebrows up and down suggestively.

'He figured it out himself, maybe, even before I did? It was the last thing I said to him before I slammed the door in his face. I said it just to wind him up ...'

'Stop it. I would have loved to have seen the look on that prick's face.'

'You know what, Rose? I don't think he was that surprised. He said it when we were arguing! But, I still like men ... I think that makes me bisexual?'

We burst out laughing and clink our cocktails together. Rose tells me the best sex they ever had was with a bisexual woman and that they had never understood why lesbians get weird about bisexual girls. 'We should be kissin', not fighting, for fuck's sake!'

'I knew I was unhappy with him, Rose, but I couldn't admit it out loud. I thought I'd lost my fucking libido. I'd avoid sex with him all the time. I'd literally SWAT his hand off my thigh like a fly if he touched it, and then when I saw that girl ... in my fucking T-shirt ...' I shake my head. 'I felt this rush, a complete ... overwhelm. I realised it's not that I don't want sex ... but that I don't want sex with him. He was *vile* to me, Rose, *way* before he cheated on me. He made me feel like I was going crazy. He would belittle my designs, make me feel small, and then when we were in front of others he'd be bigging me up like he was this incredible supportive boyfriend.'

They place their hand on my thigh and squeeze gently. I continue, 'I just don't want to be seen as this fucking bitch who broke up with her boyfriend. It's not like that. I've always felt this way. It was much more complicated than that.'

'We could all see the type of man he was, and everyone who cares about you will be happy you're out of it.'

We talk for hours about the messiness and the complexity, everything I've ever wanted to tell them about Matt but have been too busy defending him for. There's no going back. No friend would ever let someone go back after hearing what I tell them and all the half-told truths I have been concealing from them over the years.

Eventually, I press the lock button on the side of my phone and see that it's 1.37 a.m., and Rose and I are getting drunker by the minute on a third round of my vodka coladas. I gave up on measuring the ratio of spirit to mixer hours ago. Rose puts down their drink and their eyes start rolling back like they're about to deliver a sermon; they clutch my hand and slur a speech.

'Eartha … you NEED to make some art … about HoW YoU fEEl about GIIIIRLS.'

I shake my head slowly in response. A resolute no.

'Maybe do some stuff 'bout Matt. Y'know? You've got to find a way to work through all this shit. I reckon you should do something with your pain. Help OTHERS, even.'

'Imagine if I could get others to see that they don't need to put up and shut up?'

I think of Mum. I think of what, or who, it might have taken for her to leave Dad all those years ago. Could I be that person?

'I want to set every woman in a baaad relationship FREE!'

We sound like two bitter, battered man-haters. Perhaps this is what men mean when they say they hate feminists: they're afraid of us realising that the game is rigged in their favour, and that we're actually going to conspire and do something about it. Rose keeps egging me on. 'Come on, then! Let's shoot some ideas - rIgHt NoW.' They sit upright and form their hand into a fist, holding an imaginary microphone. They tap it and then cough, 'Is this thing on? Okay, Ms Eartha, knowing what you know now, that men are ...' Their eyes look into the distance, searching for words.

'Fucking useless ...'

'What would ya go back and tell you in your past relationship?' They take another big gulp of their drink, still with the microphone under their mouth. 'Shite, sorry, here ya go.' They gesture, passing it to me. I take the imaginary mic.

'Thank you, Rose! I would say ... *Dearest young woman* ... listen to your body, if it is LITERALLY repulsed by the man: LEAVE!'

Rose starts silent laughing, smacking my leg. They snatch the 'mic' from me.

'YES. Or, if ya fantasising 'bout girls, you probs like 'em.'

We're in fits of laughter.

'WE nEeD tO fIlM tHiS'. Rose opens up my laptop's camera and places it on their knees to start recording me from below. I look down at my face in the screen and all of the chins that appear and yank all the pillows off my bed and shove them onto Rose's lap, placing the laptop on top so it's facing me. The screen covers Rose's head and I can't see their face, just their arms dangling at the sides of their lap. They now reach their arms around the front, struggling to press record.

'Right, Eartha …'

3, 2, 1 … ding!

The laptop starts to record. They hold up their imaginary mic again, this time in front of the laptop camera so their little tattooed fist is in front of my face on the screen. 'Everything you wish you could have told yourself to save yourself years of misery! This video can inspire your next collage, a gift from drunk Eartha to sober Eartha. You can cut up some pictures of men and chop their heads off.'

I begin ranting about Matt. How our entire relationship felt foggy. How I couldn't pinpoint exactly what he did to me, but that I was always left feeling confused, and relieved when he would 'make it up' to me. That I felt I had been tricked into being with someone who had never deserved to be with me. How he used the threat of suicide to control me. I go on and on, my feelings pouring out of me – talking for the first time about how he had physically hurt me. I start crying and Rose's hand flops to the floor: I look up suddenly and their head is drooping. They've slammed the laptop shut with their head and fallen asleep.

For a split second I'm offended they've collapsed in the middle of my dramatic monologue, but the disappointment is fleeting and quickly turns into adoration. They're an absolute mess, and I love them. I slip the laptop out from underneath Rose and help them up onto the bed before playing back the video. I hadn't realised I'd been speaking for so long and my eyes start to prick with tears as I'm watching it back. The room begins to spin, so I fetch a drink of water. I keep watching the video and I think absolutely everything coming out of my mouth is pure fucking brilliance. Iconic, even. In the video Rose's hand occasionally comes out of the frame as they reach for their drink, and you can hear them sipping it; at one point, you even hear them belch. The whole thing is a perfect mess. I shake Rose to wake her up, but they look disoriented.

'Should I post this on Wonderland? Don't you think I sOund RealLy clever?'

Rose grumbles at me and watches the first minute of our video through one eye.

'Yeaaah, GO on! The GirLs are goNNa fucking LoVe you, Eartha.'

There's a smile on their face, framing the drunken delusional confidence of two friends who say to one another: 'We should start a podcast.'

I download the video to my phone and caption it: 'tHiS oNe'S fOr ThE gIrLs #CumingOut'.

I upload it on Wonderland and then close my eyes with my phone in one hand and Rose's in the other.

CHAPTER 7

THAT COULD HAVE STAYED IN THE DRAFTS

Wonderland followers: 90,389

I wake up sharply to something moving very close to me. My half-asleep, hungover eyes can't pull into view what it is; all I make out are a pair of dilated pupils.

'Eartha, WAKE UP! THIS. IS. FUCKING. B-r-i-l-l-i-a-n-t.'

Rose has a manic hangover, they're restless and laughing their head off at my laptop, sat in their vest and boxers.

'What is?'

I blearily peer around at my bedroom.

'The video you put on Wonderland last night. It went VIRAL, BABY.'

'A video, what the bloody . . . ? What are you on about?!' I reply. My mind is scrambling to piece together the scenes erupting in front of my clouded mind.

But then a sinking feeling starts to take hold. I can't remember the video – or, more precisely, anything I said in it.

'Look at how many fucking people plugged in to watch. Look at all of these people! Listening to YOU NOW!'

I look over at the screen. I open and close my eyes again; there's an acrid coconut taste in my mouth. I do a double take: 489,000 people have plugged in to view. In eight hours. I imagine them sitting there, staring at their phones, their pupils flooded with my image.

'What-the-fuck-am-I-talking-about-what-the-fuck-am-I-talking-about-tell-me-now-fuck-fuck-fuck?' I say, facing the back of the laptop screen.

'ROSE, STOP! HOW BAD IS IT?'

Rose is still watching it.

'ROSE, give it here.'

'Wait! You have GOT to start it from the beginning,' they reply.

They scrub the video right back to the beginning. I am burning up with panic and a sick curdled fear is now lodged in my throat. Before Rose can even move the cursor to the beginning, I yank the laptop out of their hands to assess the damage I have caused myself in front of almost half a million people.

'Oi!' they shout as I unplug them.

'I can't wait,' I explain.

I take a breath so deep that it fills my lungs with oxygen enough for two underwater lengths of a pool. *Please, do not let this be a drunken coming-out video that has been seen by the same amount of people as the population of Liverpool.*

Original script from the 'Eartha goes viral' video

An unsteady Rose struggles to keep the camera still as they film Eartha sitting on the bed. Rose shoves their fist into the video frame pretending it is a microphone. Eartha appears on screen, swaying a little as if she is preparing to slow dance.

Eartha talks into a tattooed fist.

Rose: Babe ... fuckin'... go for it.

Eartha: Okay, my name's Eartha. I am single. Twenty-five years old. Officially done with men. Well, not entirely. I still fancy them.

Eartha puts two fingers into her mouth and pretends to be sick

But I'm done with them on a spiritual level. Does that make sense? I've recently left my boyfriend. He was like stale fridge cheese you really need to chuck but never get round to. Finally. I think it was the hundredth fucking time I tried to. Why do we do that? Why do we stay with these men? Even after they have hurt us?

Eartha half closes her eyes for a few seconds with her finger pointed at the camera

We stay with shitty men because it's all we've ever known. We learned it from our mothers, they learned it from their mothers, we don't know anything else. My mum taught me with my dad and my grandma with my grandfather. I mean I had to ... pick up ... his boxers ...

Eartha pinches her fingers, gesturing picking up boxers

... around the flat every day. Like his fucking mum. Who wants to have sex with someone that you're also mothering? THAT is messed up.

Eartha blinks slowly

I really want women to know that we're allowed to leave relationships when we're unhappy. It is not the crime of the century that you think it is to leave a man that makes you unhappy.

Eartha swigs her drink

But anyway, HE knew that I was the kind of girl who wanted to be seen as a good person and so I would apologise for EVERYTHING! Just in case it was my fault. Which meant I became a passive ... little ... doormat ... to his big fucking FEET!
Eartha gestures the size of his feet with her hands
He had such long, brown toenail energy. LGBT. Wait, no, long, brown ... LBTE! Well, I might as well move onto THAT topic now that I'm here ... L ... LGBT...
Eartha sways and closes her eyes
He cheated on me. That's right. He had sex with someone else. And you know what? The girl was beautiful. Just ... beautiful. When I saw that girl with the pink hair that slept with my boyfriend ...
fists cocktail glass and sucks the froth off each finger before finishing the sentence
THAT'S when I realised I'm probably a bit fucking gay, actually!
Rose starts to laugh sporadically as though they're high. Eartha looks back at Rose behind the camera, trying to get their attention to stop laughing
So, to anyone else out there wondering if you like women because you, like, can't stop fucking thinking about them all the time ... and want to kiss them ... you probably do. Ladies, never let a boyfriend stop you from kissing girls! Wait, no. That's ... not what I mean ... what am I trying to say? I'm bisexual! And my boyfriend had me on a LEASH! Well, he had me on a psychological leash, where the quality of my days was measured by his mood towards me. It was the stealthiest form of control – he didn't even

have to ask me to do anything, I was already trained to do it. The beauty and horror of it all is that when you appear to be the one in control, to everyone watching it looks as though it's your choice. 'No one asked you to do all this!' 'Why are you moaning about it? You didn't have to do that!'

Eartha screws up her face, impersonating people

But I did have to. He didn't have to say it or tell me what to do ... because he had me living in fear of not pleasing him. Not once did I slow down ... on his silly little treadmill of servitude as he continually moved the goalposts, dangling his love and his COCK as a reward in front of my face, the whole time I thought to myself, *If only I can be a better more loveable girlfriend, then I'll get his love*. NOTHING ...

Eartha points at the screen aggressively

... I ever did was ever good enough. But it was never about me not being 'good enough', it was about keeping me distracted so I never woke up and realised that I already am enough. Without him.

Eartha sways her hands slowly to change the subject

I never want to give a passive-aggressive hand job in my life EVER again.

I guess this is why I am cuming out. Now. Because I can, finally.

Eartha cries and drinks

ENDS

My mind scrambles. Those disordered words. To thousands of people. To tens of thousands, no, wait, to hundreds and hundreds of thousands. I'm bisexual. I wonder if my mum has seen the video, or whether any of her work colleagues have sent this to her? Or texted her? *Hi love, just seen Eartha's video! Congrats on your offspring being one of those bisexuals!*

The worst part about it all is that I uploaded the video all by myself. I have no one to blame. No one but myself.

I click below the video on 'see more' to drop down the comments. There are hundreds and hundreds of people's faces looking back at me from the screen.

'Look, look at this one.'

Rose raises their arm for me to snuggle in and reads out one of the comments left on the video as I tuck myself in.

> *@Jen57_* You've just summed up the last 10 years of my life that I've not been able to put into words, let alone say out loud. You're so brave.
>
> *@Wallflower399* Uhhhh, did you just out your mother being in an abusive relationship for clout? Lol, what a 'feminist'.
>
> *@BIAS_EDITONS* Where did you get your top from?
>
> *@Jessygal789* Commenting from my private account because I'm not comfortable coming out yet, but I have felt this way for so long about girls and this has made me feel less alone <3
>
> *@ShyamQant* Yeah ... this could have stayed in your drafts. You're a fucking mess.
>
> *@ChristianJessica_78* You'll return to the truth one day, sister #PreachJesus #HomosexualityIsASin

'Did you see that? BRAVE!'

'I was drunk with a delusional amount of courage! I could never do any of that sober.'

'Who cares? Look at this one. Macy from Texas says,

"I definitely have a lot of girl crushes ... you've got me questioning my entire life this Sunday morning girl."'

I throw a pillow over my head so I can think this through for a moment. I've not even been on a date with a girl yet. I'VE NOT EVEN HAD GAY SEX! Do I still have time to take it down so that it disappears without a trace?

'How many people have seen it now, Rose?' I ask, squinting my eyes. Bracing myself. They hit refresh.

'Half a million people.'

'How on earth did this get out there ... so fast?'

'I reckon some big influencer shared it, you know? You've only got, like – what? – a thousand followers on your page. How else!'

'WAIT, CHECK IT NOW!'

'Check what?'

'How many followers my page has! Where's my phone?'

I think I might have left it to charge on the counter again. I leap out of bed and head to the kitchen. It's not there. I dive back onto the bed and flatten my body down on the mattress, rummaging my hands under the pillows and the duvet. I find it in between the sheets. My hands are trembling as I unlock it.

Text message from Phaedra to Eartha

08.45

So ... you have a crush on pink hair girl then huh? ;)

08.45

Also, I'm dying at your comparison of Matt to stale fridge cheese in that video.

08.46

At least he has had the courtesy of unfollowing you back. Next thing he will do is block you to protect his ego.

FUCKING HELL. WHAT HAVE I DONE? PANIC COURSES THROUGH ME.

I AM SWEATING COCONUT VODKA.

STALE FRIDGE CHEESE?! HAS MATT SEEN THIS VIDEO?!

I open up Wonderland. I scrape back my hair to get a clearer view, it can't be …

'Rose … I've got 90,389 fucking followers.'

I shove the screen in their face.

I start screaming and click on some of the people following me.

@fishsticks8 followed you 10 seconds ago.

She has 732 followers and lives in Philadelphia. What does someone in Philadelphia want to do with me? Her feed is filled with pictures of pre-birth yoga videos.

@venusparadise followed you 8 seconds ago.

She has 300k followers. I click to see if we have any connections in common. Rose follows her. I wonder if they've slept together? I can see that Rose has commented the sweaty-face emoji under every one of her selfies. I start smirking into my phone.

'What?' Rose nudges me.

'Way to play it cool, mate …'

'OH MY GOD, DID SHE START FOLLOWING YOU? My God, Eartha, you've got to get me in there …'

'Rose, she started following me, like … ten seconds ago.'

I retreat and plug back into Wonderland. There are more and more names. I search through their profiles. People who have never paid me attention before let alone knew of my existence. All flocking towards me, to find out who I am, what I have to say. I refresh the page. 110,010 followers.

'It keeps going up! What does this even mean?' I squeal.

'It means ... that people are gonna be gagging to buy your collages now. Be careful what you wish for, baby,' Rose replies.

I click to read my message requests on Wonderland. Over 1,000 new messages. I'm not sure what to expect opening them. Did I use all the politically correct terminology? I was so drunk. So unfiltered. Such a state. Are these going to be hate mail? I may have been dropped in my sleep before I even became anybody. Thousands of people forming an opinion on me as I rest soundly, completely unaware. My eyes scroll through all the usernames.

@Babygirl-69

@HannahStorm

@girl2000

*@phallic_*

@fuckthegenderbinary!

@DaisyCottril

@Dykes_r_us17

All of these strangers piling in furiously to talk to me. Some of them are telling me I've changed their lives or their minds. I can't quite comprehend it. I decide to start with *@Dykes_r_us17* as the username's caught my eye.

Hey Eartha! ...

... I've linked your video to some of my 'straight' friends who are in the same position you were in with your boyfriend. Sometimes it takes hearing it from someone else for it to sink in. I think you're going to liberate a lot of women with this ☺

P.S I'd love to take you on a date if you're up for it ;)

No one's ever hit me up through Wonderland in my life. I suppose they wouldn't bother flirting with a collage. Should I reply to all of these messages? Is that what influencers do, do they reply to everyone?

'Has a Dyke Daddy asked you out on a date?' Rose asks, hovering over my phone.

I was about to say the D-word, but I don't think I'm allowed to. I pass my phone to Rose to show them the message.

'You don't have to go, you know? You're probably going to get a lot of these.'

They scroll through my inbox and start leaning back onto my bed. I put my head in my hands as my mind scrambles to keep up with the information I am trying to take in. I look up at Rose to find their eyes closed and their face pressed down into a pillow.

I pick up my phone in an attempt to regain control from this whirlwind mess that is erupting out and spilling all the way into the privacy of my bedroom.

I scroll through more and more messages, reading them less and less until I see one from someone with a black box next to their name, she's black-ticked on Wonderland, the subject is '*YOU BRIGHT SHINY THING*'. I open the message, half expecting a spam pop-up to appear of a naked woman or a pumping cock promoting a dick-enhancing drug.

> Hello Eartha,
>
> My name's E.V. I want to start off by saying that I deeply admire your courage in posting about your sexuality to Wonderland. It takes a lot to speak about these things online and I think you're going to be an extraordinary voice for young women.
>
> Saying that, if you're not careful this industry will eat you alive and swallow you whole. Especially as a woman on the internet, you're going to get trolls and all sorts

of abuse just for speaking up about what you believe in. I would love to take you for lunch and discuss some protection and guidance that I believe I can offer you. I have almost two decades of experience working with talent and I really believe you have something to offer the world. If you let me, I think that together we can make you one of Wonderland's shiniest brightest stars.

I'm free this Monday at 1 p.m., The Firestone, if that suits! I look forward to hearing from you. Best, E.V

She signed the message off at the bottom with her details, phone number and 'E.V – Special Talent Division'.

I type E.V's name into Google. I stare back at a picture of her with her arm around Ed Sheeran. I'd have thought it were Photoshopped if it wasn't for his fire emoji comment underneath.

I reopen the message on my phone from E.V and start typing . . .

How's this Tuesday?

DIRECTOR'S NOTE

Eartha's head is spinning so hard that it throws itself out of orbit from the conversation with Rose, out of the bedsit she is sitting in, out of the part of town she lives and works in, and out wider and wider, and further and further.

The screen is filled by Eartha lying in the middle of her bed with all these other people surrounding her and running towards her. We see Macy from Texas from earlier and Dykes_r_us17 and Christian Jessica.

EARTHA: I've gone viral. Thousands of people know about my sex life and my sexuality ...

THE CROWD OF FOLLOWERS (multiple voices in unison, talking over each other): Eartha, you're an ICON, you have changed my life, where did you get your jewellery, I FEEL THE SAME IT'S LIKE YOU'RE READING MY MIND, where do you live, you're going to hell.

Camera A moves over Eartha's body from the feet up, hovering above. She looks up at the camera and it descends closer to her face until it is millimetres away.

ENDS

CHAPTER 8

BRIGHT SHINY THING

Wonderland followers: 202,232

I post a collage I've had in my drafts onto Wonderland for my new 200,000-strong following.

> This one's titled NO GUTS NO GLORY! I feel as though it has taken all my guts to get to this new threshold of existence, but the glory isn't immediate: I miss being in a relationship. But I know this is good for me. I feel like I'm fighting an uphill battle with all the things I've been avoiding over the years, which have come crashing down, finally making themselves confrontable and SEEN! What haven't you done yet that you've always wanted to do? What's stopping you? Are YOU scared of what life has to offer because of a person you're attached to? #IsBeingSingleHotOrTragic?

I press 'post' and get myself ready for the first business meeting of my life, imagining how men in suits called John do this every day without feeling an iota of the imposter syndrome that currently swills around my stomach.

When I try to visualise a 'business meeting' it's always a John and a gathering of other men in suits. They're all sitting in a soulless room with a muted grey office carpet, which has a coarse texture that makes my teeth feel sensitive even thinking about it. A guy at the head of the table will crack a joke about 'the missis' and how much of a nag fiancées are, before some big bloke forces a harsh laugh that fades into '... so, let's get this show on the road, shall we, boys? The focus of this meeting is how to make more profit by doing less and cutting staff costs.' A man who sits opposite John nods repeatedly as he replies, 'Interesting, John, that's a real growth mindset you're showing up with today', and a faceless woman in another shade of grey types up the meeting into an email. All the men in the meeting will leave – headphones in, world out – feeling as though they contributed the most.

I've spent the rest of the weekend replying to anyone and everyone who has reached out to me on Wonderland for commissions and I have had to make a waiting list of people who want me to design collages for them. The internet really does love it when you open up. I've started to do it more often. I imagine it can become quite addictive to bare all when there's a chance you will be rewarded for it. I normally take on about five commissions a week, but who knows how long this burst of popularity will last? Tomorrow I could slip up and wake up to find the internet has found someone new to obsess over. Another avatar discarded into Wonderland's refuse, left out as roadkill for the trolls to feast on with their hot takes about *why I deserved it* followed up months later by *what Eartha's descent taught us about internet culture* for one last squeeze of the likes. I've decided to take on ten commissions this week. I'm going to work into the evenings to get them all done – I need the money.

By some miracle Phaedra seems charmed by my drunken revelation that I have a crush on her (that's now been watched by over two million people). By anyone's standards it was a wildly inappropriate thing to do. Rose has even gained some new followers, too; everyone was commenting underneath the video – *Whose fist is that?* and *I want those tattooed hands to finger me* – so I tagged Rose and threw them to the horny wolves. Mum saw the video and she's told me that she's upset with me for referring to her relationship with Dad. I tried to assure her no one knew who they were. She rang me and told me that I 'didn't need to drag her into it' but that she's proud of me for 'inspiring all those lovely gay people'. And Matt? Well, Matt blocked me and apparently he's going to share his side of the story in a poem he has produced beats to. I'm hoping he will resurrect 'The Yin to my Yang' to try to gain some more followers and accidentally drop himself in the process.

I examine myself in the mirror while I wait for my lift to show up, trying to get the measure of the woman I see there. Why did she get this opportunity? I hear the noise of an engine idling outside my flat and peer out of the dust-laden window. I've never had a car sent for me before and I've never been to a place like The Firestone. In fact, the most I've ever spent on a dinner is thirty quid, and that included drinks. I saw in a video on Wonderland that the hand soap at The Firestone is so expensive they have to lock it into holders to stop people from stealing it. Someone like me doesn't belong in a place that has to lock up soap.

I stare at myself again. I look smart in this blue faux-fur cuffed coat that I nabbed at a charity shop. My entire back will be drenched with sweat by the time I arrive, but it's part of the look and I'm not willing to compromise. This is my power outfit, a cloak of artificial importance to mask the deep-seated feelings of inadequacy.

Since the message I've been furiously writing and erasing notes in my phone for the meeting, curating the version of Eartha I want E.V to meet. I've rinsed her social media for details about her life. She has no tagged photos, which I imagine is to protect her famous clients. Either she's really good at hiding her relationship or she doesn't have one, as I can't seem to find any images of a love interest. But the way she talked about my sexuality like it was a trendy commodity tells me she's straight. I noticed through my incessant stalking that she took a big break from posting for an entire year and then came back with an elusive Albert Camus quote:

> *In the depths of winter, I finally learned that within me there lay an invincible summer.*

It received 1,328 likes and comments from some black-ticked users saying, 'Welcome back <3' and 'There she is!' and 'Love the new haircut'.

What happened to her during the depths of her winter? Whatever happened didn't break her. She's followed by a lot of people I look up to as well: political leaders, feminists, celebrities. Which makes me wonder what on earth she wants to do with me.

A text pings upon my phone.

> ERIK, your driver, has arrived.

*

'Here you are, Ms.'

My world is brought back into sharp focus. I realise it's been raining and the windows are covered in the weather's tears. I've been somewhere else entirely during the journey, drifting along the seemingly endless roadmap of different outcomes that my life could go down after today – and of what kind of woman E.V might turn out to be. Olympia didn't look the same from within the interior of the car; I've only ever seen it from a bus. In the hired cab I felt finally as though I was in the right lane of the city, a part of its inner workings.

I scoop up the bottom of my coat and turn to shut the door behind me. But it won't close. The driver starts laughing at me like I'm a stupid, silly woman who can't close a car door. I throw him a glare.

'It's electric! Let go, darlin'. I can close it from in here,' he says.

Oh. Right.

I jump back, release my hand from the handle and watch as the door closes in one seamless motion into the car's body.

As I approach the black doors set within an ornate marble arch, my stomach starts doing little backflips. A concierge smiles at me and gestures his hands for me to enter; I nod and walk through the entrance. As I brush past, I feel his hands on my shoulder. I jump out of my skin and he raises his hands as though he's surrendering.

'Mademoiselle, I apologise ...'

He is beautiful.

'I thought you nodded for me to remove your coat. *Je suis désolé*!'

That must be some kind of posh, universal sign language I don't know about.

'Thank you, but I'm keeping this one on. It's part of the outfit.'

He laughs.

'I agree ... and with those boots too, Mademoiselle!'

He flicks his wrist and leads me through a downstairs lounge. We walk down a long corridor and I can almost smell the wealth in the building's pores. My eyes scan the walls, admiring the grand paintings and abstract sculptures that are dotted around the lobby.

'Your reservation is booked for eighth floor, the rooftop. Walk through the corridor and take an immediate left. She'll meet you on the terrace.'

He pushes the number '8' button in the elevator.

The lift opens.

'Thank yo—'

The doors close and I jab my hand into a half wave.

1

2

3

4 …

I wonder if she's as glamorous as her online 8 × 4 cm red-carpet images?

5

6

7 …

Floor 8

The doors open, revealing a green-tiled corridor with a mirrored ceiling lined with plants which leads out onto the top-floor restaurant, bustling with people having lunch and taking meetings. The place is pulsating with phallic energy. Everyone looks like they're here to make something 'big' happen. Even the way they're all sitting on their chairs: leaning right back with their arms resting on their necks. The chairs look like they have been custom made to fit each of their sprawling, powerful inhabitants. There's floor-to-ceiling glass walls and the air is thick with the smell of vanilla bean and shaved truffle on hot food. Above the shiny bar is a wall covered entirely with portraits of women sitting inside gilded frames. It seems as though these animated, suited men are here to make the world work and the women mounted on the walls are watching on powerlessly. The eyes of the women in these photos look lifeless, as though their souls are elsewhere. There's a chorus of ice clashing against metallic cocktail shakers as bartenders make espresso martinis and alcoholic drinks with no mixers. This is where the city makes things happen, it could be 2 a.m. or 2 p.m. in here, it could be day or night, you could order a full English and a negroni and no one would bat an eyelid. I feel very small and feminine in among these men and their moneyed lives.

The French guy said to go left, didn't he? I make my fingers into 'L' shapes so I can get my bearings. There's a small door made from the same glass panels that has no sign or handle, but it seems to be leading onto a rooftop patio. As I step out, I can see a woman in the corner table smoking a cigarette and looking pensively out at the view. There are other groups of women at tables scattered around, but she surveys the city below, on her own. It's definitely her. She wears a neck scarf and big round sunglasses, each in coordinating shades of orange, a waistcoat for a dress and a large white shirt underneath.

'Eartha!' she exclaims as she jolts out of her seat, frantically stabbing out her cigarette and gesturing with her free hand for me to come and join her.

'Sorry about that,' she says, swatting the smoke away with her bejewelled hand.

'Oh, don't worry ...' I pull out my baccy pouch. 'Me too.'

'Sit down! Sit down!' she says, pointing at a seat opposite her.

She reaches into her waistcoat pocket and tucks her lighter away. It's then I realise that a real full-scale palm tree grows from within the table. Not the fake ones they put out in the summer at the pub down the road from me.

'Thank you so much for the car. I'm so grateful,' I say, jerking my head to the right as the palm tree now blocks my view of her.

'Oh, plenty more where that came from. I just like to know you're getting here safely. I feel very protective over you. Which is partly why I wanted to meet today,' she says quickly, swatting the words lingering on the tip of my tongue away like they are leftover cigarette smoke.

'You might not feel it yet, but I see something special in you and I'm just going to get straight into it … I think you're *it*. Unfortunately, none of us realise till much too late how much we were capable of. We remain stuck in the fifth chapter of the book that is our life, living out the same mundane routine … not realising that there are hundreds of pages left. My trick is that I can see the full story, how it will all play out, which plotlines will disappear and which ones need to be enhanced, so that *you* become the central character in your story.'

She pauses to light another cigarette and has this strange, impassioned expression on her face. *The central character* … It feels as though those words were designed especially for me.

'I see things in people that they don't see in themselves and help them make a fuck tonne of money from it. Like working on an oil rig, darling, but fracking for TALENT! Finding the best product.'

She smacks her hand into the table enthusiastically and the silver cutlery jumps around us.

'I want to offer you up to the world of Wonderland as someone to fall in love with, someone to follow … someone it wants and needs. You know how we can latch onto someone new every week: so-and-so's new girlfriend or *this* new TV show host? *You*, however, I want to build *you* to last.'

She blows out more smoke.

'I don't do it for free, of course. It's my job. I charge a commission. My skill is to get you to see *your* skills, and build empires out of people's fucking lives.'

An empire?

I decide to confront her sweeping statements with some cold hard truths.

'A rat from my balcony got at my bins last night and spewed a week's worth of food all over my kitchen floor. I appreciate your vision, but I don't have the space, lifestyle or money to build an empire.'

'Godddddddddddddddd, that's great! That's great, really great and original. Put it all into your art. That's why people will love you. The stuff about fancying the girl who shagged your ex, too: GOLD DUST! Brilliant!' she says as her teeth clatter to keep up with her mind, revelling in the grit of a working-class, low-rent, minimum-space, downtrodden existence.

She stabs her cigarette at me and looks at me coolly.

'You're so down to *Eartha!*' she says and laughs at herself. I want to soak in her mannerisms in the hope that they become my own. Her eyes don't search mine for approval. She just carries on. Smoking. Talking. Smoking. Big talk. Smoking. Planning. Smoking.

'I call myself a talent enhancer. You have all the talent; I'm here to show it to the world. We have to think ahead and think beyond what the world already has on Wonderland and what it might want next, or who people will want to follow down the rabbit hole next time. Who the girls will want to obsess over!

I seriously believe that person could be you, Eartha.'

She pauses to get the attention of the waiter, who I realise must have been hovering to take our order all this time. She raises her eyebrows and gestures with her hand that we're ready for him now, her bangles clattering like her teeth.

'To put it bluntly, your collages are great and people will buy them. They're so fresh, so new, so mixed medium. Binding together all the worlds which have previously lived so far apart: print, painting, video, textiles. It feels like a whirlpool of creativity where no hierarchy exists, only the one you chose to give space to. I know this might all sound a bit much, a bit … upfront for me to confess my admiration to you like this, but I see something in you …'

She points at me with her cigarette between her fingers and her eyes lock onto mine.

'A younger, braver version of myself. I feel a responsibility to help you realise your potential; I feel it would be a great disservice to the world if you didn't go for it. It's going to be a lot of work at first, but one day you'll be paid to just appear. That's the level I'm talking. I believe that there is something you and I can do to change the way Wonderland speaks and thinks. I think we can help women, I think we can heal women, and I think we can set women free. You opened up a portal when you uploaded that video, a portal into how we can live and think differently about each other. We need to seize this moment where everyone is listening to you and use it to expand people's closed minds and take back their power. When I was younger, women didn't have access to other women or their truth and vulnerability in the way that your generation does. My job is to ensure that these voices are heard among the chatter and reach the people who need it most. We need to see more of YOU and the "you" we need to see is someone who you and I can work on from today, we can curate and create the best bits of Eartha together to help women everywhere, and then, I think we might have Wonderland's next *bright shiny thing* in our hands.'

E.V finally turns her attention to the waiter, who has been dawdling next to us. She orders two duck wasabi somethings from the menu.

Reverberating around my head are the words:

BRIGHT SHINY THING.

BRIGHT SHINY THING

BRIGHT SHINY THING.

BRIGHT SHINY THING.

BRIGHT SHINY THING.

BRIGHT SHINY THING.

BRIGHT SHINY THING.

BRIGHT SHINY THING.

BRIGHT SHINY THING.

BRIGHT SHINY THING.

BRIGHT SHINY THING.

BRIGHT SHINY THING.

E.V lights another cigarette. She's studied and spent time thinking about how and who I am in a way that no one has ever done before, she has reached into my core and has found out what I am capable of. I feel as though she's now taking her chisel to carve this sculpture out of me that I have been fighting so hard to find. I see the disparate pieces of my life falling into place. A once dark, blank void of the unknown now starts to knit together as the bright, glamorous, enriching life I've always dreamed of. She's the kind of woman to force you to reach your potential. She believes in me as much as I now do myself. I look back into the restaurant and my gaze is met by the sea of women sitting in portraits, lining the wall of the bar.

CHAPTER 9

DO I HAVE TO BUY A STRAP-ON?

Wonderland followers: 281,063

'She called you a what?' Rose says as we sit huddled up in the front window of the coffee shop, perched on high stools. Our legs are mangled together and we're watching the city play out in front of us. I look into the middle distance, fixating on the cyclists and dog walkers in the street, all blurring into one colourful haze through the steamed-up window. I think of the other world that exists within The Firestone, so far removed from this coffee shop and Rose. High above the city. The thought of being part of that world makes me feel wet with yearning – the idea of my future finally arousing me more than Matt did in the last years of our relationship.

'What's wrong with that?' I reply.

I feel a Rose-shaped hole burn into the side of my face.

'She referred to you as a *product*, Eartha,' they say, sounding exasperated.

'She didn't *call* me a product, she said being an influencer is a bit like being a product – you have to market yourself. She's a genius!' I explain.

Rose's hair is tousled in front of the translucent skin of their face and their eyes pierce through the strands. They're so composed that I feel like a crushed bag of cheap crisps in comparison. I instinctively sit up and straighten my back. Sometimes I wonder if I ever even fancied Rose or if I just envied them.

'So … this E.V wants to objectify women and she wants to make it profitable?' Rose goes on.

'Exactly. I'll be the one making money, she just takes a cut. I thought you were all pro people doing whatever they want with their bodies? I'm selling my image, my online identity, and I still get to retain it. It's still all mine,' I explain.

'I get that. But I just think it says a lot about how she views you, you know? It doesn't sound very ethical to me … Does she even see you as a person, or just a cash cow she wants to milk?' They raise their eyebrows at me.

I flinch as they say this and then try to lift my glass from its coaster, but its suction is fusing the two together. When the coaster finally falls off it lands awkwardly on the counter, like a rocket's discarded engine as it goes into orbit. I apologise quietly and then stir the espresso up with the oat milk until it's blended into one.

'Whatever the answer to that question is, I don't care. It's a business relationship. Rose, she is proper magical.'

'I just want you to be careful.'

'But that's what *she* is there for. I really appreciate the advice. But she sees something in me; who am I to tell her otherwise?'

Rose rests a hand on my leg.

'That's not what I'm saying. You deserve to be huge, Eartha. But you were on that track before she came along. You need to know that. I just question what her motive is …'

I look down at my coffee now sitting derailed from its coaster and I turn my phone over to see that another 2,012 people have started following me on Wonderland. I trust Rose but E.V's reputable; she's black-ticked and she's got 500,000 followers. This is an opportunity, one which could offer the very life I've left Matt to chase after. It's so tantalisingly close I can almost taste the *real* champagne I'll be drinking. This kind of opportunity is a one-off and I'd have to fight so hard to do it all on my own. I need E.V.

'I'm not trying to deflate you. You know I want you to have all your success … Go on, tell me more about her, then,' Rose says.

I actually don't know much about E.V, or her story. All I've seen are Google images I've hunted down. But I fill Rose in as much as I can with a few extensions of the truth.

'Just don't jump into bed with her until you've weighed everything up,' they quip.

'Of course not. But I do need to jump into bed with *someone.*'

'Have you been on any dates with girls yet?'

Their eyes glisten, every cell in their body taut.

'Well, actually … there's nothing going on right now.'

They drop their head in disappointment. But at least they don't have to hear another story in which I am forced to paper over the Matt shitshow.

'I'm sorry to disappoint. I can't stop thinking about that Phaedra girl … I feel really weird about it! I don't know if I'm obsessed with her because of what happened, or if I actually like her? I just don't know how to be single. Let alone be queer and single, and …'

I glance sharply towards the counter: my monologue about bisexual singlehood has been bulldozed by a barista who's just turned on the coffee grinder. I raise my voice so it travels over the racket of blitzing beans.

'How do I flirt with girls? Are the thirst traps you post on Wonderland supposed to be different? How do you even slide into a girl's Wonderland inbox without being creepy?'

I'm now having to shout to make my myself heard over the racket.

'Do I have to change my STYLE now? Because I LIKE the way I dress, but no one's going to clock me as someone that likes GIRLS if I dress this way.'

I can't keep up with my thoughts as they explode out of me.

'How do I remain myself? I've not even tried "being myself" with girls, because I've not tried dating girls yet. I've not got any experience under my belt and I know that's super UNATTRACTIVE. But maybe it's all about confidence. Do I have to talk differently? Should I start wearing Y-fronts? LIKE, DO I HAVE TO BUY A STRAP-ON?!'

The coffee machine stops and everyone's eyes dart in my direction. Rose's face creases up, trying to stop their snorts of laughter from filling the stunned silence of the customers who are now pretending to scrutinise their phones. I lower my head closer to theirs so I can whisper.

'That fucking barista. Rose, I swear, she did that on purpose.'

Rose laughs and grabs both of my hands. We're now huddled so close we are one silhouette.

'First of all, that coffee grinder is on a timer.' I roll my eyes and tut my tongue, releasing my grip from their hands. 'I'm not finished.'

They grab my hands back to the middle of the table. 'Second of all, you do NOT have to buy a strap-on.' All the customers who are trying to erase the image of me wearing a harness by sending formal work emails seem to relax.

'You don't have to do anything you don't want to do. And, if you want to meet girls, you're gonna have to download FIRE.'

'One of the girls at my old job used that thing to meet some bloke and it ended in tears. He lied about having hair!'

'Okay, but that's straight FIRE. Straight men are a different breed. Also, most apps let you connect your Wonderland page to your profile now so you can verify that they're real. You can check if they've been dropped, too, so you're safe! Listen, you've been in a relationship for years. Shit's different now. It's almost impossible to meet girls any other way. Sure, you can go to a gay bar, but they're likely the same girls that all of your friends have been with,' Rose explains.

'You just don't want me to hook up with any of your exes!'

'Well, duh! But not to sound vulgar, mate …'

They look around to check no one's listening, point a finger in my face and murmur, 'You're fresh fucking meat!'

I think of a T-shirt I once winced at in a street market that said 'Dip me in chocolate and throw me to the lesbians'.

'Being fresh meat is hot. Everyone's been with everyone in this small scene in Olympia, so the gays all love it when there's someone new around! If you haven't been with anyone that they have, your value goes up. We should make you a FIRE profile. Give me your phone.'

I look around.

'Here?!'

'Eartha, we're logging you on to a dating site on your phone, not having sex on the counter,' Rose says indignantly. 'Everyone's got their head deep in Wonderland anyway.'

I look around the café; everyone has the same doped-up smile on their faces as they stare into their phones. Little white rectangles fill the reflection of their irises. They're all plugged in. All of them are unaware of what's going on around them or who is in front of them, collectively yearning for acceptance from their phones. I wonder which rooms they're inhabiting online instead of the one they're in here, now. I see the guy sitting with a black scarf round his neck, black trousers, a backwards cap and a slouched hoodie; I wonder who he is on Wonderland. It's so hard to tell who's being themselves and who's lying. Who's a real person and who has bought into their Wonderland avatar, convincing themselves that they're happier online. There's a woman sat a little further along the bar in a slackish grey suit and dishevelled bob. I glance down without moving my head to look discreetly at her screen. She types –SCREAMINGGGGG– slamming her thumb onto the –G– multiple times with the most deadpan look on her face. She exits her texts and opens up Wonderland, uploads a 3D image of the component parts of the salad she ordered in front of her, along with their calorific content and salt measure, typing up with the caption '#HealthIsWealth'. She posts it, turns around to call for the waiter and requests they bring her a portion of fries. There are bags under her eyes, she doesn't look like she has unplugged for days.

Rose is already building a dating profile on my phone with the maniacal conviction they apply to everything they set their mind to. As they type and tap away, assessing me, they ask if I mind curating the truth a little bit. I say 'no' without thinking.

Rose finally comes up for air with a smug look on their face and claims they've chosen the photos I look hottest in. I take the phone from their hand and swipe through the selection; there's a picture of me smiling with Rose in the sun, one of me at my desk, a selfie with the good natural light I took in my bathroom, and there's—

'What the hell, Rose?' I shove my phone in their face.

'Your hands!'

'Yes, a picture of my hands. What were you thinking?' I look back at the picture.

'Wait, hold up, did you just take this picture?!' I ask.

'Yup, while you were staring at a customer. They look really good, and your hands…' they hold out their hands either side of their head and turn them into guns pointing up towards the sky … 'are your dick.'

They start aggressively pumping them up and down, squinting their eyes and biting their lip.

'Rose, stop being so loud,' I say, pushing their hands down into their lap.

I extend my arm out in front of me and tilt my head, examining each of my fingers. I turn it around to look at my palm, lowering my middle and index fingers. I think of what these fingers will feel. What they might plunge into. I think of what it will feel like to be inside a woman.

'All right. Let's keep the dick pic in!' I shrug as if they are forcing me.

I pass the phone back; they reject it and push it away.

'This bit's for you, you have to write about yourself, what you're looking for …'

I type while they're talking.

'Done!' I say.

'Twenty-five, looking for fun, friendship or make-out sessions—'

'Friendship? Come on, don't be one of *those* people. There's nothing worse than meeting a girl for a date and then it turns out to be all "I am just looking for friends". You're looking for a hot date, right? Be honest.'

'Okay, *looking for hot dates and make-out sessions*.'

'HOT! Maybe also add that you're new to this. Some people will be looking for hook-ups and don't wanna be teaching you how to "be gay"... they'll want a girl with more experience.'

The comment stings as it lands; the thought of being bad at sex scares the living orgasm out of my body. Matt would always tell me how useless I was in bed when we were in the heat of a row. *What if I'm just as bad as men at fucking girls?*

'Look, I'm just here to impart my wisdom. You can take my advice or not. It might actually be better if I back off a bit. I think you'll learn some of this stuff better on your own.'

I feel suddenly defensive. I want to be left alone to do my thing. In private. I activate my account.

Ping

'Oh shit, has someone messaged me?' I say.

Ping

Ping

Ping

Rose grips the top of the chair between their legs and stretches back.

'What did I tell ya ...?' they say.

They stand up from straddling the chair, grab their bag, put it over their shoulder and give me two pats on the back while looking me dead in the eyes.

'Fresh. Meat. Let me know how you get on with all of those fingertips ...' They walk back to the counter. I return my gaze to my phone, hypnotised by the little red bubble above my inbox that reads '19' climbing higher and higher every few seconds or so.

20 new people have liked your profile.

21 new people have liked your profile.

23 new people have liked your profile.

26 new people have liked your profile.

35 new people have liked your profile.

I click on one of the profiles. A woman who looks way too much like my mum to make it normal for me to date her. Only one man has liked me, Sebastian. I skim past his bio and go straight to the link at the bottom that leads me to his Wonderland page and ... his account's public. He follows way more people than the amount that follow him back. A little opportunistic, the kind of guy to follow and unfollow to see which ones return the favour. I click to see if we have any connections in common. He follows a few of my favourite musicians and media outlets that would at first glance suggest he's a feminist. I click through his tagged photos to see if there's any ex-girlfriend's old tagged pictures lurking around. Let's see if he has a type. If *I'm* his type. There's a group picture of him and his friends. All men. Same sort of style. Long hair, tattoos, probably all in a band. I click on one of his friends who looks familiar, he's called Sam. I screw my face waiting for it to load. Sam, as in, SAM. Matt's friend Sam? Fucking hell. Absolutely not. I shudder and reject him. The next profile is Victoria. Wow, she's hot. Or, they? There's a bit of an androgynous vibe going on. I scroll down and check. *They/them pronouns.* I click through to their Wonderland page. Shit. They have 20k followers and they follow 100 people. I click on their 'following' list and we have no mutual links. Probably because they know cooler people than me. I read that they're a drummer. Their feed is full of pictures of them in different locations. Mirror selfies, in a studio somewhere, pictures in the street, pictures with their ... girlfriend? Wait, hang on a minute. I return to Victoria's FIRE page and read the bio. *Couple looking for a third, let us take you out!* I laugh and forward the profile on to Rose.

Text message from Eartha to Rose
17.32
Don't wanna throw myself in at the deep end with a couple, but they might be your cup of tea ;)
(Link to profile on FIRE)

I watch the notifications ping up one by one, sometimes two or three at a time, just like they did when my video went viral. All of these different usernames, all of these faces flooding in, to talk to me. It's the complete opposite of rejection. My mind is going wild with the abundance of offers all served up on this shiny platter of a phone screen.

I wonder if this is how Rose feels every day; being as hot as they are, you never get to experience the real world of being rejected. You just live in a sort of bubble where everyone loves you. I wonder if this is what it feels like to be the chooser and not the person sitting on a shelf waiting to be *chosen.*

DIRECTOR'S NOTE
Eartha locked in.
Eartha sits staring at her phone, just like the people she was judging a mere twenty minutes ago. The imprint of the white rectangle is now etched on her eyeballs, too.
Camera A zooms in.

Camera B captures a new girl liking her profile every minute.
She flicks into the notes section on her phone and types a draft post idea for Wonderland: *Being hot? Form of romantic nepotism for your love life?*
She goes back onto FIRE:
A profile catches her eye.
Mona.
Casting director notes: Mona has a septum nose piercing, long dark brown hair that goes past her waist and an irresistibly sleepy gaze that looks like she wants to either fuck you or kill you. In some of her photos she's pictured wearing fringe shawls and dresses, in others she wears polo shirts, baggy suits and Doc Martens. She's put her top two artists as The Stone Roses and Jefferson Airplane, which perfectly mirrors her niche blend of aesthetics. She's cool, intimidatingly cool.
Eartha starts typing a message to Mona.
'Hi Mona, what are your plans for the weekend?'
ENDS

CHAPTER 10

MONA

Wonderland followers: 390,763

> A picture of Eartha fresh from a shower with toothpaste on her pimples.
> Caption – Selfie Care – is uploaded onto Wonderland
> Comments:
> *@LostInWonderland* Can we expect a tutorial any time soon for that eyeliner look?! <3
> *@StaceyFooly* SKINCARE ROUTINE!
> *@GenerallyDoingAlright* UR A VOICE OF AN ASSHOLE GENERATION.
> *@VeronicaEscher* Give the girls what they wantttttt (make-up tutorial).

18.32
My only form of skincare routine has been to buy the cheapest moisturiser I can get hold of in the chemist and then try to remember to put it on before I go to bed. It's not going to make a video-length tutorial. There are so many replies to the picture I uploaded. *YES! Skincare routine coming soon*, I reply, mentally

extinguishing the theories around female beauty and its links to oppression that I've just read about this morning in *The Beauty Myth*.

I need to give the girls what they want!

> *@E.VTalent* You look gorgeous, darling! Look at your inbox ...

I check my email to see one from E.V titled 'Sign here for the life of your BLOODY dreams'. She's asked me to read it through before tomorrow's meeting so she can start reaching out to 'brands'. I'll give it a couple of hours before I send it over with a signature to at least *look* like I've considered this. But I don't need to think twice. This is the life I want.

18.44

I'm going on a date with Mona tonight, that girl whose Wonderland page should be titled *A portfolio collection of why you should date me*. Before I shut down my laptop I look back at a list I've made of all the things I could ask on my first queer date tonight, just so we're not stuck in any of those date-doom silences.

I've been inhaling online tutorials about dating and fucking as a queer woman. When you come out later in life everyone else has already 'worked it all out' through trial and error – not knowing what you are doing stops being a cute affectation. I don't want to make any obvious errors and I'm also neurotically panicking that I will be shit in bed. I feel like a virgin all over again. I wish that men thought to undertake this amount of prep before they had sex with women. I wish I hadn't been told to just 'expect' my first time to 'really hurt' to excuse inadequate foreplay, allowing men to explain my own feelings to me, right down to the pain experienced in my own body. I wish it was men that watched YouTube tutorials on how to make women comfortable, instead of how to get them into bed. I wish men cared this much about making sure they're good enough for women, before they enter into their lives as unfinished projects with mummy issues, looking for a woman who'll make it their mission to fix them. I wish men walked away from women the second they realise they have nothing of value to offer and I wish women didn't talk themselves out of things, places and people they don't think they deserve. Why does the responsibility of compassion and consideration constantly fall onto our shoulders?

My form of protest against this double standard won't be to start acting like men on dates. I don't think I have it in me to not care how a woman might feel if I ghosted her. I refuse to offer any woman the bare minimum. But I'm used to *being* courted and not *doing* the courting. (And by 'courted', I mean showing up to a pub and taking it in turns to buy drinks with Matt.) I'm not used to having to be the one to impress a woman on a date. I really want this girl to like me and I know that she'll be harder to impress than a man. I can usually lean into a man's ingrained sexism to impress him as he assumes he will be more intelligent. A guy once tried to get my number by calling me 'different' because I knew which IPA I wanted to order at the bar. Men never expect a woman to have fully firing synapses. But Mona, a woman herself, will *expect* me to be a full human.

I made a reservation at Some Velvet Morning, a new bar that has opened in Tangerine Yard named after the Lee Hazlewood song. I wouldn't have known it even existed if I hadn't walked past one evening last week. I was on my way to buy a patchouli and vanilla-scented candle to send home to Mum for her birthday, with the note 'a little bit of you and a little bit of me'. There was a warm orange glow emanating out of the front-facing windows, I could make out a few candlelit tables and, above the shelves of spirits, a neon orange sign spelling the name of the bar in cursive font. Rose told me later that they play 'sexy as fuck French music that will make ya knickers wet'. So I booked a reservation.

19.05
I flick on the lamp next to my bedside table and open my wardrobe to work out who I should be tonight. Mona will probably be wearing one of her fringed jackets, but what if she shows up wearing the more masculine tailored looks I have seen her donning on some of her Wonderland plug-ins? Who's going to be the 'gay' one? Or can we both be the gay one? I don't want to look like I'm copying her, but I also want her to fancy me. I slip into a cream silk slip dress with a low back and lace at the cleavage. You can see my nipples through the lace but that shouldn't matter if the date is lit by candlelight, a little bit of visi-nip never killed anyone. I curl the tips of my hair away from my face, tie it up in a loose bun and leave my layers at the front. I add a pair of black ankle cowboy boots and an oversized blazer, spraying myself with Rose's signature musky perfume that they left here.

I'm trying to perfect my eyeliner matching the angles of the other eye's flick.

Ping

The eyeliner splatters across my cheek. I place the lid back on and reach for my phone.

> *Text message from Mona to Eartha*
> 19.21
> Really excited to meet you! See you in an hour.

I hurriedly check the top of the screen for the time.

It's 7.22 p.m.

I'm going on a *queer* date in an hour's time.

People are going to see me as a *lesbian* in public.

I pause and notice how that word exists uncomfortably inside me. Why does it feel like a dirty word? I've been so focused on acting the part and gorging on tips and information online that I haven't considered *being* the part.

19.26

With an entire face full of make-up to redo, I reply to Mona:

> *Text message from Eartha to Mona*
>
> 19.26
>
> Me too. I'm on my way. See u soon ☺

I take a deep breath. Inhaling for four seconds.

1

2

3

4

Breathing out again.

1

2

3

4

I re-apply my eyeliner, opting for a more feline look and smudging it underneath. I look around to check I've got my things …

Keys … money … phone.

Right, I am ready.

But not really.

Ping

Text message from Matt to Eartha

19.53

I miss you.

I turn around to check he's not following me.

It's like he knows I'm about to move on.

I shake my head.

I miss you.

Ping

Text message from Matt to Eartha

19.54

Can I get that Fleetwood Mac vinyl back? I need to sell it for rent.

There it is. I reactively punch out a text into my phone: *You stupid manipulative prick, do you think I'm thick? I know what you're doing, trying to wind me back into your life. What a pathetic excuse of a man ...* But the remaining ounce of self-respect that's been growing in me since he left grabs the steering wheel. I 'select all' and delete our entire message thread instead. I drop my phone into my bag, lock up my flat and turn from my door to the street.

Something about being single, moisturised, freshly shaven and dressed up feels like the pinnacle of being alive. I can't remember the last time the world felt as though it belonged to me in this way. The night feels so seductive, as though it's holding its climax back from me. As though it understands the kind of foreplay most men don't have the patience for. I move through the streets I have claimed as my own over the last few weeks and I realise that – although yes, I do miss being in a relationship – nothing, *nothing*, NOTHING, compares to being single in this moment. I can't believe I ever forgot how powerful and delicious it is to be female, dressed up and hot for sex. I could do anything I want. I could even put my hand on the crotch of that man's who's eye-fucking me from the side of the road and ask him if he wants to 'get out of here'. I won't. But I could. And that's the fucking point. I wouldn't have allowed myself to think this freely a month ago. I walk along the cobbled stones that lead to Tangerine Yard among other groups of people and their dates, like moths to a flame towards Some Velvet Morning.

19.57

Rose was right about the French music. When I'm seated in the soft orange glow of the bar, I order a Paloma from a velvet-covered drinks menu. I observe everyone around me and reckon I can tell who's on a first date and who's not. There's a girl frantically nodding her head, really showing the girl she's on a date with how much she's 'hearing' her. A couple in their late fifties are sitting in the corner by the window and I get the sense that the wife is desperate to get her husband's attention, but his eyes are focused on my chest. She points out to him the twisted-stem martini glasses that the waitress brought over and says to him, 'Recognise these?!' He doesn't reply. I watch her deflate, she wants acknowledgement for all of the unrecognised emotional labour and consideration that have clearly gone into building their home – she needs him to see her. But he is too busy gawking at a stranger's tits. It hurts. It's like I'm watching my old life with Matt reflected back on me. I mouth 'fuck off' to him and he abruptly turns his attention to his wife and I turn back to the bar.

20.05

I check my phone screen, she's not that late. I uncross my legs and cross them back over so that I look as good as possible from the direction of the door.

I overhear a waiter say, 'Right this way! Your friend is waiting for you at the bar. Can I take your coat?'

Friend.

'Oh, no, I'm good, thank you!' I hear her say forcibly.

I adjust my face to give her my side profile and pretend to look at the contents of the cocktail menu, despite the one I ordered sitting in a pool of its own condensation in front of me.

Fuck. Fuck. Fuck.

When do I quit acting?

When do I 'naturally' turn to look up.

I am very aware that I need to look up …

'Eartha?'

I slam the menu shut to look at her.

Oh, God. She is perfection.

'Is it Mona?'

'I hope so,' she says with a smirk.

Is it Mona?! Of course it's her. What a completely stupid *someone-who-definitely-hasn't-ever-been-on-a-date-with-a-girl-before* thing to say.

She raises her arms to hug me. I awkwardly clamber off the bar stool to stand up and hug her back. She's a few inches taller than me. She smells so good.

'You smell *so* good.'

DID I JUST SAY MY THOUGHTS OUT LOUD?

'Thank you. I love your eye make-up.'

'Thank you, I actually had to redo it three times …'

What the fuck am I doing? I might as well write 'gay virgin' on my forehead.

'I love yours, too. Your hair looks beautiful,' I say, reaching out my hand to grasp my cocktail glass.

'Thank you, my mum braided it for me and helped choose my outfit, so I can't take any credit for this work of art.' She swoops the dark brown braids over her shoulder before seating herself on the stool. She crosses her long legs, which glow a glittery umber in the low light of the bar.

'Anyway, what are you drinking?' she asks as she adjusts herself on her stool.

'Oh, this is a Paloma!'

Her eyes are now fixed on the menu, her finger tracing each drink from the top to the bottom. My mind starts whirring and racing, trying to think of the questions I had written out in prep.

'So how long have you—'

'Hold that thought . . .' she says.

She closes the menu and looks up at the bartender.

'I'll have the same please! But with salt, two limes and more ice.'

She says this with the confidence of someone who can order complicated, off-the-menu drinks without fumbling or apologising. An uncomfortable mirror of how far I'm yet to travel on the road to becoming.

She turns to face me.

'How long have you lived in Olympia?' I ask.

'I'm born and bred! Although I don't have many childhood friends around. I outgrew everyone I went to school with but didn't fancy living anywhere else. You see a lot of people pass through and it can get quite lonely being single here; no one really seems to stay in Olympia. Plus . . .'

She turns around to look at the restaurant, and with her head points towards the guy in the corner on his phone.

'Everyone's head is in Wonderland.' She swirls her index finger beside her head.

I start to wonder how many people have commented on my most recent post and whether people have reshared me. How many could it be?

EARTHA, CONCENTRATE ON YOUR DATE.

'Why are you using dating apps then?' I ask bluntly.

I should probably ask myself this question, too.

'I'm not against them, I love them!' she continues. 'But everyone being on their phones all the time just makes the city more isolating; no one's really … present.'

'That makes sense. I had a video go viral a couple of weeks ago,' I reply, 'and I'm just getting my head around it, and also getting my head around being …'

Shit. Don't say queer. I don't want her to know I've never done this before …

'… being someone that strangers know from a stupid video! It's weird. My friend Rose told me to get onto dating apps if I want to start meeting more women, so that's why I joined.'

Nice pivot.

'Whereabouts are you living, then?' she asks.

I'm still fidgeting with my arms. I have no clue where to put them. I've worked up a nervous sweat and droplets have found their way down to my lower back.

Fuck it. I'll take my blazer off.

'Well, I actually live round the corn—'

I extend my arm out to remove my jacket and hit the tray of a waiter walking past. The knives and forks on serviettes splatter across the floor.

I leap up to help the waiter pick up the debris.

'I'VE GOT THIS!' he erupts.

I look up at Mona and we simultaneously purse our lips, trying to contain our laughter.

Our first inside joke. I'll reference this later to make her laugh.

The waiter collects the wayward cutlery and tries to move past Mona. It's a tight squeeze between the bar and the tables, so she puts her hand on my lap to steady herself as she leans in to make way for him. We both start laughing and when he's past, but she doesn't remove her hand. We look up at each other and our eyes meet.

20.22

'I wanted to say, Eartha, this is actually my first date with a girl. And, I think you're really cool, but I was quite nervous about tonight.'

'No really ...? This is my first date with a girl too!' I place my hand on top of hers as I say this, so our hands are now resting just above my knee. It appears that my clumsiness with the waiter has released the nervous energy between us. 'I'm bisexual. I mean, I think ... my attraction to men at this point is hanging on by a single puny thread.'

I slowly press my fingers into hers, so that they start to interlock. Our knees are now enmeshed.

I can't believe I was ever worried about this.

I love this.

No, I am *obsessed* with this.

20.34

Mona continues to tell me things about her life: her coming-out story; her parents' divorce; how she feels powerful dressing like a skinhead from the Eighties because they would have hated a girl like her; how her life is a daily struggle between committing to self-improvement or living in the moment and going with her desires, however impulsive they may be. I tell her that I'm only just learning how to do both too.

21.01

We begin to move closer and closer together. Our fingers lingering and testing boundaries to gauge how the other person is responding. I use my fingers to stroke hers while she talks.

Look at her eyes, not her lips, Eartha; this is rude, she's talking!

It's like staring at someone's tits when they're talking.

Shit, I JUST LOOKED AT HER TITS.

Say something.

Anything.

'You're … gorgeous,' I say.

REALLY?!

'Oh, thank you,' she replies.

'Sorry, I know that has absolutely nothing to do with what you were just saying.'

I AM PANICKING.

She dips her head in embarrassment and then raises her eyes to meet mine. I feel completely and utterly lost in her. My body has a new frequency coursing through it, every muscle is trained on her.

'We're about to kiss, aren't we?' she says, smiling.

ARE WE? DID THAT 'GORGEOUS' LINE REALLY PLAY IN MY FAVOUR?

Our faces are close.

I can smell the tart grapefruit from her Paloma on her tongue.

She pulls me in by my waist, finally opening her mouth to meet mine.

And everything makes sense.

It just makes fucking sense.

Kissing a woman at a bar.

Makes sense.

21.06

She pulls away to take a deep breath and tightens her grip on my legs.

I look around to see that we've attracted the attention of people in the room, who upon seeing my gaze all retreat back to their own worlds. We have become an unintentional spectacle.

'I'm really trying to control myself,' she says finally.

Where do I want this to go?

I stroke the back of her neck while I figure out a response. I look into her eyes.

'Wanna get out of here and have some fun?' I ask.

CHAPTER 11

@HAILEY3000 CAN FUCK OFF

Wonderland followers: 430,939

I kissed a woman. I kissed a woman in public. I stick my hand out from my make-up-sullied bedsheets and slam it around my nightstand to try to locate my phone. It's not there. An arrow of dread shoots through me and I sit up immediately – a fear of where it is and what I may have done on it the night before now triggers my bodily instincts into gear. I spot it on the floor near the door, among the spewed items of clothing from last night. I drag myself up to get it, before retreating into the warmth of my duvet. I notice a crumb-scattered plate on the floor and a knife smeared with butter sitting at quarter-to on it. *Did I eat?*

I plug into Wonderland and my gut twists back into itself. I have uploaded three stories: at 11.21 p.m., 12.43 a.m. and 1.12 a.m. And they have each been viewed by tens of thousands of people. I recoil from my phone. A dirty festering panic claws at my skin as I click on the first post:

23.21

A picture of a shot glass with a caption:

I love woman more than tequila;::!

That's not terrible, I can live with typos.

00.43

A selfie of me doing a peace sign in a really gross sink loo mirror with pink neon lighting. My eyes look out of focus and my make-up has begun to slip off my face.

Okay this is terrible but still it's not inexcusable.

01.12

A video of me dancing home singing 'like a queer virgin' with some chips in my hand.

01.13

The screen tumbles out of view as I scream 'faaaack'.

I want to vomit. And be buried.

It's wild that picking up a thin, rectangle slab of technology can be so assaultive to my brain, producing such an overpowering cocktail of intense emotions.

Text message from Rose to Eartha

19.54

Have fun tonight doll. You've got this! Text me when you get home safe.

19.54

Also, forgot to say on the phone. I'm on my way to meet that couple you sent me on FIRE. Hopefully we both get laid tonight ;)

Missed call from Rose

23.51

Text message from Rose to Eartha

01.14

The only acceptable reason you've not texted me is because you're tits deep right now after your queer virgin little jig. I'm going to sleep. Text me in the morning.

Text message from E.V to Eartha

07.57

You need to be careful about posting such personal content on Wonderland FYI. The last video has the street name recognisable 0.03 seconds in. Be street smart and don't get so drunk in public. Would be great if you have read the contract before our meeting today at 6pm, so we can discuss together when you get here! I am on 21 Fashion Place, O15 2BE. See you then. VERY EXCITED!

Text message from Mum to Eartha

08.39

Morning love! Rose can't get hold of you, everything ok? I've seen your Wonderland posts. They said you were out with a friend. Please let us know you are safe and sound x

Text message from Phaedra to Eartha

09.56

I can't believe you love Talking Heads too. Saw you posted their stuff on your Wonderland story last night. Hope you prefer that to Madonna – nice singing voice btw. We should totally get together some time.

Wonderland messages (39):

@EmilyTrish9 Hi! I'm in LOVE with my collage, Eartha. Super original. My mum's going to love it. Or hate it. I'm not sure. I'm in the process of pushing my political agenda onto her so we'll see about that one lol. I love you!

@G.Mapsteadx Waiting patiently for that eyeliner tutorial babes! PS can you do a day in the life video ASAP? x

@Bethhh__ Eartha, after watching your video more times than I'd like to admit, I've finally taken the plunge and left my boyfriend. I needed to hear it. Thank you. Do you offer therapy sessions or anything like that? I feel like you're the only person who really gets me.

@Paleblueeyes Did I see you at Some Velvet Morning last night with some girl?! I was on a date there too, the girl sat at the front with the red mullet. My date didn't go well. If you're down for it, I'd love to take you out instead.

@MADmadonmadonna You have ruined Like A Virgin forever for me. Thanks. I am blocking you.

@Hailey3000 Bestie that plant in the background needs watering. Don't buy plants if you are going to neglect them, it's cruel.

@InteriorsSlag Flat tour, do you live on Lots Road?!

I delete the last video and admit defeat with the other two. E.V's right, I need to be more careful. How do they know where I live? I look around my bedsit and imagine the sorry excuse of a video I'd produce of a flat tour everyone's been asking for. People must be under the impression that having followers equates to income. 'Not much flat to tour,' I reply to the message. Then I look up to spot the dehydrated plant above my wardrobe and I want to tell @Hailey3000 to fuck off. I unplug from Wonderland, deciding I can't handle the influx of demands from my new audience this morning. I'm too dehydrated. I'll read the rest of them later. I voice note Mona instead to make sure she got home safe.

Voice note from Eartha to Mona (10 seconds)

14.06

I just caught a glimpse of myself in the mirror and ... I didn't take my make-up off last night, and your lipstick is still all over my face. It's also all over my pillow. I feel rough. How are you holding up? Also, one of my followers saw us at the bar last night. SO CREEPY!

14.06

Photo of Eartha's face with red lipstick all over it with a caption:

What do you think, should I upload it to Wonderland?

Voice note from Mona to Eartha (20 seconds)

14.30

Goood morning! Do you remember what time we got in last night? I woke up a couple hours ago. I'm exhausted too babe, like deep in my BONES tired. But I had so much fun with you it was a right laugh hanging out. Also, when you said you went viral, I didn't know it was THAT viral. I've never been SPOTTED before, that's hilarious.

Text message from Mona to Eartha

14.31

That should definitely be your new FIRE profile picture ;)

Voice note from Eartha to Mona (2 seconds)

14.32

Like ... 2am I think! And also—

I receive a notification on my phone and see that Mona has started following me on Wonderland. I follow her back.

Voice note from Eartha to Mona (1.12 minutes)

14.33

Sorry, I don't know what happened there, my phone just cut me off. Wait, doesn't that make our date, like, a six-hour date?! I'm trying to piece the evening together, I think I remember something about an old man called Gareth. It's all coming back now. He was being a big man to his mates and we were having none of it. Didn't we refuse to let him buy us drinks too? Thank fuck, he seemed like a right spiker. That's not to say I had a bad time. Because I actually had so much fun. I'd love to see you again, if you would too ...

I dimly remember taking her to this little karaoke bar where we belted out the lyrics to 'Like a Virgin', which must have inspired my impromptu Wonderland solo gig. Didn't they also play Ed Sheeran? Yes, they did. And I decided to take it as a sign to hire E.V as my social media manager. I remember, now. She's friends with him. That's got to mean *something*!

How do I *feel?* I make myself a cup of tea to rejuvenate my brain and think about last night while my yellow kettle boils. I reach for a mug with one of my collages etched across it that Mum got me for Christmas. I want to see Mona again, of course I do. But the reality is it's Phaedra I can't get out of my mind. God. I'd be shit at polyamory. I feel guilt for cheating on a girl I haven't even kissed yet.

Voice note from Mona to Eartha (23 seconds)
15.17
Just on my way back from the food market, had to get myself something, our late night knocked it right out of me. Oh my God, yes, GARETH! He kept on trying to buy us those house cocktails with umbrellas in them? Loving your Wonderland content too. We were drunk, weren't we? So, anyway, Eartha, I was just thinking ... I *do* want to carry on seeing other people. You were my first proper date with a woman and I think I still need to explore my options and find out who I am and what I want first ... Sorry. I am eating noodles and things got

a little precarious back there. But yeah, I feel bad. But I also know it wouldn't be fair for me to let you feel that this could be something more and keep on meeting up with you and giving you the wrong impression. I proper rate you.

I stop listening and put my phone down next to my lampshade and mountain of used mugs, flopping back onto the bed and stretching my arms above my head. A yellow polystyrene box from last night falls onto the floor, exposing its mayonnaise-and-lettuce-smeared innards.

How much did I eat last night?

Why do I feel so upset? Technically this is the nicest rejection ever. It's basically like 'I think you're so cool that I don't want to fuck this up and I want to keep you in my life for ever!', right? That's basically what she's saying here? Isn't it?

Voice note from Eartha to Mona (1.08 mins)
15.30
I would love to be your friend. I'm desperate to form a new group of friends and I think you'd get on with my mate Rose. But after last night we might need to ... make sure we don't kiss again if we want to keep this platonic? Or whatever you want! That's good with me.

Voice note from Eartha to Mona (10 seconds)
15.32
Well, actually, no, that's not true. Sorry. This is really embarrassing. I'm working on asserting myself. I definitely think we should NOT kiss again if we're going to be friends. Oh, and for the love of God, sort me out with that noodle link. Do they do pad thai?!'

Voice note from Mona to Eartha (10 seconds)

15.36

Yes, they do pad thai! Let me send you the link.

Link attached from Mona to Eartha

15.36

(Link)

Would love to hang out.

Voice note from Eartha to Mona (5 seconds)

15.39

Are you free this Friday afternoon?

CHAPTER 12

ENGAGEMENT!

Wonderland followers: 487,761

6 p.m. later that day.

I'm back in the real world, the one that exists outside the comforts of my duvet and the odour of last night's kebab and chips (I had to eventually check my bank account to work out where I had picked food up from: a supermarket and two different takeaways cafés). The sky is a lifeless blank canvas and a loneliness has crept inside the marrow of my bones as I walk over to E.V's flat. The heartbreak of Mona's rejection is sitting in my throat and it makes me realise I feel rudderless without Matt. I need someone or something to latch onto. I'm not sure how much longer I can hold out before I cling to the first, even slightly tempting person-shaped raft that comes into view.

I pull up my texts from E.V to let her know I am nearby.

I start typing:

I am just 5 minutes away now! ☺

I check before I send it and think that the ☺ makes me look too young, so I replace it with 'E'.

I look back at the map, following the little blue icon to work out which way to turn next. I exit the map and check Wonderland quickly – I've not plugged in since this morning's exposure. My mind floods with the over-stimulation of names, people, faces, places, numbers and colours all popping out in front of me as I enter. I wonder if anyone else has figured out my address.

Over 150k new followers since my date with Mona.

387 new commission requests.

13,566 new comments.

2,208 new messages.

How on earth will I find the time to do all of my commissions and respond to all of these people? I've not even had time to tell the girl who said my plant was dying to fuck off yet! *I wish there were two of me.* As I exit my inbox, my feed loads a new post that stops me dead in my tracks. It's Mum. She's uploaded a picture of her huddled up to Dad sitting in his leather armchair with his feet up, raising a glass of wine in the air captioned 'Cheeky bottle of wine with this one!' A comment appears below, made five seconds ago from Jane, Mum's old school friend.

Oh, Susanne, he's such a silver fox! Lucky lady. Hope your young one is well. Xxx

Mum doesn't have any actual friends, because if anyone were to get too close they'd see behind the smoke and shattered and replaced mirrors. I wonder what's 'cheeky' about an alcoholic cradling a bottle of wine, knowing another bottle will end up smashed on the floor or against a wall by the end of the evening. I thought she said he was supposed to be sober, that he was going to his meetings. But there's no incentive for Dad to become a better person when she is bending over backwards to protect him. Worse yet, who would ever believe how horrible he is to her, when she's the one telling the world how perfect their life is?

The picture was uploaded five minutes ago. I imagine Mum sitting glaring into her phone, the glow awash on her face as she loses herself in the Wonderland version of her perfect marriage. Without liking the picture, I lock my phone and put it back into my pocket. I already suspect she will text me later to 'check in' because she has a guilty conscience. It's happened before.

I carry on walking, but my feelings are all knotted and matted together, and it feels as though they are slowing me down. An invasive voice has crept into my mind: *I hate the way I look*, it tells me. *I couldn't even get a second date with Mona.*

I didn't have long to get ready because I 'accidentally' spent hours doing another deep dive on Phaedra's profile. I want to know everything. Where she buys her clothes. Who cuts her hair. Does she prefer milk alternatives in her coffee? I've been chewing over the idea of a date with her like a stick of juicy strawberry bubblegum – waiting for it to lose its flavour so I can spit it out. But it hasn't.

I turn left and spot a red car with a convertible hood to the right and walk over to take a selfie by it. I lean down to check myself out in its window. I catch a glimpse of the contents of the car behind the window. The glove compartment's open and there's a pair of men's shoes at the passenger's side. I fluff my fringe in its reflection, tuck some strands of hair behind my ears and wipe my index fingers to remove the black under my eyes. I realise they're just dark circles from staying up all night with my new crush-turned-date-turned-friend. Being queer really is as confusing as Rose said it would be; not that you'd see this on their Wonderland account, where they assert they are a god-like baker of vegan treats who have their shit together.

'EARTHAAA!' E.V shouts. Half of her body is leaning out of

a glass-fronted door thirty metres down the road. I jump away from the car window and walk over to her, smiling. Her building towers over the street; it's about ten floors high and has an all-glass-panel exterior. The other buildings on the street – identical traditional red-brick houses with different pastel-colour doors – are dwarfed by it.

'I thought I saw you out the window! What were you doing looking in my car, eh?' she says.

I look back at it.

'I was just checking myself out in the window.' I try to remain jovial.

'Have a fun night?' she says as she gestures with her arm for me to come inside. A waft of the tobacco-sodden fringing on her kimono hits my nostrils.

'You could say that!' I reply.

She holds the door open.

'Good for you! *I hope you got laid.*' She winks. I cower my head. Do I tell her I was actually rejected?

'You don't have to be a prude in front of me. You don't have to be presentable and all that bollocks …' she says as she gives me a proper embrace. I feel the urge to tell her everything: about my first kiss with a woman and the rush of it all, how angry my mum's post has made me and about the loneliness lapping at my heart.

'I have been plugged into Wonderland for hours, practically this whole afternoon …' she says. 'It's so nice to see a human face, particularly yours.'

She lets go of me and holds me at arm's length as she absorbs me fully. She's taking me in, not as a date, as a daughter, as a friend or as a girlfriend, but as a full person. All of my parts. I think it's the first time anyone has ever examined me in this way, as a oneness.

DIRECTOR'S NOTE
Flashback to E.V earlier in the day.
Camera A: Birds-eye view of E.V typing Eartha's Wonderland information and statistics into a website called www.WonderlandStats.com on her laptop, then collating Eartha's highest engaging social media posts.
Camera B: Zooms in slowly on E.V's eyes as the numbers flash in front of her eyes. Then she's unplugged and her pupils return to their normal colour when she receives a text.
ENDS

E.V places her arm around my waist and ushers me across a small, metal bridge that arches over an indoor pond in the middle of the lobby. Around the water feature there are palm trees which tower over us, bending towards the skylight right at the top of the building. You can hear the filter in the water burbling at the edges of the pond and the sound of birds, coming from a speaker above. It's an artificial rainforest. I didn't know apartment blocks like this existed. How much money does she make?

'Unreal … How can you afford it?' I ask.

My eyes are wide, scouring the lobby.

'Oh, you're not one of those, are you?' she sighs.

'One of those?'

'One of those people who resent the thought that a woman can do brilliant things on her own and achieve success without the financial aid of a man or her father …'

'No. I'd love this life for myself. Truly. I want to know how to achieve it too.'

'I bought it in the birth of my divorce,' she explains.

'How long have you lived here?'

'I've been here for a year ... *Smart* women get fucking prenups.'

She widens her eyes and looks at me.

'I'll be sure to take on the advice. But I'm not thinking about marriage quite yet ...' I reply.

'Of course not. You've got a legacy to build. In fact, do PROMISE me you'll stay bloody single!'

But I do want to be like you.

My feelings towards her are so charged, I don't know what to do with them except channel them into a singular beam of awe. It feels as though I am looking into a mirror.

'Maintenance charge on the place is a RIGHT pain up the arse, though; most of it gets spent on keeping the fucking palm trees alive and cleaning that SODDING pond,' she goes on.

The lift arrives, we step inside and she pushes the button that says '10'. The doors close, the lift glides up and the view of the palm trees below us becomes smaller and smaller, until we're the ones towering over them. How did I get such intimate access to this woman's life?

Ding

She makes way for me to leave the lift and follows behind as we arrive into a small room with a hallway table and one yellow door. She puts her key into the lock and just as she's about to turn it, she faces me.

'You didn't come back to my message last night ... I'm so glad you're having fun, darling! With that girl and everything. But you can't post irresponsibly again. It's for your own safety – not letting people know exactly where you are ... but we also need to be strategic about what you're giving to Wonderland and how much you reveal from now on ... Mystery sells.'

She's flourishing her hands in the air, like she's somehow plugged into Wonderland with all the names, numbers and people scrolling in front of her.

'Work must always come first if you want a life like this, you see. Girls are fun, boys are fun, sex is fun! You're young and hot and every fucking living breathing SECOND of this era of your life is invigorating … but be careful that these flings don't distract you from your path.'

She turns back round to unlock the front door.

'All right, Dalai Lama, I won't get distracted from my "path",' I say.

And with that her voice lightens immediately.

'Speaking of the Dalai Lama … I met him at a world peace conference. He told me that I had a gift, that I can turn things, people, anything I wanted into gold. The rest is history!'

She pushes the door open and walks into her apartment.

Holy shit. Her apartment really is the entire floor of the building.

I can hear some music playing faintly as I follow her in. I spot a disc spinning on a vinyl player in the corner.

'The Doors!' I exclaim.

'I shagged him.'

'You *what?*'

'Jim Morrison. Shagged him.'

She swells her nostrils and flicks her kimono sleeve, walking further into the apartment. I shake my head in disbelief at her and her flat. The whole *floor* is hers. It's a double-height ceiling, glass box floating on top of the city. It looks like a millionaire's greenhouse. My flat could easily fit in this space at least twenty times over. The floor's tiled entirely in a black-and-white chequerboard. There's a lit candle on a mid-century coffee table surrounded by three yellow velvet sofas all covered in green cushions. The whole apartment looks freshly decorated.

'Can I make you a tea?' she calls from a marble-topped kitchen island, pouring herself a pot of loose-leaf tea from a yellow kettle.

'I'm still tired from last night and I think it might mellow me out a bit ...'

'You want anything stronger? Espresso?'

My eyes light up.

'STIMULANTS! Yes, please!'

'Sit there,' she says, directing my eyeline to one of the sofas.

I sit myself down and she walks over with a floral teacup and saucer. It's pale blue with little red roses and gold lining around the edges of the saucer and rim of the cup. It's the only thing I've seen that doesn't look like the price tag has just been removed. Even her vinyl player looks brand new.

'That's beautiful!' I say, admiring the cup.

'It's part of a set, I inherited them. I don't think I'll ever have kids, it's too late for me ...' she says with the lightest of shrugs as if the store doesn't have her size of shoe in stock. 'So how about you can have the set when I die?' she says. The sound of the espresso machine rattles in the background.

'I'll have no one else to give them to,' she goes on.

She says the words *no one else to give them to* with so little emotion that it takes my breath away. My initial suspicions, and thorough internet stalking, were correct – she isn't in a relationship. It doesn't seem to have negatively impacted her life, though, she doesn't seem lonely without a husband or a family. In fact, it all looks very appealing, the decadence of her unburdened existence. She's the kind of woman I imagine Mum would have been if she'd had the courage to stay away from Dad.

She briskly returns to the kitchen area and flips off the espresso machine, swivels on her heel back towards me and slides a tiny cup over the table towards me. 'Here's your espresso.'

She lights herself a cigarette and offers me one. I decline on account of my ruinous hangover, knowing that, paired with the coffee, I'll be in her no-doubt-spotless bathroom within five minutes. She blows onto her tea.

We talk about Wonderland and how much it's been consuming me and the questions and demands I receive every hour from strangers who she refers to as my 'community'.

'Wonderland is overwhelming you. But you are making people enthralled by your existence. It's like dating 587,000 followers! I'd be worried if it didn't feel that way. But … all of this …' E.V pauses. She places her teacup down onto the table, flails her hands around and then snaps her fingers. 'All of this crap – about your skincare routine, what you eat – you're more than this. *Yes*, I know people still ask for it, these things can be fun sometimes and it lets people connect with you. But, like you're saying, *you're more interesting than that.* Soon enough they'll be draining you of every fucking detail: asking you where you live, what places you like to go. You'll have nothing left, nothing that *belongs to you.* I don't want that to happen to you. It's like waking up to thousands and thousands of people in your bed every morning. Too many people asking too many things of you, needing more of you until you are just an empty bag with its contents entirely spilt out for people to pick over …'

Before I can add anything, she continues.

'Which is why we need to CREATE you, so you don't lose yourself! We need to keep the real Eartha in this room, here with me. I am here to know YOU. But the rest of Wonderland doesn't deserve to, they can know what you are comfortable exposing and nothing more. Everyone nowadays throws the word "boundaries" around, I call it screening. Let people see all you want on the screen and THAT. IS. THAT. Screen yourself like you would your ex's calls. Which, by the way, I hope you are screening, Eartha? What a WRECK of a man.'

The room is crackling with static energy. Her eyes glisten excitedly. She pulls out a laptop from underneath the sofa we are sitting on.

'I've come up with a list of all the things that are resonating and our job, together, is to think of how to ... *accentuate* them online!'

'Sure, hit me,' I say.

She pulls up a list with graphs and charts and begins reading them frantically out loud, pointing to a chart that spikes randomly as she does so.

'So, when you talk about your ex, you receive thirty per cent fewer messages in your inbox; when you post a picture of yourself, you gain a few thousand followers; you lose followers when you talk about being lonely ...'

I follow her finger as it moves up and down the line on the graph. She pulls up some of the posts that I put up since I went viral: my reflections on a woman's place in art, my book recommendations, my outfit pictures and my musings on being alone, which I already feel self-conscious of. She tells me that my spontaneous updates and my diary-style captions receive the most engagement, that my top three posts all have the word 'confused' in and that my lowest have the word 'men' in them.

'THEN, when you mention your queerness we see a rise of forty per cent engagement across your stories, likes and comments. All of this, of course, dips when you haven't been posting for a while, though … or when you're talking about men,' she explains. 'So, we need to come up with a plan which allows for you to be as online as possible without it taking up too much of your time. If we want brands to work with you and pay the big bucks, we need you to be constantly posting so your audience know what you're up to, but it won't be "you", it will be a version we create that's … you, but a little fabricated.'

'But … E.V,' I say, putting down my coffee. 'One of the first things you noticed, about me … is how authentic I am online. How can I keep doing that? That's who I want to be. I don't want to be like these people that plug into Wonderland and become someone unrecognisable, someone that lies about how happy they are … an avatar.'

The image of Mum and Dad drinking together flashes in my mind. I redirect my train of thought. I explain that I want to continue my art, but I am struggling to keep up with the commissions, doing my own work and Wonderland. E.V turns her head quickly to face me and removes her sunglasses. This is the first time I've seen her eyes.

'So QUIT.'

Her eyes are piercing through black pencil-lined lids. E.V *without the frames*.

'I can't,' I stutter.

'Do you say that to *everything*?'

'What?'

'"I can't." No, really, do you? Because, darling, if there's one thing that you need to know about me, it's that I'm going to force you to be great. Call it tough love.'

She stubs her cigarette out.

'I chose you as my client, no, not chose …'

She is moving her head in a different direction every few seconds as she talks, like she has an audience.

'I felt instinctively drawn to you because I loved that *vigour*, that energy. The fire I saw in the video of the girl expressing years of repressed desire, anger, rage … It's like you were speaking the pain of a thousand women. It was such a divine feminine expression! And you're *lucky*. It took me years to figure this out and my philosophy on life's not even *half* as baked as yours. We now need to find a way of bringing that *fire* out of you and sharing it with the world. This is what you can do to change the narrative and the lives of women. Don't get stuck in the loophole of how women can look and feel better about themselves with this or that self-care routine, or this hair product or that make-up tutorial bullshit; instead you can create an online world that's fit for them in an offline world that isn't.'

She holds me in her gaze and I realise a whole new world is opening up before me. One where my voice matters. One where I'm listened to and appreciated and a man isn't slamming cupboards to coerce me into cooking dinner.

'E.V, I think I should remind you that this "vigour" that launched me into virality was influenced by pina coladas and Rose hyping me up behind the camera,' I confess.

'Behind *every* brilliant woman is a butch lesbian hyping her up.'

'I'm not sure that's how the saying goes.'

'Fine. It isn't. But it doesn't matter. You're brilliant with or without the influence of alcohol, or your friends. You're *Eartha*, for fuck's sake. So, take the leap, dammit. Just like you did with your ex! Only this time, you have a safety net. You have me.'

Something warm and oozy pours over my loneliness when she says this.

'Working with me will be an intense crash course in people understanding the "Eartha" we want them to fall in love with. We need to launch and evolve you and your audience in tandem. Now, I understand you are bisexual, of course, but really these things *do* work better when they're a little more … more … binary, online. More potent. After all, that's how the internet operates, in binaries, 1s or 0s. Don't confuse people with too many halves.'

'You want me to be straight?' I ask, screwing my face up in confusion. *I've just come out and now I'm being forced back in?*

'NO! Lean into your queerness more and talk less about "your past". Your mean ex is so over and it's boring, so Nineties Bridget Jones. I told you, darling, your engagement *soars* when you talk about your confusion and finding yourself. We need to look ahead and think about what makes *you* the voice of a generation on Wonderland. Let's not cater *for* men any more, let's live *despite* them.'

Voice of a generation?

I try to take this all in and wonder whether now is the moment to tell her I feel ashamed of the video. That I'm uncomfortable with the amount of influence I have. Thousands of people hanging on to my every word and I'm not sure what to tell them; I am struggling just like them.

She stands up and begins to wander off through some doors that lead onto a balcony. I follow her out of the tall glass wall of the apartment. To the right of the doors are two mimosa trees in giant concrete pots. I stroke their yellow fuzz and they're crunchy to the fingertip. They must be artificial.

She stubs her cigarette and throws it off the balcony edge. My jaw hinges wide open. That could land on a child. A car. A cyclist.

What if it didn't go out properly, it could start a fire.

'I know what you're worried about, Eartha. I can see what's going on inside that head of yours. But I'm here to help you get your money! That's my job!'

She places her hands on either side of my head like a mother does with their child. She looks deeply into me once again. 'Look, I'll be able to get you your first brand deal within a week. You'll be posting more content by then because you won't be weighed down with commissions. I want to see you *free*, Eartha. I want to build you up because I believe in you, in a way no one ever has before. I see your light and I want to enhance it. But you need to make sure you use your time wisely. If I need you to be somewhere I need you to be there. Don't let all these people you're fucking distract you!' She throws her hands in the air and the fringed sleeve of her kimono thrashes the railing.

I turn around and lean my back against the wall, looking out at the entire city sprawling beneath us. 'More than anything, I just feel scared about leaping into something new. One thing I know for certain, I never want to be in a position where I'm relying on a man like Matt ever again. Or forgiving a man who hurts me. I'm done with them all. I want a delicious life,' I tell her.

'Good for you. There's something so maternal in the way that women continually forgive men. Unconditional love should be reserved only for *children*.'

I feel like clapping.

'If you stick with me, darling, you won't have to think about him, or them. Or filling his spot with some other fuck who doesn't deserve you ... So, the next steps ... I need you to talk less about your ex, maybe start a few arguments with high-profile men's rights activists to get the ratings up on your Wonderland page and make it clear your video was your coming-out moment.'

Arguing with men? Getting paid for it?

'Fuck it, I'm in,' I say as I feel something hot seeping from between my legs.

'E, I'm bursting for the loo, where is it?'

'Yes, of course, darling ...'

She puffs on a newly lit cigarette, leaning on the rail. She points with her arm down the hallway.

I walk towards the stairs to find there's another short hallway leading down behind them. Is this where she meant? Down here? I think my period has just started and I really don't want to leak through my trousers or, worse, onto her sofa. There are three doors: one on the left, one on the right and one straight ahead. I poke the door on the left open slightly. The room is carpeted, it's full of cardboard boxes with a '*HOMEMOVE*' logo in blue on the side and clothes in plastic zip-up bags. No toilet. I close the door, clench my pelvic muscles and turn to try another door. I find the loo behind the next one down. I pull my trousers down and squat on the toilet. I tear off some tissue from the holder and pull it between my legs. It's got an early brown stringy smudge on it: I've got time before I really start bleeding. I roll up a piece of loo paper tightly and pad it into my knickers, and then look straight ahead. What's that? I squint my eyes. A picture of E.V and the Dalai Lama. I laugh silently. Away from the disorientating business talk, my thoughts settle like sediment at the bottom of a glass. With renewed clarity, my attention returns to its main focus: Phaedra. I pull my phone out from my trouser pocket and check to see if there are any new pictures or updates from her on Wonderland. Nothing. I lock my phone and catch a glimpse of myself in a full-length mirror next to me, hunched over the loo, cradling my phone, with toilet paper stuffed into my gusset. I don't look like I'm cut out for this new glamorous world. But I know more than anything that I want it. I want my own fucking marble kitchen island. I don't want to have to heat my apartment with my oven any more. I have a fire pumping through my veins. I want to have this life. I will make it mine.

I wipe myself dry, flush the loo and walk back down the corridor into the reception area. The door to the balcony is still open and it's blowing the smells of the city into the apartment; wafts of bins and fried chicken filter up.

'There you are.' E.V's voice emerges with her body out of a room to the side.

'Here I am!' I say, wiping my hands dry on my trousers.

'So, what do you say, darling?'

I inhale deeply and my shoulders rise up towards my ears. I release my breath.

'I'm ready.'

She starts flapping her hands excitedly.

'Here's your contract. It's very short; you can sit here and read it again if you need to. Take as long as you need!'

She pulls up the prepared two-page document from her laptop. I'd read it briefly this morning in a hungover daze from bed, it seemed reasonable. She gets her 20 per cent, like she said when we met. I lift my hands for her to pass the laptop to me.

'Just like that? Are you sure? Is there anything you want me to explain?' she asks gently.

'I read it this morning. I don't have to think about it: I'm sure.' I rest the laptop on my knee.

She raises her teacup excitedly.

I pause her cheers. 'If, like you said, you can get me some work within the next week?' I check.

'You know that's part of the deal, darling! If you don't make any money, then neither do I. Let that fact alone allow you to trust me.'

I smirk and drag the cursor along the dotted line to scribble my signature.

Signed.

Buzz

Buzz

My phone vibrates in my pocket. E.V looks around the room as if to swat the noise away. I pull my phone out and the screen glows in my face as I unlock it.

Text message from Mum to Eartha

19.32

Hey love, how are you today? Just checking in ☺

As predicted.

CHAPTER 13

TO BE LIVING ON THE CUSP OF EVERYTHING

Wonderland followers: 490,871

DIRECTOR'S NOTE
Eartha is walking down the street in a pair of denim hotpants and a silk racer top with red lipstick on. She doesn't notice it, but she is attracting attention from passers-by as she takes selfie after selfie sprawled across the city in the heat. In some pictures, she poses near parks, in others she walks down the pavement with a joyful lust for life that other people don't seem to quite have, even on the hottest day in June.
She pulls the scene around her and becomes the source of gravity as she drifts obliviously through the baking pavements and strobe-lit parks.
ENDS

4.19 p.m., Friday.

The air is tight with the sun's heat emanating from Olympia's concrete. The city's pores are wide open and we're all being sweated out of our flats. Dripping out of the brickwork are half-naked people off to expose themselves and let the sun pounce on them in parks. This sweaty armpit is my city and everyone's trying to find a place, a crevice, on its surface to soak up the rays and sweat out the heat. People crowd together in the slither of sun that hits the corner of the pavement, they move with it as the shade creeps around them. The outdoor tables are covered in empty pint-glass towers.

My mind flits to Wonderland and I wonder how my last post is doing, I spoke about the first crush I had in school – I'm sure Rose will be upset to discover that it wasn't them – and asked people to comment with their own crushes. My following is going up every single day and I now have over 490,000 followers. I've been following E.V's advice, trying to open up more and give people a little of my real self, or rather the self they seem to react best with. I suppose the definition of 'intimacy' is a little blurry now that we all share our deepest desires and insecurities online. Parts of ourselves once confided to a therapist or a partner after months and years of relationship-building are now shared freely with thousands of strangers. E.V sent me a voice note during the week saying that I should think about what I'm comfortable with sharing and what I'm not because *internet boundaries are important, darling!* I'll never share pictures of my family or my bedroom. I can't imagine 450,000 people having access to the most private pockets in my life. But still, the offline and the online are the two parts of my life that are spilling into each other and I don't really know which part belongs where.

On my way to meet Rose and Mona I walk past a tattooed girl sitting on a low wall, waiting for friends. She's wearing wide-leg black trousers and a white cotton shirt that's unbuttoned all the way down, exposing a wide, bare strip of her tanned torso. She has an unfair amount of sex appeal. I look at her and quickly retreat my gaze. Then I remember, I don't have to any more. I allow myself to check her out and she smiles back at me, making a cool salute with her two fingers. It's as though my sexual desires are blooming in front of me, finally given the fertiliser of my newfound singledom.

I tasted myself the other night, trying to imagine what it will be like when I finally go down on a woman. Every new encounter contains a multitude of possibilities about what it could become. The potential for friendship, a good shag or to meet the love of my life lingers seductively in the air. Perhaps this is a bisexual thing. Now that I've accepted my capacity to be attracted to people regardless of their gender, I'm seeing the beauty in everything. Or perhaps it's just that I now see life as beautiful, no longer living according to someone else's mood.

'Thereeee she is!' Mona sings out, interrupting my thoughts. She's waiting outside the café as the sun glints off her angular face, her eyes squinted to shield themselves from its rays.

'Hey, you!' I reply.

I'm unsure of how to act around her. How do you code switch from wild-make-out-session to deciding-to-just-be-friends mode? I reach my arms around to hug her and then Mona heads for the wrong door.

'It's this way!' I say, guiding us into Rose's café.

I didn't plan for us both being awkward. She doesn't know what to say either, does she? The café is less busy than normal, probably because it's baking hot and there's no AC in here. Plug-in fans placed along the tables closest to wall sockets whir noisily in the background. There are lots of tables for us to pick from and we choose the one closest to the fridge, filled with perspiring fruit juices. I see Rose serving beautifully decorated floral cheesecake slices and matcha lattes to a table of three women. They're all giggling. Rose says something and one of the ladies pats them on the arm. 'Stop it, you!'

They begin to walk over to me with a look of mild confusion.

'Ah, hold on …' I say, turning to Mona. 'ROSE! I've got someone to introduce to you.'

Rose throws their towel over their shoulder and walks on over with their thumbs hanging off their belt loops.

'Oh Mona, I've heard so much about you!' Rose teases. 'So, are you two ready for your first gay night out?' they continue, covering the silence they have created. 'We're going to Slinky's. I don't recommend it as a *good* place to go, but you've just got to lose your gay bar virginity there.'

'I thought you hated that bloody place?' I say.

'Well, yeah. But it's the *only* lesbian bar around here. They've literally shoved us into a club in the ground, under some porn shop. But it's still ours. All ours. No men allowed in. They're protective over trans girls that come too, so it's safe for everyone and they don't take any bullshit. Proper inclusive and all that,' Rose says, piling some leftover coffee cups into the crook of their arm.

'It sounds great, why don't you like it?' Mona asks, tilting her head curiously.

'Well, it's just the people that go there.'

Mona crosses her arms against her chest. 'Ohhh, shagged everyone in the room, have you, Rose?' she teases.

'She's gutsy this one …'

We all erupt into awkward laughter and it successfully dispels the tension. My laughter is sheer nervous relief.

'It's a bit like walking into a room full of people with expectations of you, people who are mad with you, people who are in love with you … It's not my fault either, is it, Eartha? I can't help it, it's just who I attract.'

I roll my eyes playfully and place my hand on Rose's shoulder.

'Yeah, not your fault at all! You just have a thing for sleeping with girls and not texting them back. Or fucking entire friendship groups and causing a path of chaos wherever you go. It's not you, it's totally them!'

I square up. Rose glares at me and gets called over by a customer, leaving Mona and me alone again. We both pull our phones from our pockets, hungry for distraction from whatever weird, non-definable tension there is sitting between us. In a moment of procrastination before leaving my flat, I had clicked on Phaedra's profile picture and zoomed all the way in on her face. The picture is still taking up my entire phone screen.

'Is that someone you're interested in?' Mona peers over my shoulder.

I weigh up the consequences of telling her about my messy situation with Matt and the pink-haired girl he cheated with that I can't get out of my head.

I decide to tell her everything. Mona starts smacking the table, her eyes fixed on me, waiting for what comes next.

'… then I finally kicked him out and now I can't stop thinking about her; it's like she's stuck in my mind, she consumes all my FUCKING thoughts.'

Rose interrupts us with two Irish coffees which they put down onto pink coasters. Mona counters, 'Shagging the girl your boyfriend cheated on you with sounds *very* feminist to me!'

'Does everything have to be a feminist choice?' I wonder.

'Mate, I was kidding! Maybe it doesn't have to be feminist, it can just be … what Eartha wants to do,' she replies. 'If you can't get that girl out of your mind, you should do something about it! Or am I just pressuring you into doing it so I can live vicariously through you?' She leans her chin on her knuckles.

'No, I want her. I really do. I just … well, I might need a bit of Dutch courage first.' I sip my Irish coffee. 'What happens if she rejects me or doesn't even fancy me?' I ask, reaching for my phone again.

'Then, so what? At least you can say you went for it. You can move forward with no regrets and all that,' she replies.

Her phone's FIRE notification takes her focus away from me. I'm hit with a pang of envy at how quickly she's moved on from our date. I need to do something. I look down at my phone and open up my chat with Phaedra ... All those hours of passively posting her favourite songs on Wonderland and staring at her profile …

Text message from Eartha to Phaedra

18.01

I'll be at Slinky's in a few hours if you're around. I'd love to see you tonight.

18.02

SLINKY'S LOCATION PIN

CHAPTER 14

SLINKY'S

Wonderland followers: 506,582

I've already downed two tins of pre-mixed G&T and Mona's pissing behind the bins while Rose stands guard, one hand in the pocket of their leather jacket and another cradling a can of overwarm Stella. I imagined three queers out on the pull would look a lot more sophisticated than this. Phaedra hasn't responded to my text. It's been two whole hours. If she doesn't get back by tomorrow, I will tell her I was drunk when I texted her and apologise. Or maybe if she turns me down I can explain that I meant it as friends? Having a crush is so humiliating and all this yearning is exhausting.

The air is still warm but I'm jittery and keep moving my body to rattle out the nerves inching their way across my chest into my arms and legs. I pull out another can from my pocket to calm myself down, but it's empty.

'Rose, you got another tinny I can pinch?' I ask.

With their back turned to Mona, Rose reaches into the lining of their leather jacket, which has torn through years of wear to form one enormous pocket. As they feel around their back for a can they squint in concentration. I can hear loose change rattling around the bottom of the jacket.

'Here ya go.' Rose hands me the can. 'Euuuughh! MONA!'

A stream of urine trails between their military boots.

'You should see your face,' I say, suddenly doubled up in hysterics.

'I'M SORRY!' Mona yells from behind us, like a bin troll.

Rose flicks their boots dry and reaches for my blacked-out glasses to take them off my head. I snatch them back and my phone buzzes in my pocket. I unlock it immediately. More followers pour into my life.

Mona sorts herself out and we continue along the street. Apart from the streetlights lining the pavement, the road ahead is dark. There's a man on the right pulling down the metal shutters to protect his glass-fronted newsagent.

'Right, here we are. Give us your cans; I'll put them in the bin.'

'What do you mean "here we are"? There's … literally nothing?' I say to Rose.

Mona downs the rest of her drink and wrinkles her nose to adjust her septum piercing. Rose holds our gang of cans between their fingers and shoves them into a full bin.

'I told you, it's underground!' they shout.

Mona and I glance at each other.

'Oh, come on! It's here …' Rose gestures.

As we're approaching the door, my nerves kick up a gear. The street is still empty, there's no one around. I can't even hear any music.

'ROSE! You promised me lesbians, but there's no one here. Look!' I throw my arms into the air, pointing at the nothingness. 'Where are the lesbi—'

I'm cut off by a door bursting open and the thud of music pumping out from below. Out come two girls, one walking backwards while the other clutches her waist. They're so close to me that I feel like I'm in their kiss. The night slows down. I can see their tongues slowly folding into one another's mouths, revealing the whites of their teeth as they smile at each other. I don't think I've ever kissed someone like that. They both want nothing more than each other. I want someone to want me like that. *Badly*. The girl walking backwards suddenly becomes aware of the pavement edge and steadies her feet, breaking the kiss to look behind her to ensure she doesn't fall onto the road. I keep waiting for someone to tell them to stop. Expecting someone to come over and tell them to take it down a notch. For the gay police to pop out and say, 'That's *too* gay.' But I realise the only 'gay police' here, right now, are in my head.

A car pulls up and the first girl turns around to let her date inside. Within seconds the car zips off down the dark road into the night, its rear lights becoming more and more muted in the distance. I watch as the girls are swept off in their carriage, taking them away to whatever glorious, sweaty adventure awaits them between cotton sheets – or if they can't make it that far, the living-room sofa. I imagine they've probably not even put on their seat belts as they guide their hands over one another's thighs, their heads reaching towards each other into the middle of the back seat.

'Eartha, shall we?!' Rose's shouts, waiting for me.

'Okay, fine, this place looks great. Let's go,' I reply.

'*Where are the lesbians! Where are the lesbians!*' Mona chimes a high-pitched impression of me. Rose and Mona both laugh.

Rose gestures for us to follow them inside and we're met with a fringed and beaded floor-length curtain. Rose peels it back to reveal a neon-lit staircase plummeting into the basement and begins walking down.

'Come back; it's five pound entry!'

I follow the deep, sexy voice and find that there's a woman to the right of the curtain sat on a tall stool behind a counter. There's a small tin in front of her with different sections for notes and coins and a faded sticker that says 'NOT DRUG MONEY'. Her hair's a shaggy black mullet, she wears a black vest and a little silver hoop in her right ear. There's a tattoo of a deck of cards on her neck and words I can't quite make out on her hands written in Old English.

'Rose, have you got any cash?' I shout through the curtain, letting go of Mona's arm and patting my pockets.

'Oh what! *Rose is here*?! ROSE!' the woman exclaims, leaning her torso over the counter to peer down the staircase. *Of course* she knows Rose. Rose runs back up the steps and pops their head through the curtain.

'Come here so I can stamp you and your … are these … new mates?' The woman looks over at Mona and me as though she's trying to figure out which one of us is fucking Rose. Or whether we both are.

'This one's my best mate, Eartha! She's just come out, finally …'

The woman pushes the stamp into an ink pad, hovers it in the air and then presses the ink quickly onto my wrist. Two interlocking Venus symbols in pink become imprinted onto my skin. She dabs the stamp onto the ink pad again and looks up at Mona.

'What was your name, gorgeous?'

'Mona.'

The woman lingers a little longer on the stamp than she did with me.

'All right, all right, come on, we haven't got all fucking night, give us a stamp, then!' Rose jokes, yanking up the sleeve of their leather jacket and smacking their arm onto the counter like they're about to receive a jab.

'Rose, say hello to Eve downstairs, won't you? She'll die that you're here. She's on the bar tonight.'

'Course. Come on, you two.'

We walk through the beaded curtain and down the dark basement staircase, each step lined with a red neon strip. Another two girls holding hands run up the stairs. *This place must have a good success rate.*

When we reach the bottom we're met with a chipped red door and I can feel the thump of the bass on the other side. Rose pushes into it with their shoulder and, all of a sudden, the music and voices are no longer muffled, we've walked onto a balcony that overlooks the entire dancefloor. The room has an artificial fruity smell, probably to disguise the sweating bodies within it. The balcony floor is a red furry carpet before it hits a staircase that leads off and curves around to meet the dancefloor. A large, gold disco ball rotates from the double-height ceiling above it. We take the staircase down and I place my hand on the curved edge of the banister so I can survey the crowd of women dancing, searching for Phaedra among them. The song starts to fade and another begins, a jingly guitar riff with male vocals causes the women who were sitting on the sides to slam down their drinks and end their conversations, running to the middle of the dancefloor.

'AND SOON I WAS DANCING IN THE LESBIAN BAR,' plays through the vibrating speakers.

We reach the end of the staircase and land on the side of the dancefloor. Rose pulls me in to share their view and points at the back of the room. 'I might be a while; I'm gonna say hello to Eve. You good?' they ask. I reassure them and they kiss me on the forehead before disappearing into the crowd. I feel lost for a second, then Mona grabs my hand.

'Come on, then ... Let's dance in the lesbian bar.'

She lifts my hand and spins me around. I'm wearing platforms so I wobble a little, but she catches me as I twirl. It's so different to dancing in a room with men, I feel the women looking at me, but their gaze doesn't cause me to suck in my stomach. I don't feel the need to be doll-like or attractive for anyone else. I don't think the muscles in my body have ever felt this relaxed in public.

Mona and I take turns belting the lyrics to the song. I point at her and bellow: *'SO CONTROLLED!'*

She shakes her braids to the beat, points at me and shrieks back: *'WAY WAY BOLD!'*

We point at each other and yell: *'I WAS DANCING IN THE LESBIAN BAR!'*

No wonder they don't want lesbianism to be legal across the world. Look at all the fun women are having. *Without men.*

'SHOTS!' Rose appears out of nowhere and offers the shots up to us. We each take one and cheers before knocking them back.

'Right, I need a fag,' Rose insists, patting their pockets.

'Well, I'm RIGHT HERE,' a random butch girl dressed in leather shouts and I chuckle, not used to this casual reclaiming of gay slurs.

Rose leads the way through the crowd to the smoking area, which is just the pavement outside the venue. As we walk hand in hand up the neon staircase, trying not to lose each other in the sea of lesbians, I feel my phone vibrating in my back jean pocket.

Buzz

Buzz

I've got signal! I stop midway to check my phone. Both fear and excitement rise up in my chest as the endless possibilities bounce off the walls of my mind. There are groups of girls coming down the stairs, aching to get past, but the brightness of my screen blinds me.

'Eartha, can you wait until we're outside?' Rose asks.

I lock my phone and quickly put it away. Now at the top of staircase, the bass of 'I Feel Love' by Donna Summer becomes a blurred, unrecognisable murmur.

'Hey, gorgeous.' The woman from the ticket booth pulls Mona to the side.

Mona winks back at me to let me know that she's good, before leaning over the counter to talk to her. I watch the woman's tattooed, calloused hands writhe around Mona's back and grab her in places that, just a few nights ago, I was touching. I don't have hands like that. I want hands like that. I want to be involved somehow. *But a good wing woman knows when it's time to fly.* I leave them to it and walk outside to find that Rose has already lit her cigarette from a naked flame offered to her face by a tall, glamorous woman with blonde hair and pencil-thin eyebrows holding a bejewelled lighter. Rose's friend is eyeing me up and down like a snack. I lean my back against the wall next to the entrance. Rose removes a cigarette from the packet and places it near my lips. 'Open wide!'

'It's never gonna work,' I say, as I open my mouth and Rose tries to wedge the cig between the gap in my two front teeth.

'Well, what *can you* fit in there?' Rose's tall friend says, in a thick New York accent. She reaches over to light my cigarette.

'I managed to get 5p in there once.'

She's the most glamorous woman I've seen at Slinky's so far. Her fingers are long and spindly, and adorned in a full set of pink acrylic nails, apart from her right middle and index, which have snapped off on the ends.

'What happened to those?' I stroke her broken nails with concern.

She and Rose open their mouths and throw their heads back, erupting in laughter.

'What?' I ask, a little embarrassed.

The tall girl drags her platinum hair back with her pointy claws and throws it behind her shoulder. She crouches down to my height, leans in closer to my face and lowers her voice.

'Those two are for having fun.' She takes a drag of her cigarette. 'If you're lucky you might figure out why they're shorter later.'

Buzz

Buzz

My phone's starting to vibrate in my pocket again. I frown and pull it out, walking to the other side of the door leaving them to laugh among themselves.

ALL my notifications are from E.V.

Text message from E.V to Eartha

22.14

Eartha, how are you? Let's get in our meeting to discuss the POA re turning you into a star!

Missed call from E.V

22.47

Text message from E.V to Eartha

22.47

Hi, Eartha. Sorry to text you twice, but I'm at a party, you need to be here, NOW! There are lots of important people who can help build your career on Wonderland.

22.50

They all really want to meet you, Eartha. It's at The Firestone. Come as soon as possible!

Missed call from E.V

22.52

Text message from E.V to Eartha

23.01

Eartha, I just don't want you to miss out on this opportunity, this is the time for you to be networking your arse off! Where are you??

'What's going on? Are you all right?' Rose calls out to me.

'It's nothing, just E.V, she's … It's nothing,' I say again.

I lock my phone and put it in my pocket. Rose raises their hand to their forehead, half-salutes me and turns back to their friend. I finish the last few drags of my cigarette while I stare blankly at the opposite side of the road. I'll get back to E.V in the morning, it's not working hours after all and I'm having fun. I'd much rather be here with my friends.

But what if this really is an important event?

Ah, fuck it. I don't want to go and socialise with a bunch of people from Wonderland. That's it. I've decided. I'm staying. I blow out the smoke from my last drag and throw my cig on the floor, stubbing it out with the heel of my platform. I feel a hand pull me gently by my waist. *What does she want now?*

'Eartha …'

That's not Rose, that's—

'Don't look so shocked, you did text me earlier.'

It's Phaedra. She's even more heavenly than I remember.

'Oh my God, no, of course, I'm ... I'm so happy you're here.'

I'm a little buzzed from the cigarette. I raise my arms to hug her and squeeze her tightly. When I release her she takes both of my hands and our fingers slowly interlock as she walks forwards into my body.

The more she smiles the deeper the dimples in her cheeks crease. *I want to curl up in those creases.* The red light from the Slinky's sign is glowing on her face, revealing more of her freckles. I've forgotten how to fucking breathe. I have *switched* to manual breathing.

Inhale.

'Wanna get a drink?' I ask.

'Yes, please,' she replies.

Exhale.

She lets go of my hand, which has become tacky from my sudden nervous sweats, and holds onto my other one instead. I lean on the door with my hip to open it and quickly check on Mona. A night out with women is like a tag-team system. You're constantly evaluating the situation: *Is everyone okay? Has anyone pulled? Did my mate make it out of the toilet okay or is she still throwing up in there?. Is anyone currently being cornered by a creepy guy and needing help*? I turn to see that Mona's sitting on the counter, with her legs now wrapped around the woman's torso and her arms around her shoulders.

'You good?' Phaedra smiles at me.

'Yes, just checking on my friend ...' I nod towards Mona.

She looks at them and then back at me, with a soft, seductive glint in her brown eyes that suggests she hopes to kiss me like that, too. It's a miracle my knickers haven't already flooded the basement.

We trot down the stairs and towards the bar, still holding hands. 'Shots?' I ask, copying Rose's tenor of voice for confidence.

Phaedra smiles and places her hand on my lower back and strokes it gently while I order. *How am I supposed to form a sentence when every cell in my body is close to erupting?*

'Hi, can I get ...'

My body quivers, her hand is moving higher and higher up my back.

'... two shots of tequila, please?' I manage to squeak out.

'Sure, darlin', you want salt and lime?' the bartender asks, their arm stretched out holding an LED card reader.

Phaedra's now stroking under my shirt, her fingers tracing my ribs. 'YES,' I almost scream in response as I feel something trickle between my legs.

It's all happening.

Her touch feels better than it ever did in my head.

The bartender looks slightly concerned by my jerking and erratic movements but Phaedra keeps moving her cool hand further and further up my top. I pick up the salt from the bar and prepare to lick the skin between my index and my thumb. I open my mouth and start licking before I sprinkle the salt on top. As I do, I think of all the girls I've ever wanted to make a move on, all those girls I fancied and watched go home with boys, or didn't have the nerve to go for. It's as though all of those suppressed urges are arising in this one moment. I grab Phaedra's hand and take the salt, lick and sprinkle it onto her hand. She inhales sharply and her mouth expels a whispered '*fuck*'.

We clink our shot glasses and tap them down on the bar before throwing them back and plunging our teeth into a lime wedge each. I screw my face up at the sour taste. She reaches her hand over to grab the back of my head.

'I think ...' she says, looking at my lips '... you know exactly what I want.' She looks back up to my eyes.

We lean in to kiss each other and I completely let myself go. I forget who I am. I forget where I am. I forget everything leading up to this moment. I open my eyes, to make sure this is actually happening. I'm not close enough to her. Her clothes are blocking me from her warmth, her taste, her touch. She slips her hands into my back pockets and spreads her fingers onto my ass.

'Wanna get out of here?' she grins, kissing me on the nose and lifting my chin.

She stares at my lips.

And kisses them.

A tender, slow, lingering kiss.

I'm lost for words. She has stolen them from me.

'Eartha?'

'Fuck, sorry you're so ... Yes, let's get out of here. I can't even think straight.'

'Well, with the night I'd like to give you, the *last* thing I want you to be thinking is straight.'

CHAPTER 15

KISSING THE PINK

Wonderland followers: 517,586

Phaedra is buying us a bottle of red wine from the corner shop near my place while I sprint in my platforms up the dusty flights of stairs in my building to spruce up my bedsit. I know there's a half-eaten hash brown still greasing up in the pan I left out on the hob that I need to dispose of. I rush in to clear the bins and dishes and on my return I panic light a floral incense stick, make my bed and plaster some shimmery moisturiser over my legs.

I am still smoothing out the pink wrinkles of my bed when I hear the buzzer go off. I run over to the video intercom to let her in.

'I hope you have glasses, I can't drink wine from a mug,' she says as she walks into the flat, raising the bottle of wine in her hand.

It's a screw top. Thank God.

She walks into the kitchen and looks around. I've never had a stranger back here before. What do I say? Moan about the extortionate price of rent and the mould the landlord refuses to address? It's all so real with her in my flat, alone.

'Feel free to sit down ... here,' I say as I pull out a chair from the tiny kitchen table pushed up against the wall. I fetch two glasses from the cupboard and join her at the table.

'You have a lovely place,' she says, smiling at me.

'It's not huge, or particularly spacious,' I bluster, pouring the wine.

I walk the two-stride stretch from the kitchen table into my bedroom.

'Well, that's the grand tour!' I say, handing her a wine glass.

'Wow, I feel so privileged! I know that people have been asking for one on Wonderland for weeks ...'

I smile at the thought of her being just as obsessed with checking my profile as I am with hers. She cups her free hand on the side of my waist, rolling her head around to kiss my cheek.

'We should make a pact to not discuss *what's-his-face,'* she says, grimacing, then stretches her arms back onto my bed with her legs spread. 'The elephant in the room ... the piece-of-shit DJ that brought us together,' she continues.

'He's a waste of space, time and energy. Let's pay him none of it,' I say.

I don't want to think about the betrayal. Not now. I don't want the feeling of shame to penetrate the connection between us. It's like a needle, hovering around the edge of us, threatening to burst and destroy this moment.

We clink glasses and take long sips.

'Is that your art?' she asks finally, sitting up to walk over to my desk. She reaches out to examine the one that Matt grabbed with his wet hand. She runs her eyes over my wall of collages while I sit in silence. Although she's yet to remove a single article of my clothing, I feel naked.

'Oh, please, ignore that one, she's a bit wonk—'

'I love how you've drawn her with unequal tits. That's how they really are!'

I unclench my toes.

She places her glass and the picture down onto the table carefully. 'Do you have any more tape? This lady needs to be put up.'

That's the last time I ever let a man tell me what is and isn't art.

I pull the tape from the drawer and Phaedra tears off a piece and sticks the unframed woman onto the wall.

I flick through my collection of records and decide on Mazzy Star. I place the disc onto the player and lift the needle into place. The vinyl lets out a static crackle on the first few rings and then the guitar gently kicks in.

She grabs me from behind, turns me round and pushes her tongue gently into my mouth and I begin to kiss it. I'm fighting every muscle in my body not to glance at our reflection in the mirror to see how she looks, holding me like this. I've been dreaming about this girl all my life it feels, now she's in my arms, in my bedroom and it's better than I could have ever imagined. My wine glass is cradled in my hand behind her head, while my other hand fumbles down into her top and finds its way under her silk shirt, pushing my hand onto her soft breasts. My fingers dance around her nipple piercing, flicking it gently. I want her to know how much I want every inch of her. But I'm afraid to say it out loud in case she senses my nerves. She pulls me in closer by my neck and the wine glass in my hand tilts horizontally.

I look over her shoulder at the rug now streaked in red wine.

Fuck. That's gonna be a stubborn little cunt to get out in the morning.

Stay in the moment, EARTHA!

She turns around to inspect the stain, but I pull her chin back.

'It's nothing. Kiss me.'

Her lips part and she plants wet kisses up and down my neck.

We move to sit at the foot of my bed on the floor, in front of the mirror. I put the glass down while her face buries itself into my nape.

'Here,' I say, pointing to a spot underneath my jawline.

'You want me to kiss you there?'

She traces her tongue from my collarbone and onto the lowest part of my neck. With every stroke her tongue's getting closer and closer to the spot. If she can do this to my neck, what is she going to do to my…

My body quivers.

She's teasing me. Every part of my neck has had her lips on it, except for the one spot I told her to kiss. She starts to lower me down with her arms until I am fully laid on the floor. Her fingers trace down from my neck, between my breasts and down my body. They've landed at my lower stomach, my pussy opens up like a rosebud at the sensation of her touch. I can see her reflection in the mirror, straddling me, with one knee to the side of my body. She aligns her crotch against mine and gently thrusts her hips into me. I feel the seam of her trousers push into my clit and moan.

The candlelight is flickering on the walls, dancing off the reflective threads in her silk blouse. We're in our own kind of rhythm, drinking up each other's yearning. Her hands are still moving around my body while she kisses my neck.

I move my hands down her back, feeling for the curve of her hips, then start to trace my finger under the leather belt of her trousers.

'Mind if I take these off?' I ask.

She stands up, maintaining eye contact. Her trousers drop and her belt jingles when they hit the floor. I quickly glance down at my nipples. They're hard.

She lowers herself onto me in her shirt and sweet cherry-embroidered knickers.

I hope Matt didn't get to see these.

'Can I take that off as well?' I ask, pulling on the hem of her shirt.

Without thinking, her hands start unbuttoning it. I unfasten my own and the ties of my shirt fall to their sides. She has a small tattoo on her ribs that says 'IT GIRL'. I look up at her and she's a figure worthy only of complete worship. She melts into the backdrop like the flames which burn behind her.

Wait, was she this intimate with Matt? The question sits on the edge of my tongue, trying to crawl out of my mouth. I swallow it down and focus on the moment. On her.

Still holding hands, I try to pull her down but she resists. We stay here looking at each other's bodies while the tendrils of incense and music swim around us. Is this part of queer sex?

I am in love with this woman, she's perf—

Wait, NO. I'm definitely not in love.

Shitting hell, Eartha, control yourself.

'I feel so lucky to be here with you right now,' she says, tracing a line on my stomach.

My anxiety simmers down. This *is* tender and special. She feels it too. I didn't realise it was possible to feel so sexually alive and be seen as a full human being at the same time.

'Me too ...' I reply.

But I really hope she didn't feel this with Matt. Shut up, Eartha.

Concentrate.

She lowers her body onto mine on the floor and I feel the hard metal of her nipple piercings as they press into my flesh; it sends a streak of electricity down my spine.

'Where were we?' she whispers in my ear.

'You were going to kiss me, here,' I say, pointing to my neck.

'Keep these up here ...' she says.

Her words place invisible handcuffs onto me as I raise my arms above my head.

I jitter as her fingers trace up my thigh, near to the tip of my thong. She teases the outline of the fabric, the only boundary left to cross is the line of my underwear. Her fingers spread over the top and she hovers her hand over my pussy. She thrusts her hips into mine and presses her fingers onto my clit. I almost scream. Expelling the life-long urge to be touched by a woman.

My arms are still above my head.

Our lips touch but they don't kiss.

I'm ready.

I'm looking up at her, with my arms still obediently above my head.

I'm on the brink. She lifts me and turns me round so I'm facing the mirror with my back to the bed. The pink light from my lamp reflects off her dewy skin, a single bead of sweat makes its way between her breasts.

We're looking into each other's eyes as she slides her fingers under the elastic of my thong.

Our faces are an inch away from each other.

She sinks her two fingers slowly into me.

She pulls them out and slowly thrusts them in again.

Our faces are pressed up against each other, kissing messily, panting into each other's mouths. Every cell in my body is tingling.

I grab her waist and hold onto it while she fucks me.

I'm watching us in the mirror.

YES,

YES,

YEEEEEEEES,

YEEEEEEEEEEEES,

I scream.

My body is writhing in rapture.

She looks me in the eye while her fingers plunge into me.

It goes on, and on and on and on.

Her fingers take me to a real peak of release.

My body's convulsions start to slow down like waves crashing against her thigh.

She raises her hand to her mouth.

Looks me dead in the eyes.

And sucks her index and middle fingers clean.

Ohhhhhh.

So that's what the cut nails were for.

*

It's an hour after she made me cum, twice more. I think it's around 5 a.m. judging by the colour of the sky, which is becoming more and more rose-coloured by the minute, criss-crossed with chemtrails from aeroplanes like a swirly pink latte. The only light from the room is coming from the candles, which are barely flickering; the pools of wax that have collected at the bottom from hours of burning have almost drowned the wicks. We're perched on the edge of the windowsill with our backs leaning on each side. I've got my leg hitched up on the sill with my knee pointing up and my other foot on my bedroom floor, she's mirroring me on the other side of the ledge with one arm hanging at her side and another wafting a cig out the window. Our feet meet in the middle, separated by a chipped ceramic ashtray we occasionally tap our cigarettes into. She has her knickers on, a pair of fluffy socks that she asked to borrow and nothing else. My knickers are off, somewhere on the floor where they were discarded. My thighs are still sticky from sex and the room smells of us. I'm sat gazing across from her: the colour of her hair and the rosy sky seem so impossibly matched that it feels as though all my actions over the last few weeks have led me here, right now, to witness this synchronised beauty.

'It feels like we've been up for hours,' she says, taking a drag of her cigarette. She looks over her shoulder and out into the gradient sky as if trying to read the time from the early-morning light.

'We have. I'm so tired I'm delirious,' I reply. I reach for her free hand to hold it. I pull her gently into the middle of the windowsill to kiss me, above our knees. 'I love that I can just kiss you like this,' I say.

'Me too ...' she replies, but she sounds a little confused.

'What I mean is, I didn't come out that long ago. So ...' I look at our hands holding each other, tracing one another's fingers. I smile. 'So this is really fucking nice. Plus, I've been wanting to kiss you since I first met you.'

'Me too! I mean, at first, I thought you were gonna knock me out when you found out I—'

We both go silent.

Suddenly protective of this little sanctuary we've created in my bedroom, where everything's pink, men with dangly earrings don't exist and she definitely did *not* fuck my boyfriend while I was waiting for him to come home.

'It's fine. I mean, we can totally flip this nightmare situation around . . .' I let go of her hand to sit up straight and start swaying my hands, as I attempt to conjure up some enlightening perspective on the messiness that brought us together. 'Maybe we can find a way to be grateful for him. We can actually *thank* him for what he did.'

'Yeah! If I didn't go to that gig, I wouldn't have met you.'

'If *he* didn't fuck you, then *I* wouldn't have fucked you.'

'Now that would have been the *real* nightmare situation.'

She drops her head and kisses my knee softly. I pull myself back to lean against the window and admire her again. 'I want to be closer to you,' I say, stroking the imprint the carpet left on her skin.

She removes one fluffy sock, inches her toes closer, bridging the gap between our feet. I meet her in the middle and our toes touch and interlock. She places hers over mine.

We both look at one another other, our eyes holding each other in the moment. This is intimacy like I've never experienced before.

I want to have her, again.

'Wanna get into bed?' I ask her.

'I don't think I can sleep right now.'

'The *last* thing I want you to do is sleep.'

CHAPTER 16

SEXIST MARKETING SCHEMES

Wonderland followers: 568,309

I've been locked into Wonderland for days, since Phaedra left the other afternoon. I've been mostly arguing with men for hours at a time, peppered with intervals of checking her page to see what she's up to. I find myself reading every article she shares, trying to swim deeper into who she is and what she wants from the world. I want to be enough for her.

We stayed in bed the whole day after, basking in the sweaty, warm cocoon of my duvet. The morning was full of sexually satisfied laughter and kisses thick with morning breath. I'd forgotten what it felt like to share a bed with someone whose touch you didn't want to escape from. To be in a sweaty entanglement of each other's limbs and choose each other's hot bodies to sleep on despite the cool, vast expanse that lies around you. I have an impulse to throw away my life ambitions and create room for her in my life.

But my following has doubled since I met E.V, I'm now at 568,000 followers, it's getting more and more addictive. I told her I'm starting to become exhausted from plugging in for hours and she sent me some sheet masks she got in a PR goody bag to get rid of my eye bags.

> *@Menhurt_22* Women who go outside and wear unsensible clothing are deliberately trying to encourage alpha males to harass them. It's a fact of life. If you don't want men to harass you, cover your ass up! #Alpha

I reply:

> Men who go online to deliberately harass women in their spare time are encouraging feminists to expose them! Cover your ass up, @Menhurt_22 – I'm coming for you. Stop hiding behind a username and put your face to what you're saying. Or are you too scared to face the judgement of other people, like you, who come on here to spread hate?
>
> *Wonderland comments (54):*
>
> *@Girl_Wild* YESSSSS EARTHA!
>
> *@Deandra* Didn't think I could love you any more, but you've outdone yourself ... LOVE YOU EARTHA!
>
> *@VeronicaEscher* Eartha please keep rounding up and collecting these MEN!

It's late, judging by the sky's hue. Cracker crumbs keep appearing on my keypad but I leave them for future Eartha to deal with. I need total focus as I conjure up these powerful put-downs to people I'll never meet in real life. I figure if these sexist men are brave enough to shout their bigoted opinions on the internet then they must be ready to face the consequences: me. When I find them, I start smashing into my keyboard in order to get into arguments with them. Apparently, the more confrontations I get into publicly online, the more I can get people charged and riled up, the more engagement my Wonderland profile will see and the higher the chance I'll be boosted into the trending category. I ignore my ethical concerns. A bit like scrolling past one of those awful slaughterhouse videos when they come up on your feed, so that you can continue to eat burgers without feeling like a morally debased person.

But I reason with myself that this is different, because I'm doing the right thing. I'm doing it for a good cause. I'm exposing misogynists, racists, homophobes, transphobes, and raising awareness all at the same time. I'd be complicit to just let all of this happen without bringing attention to it! People *need* to be angry about this. People *need* to see this stuff. We can't keep letting powerful people ruin others' lives. I'm doing the right thing. But as soon as I shut one man down another army of angry men come to his rescue.

E.V has promised me this will eventually lead to paid work with brands; the more I keep at it, the more people will see that I care about this stuff. She told me over a brand lunch last week (where I was collected from my flat for breakfast in central Olympia) that someone with the username 'Joan of Narc' was blowing up for exposing men online. E.V thinks that 'Wonderland Eartha' needs to latch on to this trend. So I did some digging, and at 3 a.m. that night I found out about 'incels'. I almost added vomit to the multitude of colourful stains now on my rug. These are the men who aren't able to have sex with women but believe it's their *birth right*. They are 'involuntarily celibate'. They're now listed as a terrorist threat and, as much as it hurts, I can't stop reading about them. I haven't slept. I've lost track of time. Where's our voice, our needs, our right to say no to men? We have a right to be given the same freedom of choice as them. I turn my phone over to show the screen-side facing up.

Wonderland notifications (98):
@WstedLife Shut the fuck up. We get it. Your boyfriend cheated on you. Heal and move on.
@Sickly_Sexy YA'LL WHO HURT HER?!!!
@FeminazisSuckMyCock This bitch really thinks the world is out to get her. She's crazy.
@SamanthaSanders Eartha, don't listen to what any of these people are saying. You're giving women like me a voice. I'm with a man who once threatened to kill me if I tried to leave. I can't speak up. But you can. Keep going.
@BelowTheKnickers Skincare. Routine. Now.
@WolfPack #MGTOW are coming for you, you filthy slut. Just admit you're a lesbian because men don't want you anyway.
@matt_the_shaman My life is so much better since you're not in it #FollowingMySpiritGuide.
@Champagne_taste_lambrini_budget Bestieee where do you buy your clothes?
@BelowTheKnickers SKINCAAAAARE ROUTINE PLSSSS!!

The comments roll in at the top of my phone, replacing the last notification with another, after another, after another. *Did I just see that Matt has rebranded as a shaman?* Jesus. I need to text Phaedra; she'll get a laugh out of that. I've been repeatedly typing the word 'sexism' into Google and clicking on my 'News' tab, to see if there's anything going on or any scandal I can comment on or attach myself to. I feel like a feminist vampire, sucking the toxic blood out of these men. But now I've been doing it every hour, of every day, for almost a week, and I'm starting to feel like I over-ordered too many misogyny platters. I've reordered the search to 'newest items first' and there's a tidal wave of new articles published, daily, about some misogynistic pig who's been accused by multiple women of assault or has made sexist comments at his workplace or is inciting hate against women through 'Men's Rights Activism' YouTube channels. I didn't realise how much anger men had for women until I started deep-diving into their loathing. I knew that there were men who raped women and killed women and I'd always assumed it was about power. But these faceless men genuinely do not believe women are human beings.

It's got me realising how I also tolerated this disrespectful behaviour from Matt. From Dad. How did I get six years into a relationship with Matt, who cheated and manipulated women into a false sense of security so that they would fuck him? And I *chose* him. Every single day. I felt responsible for him, his life, his success, his happiness. I believed he was as good as it was ever going to get.

I've ended up falling down rabbit hole after rabbit hole of articles about violence committed against women. And most of those articles feature the term 'emotional abuse'. I think of Matt and me, the pictures of us smiling together in the sun on a holiday he'd planned (to make up for ripping up my collages). The bouquet of flowers he brought to my studio in front of everyone (the morning after he threatened to kill himself because he saw me walking home with that photographer). I posted the flowers and the holidays and no one knew any better. The addictive approval of people on the internet became a salve for my real-life misery. But all the nice things Matt did for me were just an extension of his manipulation. Reeling me in further. Hurting me privately, with the acts of kindness made public. Our relationship was the perfect scam.

I've found a good story on Google and I click on the link.

GYM BUDDY: NEW TRAINING PROGRAMME OR SEXIST MARKETING SCHEME?

I screenshot it and open my phone to take a selfie. I pull a sarcastic smile and flip my middle finger up for the picture, swig a gulp of wine, slam the glass down onto the floor next to the bed and open the Wonderland app on my phone.

Here we go. I start typing up a caption:

What's this? A male-owned gym offering free memberships to women over a size 12 and mums post-pregnancy? Yeah, because women exist exclusively to look beautiful and not at all for the things that they're capable of creating and bringing into the world, like, oh I don't know, art, or music, or living breathing human beings? Women are more than their bodies. Fuck right off @gymbuddy2030

Women who are already pressured to be perfect by ads glaring at them everywhere they look don't need another guilt trip #StopSellingWeightLoss #FuckGymBuddy

I reread the caption typed into my phone. I change the hashtag from *#FuckGymBuddy* to *#DropGymBuddy*. That might be taking it a bit too far but I think E.V will like it. I attach the two photos, one of the article and one of me giving the finger. I swipe back and forth between the two pictures, checking for their imperfections. I recrop it to make sure everything's tight and turn the brightness/contrast up on my finger-flipping selfie. Content locked and ready to go, I press send, watch and wait. One by one, people are reacting and their comments are flooding onto my phone screen.

@willyplonkaz What an absolute disgrace, cancelling my

membership right now. Thanks for letting me know about this Eartha.

@VeronicaEscher Sexist pigs. Do these men not remember they all come from women?!

@FeministC4nt If we all ring up and complain, they'll have to take it down!

I glare at my phone as a wave of self-righteous vitriol washes over me, watching all of these women becoming engrossed and enraged. There are two comments every minute. Then five. Then ten.

These people think that what I have to say matters.

Ping

Voice note from E.V to Eartha (1.01 minutes)

22.53

EARTHA! I love what you've been doing on socials over the last couple of days. Absolutely DELICIOUS! I've been watching your insights and stats like a bloody HAWK, they're just going up and up every time you talk about your coming out, but your new post today has been soaring. #DropGymBuddy is TRENDING! Don't mention the ex any more. Oh, it's all happening just like I said, darling! You won't believe what I've managed to secure for you … Our hard work is already paying off. AHHHH! You're going to be so pleased with me. Let me know when you're free for a call. I have some great news. Speak soon.

I immediately call her.

'Hellooooo.'

'E.V, I just got your voice note! What's the news?'

'You use the dating app FIRE, right? So, I reached out to them, sent them your profile and, as chance would have it, they're looking to push queer dating on their social media channels to encourage more queer people to use their app! I've looked through the brief and it is FANTASTIC! I told them you already used the app and they were thrilled. It feels like such a perfect fit. You've not even heard the best bit yet, the budget ...'

'Yes ...'

'They're paying you twenty K to be an ambassador for their brand for a term of ten weeks and—'

'Did you just say twenty grand?'

'I sent over your recent interactions and the stats from my intel; they saw how engaged your audience has been lately ... They ate it all up, darling. They just want some organic-style content of you using the app on your Wonderland page, screenshots of positive interactions and talking about why you love the app and all that. I'll send you over the contract soon.'

'That's ... a salary.'

'There's some red-line stuff in the contract that you'll need to read about your public image and some things you can't ...' she says, cutting me off.

I'm staring at myself at the end of my bed in the mirror. Her words are trailing off, I'm not really listening to what she's saying. *Twenty fucking grand.*

'Eartha? You there, darling? OH, FUCK OFF!'

'Excuse me?'

'Sorry, not you, darling, a BLOODY man just cut me off on the street. I'm so glad you're collecting these rodents online, darling. Teach these men a lesson or two ...'

'I mean, that's technically my job now ...'

'I'll send it over to you once we're happy with it, okay?'

'Yes, oh my God, thank you ... Twenty thousand?'

'Well, it will be sixteen K once I've had my cut, remember, darling! I'll talk to you later.'

E.V hangs up before I can finish my sentence.

I return my eyes to the glow of my phone.

> *@GymBuddymediadesk* Hi Eartha, my name is Greg, I work for Gym Buddy and we made this programme to give mums, post-pregnancy, a sense of purpose and community. Please remove this post so we can talk privately to handle this. We're very open to learning.

I roll my eyes and delete the message.

A sense of community.

What about specifically targeting women over a size 12? And isn't a new mum's *purpose* to keep their baby alive and raise an actual human being? Not to buy into a gym class run by men who think women can only have purpose at a certain size or form.

I delete the direct message and return to my laptop, tapping away at the keyboard, searching for more sexist articles, more statistics, more things to be enraged by.

My phone starts to ping.

Over and over and over.

The Gym Buddy post is picking up. I reach for my glass of wine and take a sip.

I want more.

I want revenge.

CHAPTER 17

DADDY'S HOME

Wonderland followers: 662,921

I open my window to let some air in as my room is thick with the stench of hairspray. For Mona's friend's warehouse party, I've dressed up as Brigitte Bardot – but if Brigitte Bardot had just killed a man, stolen his suit and gone home to fuck his wife on the kitchen table. I picked this Sixties men's pinstripe suit on a thrifting haul with Rose and Mona on Sunday because Rose said they 'know' (translation: *have fucked*) the girl who works at one of the best vintage stores in Olympia. We received a mighty discount and Rose walked out without paying for a *thing*. I wanted the suit to be oversized but the waistcoat needed nipping in, so I've added some safety pins at the back. The outfit makes me feel powerful in a way I've not experienced before, as if I'm cosplaying male privilege and borrowing an ounce from its previous owner.

I've recorded a video trying to put on the blazer seductively fifteen times. The idea of talking a bunch of strangers through my outfits and where each piece was 'sourced' once felt humiliating and pointless, but now it pays my bills. I tag the Wonderland influencer's perfume I've been sent (it's called 'smells like queer spirit') and brands pay me to wear their clothes on Wonderland. Most of them have aphorisms on them, the latest parcel was loungewear inspired by 'female empowerment' – the tracksuits have 'bitch, please' written across the bum and cost £129.99. E.V asks them for thousands of pounds and they accept and I do it because I still can't believe that just a month ago I was worried about the consequences of forgetting to cook my boyfriend pasta after he came home from work.

I lean over my bed to turn up the music on my vinyl player and start lip-syncing to Talking Heads in my mirror, the way an egocentric frontman would – prancing about, crotch thrust forward, eye-fucking everyone in the crowd. In my weeks of arguing with men online, I've almost forgotten that they hold any kind of attraction for me. I suppose just from looking at me the men in tonight's environment won't have a clue that I'm Olympia's biggest online man-basher. That arguing with these men is part of the reason I now have my first paid job with a dating app. I feel like changing my Wonderland bio to *Ask not what you can do for patriarchy, but what the patriarchy can do for you.*

But underneath all the excitement there's a rattling anxiety that threatens to smother any modicum of joy that tries to light up my life. As though my own battered brain, used to chaos and drama, cannot trust the unfamiliar state of peace that comes with financial equilibrium and being happily single. My yearning for Phaedra is both the thing that thrusts me out of bed in the morning and the thing that ulcerates my stomach. Is it normal to feel nauseous when you're really attracted to someone? I'm starting to wonder whether she's fucking someone else. She hasn't plugged into Wonderland or posted anything for the last twenty-four hours, and the last time she did that was when she was in bed with me. My logical brain tells me that she's just busy with her own life and that she'll text me when she's available. But the anxious part of my brain offers the gut-churning possibility that she's fucking Matt. That the pair of them are in bed together laughing at me and my *silly little styling videos* online. I imagine them mimicking the things I say like 'smells like queer spirit all right!' or 'let your butt do the talking!' while Matt scoffs and calls me the 'BTEC version of Gok Wan'. I've internalised his voice, even though he's not here any more.

As for Phaedra, what else apart from great sex could possibly lure someone so far out of Wonderland that they forget to plug in? After I'd kissed her goodbye at the door of my flat, I ran straight to my phone to plug in. There was no active content on her profile and I felt proud that I was a distraction worthy enough to keep her away from her online life. It was the ultimate compliment – that being with me was a more addictive high.

Ping!

I run to check if it's from Phaedra.

> *Text message from E.V to Eartha*
> 21.39
> As promised, just emailed over the contract from FIRE! Please have a read through as soon as possible and get it back to me when you can so I can invoice them for signature payment. There are a few key points you really need to read over in there. Especially the clause ...
> *Read more.*

Knock knock knock.

'It's ooooopeeeeeen!' I shout.

I e-sign the contract quickly and send it back to E.V before my night out begins.

'Holy fucking shit!' Mona exclaims as she walks into the kitchen. 'It stinks of hairspray in here!' She places a four-pack of beer on the counter and pinches her nose.

'Yeah, it lingers around. Kind of like a date you can't get rid of,' I reply as I grab the pack of beers on the table. She laughs, swivels around towards my bedroom and sits herself down on the edge of my bed. I jam the bottle against the kitchen counter before smacking my palm down and releasing the metal cap, then hold out the opened beer to her.

'Wait, no limes?! Come on, we're not animals ... I brought one in my bag to slice.'

'I wish I was the girl rocking up to pre-drinks with my fucking limes. It's so hot,' I say, getting out a bread knife. '*Can I have a lime with my beer*?' I add in the most sultry tone I can muster while trying not to slice my fingers.

'YES, but you have to say "I'll have". It's more assertive. Look ...' She stands up from the bed and leans into the door frame, watching me saw the lime in the kitchen. '*I'll have a lime with my beer.*'

I shake my head at her brilliance. 'Where did you learn all this?'

'Please... my mum raised me this way. I'll *always* be this way.'

I pinch a couple of the fat lime wedges and shove them into the necks of our beer bottles. I catch her up on my Phaedra dilemma and she tells me she is compiling a list of all the best cinemas to get fingered in.

'*Daddy's home!*' Rose cries out as they let themself into my flat.

We turn towards the front door and they come into view, leaning against the door frame. My jaw drops.

'I know, I know ...'

Rose holds up their hands and turns a full circle, allowing us to take in their appearance. They wear a brown tailored blazer and matching wide-legged trousers. Their white shirt is unbuttoned all the way down to their waistline. They're wearing a little eyeliner, a silver hoop in their right ear and a pair of steel-toed cowboy boots.

'What's in there?' I ask, pointing at a leather sports bag by their feet.

'Change of clothes, just in case I sweat through these.'

They crouch down and pat the bag like the belly of a large dog.

I look down at the outfit I was confident in just ten minutes ago. Rose catches me running my insecurities around my head. They put their bag on the end of my bed and place their arms around my waist behind me. I rest my hands on their forearm, deflating my shoulders.

'I'm just a sweaty cunt, Eartha, don't panic.'

'We look like the gay misfits from a corny prom picture,' I reply.

They kiss me on the forehead and walk over to sit on the bedroom windowsill with their feet rested on the ledge. Mona sits on the other side, their shoes touching in the middle. The scene makes me think of Phaedra. My stomach starts to flutter and then it drops.

'Right, who wants a shot of tequila before we go?' I ask, trying to raise my spirits and erase my anxieties.

'No, no, I brought wine! You keep your booze ...' Rose insists. They point from the windowsill to their bag on the bed. I rustle through and plop the wine onto the bed in a soft *thud.*

'A BAG OF WINE?! I'm not having that,' Mona exclaims, screwing her face up.

'No, it's a *box* of wine.' Rose accentuates the word 'box'.

'Yeah, but like ... inside the box is a plastic bag, full of *wine,*' Mona protests.

'Fine, I'll have my entire plastic bag of wine and yous lot can have your fancy stuff!' Rose flicks their head and looks out of the window.

'Come on, Mona, *I'll* put in one of your lime slices ...' I say, winking.

*

Twenty minutes later, we're all stood outside waiting for a cab and Mona is cradling the bag of wine above her head with the nozzle in her mouth, milking it dry like an udder. Rose and I cheer on from the sidelines, shouting, '*DOWN IT*' and watching our friend with expensive taste ingest a deadly quantity of the lowest quality, sugariest wine Olympia has to offer. Rose is assisting her, pinching the hole at the top so it doesn't spill.

'ALMOST DONE!' Rose shouts.

Mona drinks until all that remains is a solitary, red-stained lime wedge in the deflated and crumpled bag. Too drunk to realise she's emptied its contents, she continues sucking through the nozzle and it starts ventilating like an airbag.

*

As we exit the cab we spot a frenzy of flares, leather blazers, platforms, polo shirts, pointelle collars, Canadian tuxedos, Lurex and shaggy haircuts. The queue looks like an audition for the part of 'background dancer' in a Led Zeppelin music video.

We walk past the crowd until we are outside a large, garage-sized door that's been pulled all the way up. The noise of the crowd's chatter dies down, as if someone has spun a volume knob. There's a tall man sat on a wooden stool in a black puffer coat with his hands in his pockets. For a few seconds it goes entirely quiet, then people return to their chatter.

'EARTHA!'

A high-pitched voice shouts from the queue. We stop and turn to look. I don't recognise the face of the woman who cried my name.

'Hello?'

'I love your soul! I follow you on Wonderland! I think you and I could best friends!'

'Oh, thank you! Love you too!'

Love you too?

Who the fuck do I think I am?

Another girl runs over from her place in the queue to join us.

'Hi, I'm so sorry, I just heard that girl shout your name in the queue, are you Eartha?'

'Yes ...'

'I'm so embarrassed, I don't want to be a fan girl, but can I have a picture please?'

'With *me*?'

'YES, WITH YOU, BECAUSE YOU'RE THE VOICE OF A GENERATION!'

Mona extends her hand, offering to take a picture for the girl. The girl passes her phone over and pushes herself up against me. She puts her arms around my waist excitedly, facing the camera. But I'm somewhere else; I'm out of my body, levitating somewhere above this entire scene, watching myself, completely detached. I feel a little humiliated, as though agreeing to take a picture with a stranger confirms that I believe my own hype. Even among this throng of eclectic people that I couldn't identify with more, I suddenly feel like the odd one out.

Mona takes the picture. 'Here you go!'

The fan girl waves goodbye excitedly and rushes back to her friends. The three of us walk towards the door together, as the bouncer looks at the girl in the queue and back at me.

'Excuse me, you're gonna have to go to the back of the queue ... like *everyone else.*'

'No, they don't, they're with me!' a voice says, from behind the security. Mona's friend Andrea comes from inside the venue and leans her arm on the bouncer's shoulder.

I realise now that the bouncer is actually a woman and a piercing shame hits my chest. I still have so much to learn.

'Sorry, love, you should have given me a list or something, I didn't know!' the bouncer responds.

I flash an overcompensating smile at the bouncer for my internalised mistake. We walk into another empty hall with brick walls and nothing inside it but a bookcase and the warm glow from a lamp on a side table at the back. The windows are all covered with musty-smelling, red velvet curtains ...

'This is it?' I ask.

'Oh come on, you, don't start with this *where are the lesbians* crap again!' Mona jokes as she explains, 'It's technically a speak-easy. They're not allowed to serve alcohol in this area of town because it's too residential now. So, it's secret.' She turns to review our silence.

'Don't look at me like I'm a serial killer. It's through here. This room is just the decoy in case the police raid it.'

A police raid?

Mona reads the fear on my face and rolls her eyes. She takes our hands, walks Rose and me to the end of the room and stands in front of the bookcase. She pushes on its side and it starts to move.

'You have got to be kidding me,' I say.

The bookcase revolves on an axis from the centre.

'Come on, it's down here.'

Rose and I follow Mona through the bookcase door and it swings shut behind us. We walk down the staircase and as the bottom door swings open, I hear 'Atomic' by Blondie. My eyes dart across the room – it's a dazzling mass of people dancing, sliding and spinning together.

We all grab hands and walk over to the bar; it's lit by a blue neon sign that reads 'COLD BEER' surrounded by a swarm of people not one of whom is standing still. No one's on their phones. I'm not sure you'd even get signal down here. Maybe that's the point. Actual connection.

I look out onto the dancefloor with pure ecstasy coursing through me. The walls are lined with metallic streamers and they reflect shards of colour across the faces of the dancers. Everywhere around me is pure unfiltered joy. There are men, dancing with each other, but the women are owning the dancefloor and dancing better than the boys. Everyone looks as though they're on the edge of a climax induced solely by the good energy in the room. Tonight I may actually be relieved of my burgeoning hatred for men. I spot a girl with pink hair and think it's Phaedra. She turns round, not even close.

Mona jabs me in the back and I turn around to see she is now clutching three very full pints with her debit card held between her teeth.

'Here you go,' she says as she hands us all our drinks.

We find a table in the corner and shove our stuff underneath it.

'FUCK, THIS SONG IS SO GOOD. LET'S GO!' Rose says, licking the line of foam from their pint on their upper lip.

Mona starts to dance her way over to the crowd, leading the way through the floor of people all swinging their arms, moving and stomping their feet. I start swaying my way into the crowd. Rose grabs my hand to jive, then lifts it to spin me around. I've twisted to the direction of the bar when I spot a guy looking out at the dancefloor. He's leaning onto the side of the bar, his midriff stretches out of the top of his corduroy flares. His bony face and large nose glow under the blue neon light. He latches onto my eyes. Hot, fucking, damn.

'Who are *you* looking at?' Mona teases. I haven't taken my eyes off him. She follows the direction of my gaze.

'That guy looks a bit like Jim Morrison, right?' I remark. Mona nods.

He's staring right back. I give him just a few more seconds of eye contact before returning my attention to dancing with Mona. *That should do the trick.* Sexual tension is often better than sex. Right now, he's my fantasy guy: the one who will go down on me for hours and give me multiple orgasms, the one who will take me on an elaborately planned date based on my birth chart, the one who's read all of bell hooks' books, the one who goes to therapy, the one who's super feminist and respects the hell out of my mind but also loves to smack my ass in the bedroom. In this moment he's everything because I know nothing.

'EARTHA!' Mona says, flapping her hand in front of her face. 'I know where I've seen *that* look before . . .' She points to my eyes.

*

Rose has hooked up with someone already and Mona has wandered off. I'm trying to be present and not think about why Phaedra still hasn't texted me. I'm charged from the potency of dancing in this seething mass of joy. I wonder if this charge is reciprocal or entirely in my head. I feel alive. There's a throbbing in my crotch, a combination of how turned on I feel and the fact that I haven't used the toilet since we arrived. I scour the walls for a sign to the loo and spot a man zipping up his trousers walking through a swinging door in the opposite corner of the room. I presume the ladies' will be next door. I walk alongside the dancefloor, trying not to get hit in the face by the swinging and jiving limbs, and push the door open. I'm met with four cubicles. I hear a flush and a guy walks out.

'Oh SHIT.' I've walked into the men's room.

'This is a gender-neutral toilet, anyone can use it,' the guy says, doing up his fly and holding the door open above my head to leave.

'Oh …' I reply, awkwardly walking under his outstretched sweaty armpit.

In the loo cubicle I can still hear the muted music from outside but also squelching; people are kissing in here, somewhere. I hover over the cold metal toilet seat and face the back of the cubicle door. I spot some freshly scrawled graffiti, written in lipstick. I squint my eyes to read it.

Maybe it's a girl crush, maybe you're queer.

'Now that's fucking cool,' I whisper.

I wonder who wrote this? I wonder if they did it tonight?

I exit the cubicle and roll up my sleeves to wash my hands in the sink. I look at my reflection and instead see a pair of fingertips latch themselves over the top of one of the cubicles behind me, *Oh to be fucked in a toilet.*

I reach for the soap pump as the external door opens. I can hear a shuffling of boots make their way over to the sink. I look in the mirror. It's the Jim Morrison guy. He smirks. I smile in the mirror to acknowledge him while I wash the soap between my fingers. From the corner of my eye I see him splash water on his face then reach for the towel around his neck and use it to pat his face. He leans his left arm onto the top of the hand-dryer and turns his body to face me. His crop top rides up as he stretches his arm, revealing more of his torso.

'*There she is,*' he says.

'Do we … know each other?'

'No …' He moves his arm from resting on the dryer and leans it onto the counter next to the sink, 'But I'd like to.'

I blink slowly and clench my jaw. He's so close, he's all whisky and coke, it stirs up a magnetic desire in me.

'My name is—' he says.

'Don't tell me,' I cut in.

I look around and search for anyone who might be watching. Since I've started to live most of my life online it's become harder to differentiate between when I'm being watched and when I can live. I'm pretty sure the only two people in the bathroom are the ones that are fucking. I lean in closer to him and get right up to his face.

'I don't want to know your name …'

'*Buuuut* …?' he says, as he leans in closer towards me.

'But I'd like you to kiss me,' I finish.

He puts his hands either side of my face. The kiss starts off intense but gradually becomes slower, finding a rhythm with the music from outside. We're not really kissing any more. Just teasing and touching the edges of each other's bodies and mouths. Knowing that at any moment someone could walk in makes it even hotter. He lifts me up and places me onto the sink, I sit with my legs wide open and he stands between them. I scoop up the hem of my blazer and curl it around my lap to dodge the wet patch of soapy water on the sink. His large hands caress my body, moving up and down my back and around my thighs. It feels odd to be held by a man after Phaedra. His bristle is starting to graze my chin. With my eyes closed he starts to feel just like Matt, so I keep them open. He moves his hand further and further up my chest and gently holds it around my throat, just so I can feel the pads of his fingertips. I wrap my legs around his torso and use them to pull his crotch into me. I feel the imprint of his cock press gently against me, sending one neat pulsating throb to my clit. I can still hear people fumbling around in the cubicle and it's turning me on, *a lot*. One of them is grunting while the other lets out soft moans, muted by the placement of the hand of whoever's pleasuring her. My hands run through his hair when I hear the screech of the door and the outside music erupting into the bathroom. He jumps back and we both look at each other, laughing at our knee-jerk reaction, caught in the act. I drop my head onto his shoulder as we collapse laughing into each other.

'You should have seen your face,' he says as he strokes the hair behind my ear.

I bite my lip laughing, ready to lean in and kiss him again.

'What the fuck are you doing?' says the person who has walked into the bathroom. It's the girl from earlier who took a picture with me.

'Are you talking to me?' I ask.

'Yes, I'm talking to you.'

I look back to the guy, confused.

'Seriously, what are you doing?' she says again, this time more indignantly.

'I'm confused, are you my mum or something?' I force a laugh to dispel the tension, then lift my head from the guy's shoulder and place my hands around his waist. He's still standing between my legs.

'I thought you were supposed to be gay,' the girl says. I look at him, then back at her.

'I'm bisexual.'

'You're a fucking fraud and you've ruined my night. I'm unfollowing you right now,' the girl balks.

'What ... what are you talking about?' I ask, confused.

She puts her hand into her back pocket and reaches for her phone. She loads my page up and unfollows me, then angles the camera at my face. The flash bursts out of the pinhole of her camera. I don't say anything, or move. I'm too stunned.

'What the fuck are you doing?' He reaches his hand out to take her phone. She pulls back and glares at me.

'Queer people deserve better than you,' she says as she puts her phone back into her pocket and storms out of the toilet. I shake my head, trying to process what just happened.

'Are you ... okay? What the hell was she on about?' He brushes my hair behind my ears again.

'That ... was ... Where is she going to put that picture? That was so fucking weird.' I can hardly form a sentence.

'Why would she call you gay?'

'Well ... she's only half wrong. I'm bisexual.' I shrug it off.

'Why didn't you tell me that at first? That's so fucking hot.'

'Oh, *really*? It's not exactly the first thing I say to people,' I laugh.

'Yeeeeah, I love a bit of girl-on-girl action,' he smirks, slowly nodding his head.

Oh. For fuck's sake.

I drop my arms from his shoulders and lean backwards onto the sink. 'I mean, yeah, I enjoy sex with women, but I love all the other stuff as well. I could proper marry a woman, I reckon,' I explain.

The cuffs of my blazer are starting to get wet from the edge of the sink.

'So, you don't do it with, like, other men. It's just ... just you and a girl?'

I nod. He lets go of me and backs up. He holds up his hands defensively.

'So, you're a lesbian?'

'No, I'm bisexual. I like men and women ... '

'Yeah, nah, that's a bit too—' He stops himself. I raise my eyebrow. He starts to wrinkle his face and twist his hands. 'I'm just ... gonna go back outside.'

He backs up and walks out the door, leaving me on the edge of the sink with my legs wide open, staring into the blue neon light on the back wall ahead of me which I can now see reads 'Be Yourself' in cursive neon lettering. *Brilliant.*

I can hear the harmony of a person cumming and another person grunting in the same cubicle. I can't believe I was turned on by them seconds ago. Now I feel deeply alone and bitter and am overcome with the urge to tell them to shut up.

'Here's yer knickers, gorgeous. I've just gotta go outside and sort something out...' Wait, *I know that voice.*

The cubicle door swings open so hard that it bounces back on the hinge. Rose is stood with their hands in fists, like they're ready to fight someone. 'Eartha! What happened? Was that homophobic asshole talking to you?!'

I look behind Rose: there's a girl pulling her trousers up from around her ankles. Rose immediately jumps to protect the girl's modesty and closes the door. 'Are you okay? That sounded horrible! Where is that fucker?!' They turn around then lean in closer to whisper. 'I got so angry I literally finished that girl off so quickly to come out and one-bang this cunt: where is he?'

I'm hit with a sharp pang of jealousy in my gut. I want to be the kind of lover that can finish someone off in ten seconds flat. 'It was that Jim Morrison guy, and a girl from the queue took a picture of me kissing him.'

'FUCK THEM!' Rose flings their arms in the air and goes to grab the door handle to the club.

'ROSE, calm down babe,' I shout over to them.

They pull back from the door, pinching their unbuttoned shirt and flapping it to create a breeze.

Rose embraces me with a hug stood between my legs, smothering me under a fog of their sweaty pheromones and signature scent. The cubicle door behind them creaks open. 'Right, you wanna come with?' Rose says to me as the girl they were having sex with comes up from behind them and rests her arm on Rose's shoulder, kissing them on the cheek.

'No, you go. I need a minute to get my head screwed back on.'

'You sure?'

'Yes'

I jump off the sink and turn around to face myself in the mirror. Something is creeping its way out of my chest. As Rose and the girl leave, the door to the club swings closed. I think of Phaedra. How she still hasn't texted me back and how my pathetic attempt to spread out the intensity of my crush on her has backfired. What are you supposed to do when you like someone this much? Anyone else that isn't her just becomes a placeholder. How have

I been declared both too gay and not gay enough in the space of a minute? I feel like I'm not enough for gay women *or* straight men. So, where do I belong? Everyone around me seems to know exactly who they are. What made him find it so hot initially and then literally wince in repulsion at the thought of me? Why did this woman have such high expectations of me and my queerness?

I investigate the girl I see in the mirror to remind myself of who I am. I remember the words of encouragement from E.V from our meetings. I take a deep breath, readjust my blazer – now creased and soggy – and leave the safety of backstage to enter the theatre of the nightclub.

DIRECTOR'S NOTE

Camera trails Eartha as she walks over to the bar, scouring the customers.

She catches sight of the 'Jim Morrison guy' who is propping up against the bar, talking to a blonde girl.

Her eyeline spins off from the couple and stretches out across the dancefloor where she sees Rose and the 'Rose club sex girl' on the dancefloor together.

She goes over to the table where they deposited their things, pulls out her jacket and walks out of the club.

She texts both Mona and Rose:

'Sorry guys, not feeling it. Call me when you come back this way and we can always have a drink at mine or something. But you will both be getting lucky I hope.'

She walks down a pavement still full of people queueing to get into the club, then spots a bike dock and her face is flooded with an idea.

Up-lit shot for this moment.

Next shot we see Eartha riding home on the bike, using it to make herself cum.
Drone camera then circles high above Eartha until the viewer can barely detect Eartha's outline.
ENDS

CHAPTER 18

CONTRACTUAL OBLIGATIONS

Wonderland followers: 709,325

DIRECTOR'S NOTE
Eartha has the glazed look of everyone else who is on Wonderland – not quite present, not quite focused – as though their cadaver has been left behind and their soul is wandering around online.
She types with speed and fury as though her body is a function of the laptop.
Camera A zooms into the laptop screen.
Eartha types: Hey *@gaygirlsleaze*, there's not *one way* to look queer. I heard you're not letting girls in if they're not 'gay enough' looking? Why would a queer club stop queer people from going just because of how they look? If we can't accept that queer looks different to every person, then what are we doing? We're liberating a select few and that isn't liberation. That's just more OPPRESSION. That's just more GATEKEEPING. It doesn't matter what you look like. If you like girls, you like girls. No bouncer can tell you otherwise. #BetterNightLifeForQueerPeople

After finishing, she chucks back another paracetamol while taking a long gulp of water from a glass in the café. *Camera A zooms above Eartha's head*, revealing that everyone in the café is plugged in. The couple next to Eartha with their young child are plugged into two different arenas – one on progressive parenting and the other on FIRE. Their child is plugged into Wonderlanders, an arena for children aged 0–4 years. The teenage girls at the next table are all plugged into the same arena as each other and they are talking through their avatars who they are dieting to become. The man who is unloading a crate of oat milk onto the counter is plugged into a conversation about positive impact marketing and the woman helping him is plugged into an arena about BDSM.
ENDS

I'm smashing out post after post, using buzzwords, keywords and clickbait to grab people's focus. After taking a sip of coffee, I check that no one's looking before opening up the tab to plug into Phaedra's Wonderland profile. I'm tired of waiting for her to reply. I start to type a message to send to her, 'Hi Phaedra. Thinking of you. What are you doing tomorrow evening?' I press send and feel that all-consuming confidence that comes with taking the driver's seat in your own life.

One minute passes with no reply, and a deep-seated fear of rejection has already kicked into gear and erased all feelings of empowerment. I feel sick. I check if I can unsend. I can't. She's online. She's seen it. I return to my screen and plug back into Wonderland to distract myself; my eyes gorge on the comments from my latest post that load in front of my face.

Wonderland notifications:

@WanderMaisie Can you do more content on your journey of realising your sexuality?

@GagaRaisedMeee Where's that fit mate of yours! MORE ROSE CONTENT PLEASE!

@Matt_Kinsley PREACHHHHH! I'd buy the T-shirt.

@AinzBow Why is she capitalising everything, lol, is she ok this girl hasn't unplugged for daysssss.

@ChristianJessica_78 Still have hope for you. I know you'll find your way back to God some day.

@AmeeInWonderland You are a GODDESS Eartha. You have saved my LIFE.

@VeronicaEscher You never miss Eartha.

Notification: User's time in Wonderland, 2.30hrs

I have to keep the time-log notifications on my laptop now; if I don't get interrupted I am lost for the whole afternoon, days even. I'm opening up another browser on my laptop to copy another URL link of a sexist article when I'm pulled out of my focus by a woman stood outside the café staring at me. It's E.V, but in even more enormous sunglasses than normal. Her face is contorted into an expression I have never seen her wear before. She walks in and stays standing, hovering over the bar stool in front of me.

'E.V, what's going on?'

'What is this?' She waves her phone in front of my face. 'WHAT IS THIS, EARTHA?'

Phone screen: Displaying a picture from last night of Eartha sat on a sink with her legs wrapped around Jim Morrison guy.

The photo isn't flattering in the slightest. I laugh with embarrassment.

'This ISN'T funny.'

'Wait, what? Why are you angry at me? I haven't done anything wrong ... have I?' I reach for her phone to look at the picture. 'This girl totally violated my privacy, look she—'

'Looks like someone didn't read their contract like I asked them to.'

'What contra—'

She raises her eyebrows.

'Oh, the FIRE one! I signed it last night just before I went out. Look, I've been writing this piece about how this gay girl sleaze bar hav—'

'That's great you are working so hard ...' She looks over at my laptop screen, which is plastered with the search terms *SEXISM, HOMOPHOBIA*. I slam it shut. 'But I really needed you to have looked over that contract properly, before you signed it.'

'What does the contract have to do with this?'

'If you had read it, you'd know ...'

She opens the email app on her phone to find the email containing the signed contract. She scrolls until she finds a specific clause. She points to the line in the contract with her finger, moving it along each word as she reads it out loud: 'Your contract stipulates that you *cannot be seen to date men within the duration of this contract*, as this campaign is about *championing queer talent.*'

'That's so biphobic. The girl who *took* that picture last night called me a fraud for being with a man! Now you are too? Now I'm "contractually obliged" to not be intimate with men?!'

I tell her what happened and try to laugh it off. But my blood is boiling as I remember the sadistic expression on the girl's face when she took the picture.

'I'm not saying that you're not really queer, of course I'm not. But part of the FIRE contract says that, as a growing public figure, if you're seen to be dating men, it will make their campaign seem…inauthentic,' E.V explains.

'But that's part of the problem, I'm bisexual. Kissing men *is* "authentic" to my sexuality …'

I feel so tight inside. I've just started to feel proud of who I am. I stare blankly into her lap. I feel I have failed by being myself. I want to prove to her that I can do this, that I can be what she wants, the version of Eartha that she has invested in.

'Say something, what are you thinking?'

'I just … I just … I didn't know that was in the contract,' I say eventually.

She removes her glasses, places them on top of the bar stool next to me and reaches out to hug me. She smells of lemon balm and cigarettes. I hold onto her hug for longer than I initially intend to. With my arms still around her, she pulls away to look at my face.

'Unfortunately, public opinion is everything in this job. The world doesn't care if you love yourself, if you love being bisexual, or if I love you being bisexual! It will make its own mind up about you anyway. That's why FIRE has got to be honest with their talent. They have to put these clauses in to protect themselves. When people see you kissing a guy they think, *Silly straight woman who doesn't know what she wants*. FIRE could get called out for using "fake queer artists" if you're seen to be fumbling around with these boys!' She pulls herself away from me and flaps her hands in the air.

I shake my head. *Fake queer artist.* This feels like being back in the closet all over again.

'Wait, how did you find me here?'

'Your calendar, you booked in to work here this morning. You gave me access, remember? I don't have time to be running around chasing my talent, trying to rein them in and get them to stay in line. But I really care about you, Eartha. I feel that you have such extraordinary potential. You'll slowly learn what is work and what is play and that sometimes online will leak into offline … Do you know of Velma Quinnley, darling?'

I shake my head.

'EXACTLY! If you want to *be* someone, you need to listen to me. Otherwise,' she sits back, 'what's the fucking point? You'll end up like Velma Quinnley. No one knows who she is. I tried to help her, but she just …' She shrugs and drops her shoulders again. 'She's nobody now. She got dropped.'

Velma Quinnley. I make a mental note to find out why she got dropped.

'If that picture stayed up any longer on Wonderland, FIRE would have pulled the contract and may have released a statement distancing themselves from you. You might have been dropped on Wonderland, too. People hate a hypocrite…'

'I'm so sorry. I can't believe I was so reckless. I almost lost twenty grand over a stupid kiss with a homophobic arsehole.'

I explain everything to her. I love talking to her, her eyes are so intent on mine, as though I am telling her the most impactful story in the world. She encourages me to stand up to men; she never makes me feel 'too much'. I think of my mother still attached to my father, even after the divorce. I don't believe E.V would ever adhere herself to a man who served her anything less than total respect. She makes me feel as though I am the centre of her universe, as though I am the arena she is plugged into online.

When I have finished she says, 'Well, maybe this staying-away-from-men thing isn't so bad after all, then?' She rubs my shoulder. 'Listen, you still need to use FIRE as part of the deal with them, but you just can't use it to date men at the moment.'

I've really let her down.

'I'm just so sorry I have caused such a mess,' I apologise.

'Listen, Eartha, *I* work for *you* now! This is my job. I'm here to protect you, not make your life harder! I got the photo removed as soon as possible this morning. I've had a relationship with the Wonderland team for years, I had my contacts there remove it and issued the user who uploaded it with a warning for posting defamatory allegations.'

'So … you're not mad at me?'

I couldn't bear it if she was.

'Why would I be?'

She looks at me, a genuine look of inquisitiveness on her face. As if she is challenging me.

'I just wanted to let you know I'd handled it for you in case you got any messages in your inbox. And also to try and impress upon you that the world you now inhabit has repercussions: we have to sense-check ourselves more and be accountable to who follows and pays us. I've got to go now; I'm heading into a meeting with a luxury vibrator brand who want to do something with you …!' She places her glasses back on and walks out of the door from the café. Her heeled boots making a loud, clapping noise.

Contractually obliged to stay away from men. This may well be the antidote to healing from my heartbreak, a healthier alternative, perhaps, than sleeping with the girl he cheated on me with – slowly weaning myself off male validation like a drug and going cold turkey. Perhaps all women should be rewarded twenty grand to keep away from men. If women were incentivised to stay away from them and get paid for it like this, we'd rule the world.

Ping

> *Text message from Mum to Eartha*
> 16.45
> Hey love, bit worried about all of this shouting stuff you're putting on Wonderland! Is everything okay? Stop getting too personal online! These people are not your friends! They can turn on you just as quickly as you are turning on them. Let's speak.

Ping

> *Text message from Phaedra to Eartha*
> 16.47
> Yes! Screw top!

Ping

> *Wonderland notification:*
> @Mirebelleee_ has tagged you
> Someone has deleted the picture, but she is a fake and a Wonderland planted avatar #YouHeardItHereFirst

CHAPTER 19

MORNING BREATH

Wonderland followers: 722,012

I'm fully convinced I've pulled a muscle from fingering Phaedra. The frenulum of my tongue's a bit torn up too. But I wouldn't have it any other way. There's something about seeing her screw up her face unselfconsciously while she's cumming that makes me forget about everything else. I'd break my fingers to make her happy.

She came over to mine smelling of luxury floral candles after her shift at the store and it all felt so grown up – as though she was my wife, this was our place and she'd come home after a long day's work. It's like we were cosplaying as a married couple, all political discussions over homemade hummus. I invited her over for dinner and spent the afternoon cooking her a spread of Greek mezze that she said her grandma cooked for her every summer when they visited her. I had seen someone make it effortlessly on a Wonderland arena that Rose had sent through. I thought it was a really romantic thing to do and Rose said it would be a good vegan option that I could knock up in under an hour. It took me four. I served up burnt pitta bread along with a selection of chunky watery dips that would have been better bought from the newsagents down the road. She told me about the weekend dinner she'd had with her friend Lola and I asked her normal questions like 'What did you eat?', although I knew every single detail, right down to what colour the rice was and the name of Lola's ex-boyfriend because I'd been religiously stalking her Wonderland page. The more I learn about her – her habit of eating spoonfuls of marmite with her breakfast, the difference between her fake laugh and her uncontrolled cackle – the heavier I fall and the more detailed a portrait I paint in my mind. The conversations and kisses we have shared between sweaty sheets, morning breath and unbrushed teeth are some of the most intimate moments I've had in my life.

But like an addict, I need to know when I can get my next fix. I cling onto her 'see you soon' or 'see you next week' as a real promise rather than an easy goodbye. I find myself wondering if 'next week' means Monday or Wednesday or Thursday, as I realise she didn't specify. It starts to make me feel as though her tug towards me isn't as desperate. I feel so inexperienced in how to handle the intensity of my feelings with a woman. Because I don't want to 'handle' my feelings, I want to indulge in them. I realise I still need to try and spread my feelings out.

Everything moves so fast when you date women, but it doesn't *feel* like things are moving fast because each date lasts a minimum of an evening all the way up to a whole weekend. A date with a man might last four hours: drinks, chat, then home. So technically, one date with a girl amounts to three heterosexual dates. By the end of the second date you've learned so much about each other it would be the equivalent of two months of dating a man. You've covered everything from parents' attachment styles and how they have shaped your own, to whether you've ever tried anything up the bum or would like to in the future. It took me four years to learn these things about Matt. I've only met Phaedra a handful of times, yet I'm entering depths and realms of intimacy I never experienced in my relationship with him. The beauty of it is that there's no right or wrong. Queer women never had any rules set out for them about how to love. Wanna fuck on the first date? Cool. Wanna spend hours talking about your past and then hold each other tenderly (the way you say your mother never did) after you've cried? Also cool. Wanna be introduced to all of my friends on the first date? Yep, cool. The only downside is that I'm losing 'Wonderland Eartha' in this. I don't want to date anyone else, but I *have* to. Now I've read my FIRE contract, I realise that as well as avoiding dating men I'm meant to be using the app actively, not just doing spontaneous posts on Wonderland about dating. The contract states I should go on three 'organic' dates with the people I meet on FIRE. The idea of anything being 'organic' whilst being stipulated in a contract is disturbing, but I need their money.

I need to talk about this on Wonderland as I've got five more posts to do as part of my contract with FIRE too. I upload a picture of me lying sprawled out on my bed with tired eyes from having stayed up all night.

> Caption: Anyone else get back from a first date with a girl only to spend the entire weekend together and neglect their responsibilities? Just me? #LoveInPride #FIRE
> Comments:
> @*Angelayhh* LOLLLL, pls. I didn't need to be dragged like this today.
> @*ShritiPie* Girl, the tip is to not tidy your bedroom before

a date. Then they can't come back to your place ...
@YoursTruly.Samx Come baaaaack, Eartha! We miss your face, get out of bed! ;)
@ShritiPie Hahahaha yes, or don't shave! But, I still end up caving in every time and then wishing I'd just tidied and shaved my legs.
@MichelleMmmmmmm Earthaaaaa, we want more content! You've lost yourself babe ...
@DaniellTT Smokey eye routine? Or are those just eye bags? Lol

*

I've had to make a few adjustments to my dating profile as I've been attracting quite a few people who recognise my face, so I've changed my name to 'Lily' and disconnected my Wonderland page from my profile. So far, so invisible. Though I have also now received a few messages from my followers informing me that someone's using my pictures as a catfish. I wish I could post, *I am horny and single just like the rest of you!* I matched with this girl called Jaz who seems interesting but there is trepidation, I've not tried meeting someone anonymously without them knowing who I am on Wonderland. I also feel odd going on a date with someone when all I can think about is Phaedra. I feel odd for feeling odd, because she's not my girlfriend and I definitely shouldn't feel I need to be exclusive with someone after the second date. Right?

A day or so later, having arranged a date with Jaz, I'm waiting for her at a local train station. I'm shielding from the rain near the ticket barriers. There's a man opposite me singing for spare change with a cat on his lap; he stops to wink at me and sticks his tongue out when he finishes a song. I don't have any change so I give him my umbrella. Beanie wearers, dog and moustache owners shuffle in and out of the ticket barriers. I've already been stopped twice by girls who say they recognise me. I'm relieved they didn't ask for pictures. Ever since the warehouse night the idea of people taking a photograph makes me feel anxious and disoriented. Wonderland blurs the lines between who you think is and isn't your friend. You're under the illusion that you know someone or that they're your best mate because they uploaded a video about their decision to stop their anti-depressants, because you know what they had for breakfast that morning, or because you've seen videos of them dancing on the table at their local pub with their fling of the night. You know where they hang out, if you look hard enough you'll notice the hickey on their neck and decipher that it's likely from the new person they've been drip-feeding into their pictures lately. Soft-launching their relationship. Or, in my case, you know their entire coming-out story because they voluntarily posted it. People love to play detective and I'm no exception. I've got to start being more careful; a girl who follows me turned up at a work event E.V asked me to go to last week for a skincare brand that sponsored two of my new facial routine posts. I posted a picture of my espresso martini at the bar and within half an hour a girl came running over to say she recognised the corner of the menu that my drink was resting on in my post and just *had* to run down from her apartment and ask me for a picture.

And yet I'm living off ready-meals and setting aside every last penny to be able to afford drinks and dates with Phaedra. I've still not received my invoice for FIRE yet, and people think that I live this lavish lifestyle. They have no idea it's a mirage, that it's actually a glamorous-*seeming* lifestyle, mostly led by E.V, who invites me to all the right parties and lends me her own designer clothes. But after all the events and glamour, I still return to my flat that's heated by my oven and where there's a vase collecting the drips coming from my ceiling. I'm living a double life.

The rain's getting heavier and the homeless man has stopped playing his guitar, he's popped up the brolly I gave him and he's now performing 'Singing in the Rain'. The bottoms of my denim trousers are soaked in an inch of muddy rainwater. I can see a girl in the corner of my eye, I've not looked directly at her yet but she's been standing for a while leaning up against the ticket barrier. Is that my date? I turn my head to check. She's taking a video of me … Her phone's propped up in her hands using her fingers as a tripod either side and the camera's pointed directly at me; she's trying to act natural. Her head is facing the opposite direction to her phone as though she's 'not even looking'.

'Excuse me, can you delete that please?' I say firmly but with a smile on my face.

'Is she bothering you?' A woman approaches the girl, offering her help.

'No, actually, she was bothering *me*, she's taking a video of me and I feel uncomfortable.'

'You said you were a vegan, but you are wearing a leather coat.'

'What?'

'THAT COAT IS LEATHER!'

'So what? You were filming me without my consent … You're still doing it now!' I point at her phone.

'You are a fake vegan. You did a sponsored post by a vegan cake company. The whole "Be better than butter", I shared your post. I made your cake,' she says, still filming me.

'I'm re—'

'Eartha, a baby cow was murdered so you could wear that.'

'Sorry but literally the last thing on my mind is your vegan bullshit agenda when you're filming me, without my consent, minding my own FUCKING business.'

'You are a murderer.'

'What the ... what the fuck are you on about? You're invading my privacy. Fuck off!'

CALM DOWN. CALM DOWN. Breathe.

'Look, I just—'

'YOU HAVE OUR BLOOD ON YOUR HANDS.'

'OUR?'

'Yes, us and the animals.'

'I-I don't know what to say. I apologised, what more do you want me to do?'

'I think you are a liar and a massive sell-out, you're a hypocrite.'

'I DON'T GIVE A FUCK ABOUT YOUR WANKY VEGANISM. GO THROW SOME FUCKING FAKE BLOOD OR SOMETHING. STOP VIOLATING MY PRIVACY!'

I've lost all control. I look at the smirk on her face as she watches me through the screen of her phone. I realise her hunting sport for provoking profitable emotions has been a success. 'Look, can you please just delete that? Stop filming me. That's not right; you can't just film people without their consent.'

She locks her phone and slips it into her tote bag, clutching the handles on her shoulder, and walks away. She looks embarrassed. *Good.* For once I'm not the one leaving an interaction feeling disempowered because of the surveillance of strangers.

'Hey, Lily?'

It takes me a second to remember my dating-app pseudonym and realise the voice is referring to me.

'Jaz! So nice to meet you. Did you …?'

I look at the scene, where the person filming me was stood.

'I'm so embarrassed.'

Is my cover blown?

'Yeah, I saw. Are you …?'

Please, don't ask if I'm Wonderland famous.

'Are you okay?'

'Yes, I'm … I'm okay. Thank you.'

'Why were they taking a picture of you? Are you a "big deal" or something?' she jokes, digging her hands into the pockets of her leather jacket a little awkwardly. Her hair's short, curly, black. She has bleached blonde eyebrows and a septum piercing.

'No, not at all, I just, lately … I'm fine!'

Don't get into it, Eartha.

I hate the way people's faces have changed recently when I've had to tell them I'm someone with a profile. The chilling shift in their eyes from disinterest to desire, as they learn I'm 'someone'.

'That must be so annoying?'

'Yeah, but I guess I shouldn't complain.'

'Why not?'

Because I literally *signed up for this. So I don't feel like I am able to complain.*

'You shouldn't have to deal with people invading your privacy and using you as some kind of … prop.'

Everything happened so quickly, I'm starting to panic about how I spoke to the person with the phone. *Did I say something about pig's blood?*

'God, did I lose control back there? I was … I felt … cornered …' I say nervously, looking down at the floor, my eyes darting frantically all over the place.

I realise we're not even a minute into the date and I've already made it all about me.

'I'm so sorry about that. Anyway, are you a vegan, Jaz?' I smile at her.

'No,' she replies, laughing.

'Probably the weirdest start to a date you've ever had …'

I try to stop my inner monologue being at one with my speech.

She smiles solidly and I realise how much more grounded she seems in comparison to my adrenalin-addled self. She links my arm in what feels like a protective manner as we walk to the bar she's singled out. It's industrial and looks like it used to be an old factory or warehouse with exposed brickwork on the back wall. Metal beams hold the weight of the ceiling up, forming a vaulted roof over us. There's a chalkboard above the bar detailing today's specials and house cocktails in handwriting. The bar's on the right, it's long but its outer edge is smothered with people sitting on uncomfortable but aesthetically pleasing leather bar stools. The guests every now and then are forced to readjust their backs.

'You said your favourite cocktail was a Paloma on your profile … so I brought you to one of the best mezcal bars!'

'That's so thoughtful! Thank you.'

Probably a bad time to mention I like my Paloma with tequila and that I hate mezcal.

'Hi! Do you have a reservation?' A hostess greets us in an unfriendly manner from a metal plinth next to the entrance.

'Yes, for Jaz and uhhhh … Lily.' *I need to relax.*

The waitress seats us at a table leaning against the left-hand wall, opposite the bar. Jaz pulls my chair out for me before I sit down.

'Such a gentlem ... woman?!' I say, raising my eyebrow.

Almost said gentleman. Shit.

'What *are* you! Bisexual or something?' she laughs as she pulls out her chair. My face drops. She clocks my panicked expression. 'I'M KIDDING! It says on your profile, remember ...'

'For a minute there I thought you were about to leave.' I squirm in my seat, trying to find any position that isn't uncomfortable.

'Why would I do that?' she asks as she also tries to find a good position.

'A girl literally told me that I was "a fucking fraud" last month when she found out I was bi, so I guess that's traumatised me for life now ... Anyway, enough about that! You know, I usually find chivalry repulsive, but it's hot on girls.'

My first compliment to her, served up casually, smoothly and at the expense of men. Delicious.

'Well, I'm lucky my mums raised me to treat pretty girls properly!'

'Oh, have you always known that you're gay?'

'I was raised around two women who adore the absolute shit out of each other. The gay rubbed off on me, I guess.' She laughs, leaning her forearms onto the table.

'Wow. I can't imagine having two mums. I adore my mum, the idea of having two of her to raise me actually seems surreal. I can't imagine the person I'd be ... she doesn't make very good choices for herself, but she's always made the best ones for me. I imagine that's a really beautiful way to grow up.'

'Yeah, it is, I love them to pieces. But it's also chaotic. I hate the stereotype, but there are lots of emotions involved: constantly talking about how they feel with each other. It's very healthy, but also annoyingly healthy, you know?' She looks into the distance, then brings her attention back to the table. 'Sometimes, I just wish we could have one dinner where I don't get accused of disordered eating because I haven't touched my fucking dessert.' She throws her hands dramatically into the air and I burst out a laugh, then quickly cover my mouth.

Act chill, be cool. Be aloof. Not rude. But composed.

'My mums are over-reactive and sensitive to even a slight change in my behaviour. If I am tired, they worry I am depressed. They care, but parents can care a little too much. It's an interracial relationship…' she says, washing her hands over her complexion, 'so there are also a lot of differences between them culturally.'

'That's lovely though, right? That they're so different but they choose to make it work? I can't relate to that. Well, I can to the mum stuff. But I'd have died to witness loving parents adore each other like that growing up. I can't imagine it ever being annoying. My mum divorced my dad, but she went back. She stills lives with him and I really feel this duty to live the life she couldn't, because she is still with him, you know? She only did it halfway …' I suddenly feel very aware that we've not even ordered our drinks yet and I'm talking about my relationship with my family. A slippery slope into a date-turned-therapy session.

'Actually, you know what? Let's stop talking about mums.'

'Agreed. You're right. That could get a bit too deep … So, what's your relationship like with your dad?!' she says jokingly, leaning her elbows forward and placing her head in her hands. I laugh at her and she asks me another question.

'Sorry, serious questions only now. How long have you lived in Olympia?'

And so begins the life-story spiel. She pulls it out of me, untangling it all like a ball of yarn. I tell her the whole thing. It's the third time I've told this story since being single and it feels like I'm reading a script: I moved from a small town called Hebeford. *Do you know it?* I ask. *No* is always the answer. I shrug off its insignificance, mentioning that the best things it has going for it are its cheap beer and the ugly statue they erected of Mick Jagger outside a fish and chip shop to commemorate the one time he stopped off there in the Sixties. I then go on to tell her that I left home as soon as I could because I felt that living under the same roof as my dad was co-signing what he was doing to Mum. That I worked full time at a high-street store that drained the living soul out of me to save up enough money to quit and work from home, then I quit the relationship that was draining me too ...

I feel like a machine, saying the same things about myself over and over again. But she seems really interested in me and my life. She keeps asking how things make me *feel*. Dating is a funny old dance, a balance between retaining mystery and opening up: *This is my life, this is who I am, I'll tell you what you need to know so you know what you're getting into with clear sight, but also not give away everything to preserve an element of mystery that leaves you wanting more and, hopefully, you'll come back for a second date.*

But of course, this is a queer date, so all that goes out the window. Tonight will be another night brimming with unearned intimacy and access to my life bestowed upon a stranger based solely on the fact we're both girls. We order a drink and then another, we find ourselves talking and laughing, crying and drinking...

Wait.

I'm drunk.

I'm referencing the opening credits to The L Word.

*

I ask her if she wants to walk back to my place after we split the bill. We collect our damp coats from the back of our arse-numbing chairs and head out. On our way a guy comes over to us.

'Hey, where are you going so fast? I just arrived, you can't leave now!' he says, placing his hand around the small of my waist like I'm a china doll.

'Sorry, I can't. I'm contractually obliged to stay away from men!' I say in his face before swinging the door open to leave with Jaz. We both burst out of the door in a fit of laughter.

'Is that true?!'

'Oh God no,' I reply, remembering the NDA I signed with FIRE.

We walk home in the rain, linking arms and belting the lyrics to *The L Word* theme tune I've not been able to get out of my head, until we arrive at my front door.

I sort of want it to end here but I also want to get better at sex.

I invite her to come inside. We walk up the stairs and I open the door to my apartment.

'What a space,' she exclaims as a drip falls into a vase in the corner.

'How am I paying so much rent for a leaking bedsit?' I shrug at her and she chuckles.

'Stop, you've made it really lovely here.' She looks around at the kitchen, admiring the plants I've draped from the corners of cupboards and the mismatched candles that line the windowsill in contrasting glass holders.

'Let me go grab us some towels! We're soaked,' I say, wringing my hair over the sink and dropping my wet leather jacket onto the back of the kitchen chair. I return with the towels and pass one to her; they're a little crunchy since I haven't been able to afford any softener. I throw her the softest one. While we dry ourselves off, the rhythmic patter of the rain on the kitchen skylight fills the silence and I know there will be a few puddles to clear up tomorrow. She bends over to shake her head into the towel and flicks her head up, brushing her fingers through her curly hair. She folds the towel up neatly onto the table and I stop myself from thanking her for how polite that was in comparison to the boxers I've had thrown at my feet. Mustn't let her know the bar for my standards is the literal *floor*. She places her hands either side of my body against the kitchen counter. Trapping me like a spider, inches away from my face.

'So … when were you going to tell me the truth?' she smirks.

'About what?'

She knows. She knows. She knows who I am.

'That you hate mezcal. Your face gave it away earlier …'

'I'm so embarrassed,' I blush.

She brushes the wet strands from my face and licks her lips. 'Can I kiss you? Even though I've been drinking mezcal all evening?' she asks.

I like her, but not enough.

And she isn't Phaedra.

But I kiss her anyway.

'Woooooooah!' I exclaim as she scoops me up and carries me into the bedroom. She turns on her side to fit us both through the door frame. 'Sorry, I'm so fucking heavy,' I say, cringing.

'No! I've got you!' she grunts before she drops me onto the end of my bed.

The hems of my trousers are still sodden from the rain and I can feel the damp creep onto my ankles. 'Mind if I take these off? They're so wet,' I ask.

'Well, give us a few minutes and I'm sure we can get your thong soaked too,' she says with a wink.

I remove my trousers and slowly kiss my way down her chest and onto her stomach the way Phaedra did to me.

'Can I sit on your face?' she asks abruptly.

I stop doing what I am doing to look up at her from her crotch.

'Uhh, all right, yeah!' I say, although no one has ever sat on my face before and I have no idea how it'd even begin to work.

I lean myself back onto my bed and she places her knees firmly either side of my head.

FUCK. A woman is about to use my face as a fucking seat.

Her crotch is so far away from my face, am I supposed to reach up? I stick my neck out but it's still miles away and so I grab her to pull her down, expecting her to adjust herself. Instead she exerts her weight onto my face and I plunge my tongue deep inside her. Her hips start to quiver and she grabs onto the frame of my bed to steady herself and grind her hips.

'Eat it there,' she commands. I go further back.

I've never eaten someone's ass before and all I can think about is how I wish I was doing it for the first time with Phaedra.

She eventually climbs down and wiggles herself to align our bodies. She reaches down to lie next to me and we kiss.

'Do you like how you taste?' I ask her, the muscles in my tongue are so thankful it is over.

'Hmmm, let me try again,' she kisses me again, this time with her warm, wet tongue.

'Yeah, I like how I taste.'

She pulls herself up above me and repositions herself to fuck my face again until she cums.

*

We lie next to each other, panting and looking up at the ceiling, arms above our heads. I lean over to my bedside table to reach for a hairband and my day-old glass of water. I swing it around and share it with her.

'Can I get some more? I'm so thirsty,' she asks.

You're so thirsty!

I take the glass from her hand, annoyed that my hard work hasn't been acknowledged.

'Be back in a sec,' I say.

I get up even though I'm naked and walk towards the kitchen, trying to pretend that I am used to having this kind of casual interaction. I drink an entire cup myself and refill it for her. I walk back into the room and she's hovering over her bag in the corner by the window. Her head turns sharply when I enter.

'Hey, sorry, just turning off my alarms ... don't want them to wake us up so we can lie in.'

She locks her phone and stuffs it back into her bag.

'Good shout!' I say, placing the cup on her side table.

We meet in the middle of the bed to start kissing again. We lie naked in each other's arms, my head buried in her chest and our legs intertwined. Our skin is sticking to each other's and it feels quite uncomfortable, being velcro-ed like this. I turn around to sleep on my side and she wraps her sweaty arms around me. Just as I'm about to drift off, she pushes back my fringe and kisses my forehead.

'Night, Eartha.'

'Night.'

I fall asleep thinking how perfectly my face fits between Phaedra's thighs. And how I wouldn't mind the sweat so much, if it were her arms wrapped around me.

CHAPTER 20

PROBLEMATIC

Wonderland followers: calculating ...

Razorblades of sunshine are slicing their way through the morning darkness of my flat so I can just make out the back of a dark-haired girl pulling up her trousers.

'Are you going?' I mutter foggily.

'Yes, sorry, I've got to go. Didn't realise how late it was!'

She's in such a hurry. Did we sleep through the alarm?

I sit up, tits out, forgetting that I fell asleep naked. Something about this morning already feels deeply exposing. I grab my quilt to cover my chest.

'Oh, I thought you said ... well ... maybe we can do breakfast another time then?' I suggest.

'Yes, I'll text you later!' she says without turning round.

No, I am not imagining it, there's a distinct change in the air.

Any trace of our shared evening has drained away. She pulls on a trouser leg and edges towards the door with her shoes in her hand.

'Well, how abou—'

Before I can offer her a coffee, she's gone.

Maybe not all girls like to lie in bed all day with you. That's okay, Eartha!

I try to talk myself out of spiralling into a dark self-deprecating pit, but I feel the piercing objectification of hook-up culture in the sudden emptiness of my bed. I feel like a discarded tissue you find on the kitchen floor after a drunken kebab.

Rose's Irish twang rings through my head: *Fuckboys know no gender, Eartha!*

I roll myself out of bed, stretching my hands down to my toes, with the sun falling neatly onto my spine, as though it's stroking it. I decide that today is actually going to be quite glorious. I walk with a little bounce into the kitchen to play some music for my shower. I reach over to turn on the speaker and think of the hot kiss I had with Jaz in this very spot last night by the hob. I smile to myself, grateful that the tragic memory of Matt pretending to kill himself with tonsil spray is slowly being replaced.

I reach for my phone to pick some music and check my texts. Phaedra texted an hour ago.

> *Text message from Phaedra to Eartha*
> 08.01
> Hi. Thinking of you (and THAT hummus, obviously).
> 08.02
> I'm shit at telling people how I feel. So, I made you this playlist instead. Promise not to laugh.
> https://open.spotify.com/playlist/5x0EtXrY4zqLXEes-g6vshS?si=d9bdd4aa2ea4486d

My chest leaps, I could scream. She feels the same, I knew it. I felt it in my bones. I've found the mythical, rare breed of love where both people like one another the same amount at the same time. I type her out a response, with giddy excitement.

Text message from Eartha to Phaedra

09.02

For god's sake. I made you one too, but I was too embarrassed to send it. Why are we so soppy?!

09.03

Going to listen to your playlist before I send mine...in the shower...now.

I put my phone on charge and turn on the shower. The hot water washes away the gritty feeling this morning has left me with and I focus on cleaning away the dried sweat of a stranger that lingers on the hairs of my back. I wipe the black make-up from under my eyes where it smudged between Jaz's thighs while Phaedra's playlist hums gently in the background. I can't stop smiling. I fuck myself in the shower thinking of her, brush my teeth, put my hair up into a towel to dry and walk into my bedroom to put on a fresh pair of knickers. The sun's now pouring through the window. I make my bed and throw over the pink satin throw, indulging in the sensation of the sun on my skin and freshly shaved legs. I decide to dry myself off in its heat.

Buzz

Buzz

Buzz

Buzz

I'm brought out of my state of serenity by the frenzy of notifications on my phone. I open my eyes and roll on my back to shield the screen from the sun.

Wonderland notifications

(+99)

Open Wonderland to read your messages.

Missed call from E.V

09.13

Missed call from E.V

09.14

Missed call from E.V

09.19

Missed call from E.V

09.23

Text message from Mona to Eartha

09.24

Babe, are you okay?! Xxxx

Text message from Mum to Eartha

09.24

Darling, are you okay? I have seen pictures of your flat on Wonderland this morning. Why did you take them? Call me xx

Pictures of my flat on Wonderland? My entire body turns cold and the hairs on my arms become staples. I take a deep breath and try to calm down the rate of my heartbeat. The air around me weighs a ton, I have that sickening feeling just before the pain kicks in.

Buzz

Buzz

Buzz

Buzz

'Hello?!'

'E.V, what the hell is going on?'

'The girl you had sex with last night was a fan who has posted pictures of your apartment all over Wonderland, captioned 'The bedsit from hell tour you've all been asking for #DownToEartha'. She's a wannabe influencer with absolutely FUCK ALL social media following using the handle @VeronicaEscher and she's used you to boost her presence. I'm so sorry, darling ...'

'Oh God. Oh God. Oh my God.'

I've put her on speaker, the phone resting next to my head on the bed and I stare up at the ceiling.

'I'm on my way, I got in a car as soon as I saw it, I'm so sorry this happened to you. *Excuse me, driver, to the left!*'

'She ... she only left about an hour ago.'

'THE STUPID WOMAN WAS PROBABLY DRAFTING THIS SHIT NEXT TO YOU IN BED! I AM SO ANGRY! I'm sorry, I'm almost at your doorstep now. Get ready to let me in.'

I type her username into Wonderland. I recognise her name. She follows me. Has followed me from early on. Her caption is longer than E.V made out:

> ... we met as connects through wonderland and had a few too many drinks. ended up hooking up drunkenly and one thing led to another... she is queerly inexperienced, definitely the first time she's given head...

I'm still lying on my back. The room is spinning. There is a ringing in my ears. I can't feel or think clearly. A few moments later, the video intercom rings and I can make out a hammering sound.

I realise I'm still naked. I grab my flannel dressing gown to wrap around my body, tug on some underwear and then run over to the door.

'Eartha, I'm so sorry. I just had to come and see you!' E.V shouts from behind the door. I let her in and she throws her arms around me and I rest my head on her shoulder: it feels and smells like one of those warm lavender-scented pillows Mum used to put in the microwave and send me to bed with when I had agonising period cramps. I hug her and don't let go.

'You're safe, it's okay. I'm here. I've got you.'

I don't let myself cry. 'Why would someone do this to me? What's … what's happened?' I muffle, my mouth covered by her coat.

'What was that, darling?' she asks, pulling herself away with a look of concern on her face. I repeat what I said and she walks over to my kitchen table, pulling us both out a chair.

'Sit here, darling, won't you? Come on.' I sit next to her at the table. She holds my hands while we talk. 'What happened? Did you have any idea who she really was, at all?'

I loosen my grip on her hands, suddenly feeling unsafe at the suggestion that any of this was my fault. 'Of course not, what do you mean? How was I supposed to know this would happen? We matched on FIRE, you told me to continue to date girls and that's exactly what I've been doing. I know I'm contracted to date three people so I went on one. How was I supposed to know this would happen? I even dated her under a pseudonym, E.V!'

'None of this is your fault. I'm just trying to make sense of things. You can't even point to a moment where it felt a bit … odd?'

I think back to her crouching over her bag with her phone when I left the room to get the water she asked for. I lean myself forward into my chair to peer into my bedroom. The glass of water I got her is still on the bedside table. It's full. That's probably when she took the pictures. I feel a punch in my gut so deep I worry it will take a lifetime to heal. Phaedra will see the pictures and know I was with someone else …

'What on earth should I do?'

'You can't be so trusting any more, darling. I know it doesn't feel good right now, but everyone needs experiences like this so they can learn to protect themselves. That's the only thing I can say.'

'How am I ever going to trust anyone?! How are you supposed to know when someone's lining you up, placing you where they want you, just to shoot you like this? Like I have a bounty on my head. It felt so genuine. She kissed me goodnight ...'

I tune out in that moment. *Wait.* After she kissed my forehead, did she say goodnight with my real name, *Eartha*? Or am I dreaming? I want to shut down and shut off from everything.

'This is a lot for anyone, Eartha. Why don't we pull this contract with FIRE if you feel like it's becoming too much ... There will be bigger and better ones, I promise. This is all becoming more hassle than it's worth.'

I look over at the frayed edges of my stiff-as-a-board towel, folded in a pile on the table where Jaz left it. 'But this is more money than I've ever seen in my life. I can barely afford soft fucking towels any more. I can't pull the contract, I don't want to.'

'Well, darling, if that's the case, the alternative is that I can do a background check on everyone. You just can't bring them back here any more.'

'She didn't take any pictures of me *naked*, did she?'

'Not any that she's uploaded, but some intimate shots of knickers on the floor, I'm afraid. E, people who are hungry for power and fame will do anything, manipulate anyone or use anyone, to get what they want. Don't worry, I'm going to slap her with defamation and a cease-and-desist letter. Attention is a fucking drug and these people are addicts.'

I nod, pretending to know what a cease-and-desist letter is.

'Life is full of these obstacles, you're just going through all of the shitty bits and soon you'll rise from the fucking ashes. Trust me. You're lucky you're going through this now and not later. You're building a strong foundation. If you can get through this, you can get through anything. I believe in you. I do. You were born for enormous things. Try to see this as a test.'

'I genuinely don't know if I can handle this.'

I feel like there are a thousand needles in my chest and if I breathe out too quickly, they'll pierce my skin.

'Why don't I do your social posts on Wonderland for you while you take a little break? I am going to cancel our dinner tonight with the vibrator brand. We have done so many of those recently. You need some time off. I advise you not to look at any more of the pictures. Or read Wonderland direct messages. Don't go online. You don't need to see them, it would be tantamount to self-harm … There are things we can control and things we can't control, let me handle this. Email your password to me and I'll post your normal content if you send everything you had planned for today over to me. You don't need to worry about any of that today.'

The needles around me are retreating.

I agree, and she shoots out of her chair and picks up her small bag with a Hermès scarf tied to the handle. She looks around the small room that contains my existence.

'Cute place …'

'Thank y—'

'But you deserve more than this. Much, much more.'

She purses her lips and nods her head, until it's eventually still. A drop of water falls into the vase in the corner of the room, taking my dignity with it.

We hug goodbye at my door and I soak in her warmth one last time.

She turns to me before the door closes and says, 'We just need to stick together and we will get through this, you'll see.'

She meets my eyes and I can see the worry in hers.

*

I open up my emails and forward my login details to E.V, then collapse back onto my bed to stare blankly at the ceiling. I try to breathe through the surging numbness across my body.

Jaz, wait Veronica, must have been studying me for weeks, her story was so convincing. Was everything she told me a complete lie? I thought we had so much in common, but maybe she built herself entirely off what she knew about me from Wonderland. She must have plucked her favourite books from a Q&A I did. Now that I think about it, every single one she said was on my public list. I can't find her real Wonderland page anywhere, she must have blocked me. I can't even see the post she uploaded. I check my inbox: like a crime scene splattered in blood without a body, it's filled with the debris of my own public humiliation.

> *Wonderland messages:*
> *@AlphasUnite* Sucks to be you right now! This is what you deserve for all of the men you've tried to make look evil. Feminists are going to hell.
> *@Amelia-Bracken* I spotted the building in the back of one of those pictures. We know where you live.
> *@ClausiePrice* Unfollowing. Purely because you have shit interior taste. Lol.
> *@DarlahBrown* You don't even wash your period stains from your pants. What self care?

@JohnnyMarrIsDaddy You're a fucking fraud. I can't believe I ever looked up to you. How could you kill innocent animals?

@FishAreFriendzNotFood How much u must hate urself to be such a hypocrite. MURDERER.

@BeKind_38 Die, bitch. Do us all a fucking favour. I think deep down part of you knows the world will be better off without you.

@WashUrStrap Don't think we didn't see that picture of you kissing that guy too, Eartha. Stop calling yourself queer when you're bending over and taking dick in the toilets.

My comments sections are being flooded too.

*@smallie38_* Anyone else feeling really betrayed by Eartha? I looked up to her for so long ...☹

@bettyboob I really loved Eartha nooooo why is she getting dropped ☹

@TruffleOilSoakedTiddies Don't know why anyone's surprised. Eartha's friend spat on me and called me ugly when we were 12 and she did NOTHING about it. Guess she hasn't changed ...

@yourbestfriendisgay Lollll, big yikes. Who bets she got that girl to upload those pictures as a distraction from the ugly murder scene truth?

The truth? I throw my phone onto the bed. I don't even know what half of these messages are referring to. There's a heavy emphasis on me being a murderer? Did I miss something? Just as I'm sorting through my thoughts, E.V rings me again. I manage to lift my hand and reach for my phone. I press the green phone icon.

'E.V, it's fine, I'm alive!'

'Eartha, there has been another post, a copycat if you will,' she says, in a tone that let's me know me this is somehow about to get worse.

I lie back, staring up at the ceiling while she talks into my ear. There's silence for a few seconds, I can hear the sound of the car in the background. 'Today's post has prompted another video shared of you, by another account. You've been caught being anti-vegan on camera and the left-wing pundits are framing it to look really bad, the girl is saying you bullied her. You don't look too good in the video, darling. You're losing quite a lot of followers, too. People are now saying you staged last night with Veronica so that people wouldn't pay attention to the other video ...'

'Right.'

My body weighs a tonne. I can hardly move.

There's silence on both ends of the phone.

'Are you okay?'

People think I staged one of the most intimately violating experiences of my life.

'I don't know. I don't even have the energy to defend myself, to set them straight.'

'Please, can you be with someone today?'

'I'll ring someone.'

'Can you just tell me the full story?'

I tell her and she listens without interrupting.

Finally, she says, 'Promise me you'll see someone, Eartha?' with a thinly veiled steeliness.

'I promise,' I say, before hanging up.

I've never felt like I wanted to stop being a part of life before, but now it doesn't feel like such an awful thing. Anything to escape this piercing, all-consuming sensation of shame. My entire body feels heavy. Like I'm full of sand and it's all pooled around me, crushing me. I can't move my arms, not even if I wanted to. I feel paralysed and afraid of running into all of these people. Veronica was one of the people whose name had been rattling around the comment sections of my page for so long, I feel the loss of that relationship too. Of who I thought Jaz was and who Veronica isn't. I want to shut off. I never want to log into Wonderland ever again.

But I reach for my phone and do the worst possible thing.

I plug into Wonderland and I read about 'the real Eartha'.

CHAPTER 21

TWO-FACED MEAT LOVER

Wonderland followers: 455,987

> *Voice note from Mum to Eartha (44 seconds)*
> 17.40
> Eartha ... sorry ... trying to get good at these voice clips. I'm so worried about you. I can't stand to read all this stuff about you online. Can you promise not to mention anything more about me or Dad? All these eyes on you ... it's starting to make me feel scared for myself too. I know my old friend Sally from school is probably loving this shit, the stupid jealous cow. You know she rolled her eyes at me pushing her shopping trolley the other day in the vegan frozen isle? I wanted to open a pack of mincemeat and shove her stupid smug face in it ...

Like mother like daughter. I want to get back to her, but I don't have the energy for more *I told you so's.*

It's been a week since I left my flat. I've been a silent bystander to the angry storm that's surrounded me online. E.V and my new publicist, Ellen with the whiter than white teeth, have said there is no way in hell I'm apologising for something this ridiculous. I've got Ellen on a retainer now at £2,000 a month – twice the amount of my rent on paying someone to 'manage my public relations'. I've been advised by her and E.V not to defend myself as it will only further fuel the clickbait fodder, and people will pick flaws in anything I say. The expression 'take it lying down' has been thrown around by my new publicist more times than I'm comfortable with. I'm not sure why I'm paying her so much to just tell me to do nothing.

But that doesn't mean I haven't seen every comment, every sub-group discussion, every attack, every unfollow. I am now a world expert in the public opinion of Eartha. I could recite reams of online conversations by heart if anyone wanted me to. The words echo in my mind and I find myself mistaking them for my own sentiments.

Friends who I have laughed and cried with have now joined in to either throw dirt in my direction or silently unfollow me.

Customers have uploaded pictures of them ripping my work in half 'to stand in solidarity' with animal rights activists. Rose is being shamed publicly and constantly pushed to denounce me, with people commenting and harassing them on the pictures of us together. One of these pictures is from the night I'd come out to them, where we were lying together on my bed smiling, just before I uploaded the video. I look so happy. My eyes look so unexposed to the world, I had no idea what anyone barring four people really thought about me.

Matt decided to hop on the bandwagon and made a video recording of a poem he wrote about me being a two-faced meat lover. It didn't go viral, but I watched it and it made me laugh, then cry, all morning.

I'm afraid to leave my flat, which, just like my online persona, also feels as though it has been trespassed. My bed was the last place on this earth that deeply belonged to me. My skin crawled as I got into bed the night after Veronica had stayed, as though I was having an allergic reaction. I slept on the floor and washed the sheets three times before finally deciding to order new ones altogether. But if I go out, I'm scared someone might recognise me, shout at me, spit on me, or throw a pint of fake blood on me and call me a murderer. I can't fight back. I want to disappear. I want to be forgotten. Every cell in my body urges me to pick up my phone, tell my followers I love them and apologise. That's how Eartha solved all her conflicts before. But this is a monster much bigger than anything that has happened to me before. Now thousands of people are angry at me. No part of my life is untouched as I sit at home awaiting the outcome of my public trial. What sentence will I receive? Every day I feel the executioner's block inching closer.

I want to see Veronica in person, to remind her of the living, breathing human that she did this to. No wonder she darted out in the morning. She couldn't bear to look at me; she couldn't face the gravity of what she'd done to another human being. I tried calling her so that I could get some answers, but she blocked me. There's a special place in hell for someone who sits on your face and then exposes pictures of your knickers to the internet afterwards.

I've tried to speak to Phaedra but she's yet to reply to my texts. I'm worried she wants nothing to do with a person branded 'problematic'. In her silence my mind is left to fill in the gaps and assume. I can see she's online, I can see her nights out with Lola and other anonymous people whose limbs make appearances, holding delicious cold pints that she cheers with, laughing in the background of a park or dancing in the dark at a rave. *I* want to be the person behind the camera, kissing her on the sunny grass, listening to the playlists we made for each other, her head in my lap as my fingers brush through her pink hair all matted from hairspray. A life like that – one that brings me joy – feels so out of reach now. I wanted too much.

And the messages never stop pouring into my phone; it's a deluge of anger:

Wonderland messages (99+):

@CamillaPerk89 Eartha, just apologise and hold yourself accountable and this will all go away.

@FarmBoySammy I'd still do you. If no one else will touch you.

My inbox is now full. I woke up this morning to a woman calling me 'violent'. It's the first time I have been called that in my entire life. But I see now that I've done this to men, too, haven't I? Why did I love to see men attacked in this way? Why did it cause my pupils to dilate? I did this to them just to boost my own Wonderland following, dragging businesses through the mud, taking them for the ride of their life through social justice internet hell. Did it feel this bad for them? Have I done this to another person? Perhaps this is karma. I try to justify what I did to others in my head, telling myself that they deserved it because they *actually* fucked up. Those people I came after *actually* made a mistake. But I am not sure if I believe it any more.

Ping

I check my phone to see another message on Wonderland.

@DonchesterDee: Die. I dare you.

I've been constantly plugged into Wonderland – waiting, readying myself, preparing backstage for the next take-down, the next article calling me out for not being a helpful enough asset to the online world.

Buzz

E.V calls me every hour, to check I'm still alive.

'How are you holding up?'

I look down at my arms, which are red and swollen from where I've been obsessively picking at them. 'I'm fine. I feel a bit ... shit, though, actually. I've been keeping tabs on everything, googling myself, keeping track is the only way to feel safe, to predict what's coming next, what's around the corner.'

'That's what we've got a publicist for, darling. Look, I know how horrendous everything has been for you, but we need to start inserting some of that joy back into your life. That's why I'm calling you, to cheer you up. It's not all bad, darling. I have the perfect opportunity for you! Not work, just fun. I've got a Wonderland party tonight at a private house in East Side Olympia. Very high-profile guest list; you're going to be my plus one. Can you make it?' she asks hopefully.

All the people there probably hate me, or at the very least have heard the online rumours about what a terrible person I am.

'Of course you can! Trick question, I manage your diary! You're probably disintegrating into your living-room bed right now, aren't you, darling? Oh God, come, if only for me to give you a big squeeze. I hate the thought of you being alone.'

I think of the comforting smell of her shoulders.

'But ... what about all the people *there*, won't they hate me?' I whine.

'*Everyone* going tonight has been bloody dropped by Wonderland at some point. The truth is no one else gives a fuck about what's going on with you. No one else cares the way you do about all of this stuff. I know it's hard to see when you're in the eye of the storm, but in fact half of these people bullying you would probably ask for a fucking photo if they saw you in the street. The people going tonight are all out living their lives, being present on Wonderland, earning followers, regardless of other people's problems with them! You deserve the same, you've worked so hard.'

I open the fridge with my phone wedged between my cheek and shoulder, shoving raspberries onto the tips of my fingers like little hats. I feel nothing.

'After everything I've helped you with, please do this for me … I promise it will help. Besides, you also owe it to yourself.'

I suck one of the raspberries off my finger and then spit it back out. It's spherical nest smashes onto the countertop, staining it scarlet.

'My driver will text you when he's outside in an hour, okay?'

I haven't eaten for days. Or called Mum. Or checked in with Rose. 'I don't want to—'

'Nonsense. You'll have a fabulous time. It's time to fuck the haters and RESURRECT Eartha.'

*

I roll down the window and look out, taking in the streetlights, the buildings towering over me and the people living their lives – watching TV, snuggling with loved ones, preparing for a night out. I look down at the dress I'm wearing. E.V sent it over with the car along with a hyper-pigmented, glittery lipstick. I changed into the dress and slicked on the lipstick quickly while the driver waited downstairs. The top half is a cream corset, flowing into a short, silky skirt with a ruffled hem. I added a blazer. It was wrapped in lavender-scented tissue paper with the note: 'Don't be scared by the frills! Queer it up. Your tits will look fabulous.' I realise I feel a lot smaller outside of my flat, among the lives of others – amid the chaos, feeling insignificant is beautiful. As I zip through the night, everything that has happened to me online is inconsequential. The world is moving on and I should too. The city around me is expansive; every person, every building, every pub or street corner offers the opportunity to live a new life. I've lived such an insulated existence in my flat over the last week, I forgot about the rest of the world. How is it that the online world cannot be touched, but that it can touch you?

The car slows down at a red light. A man on the pavement walking his dog and holding a carton of full-fat milk stops to peer in at me. I turn my head to look away. He comes closer to the window. 'My gay daughter loves you, keep it up!' he shouts with a warm smile. I start to cry. 'Oh, I didn't mean to scare you!' he apologises.

The driver lifts the brake and the car starts to roll forward; I wipe the tears from my face. 'No! Thank you!' I shout out of the window as we move further into the night.

I'm reminded that I'm a person with dreams, with a purpose that matters. I think about one day owning a house filled with silly, gorgeous, beautiful things and people. I think about lying in the sun with someone I love, my skin itchy from the grass. I think about all the people I am yet to meet and the kisses I am yet to have, about the soulmates who are yet to change the shape of my life and who I am. I think of the beautiful smell of pastries in a bakery. My favourite colours flood into my mind like a tsunami of optimism. I think about the most beautiful night of my life with Phaedra. I think of flowers and their sensuous petals. Of summer holidays that you don't want to end. I think about one day getting fingered at the opera by the love of my life. *What could happen if I choose to keep going? What things could I discover and what life could I lead?*

I belong in this world, I am a part of it and it has a place for me.

I belong in this wonderland, I am a part of it and it has a profile for me.

*

The night has become a sheet of darkness by the time the car pulls up to a Georgian townhouse. It's quite far out into East Side, so a few stars have made themselves visible now that we're away from the city. The door has a giant gold lion's head on the front with a ring in its mouth. The curtains are all drawn but there's a small splinter of warm light emanating from the two bottom windows. This doesn't look like a venue for a party. It looks like a family home. I unlock my phone, its glare blinds me in the darkness and I shield my eyes by squinting tight. I open up my map to check it's the correct address.

A window wrenches open above me. 'Eaaaaaarthaaaaa!'

I see E.V's face peering down, her bangles clattering against the ledge. 'Oh, it's the perfect size for you, it shows off that gorgeous little waist! What are you doing waiting outside? Ring the buzzer. I've just texted you the password!'

The sound of jazz music twirls out of the window. 'I AM COMING TO GET YOU.'

'The password? What passwo—'

The window shuts and the curtains close behind it. I realise the windows must be soundproof. I knock three times using the ring in the gaping lion's mouth and wait. I put my hands into my pockets and begin nervously tapping my feet, making a clicking noise with my tongue. I'm reminded of the reason Mum used to call me shy bird. God, I do miss her. The letterbox opens and

I can see the outline of a person's lips move from behind the door.

'Password?'

'Hold on ...'

I unlock my phone and open up E.V's text.

'DOLUS?' I say, unsure if I'm pronouncing it correctly. The letterbox closes and I hear the sound of the latch on the door opening up.

'We've been waiting for you!'

A man in a waistcoat, twisted moustache, thin eyebrows with gelled-back hair greets me. He makes way for me to enter as I walk into a long hallway with a spiral staircase at the end. It twists back onto itself like a DNA strand. There's a red velvet runner that goes all the way up the wooden steps and a chandelier hangs low in the hallway. The floor's lined with multiple rugs on top of a chequered black-and-white-tiled floor. The hallway is hung with striking portraits of women.

The man walks in front of me and turns an ancient brass knob to a heavy oak-panelled door nearest to the staircase. A cumulus of incense and cigarette smoke greets us; the entire room is cloaked in it, protecting the identities of its high-profile inhabitants. The room extends all the way through to the back of the house, the wall nearest me is covered in red damask silk and the lamps dotted across it emit a muted glow. Unlike Slinky's, no one notices me when I walk into the room, they're all caught up in the plot of their own lives. There's a woman laid out on a pink velvet chaise longue to my left while a waiter tops up her martini glass; her legs stretch out through a slit in her oyster-coloured minidress. She's locking eyes with a man with slick hair and a pair of wide-leg pinstripe trousers held up by braces. He's sitting at the end of the chaise with a book on his lap. His hands are covered in sailor tattoos. They're not smiling at one another, they're sharing something much more primal. But as soon as the waiter finishes pouring her drink she uncrosses her legs and sits on the tattooed man's lap, knocking the open book to the floor.

I look away for fear of being caught gawping. There's a grand fireplace positioned in the middle of the wall, bedecked with a gold Italian mirror that reaches up to the ceiling, dimly reflecting the room back onto itself. Indoor palms are potted either side of it, forming a feathered arch. As I look around at the other guests' faces, I realise I'm the youngest person here. I fear they might smell the inexperience on me. I reach into my pocket to capture the surreal scene that unfolds in front of me, unsure that I will believe this place existed tomorrow. I press record, smiling at the camera and spinning around.

I'm interrupted by an abrupt tap on my shoulder.

'Excuse me, miss, there are no phones allowed in here. I'm going to have to remove this from you and return it to you at the end of the night. It's to protect the privacy of the guests, yourself included, miss. No one else here has a phone,' the man in the waistcoat says to me.

He reaches his hand out and gestures with his fingers for me to hand the phone to him. I reluctantly place it into his palm and he gives me a small red ticket with a number on it: *29*. I wonder if that's how many guests are here tonight, or how many phones.

I look around trying to spot E.V and catch her face in the corner. She has both her elbows leaning back on a velvet seat covered in cushions against the windowsill. She's smoking and as she exhales she leans her head right back out of the window to blow smoke out, revealing her bare neck. I've never seen her this relaxed before. Her hair cascades around her like the whisps of smoke coming out of her cigarette. She's the glowing centrepiece of the room.

I pick my way across the room to her until I am inches away from the peel of her neck. She slides along the seat to make room for me to sit down, the air gusting in from the open window. This vantage point reveals the pleasure seekers, intellectuals and romantics around us.

She is wearing the same lipstick as me and I mimic her pose, lowering my head backwards and out of the window to breathe in the night. Our necks and cleavages become one droplet of skin. I've never seen her breasts before. They're spectacularly large. I whisper to her on my right, 'So … who the fuck is everyone?'

'The two you were gawping at when you first came in are both in relationships. He's one of the biggest directors at Wonderland and she's a top influencer …'

I recognise her. I think about how pretty, passive and perfect she is online; I would never imagine her to be draped over a man's lap with her legs open, holding his cigar between her fingers.

'When the two of them come here, they create their own little universe, out of the public eye.'

'Did you say he has a wife?!'

'No, they're both in queer relationships.'

I pull my head out of the window and, with the blood rushing back into my face, I look at them. I can see he is muttering something to her and, as they slowly spin round now dancing, I see how his words enliven her face as they pour into her ear. A shorter woman dressed all in black who's been sitting on the side stands up and walks over to them both. She brushes the woman's cheek to get her attention. They talk with one another and then the other woman leans down to kiss her. That must be her wife.

The man with the white vest and sailor tattoos continues stroking the back of the woman. I follow his gaze to see him winking at the man playing the piano in the far corner of the room. I feel like I've walked into a den of polyamory.

'The people in this room are the founders, creators and owners of the whole world of Wonderland,' E.V goes on, drawing her face back into the room. 'This is backstage for people who have to be "onstage" all the time. For people like us. They have all been through the same things as you are going through now. This ... is my life offstage ...' She looks proudly out across the sea of the room.

'But, be careful, you *can* trust everyone ... it's just ... when you want to leave ... just please grab me or message me, I'll have a car waiting to make sure you to get home safely. Okay, Eartha?' She removes her thick-rimmed black glasses and looks directly at me. 'Because everyone here has something the other wants.'

I hear her but am caught up in imagining everyone's onstage life – who they are when they are not in this room, how many people report to them, whose lives they influence. I half recognise a girl sat picking through the records. I think it's the fashion influencer Rose fancies. Or is it? She looks so different. She's usually wearing dresses, large statement earrings and bold eye make-up. Tonight, she wears a black waistcoat with no shirt underneath and a pair of trousers with the crotch cut out.

The waiter walks over to us with a bottle of champagne held upright, ready to pour.

'Drink, madame?'

'Yes, please!' E. V and I both say at the same time.

We laugh simultaneously and share a knowing look. It feels

then as if we've always known each other. As if, in that moment, there's no E.V without Eartha. She looks at me admiringly and reciprocates my feelings. It's as though I'm looking into my future and she's looking at her past.

The waiter presents two coupe glass filled to the top with champagne. I thank him and try to hold it the way E.V does, with the base in the palm of one hand, but I can't balance it right and half of it sloshes out onto my arm.

E.V laughs at me and raises her glass. 'To your resurrection …' She winks at me, and the world is ours again. Her eyes move away from mine and land somewhere out of my sight. 'And to becoming the next bright shiny thing on Wonderland!'

We clink glasses and I peer over the rim while I take a sip, trying to catch a glance at whoever caught her eye. A tall man with dark stubble and a slicer for a jaw hands his blazer to one of the waiters. He stands so upright it's as though someone is pulling a string taut through his body. His shirt is one button too undone. He begins to walk over.

He looks as though he has been on a tropical island for the last year; his eyes flicker down at me with flirtatious curiosity.

'I'm Eartha,' I say, introducing myself. We are already holding each other's gaze. I notice a tan line on his ring finger. *Divorced.* He starts to slowly curl his fingers into his palm and his right hand makes a fist.

'I've heard a lot about you.' He cracks a sideways smirk before retreating into the room to speak to the rest of the guests. As he turns, the spiced scent of his cologne wafts in my direction.

'*Who the fuck is that?* He's walking around like he owns the place,' I say, immediately wanting information from E.V.

'That's because he does.' She's sharp with me and there's

a steeliness to her voice. 'This is his house. Dylan is one of Wonderland's founders. The most powerful man in this room. In any room. Real or virtual.'

I watch him as she whispers more information in my ear about how he's someone to respect but avoid. He's shaking hands with the other men in the room, then lifts a girl's hand to kiss it while she gawks up at him from the lap of her businessman partner, who looks on with admiration too. He carries himself with a power that feels inherent, built into his core. He forces everyone to question the value of their lives when in his presence. He is the room's point of gravity.

I turn to look back at E.V. 'He'll be able to boost your profile, get you seen by more people. He's been helping us behind the scenes. He was very happy to see I'd started working with you ...'

Dylan turns his head towards me in the middle of his conversation stood by the fireplace. Our eyes lock again. I'm not used to being around attractive, older, powerful men, and this one has dangerous levels of charisma.

E.V catches me looking at him and goes on, 'Eartha, listen to me, *don't* ...'

DIRECTOR'S NOTE

Eartha walks through the crowd of egos, womanisers and coked-up party-goers and leaves the living room with Dylan. They walk upstairs in a group of people, laughing, into another room. All the guests leave this room one by one until it's just Dylan and Eartha. With his hand on the doorknob, Dylan sticks his head out of the door and catches E.V looking up at him from the bottom of the stairs. He closes the door. E.V flinches when she hears the door to the bedroom lock. She shakes her head and returns to the party.

ENDS

CHAPTER 22

A TEMPORARY DEATH

Wonderland followers: 414,219

It's light out. I'm walking back to my flat with my right shoe in my hand. I lost the other one along the way. I catch a glimpse of my reflection in a pound-shop window. I look like a walking corpse. My mind doesn't want to belong to my body. The disapproving looks I've received from parents on the school run and the remarks I've attracted from construction workers skim off me like a sheet of water. I keep walking with my head down in last night's clothes towards the entrance of my flat. I just need to get through the door.

Voice note from Eartha to E.V (1 second)

08.36

'E.V...'

08.37

Sorry. I had to start that again. I can't stop crying. Sorry. I really want to explain to you what happened last night. I don't know what to do. I fucked up, didn't I? Please can you call me.

Missed call from Eartha to E.V

08.39

Missed call from Eartha to E.V

08.41

Text message from E.V to Eartha

09.01

Hi darling, let's speak later. Try to get some sleep, I'm back-to-back today. I wish you'd listened to me.

Voice note from Eartha to E.V (32 seconds)

09.02

I can't remember much but ... you're mad at me, aren't you? I know I was drunk. You sound mad at me. I could really do with telling you my side of it all ... I don't want to rush you or anything. But ... I'm so embarrassed. I'm so fucking stupid.

Text message from E.V to Eartha

09.05

Calm down, let's keep it between us until we've spoken. It could ruin your career to be seen to ... We'll talk about this later. Get some sleep and rest. I'll call you at 5 pm.

I realise then that no one is coming to save me.

*

Wonderland messages (+99)

Without talking about it, I'm not sure if it's even real. Or if it even happened. My body feels foreign and I don't recognise my hands or my reflection. It's as though I'm a cut flower, severed from my root. I don't know how to exist without the ground that I've been plucked from. My whole job relies on me talking about every experience I have. To everyone. And now I need to be silent.

Wonderland messages (inbox almost full, limited space available)

I haven't taken my bins out for days; I'm at one with their warm, decomposing odour. I've found familiarity in it, comfort even, it's my mirror. My plants have gone unwatered and I'm jealous of how they can droop lifelessly and lose all vitality to conserve their energy. I want to slowly collapse and preserve what life I have left too.

Wonderland messages (inbox full: delete some messages to free up memory space)

Being asleep provides a sort of beautiful temporary death. My bed lies there in the middle of my room, calling out to me like a siren, the duvet beckons me to slip myself inside her for hours at a time and the pillows tell me to rest my aching head.

CHAPTER 23

I'M DISAPPOINTED IN YOU

Week-on-week follower variation: -90,728
Wonderland followers: 323,491

One week later.

I hover my finger over the Wonderland app on my phone and take a deep breath. I press down.

My eyes flood with hundreds of usernames.

There's a new message coming through every minute.

@DontTrustHotPeople Where did you get your bag in your last pic?

@Martha_Cline Can I take you out?

@DivineMadelline I just wanted to say that you've changed my life, thank you.

@RiotingTw1nk Who do you think you are, trying to be the 'face' for queer women?

@Rachel_2800 Please share my fundraiser to pay my rent, you can't call yourself an ally if you don't uplift other people. You should be donating.

@ChristiansAgainstLezzers God would HATE you if he was still alive.

@DaddyLongLegs Murderous scum
@Atomic_Smitten Your silence is violence. Why are you ignoring what's going on in Hawaii?
@Jessica2023 Just sliding in to say thank you. I wouldn't be comfortable with myself if it wasn't for you.
@LikeAVirgo00 Madonna unfollowed you lmaooo
@MyPussyTastesOfLavender Skincare routine plssss.
@HilaryMildred What do you do when you're so fed up with men? Like I genuinely don't care about them at all, LOL! Am I lesbian?
@LindaMcFartney I'm disappointed in you. I thought you knew better than to share a post by *@feminism_foreveryone*. Their owner was outed as a predator literally an HOUR ago.
@Brittany-95 SKINCARE!!!!
@Paris What plasters do u use for ur doc martens, to wear them in? Can you share a link with us?
@TakeThisTakeThat Gary Barlow would literally love u I just know it.
@CosmicDancer EARTHA, I JUST CAME OUT TO MY MUM! THANK YOU!
@DreamGirl3000 Hey, we have some mutual friends! Your friend Rose once served me coffee. Let's hang?
@SlipperySonia I need your help. This man just ghosted me after we had the most incredible night and I don't know what to do?
@Empath_Spirit Hi there ☺ just popping over a message to ask why you hang out with Rose who's a known womaniser? Surely that's not feminist?
@CandyDarling You're the only person who can help

me Eartha. I sometimes want to kill my boyfriend. What should I do?
@IsobelRose Hi, just wanted to send some love. I can see the internet's being cruel to you. Some people are just bitter unfortunately. Keep going.
@PearlescentPolyamory Fraud. I saw you kissing a man. You don't represent me or any other queer women.
@PinkIsTheHottestColour ... your plants are dying.

I read through them, trying to absorb the mass of emotional outpouring and truths firing at me.

I didn't even know Madonna followed me.

*

I've started to realise that my life doesn't really belong to anyone any more: it doesn't belong to me and it doesn't belong to those who plug into me, however close they feel to my existence through Wonderland. Instead, every decision I make is influenced by manipulations through my screen and through the deep pockets of those in power. Thousands of people know me and yet I've never felt lonelier in my life. They're all strangers to me. And I am a stranger to them. This is the kind of visibility that makes you feel invisible. I'm no longer a person. I've become a brand. A message. A slogan. I 'represent' something, something that's used to position others as a benchmark of how well they're doing in their lives. An adjunct. It's such an awfully strange feeling when *you* don't even feel that way about yourself. I really do believe it when people call me a fraud. *Because, of course, I am.* How can anyone live up to the title 'the voice of a generation'? People who are given that are set up to fail.

Everything I ever thought I wanted for myself has come true – people know my name, they pay money for me to represent their products, I'm taken out for dinner by luxury soap brands in places I could never have afforded previously in exchange for a tag on my page, I have £7,500 in my bank account, I've felt desired, adored and seen in ways that I have never felt before, I have over 350,000 people who follow me and, as much as it makes my toes curl and cringe, call themselves 'Earthalings' – and I don't want any of it. I have never felt less connected to the world.

All I want is Phaedra. I haven't heard from her since and I'm starting to think she's gone cold after seeing everything about me online. While I'm left stuck, wondering where her warmth has gone. Everything fucking reminds me of her. I want to complain about the sadness it brings me, but I can't stop playing the playlist she sent me and at this point the pain almost feels self-inflicted in its indulgence. I know too much about her to fully accept I will never be intimate with such a wonderful person again. I was so sure that I was a woman who 'knows what she wants' that I've never considered that the object of my want might not want me.

And still my Wonderland platform holds on by a thread since almost being dropped for the leather jacket incident. I need to pretend to be oblivious to the turning tide. I still need to try to engage with thousands of people every single day, who seem more disappointed and enraged than engaged. I have no idea what language to speak to them in any more. *Do they even like me?*

A girl messaged me today to tell me that she was disappointed in me for not sharing her fundraiser for a hurricane. Because the hurricane 'disproportionately affected women', she said I couldn't consider myself a feminist unless I dedicated my page to it.

I woke up to a woman calling me 'abusive' because I am yet to speak up on the difficulties of having sex as a disabled person, as though I, a non-disabled person, am the right person to do that. Even if I shared someone else's work, would that be enough? Or would I be criticised for not sharing the 'right' voice?

I've been experiencing targeted harassment non-stop for the last three days from strangers demanding I be held accountable for the 'harm caused to the asexual community' for once forgetting to include the 'A' in 'LGBTQIA+'. They told me I need to hand over all my earnings to organisations raising awareness about asexual people.

A girl posted a comment on one of my selfies: 'bring back bullying'. It received 121,471 likes and 1,470 comments. I lost 20,131 followers and received DMs saying I deserved to die. Which is apparently the only thing I do deserve.

I'm being held to the same level of responsibility as a politician for reporting on traumatic events the world over and somehow representing *every* experience that *anyone* might have, *ever.* While living entirely by myself with my phone as the main character in my existence.

Although there are also hundreds of people backing me, their messages fail to penetrate my consciousness. It's as though my mind's sole mission is to find information that confirms my rotten belief system that started with Dad and was cemented with Matt: that I am wrong to think I was built to experience joyful things, that I deserve to be expunged.

Ping

My body flinches.

Voice note from Rose to Eartha (8 seconds)

14.05

Baaaaabe, it's been a little while. I miss you! Saw the article this morning ... AMAZING! How is everything?

EARTHA: THE VOICE OF A GENERATION

Eartha, 25, made her name in a viral 'cumming out' video that has subsequently been watching 11 million times. Ever since the viral video she has been campaigning against the misogyny that continues to circle on Wonderland, despite its management takeover by the 'positive impact' senior investment group, Spartan X, late last year. Eartha is the woman making Wonderland safe for other women and is spring cleaning and gutting the extreme opinions from within the cracks of Wonderland. Since Spartan X's majority share takeover, however, the space has become increasingly extreme in viewpoints shared but this extremity has led to 200 million more users. According to recent stats released by the company, in the last three months over half the world's population logged in at least once a day. The Wonderland space, designed initially for people to speak their truth, has found more and more people getting dropped from the platform day in and day out after the Spartan X takeover, which imposed new, restrictive guidelines. Eartha seeks to 'claim back the space where women can share their truth and their stories' on the platform and has said she doesn't stand for the strict guidelines imposed on women, their views and their bodies on Wonderland.

Ping

Voice note from Rose to Eartha (10 seconds)

14.07

Was thinking of havin' a sexy gay night out for my birthday, you've GOT to join. I live by myself as of tonight, so I'd love to see you tonight or tomorrow for a beer. So much to catch up on. We can watch hetty programmes and scream at them. I invited Mona too, persuaded her with the promise of some limes ;)

The *ping* of a notification sends me into a suspicious frenzy. I've muted my Wonderland notifications for the last few days, but any sound my phone emits feels like a tripped alarm system. It feels like it could be about what happened at the Wonderland party. The party is becoming another thing that I try to ignore out of existence; like breaking up with Matt, like coming out, like telling Phaedra how I really feel.

Text message from Mona to Eartha

14.14

BAAAABE I have so much to catch you up on. Fucked Stephie again, the woman from Slinky's. Obviously (those hands??!)

14.15

Rose just said she texted you about her birthday, you down? Miss you. Come to the shop some time? I will give you a tester.

14.15

Also, congrats on that fucking article! VOICE OF A GENERATIONNNNN?? COME ONNNNN!!!!

How did I get to the point where texts from my best friends feel like obligatory admin as opposed to little angels in my phone sent to lighten up my day? Instead of replying, I plug into Wonderland.

Wonderland post

A picture of an article with a caption: Taking down more hateful men tonight! Watch this space.

Within less than a second a comment appears.

@FrenchieStoppard Would rather you just took yourself offline.

I panic and delete the post.

The adrenalin rush from people feeling strongly about me is not enough to sustain me. I punch out a generic, vague caption that alludes to my double-life situation without explicitly addressing it. I promised E.V I would stay quiet. But I wonder if it looks *too* direct coming from my own digital mouth? Rose might text me and ask, 'What's this all about?' or E.V might ask me to remove it and then, instead of comforted, I'll feel humiliated at my sad attempt to connect and be accurately accused of attention seeking. Or worse, Phaedra will see and be even more repulsed by me. I can already hear the mob in my head telling me that I'm 'playing victim'. I type in the hashtag #MentalHealth on Wonderland and refine the search so that the newest posts load first. I land on something from a mindfulness account that was posted an hour ago: that way it's more believable that I just happened to 'stumble' across it. Less strategy, more authentic.

@mindfulness_in_mayhem You never know what someone's going through. Be kind. Always.

I physically recoil at the fact I'm sharing this quote, written in cursive font on a floral background, but I don't know what else to do. My skin flares up at the thought of sharing something so glib.

I press 'upload' and put it on my Wonderland arena. That way it will only be there for twenty-four hours. Maybe people will read into it and see that something has happened to me that has changed the real Eartha. It might be the only way I can let people know there's something going on. I stare into the screen from my bed, watching the snake chasing its tail as it loads.

Drip.

A brown droplet of water lands on my stomach and trails down the side of my hip. My skin flares up in goosebumps and the hairs on my arms and legs rise in a soft layer of fuzz. I raise my head to see a new leak in the ceiling. I catch a glimpse of myself in the mirror at the end of my bed, tits out with my phone in my hand and dead behind the eyes. I tell women that self-care is important, but I've not even been following through with any of the viewings I've had for new apartments. Part of me is still clinging to the comfort of the old, sorry, pathetic life I had with Matt. The reality of looking after yourself is horrific. It's facing your biggest fears and memories; it's resisting the urge to reach out to the people who have hurt you because, secretly, part of you still wants them to love you. It's making your bed in the morning even when you want it to swallow you up. It's flossing after food. It's replying to your fucking mum, who loves you. It's washing the dirty dishes as soon as you've finished eating so that there's always something to eat from and it's definitely not putting up with the leak in your ceiling. It's allowing yourself to finally face the abuse that you experienced. It's definitely *not* trying to run on from it, posting online and creating a fucking storm around you to distract yourself. It's sitting with it and accepting that you must heal from it.

It's not you, it's me, Eartha. I avoid things. That's what I fucking do. I've accumulated years of resentment and hurt towards people and situations that I have never once attempted to fucking fix.

Your post has successfully uploaded.

I sit and wait, refreshing the feed to see if anyone has commented. Instead, a picture of Phaedra's face bathed in sunlight appears, uploaded fourteen seconds ago. I am probably the first person to see it. *Does that mean something?* I scroll through her profile, torturing myself with more pictures of her face. I remember how deliciously she wore her hangover the first time I met her in the street. How she looked when she was on top of me the first morning after we had sex. How her body felt warm, crushed up on top of mine as we fell asleep with our fingers interlocked. Her tiger eyes that I once found mesmerising now look back at me with hate and disdain. As though she is disgusted by the grasping, smothering weeds that cover and grow around me the longer I stay in my flat.

Perhaps Phaedra is drinking the internet Kool-Aid herself, or perhaps she is genuinely hurt that I slept with someone else. But she was also dating other people, I'm sure of it. I worry that all of this chaos surrounding me has left her feeling confused, or worse, that she believes it all. I have had months of people telling me they'll do anything to meet me and yet I'm sat waiting and watching Phaedra's message screen to see if she goes from 'online' to 'typing'. I swipe up through our chat to find the last voice note she sent me and replay it, just to prove I didn't imagine it all.

Archive voice note from Phaedra to Eartha (13 seconds)
17.48
Last night was so funny. I don't think I've laughed so much during sex before. Human beings are AWFUL, what did we EVER do to deserve a thing such as funny sex? I'm still thinking of you ...
whiff I think I can still smell you too, babe.

I play it over and over again, my heart fluttering as I temporarily relive the moment.

I click on her 'following' list to see who she's started following, if there are any new girls, or guys, or if she follows Matt to see whether they're conspiring against me. I type Matt's name to halt my spiralling. Nothing. I roll my eyes in relief. She's following Rose, which is interesting. *I wonder what that means.* Suddenly a poisonous thought races across my mind. My thumbs are overcome with the impulse to search for something …

Has Phaedra stopped interacting with my social media because …

She's unfollowed me?

No, people don't do that.

People you know in real life don't unfollow you without saying anything.

That's cruel!

But I should check …

I type the letter 'E' into her following list to test my theory.

I can feel my heart pounding against my chest.

A list of a hundred names appears …

I type the letter 'A'.

The circle on the screen loads.

No results found.

CHAPTER 24

VOICE OF A GENERATION

Wonderland followers: 313,096

I'm finding it overwhelming to feed myself properly, brush my hair, shower. But I know that the only way out is through. If I want to leave this flat, I'm going to have to stay online; I'm going to need to sit in this washing-machine cycle until it finally starts to slow, beeping to signal its load is over, letting the dizziness subside. I need to erase what happened at the Wonderland party from my mind: *it* can't exist if *I* need to keep existing. I finally replied to one of Rose's many texts asking me to hang out and arranged a time, instead of the myriad of excuses I've been giving:

On my period, again!
In a meeting!
Too much work!
Busy,
busy,
busy!

But as I walk towards the café a swooping sensation drops through my chest. I'm convinced Rose either hates me or has abandoned me along with the slew of social media trolls. I haven't seen them since before the Wonderland party. I'm nervous, afraid they'll ask me what's wrong and I'll explode. Maybe I'll tell them about Phaedra. Or ask why Phaedra follows them. It feels like a gulf has opened between our once-synchronised lives. I don't know how to find a way to bridge it. I keep my head down, focusing on placing one foot in front of the other, not making eye contact with anyone I pass on the pavement. It's the first time I've left the flat since the party and my body is overly sensitive, reacting to the slightest movement from passers-by, as though a single negative thought or change in the wind's direction could knock me over.

I look down at my phone, there's an email from E.V.

From: E.V (E.V@talentenhancement.com)

To: Eartha (eartha_17@gmail.com)

Subject: Checking in ...

Hello Darling,

Sorry I've been quiet the past few days. I've been sorting things my end as promised after the party. But you must understand that you've left us in an impossible and incredibly precarious situation. This should stay our secret for now. I fear that if you say something it will ruin everything we've built, they're big players, darling ...

I'm sending you over some things in the post, self-care goodies, bath bombs, a bottle of prosecco and some silk pyjamas from a brand who want to work with you, they're all gifts so if you tag them we get paid too. I don't quite know what to say to you ... a part of me feels frustrated that you didn't listen to me and went ahead with what you wanted to do. But perhaps that's not fair.

Let me know if there's anything you need, I am here. For

now, we're just going to have to pretend to the world that nothing happened so we can all move on and recover from this privately, saving your reputation. To protect you. I am deep in damage repairs with Wonderland. Take care of yourself. I'll visit soon to check in on you ...
E.V

'My baby!'

Rose shouts at me from the café door, using a foot to hold it open. I pocket my phone and instinctively run over to hug them. I get a nose-full of their hair and I inhale as deeply as I can. They smell and feel like home and I feel grounded to my root.

'Woah, are you okay?!' Rose asks, with their arms still around me.

'Yes, I just missed you.'

Their rings are hot on my skin and their hands make little indentations into my shoulder. They are my friend. The most permanent and consistent person in my life.

'I see you're posting again on Wonderland! I'm so glad that whole shit show with those self-righteous assholes (plural) is over. That girl Jaz is never going to be allowed in Slinky's again and I have told everyone to avoid her. Saw that article in the paper, too, 'The voice of a generation'. Fucking hell, babe ... you must be made up? Everyone's loving you again. Our Eartha, the poster child of the generation!'

'Oh Rose, stop it.' I blush and nudge their elbow.

'Nah, come on, what was it that they said, "The woman who is making Wonderland safe for other women"?'

Well, we definitely have very contrasting perspectives.

'Yes, yes, yes, yes ... everything's going so well, getting paid lots of invoices from smaller brand deals and coming to the end of my contract with FIRE soon, so I'll be getting that second batch of payment any day now.'

'Ooooo, what have you been spending your money on?!' they say, nudging my shoulder. They move from the door and pull out a seat for me at a table near the window. As I sit down, I hear the door to the café close on the latch behind me. I turn to look at it, drawing into myself as I do so. 'Are you constipated?'

'Oh, no, at least I don't think so.' I shake my head, trying to remember the question they asked me.

That was it.

'Well ... I've not spent an awful lot. I get clothes for free now. E.V has been sending me so much PR crap, I have a big bundle of it in the corner of my room. I should probably look for a new place, though. There are too many memories in my flat now. It's like living in an old skin ...'

I grimace and scrunch up my face.

'Yeah, shit, I get that, babe. If the FIRE job is up too, does that mean you can start fucking guys again?!'

A thick lump forms in my throat at the thought.

'You know me, love me some good old DICK.' I pump my fist to emphasise my sarcasm. Rose squints their eyes at me. 'Why are you looking at me like that?' I ask defensively.

'Like what?'

'Like I'm some annoying drunk you can't shake off in the smoking area.' I exaggerate their facial expression, pretending to be disgusted.

'You seem a bit ... well, you seem on ... edge today.'

'Too much for you to handle, is it?' I deflect.

'Something's different about you. It's not that crap online, that's not still going on, is it?' I shake my head to reassure them.

'You've not been on Wonderland all night searching yourself, have you?' They places their hand onto my wrist to comfort me and I flinch. 'Jesus, Eartha, are you high?'

I pull down my sleeve to conceal my wrist. I scrunch the sleeve over my hand and curl it into a fist. 'I'm just super tired and I've hardly slept ...'

The coffee grinder starts up in the background. I lurch in my seat and my knee hits the table. I look up at Rose, who stares at me, bewildered. I try to laugh it off and smack the air dismissively. 'Sleep deprivation ...'

'Babe, did you do any drugs last night?'

'No,' I reply firmly.

But thinking about it, perhaps it's better if they believe I'm on a comedown, they might not dig any further.

'I mean ... a little line of coke,' I say, indicating the thickness of the 'line' in the air with my index finger and thumb.

'That thick, was it?' Rose says, raising their fingers. I think they're mocking me and they grin to confirm it. 'Nah, come on, that's not it. You don't do drugs, you're lying to me! What the hell is going on? Something happen with Phaedra?'

'I went to a party with E.V last week, it was filled with major-league people from Wonderland and I guess I've just been on a real shit comedown since.'

I'm so bad at lying. *The word 'comedown' has literally never left my mouth before.*

'Last week? Mine don't usually last that long; you must be down bad!' They pat me on the back and it rattles me but I style it out as itching and they surrender their hands. 'What happened at the party? Did ya get lucky?' they ask, curious.

'Nah, it was a weird party. They took my phone at the door

because it was so exclusive, you couldn't take pictures or tell anyone anything that happened.'

Rose nods, pursing their lips to hold back their opinion.

'It was good to just let go and have no one watch or be able to spread shit about me afterwards. You know I've been going through so much lately, it's been hard to relax. A party like that … it's like mutually assured destruction. No one can say anything about anyone.'

'If you ask me, that sounds shady as fuck and also … I don't think everyone cares or is trying to take you down as much *you* think they are, honestly!'

'Yeah, well, no one *did* fucking ask you, did they?' I snap. 'I didn't come here to be grilled by you. I'm under a lot of stress with … everything going on at the moment and I just, I don't really know what to do about it so …'

'Well, let me help you?' Rose says, reaching a hand over the table to comfort me.

'Where have you been when I've needed you before now? I have been posting asking for help and you haven't got in touch with me!' I exclaim.

'Posting what, Eartha? What are you talking about? You've been posting about EARTHA THE VOICE OF A GENERATION. When have you asked me or anyone for help? Tell me, help for what? You've got over three hundred thousand followers now, you've got articles comin' out of yer arse about how loved you are … It's everything you ever wanted!' they shout in frustration.

'Yes, *Rose*, but maybe that's just it. I thought you knew me better than that. Maybe I don't have any privacy any more with these three hundred thousand eyes on me constantly and I don't want people to know every detail of my life and I feel like slowly, bit by fucking bit, I'm losing myself. I'm becoming someone else entirely and it's too late to back out now because of—'

I close my eyes and stop myself speaking to subdue the caged animal that rages inside me. *Don't*, Eartha.

Don't cry.

'I need to go, I'm still so tired and you know what? I can't take all these intrusive questions,' I say, more quietly.

'Intrusive questions? How about asking me ONE fucking question about my life, hey? I don't think you're seeing clearly, babe. Other people have problems too; you aren't the only person being affected by Wonderland.' Rose points at the people in the café, they're huddled into their phones as if they're in a passionate embrace with their screens. I don't know how to reply.

'You don't ask me anything – and I mean *anything* – about me any more. Like, "Rose, how's your day been?" You never ask me if I'm dating anyone, you wouldn't even fucking know if I was in love!'

Rose in love. I roll my eyes.

'Oh, don't roll your eyes. Lately it's been all about how I fit into your life. I've needed you too, Eartha. I've been getting abuse on Wonderland too. You never even got back to my text about my birthday.'

Shit.

'Which, by the way, is next week …'

'Obviously I remembered that.'

Fuck.

'You never ask about how I feel living alone since Billy moved out, or—'

WHAT?

'Billy moved out?! What the—'

'You're not even reading my texts?' They sigh and look down at the table, and I can't look. I can't bear to see the person I love most in this world hurt and let down by me.

'I'm sorry,' I deflate and drop my shoulders. I place my face into my hands for relief from the performance, so I can relax my face muscles. I came here upset with *them.* But *I've* been the shit friend. I want to know everything about Rose, I always have. I want to know every contour and moment in their life. How had I forgotten that? Forgotten that it's their fucking birthday next week …

'Rose, I'm sorry. Please, tell me everything about Billy, how are you making rent now? Do you need help or anything?'

'Well—'

Ding.

The bell at the top of the door rings and I hear someone enter the café. I hear the shuffling of their shoes as they walk past to stop behind me in the queue. I smell a cologne that is assaultive to my stomach and sends electricity into my wrists.

'What's that smell?' I ask, raising my head from my hands.

'What smell? Coffee?' Rose asks, looking at me again like I'm an alien.

'No, it's like …' I turn around to see a man stood in the queue. I catch his face. A relief.

'I've got to go to the toilet,' I say as I excuse myself.

'Do you want me to come with you?' Rose asks with a look of concern across their face.

'I'm going for a piss, Rose, I don't need you to hold my fucking hand.'

I can feel their eyes burning into my back as I walk off.

I enter the first cubicle and close the door behind me, but I can't bring myself to lock it. I wedge my bag between the door and the frame. I place my hands either side of the small sink and look at myself in the chipped mirror with my face lit by a fluorescent strip revealing every pore and crevice. The cologne has churned my stomach and I want to bleach my nostrils clean. My lip starts to quiver and I quickly place my hand over my mouth. *Don't cry, you stupid bitch.* I stare at myself. Trying to send muscle to my tear ducts.

Don't fucking cry.

Don't fucking cry.

My face scrunches and no matter how hard I fight I can't overcome the strength of my emotions. I bunch the end of my sleeves into balls and jam them into my mouth to muffle my sobs. I think I'm wailing but it could be police sirens outside. Or maybe it's a siren going off inside my head. My breathing becomes shallow and short. I'm choking on my spit as I try to slow my body, my breathing, my heart and my mind out of acceleration mode. I miss my mum. I remember our phone call after I broke up with Matt and how she calmed me down.

Breathe in.

Breathe out.

I splash my face with cold water and wait a few minutes to cool down. My hands are shaking. I rip off a few squares of toilet paper and fold them into one neat thick piece to blot the inky tears under my eyes. I look into the mirror again and assess the sight in front of me. I briefly feel sorry for this woman. But then I remember I've been such a shit to so many people. *It hurts me to hurt you.* That's what Matt used to say, not that he ever meant it. I can't believe I'm on the other end of that now. I turn my head to face the door, then quickly back to the mirror again as though I've just been introduced to myself, to check whether people will think I've been crying. I think I can get away with it. I unlatch the door and walk out with a gleaming smile on my face.

'So ... I'm gonna head home now!' I announce, placing my hands firmly on top of the table. 'I just have so much work to do. We'll have to catch up another time!'

I can see Rose's smile drop in the corner of my eye as I glance down to fiddle with my bag. I'm avoiding looking at them. If I see how upset I've made them, I'll cry. So I'm talking, filling up the space, pretending to look for lip balm in my bag.

'What's going on? You can't just avoid me for ever,' Rose says, their eyes looking up at me and searching mine for a flicker of the reciprocated affection. I see their hand move closer to my wrist to console me. I swiftly move it out of reach and clutch the handle of the bag on my shoulder.

'I just need to be alone, I think, too many eyes on me all the time ...'

I look frantically around the café. There's a girl in the corner who's been watching me like a hawk since I entered. As soon as I look up, she tactically looks back at her laptop. Was she actually looking? I blow Rose a kiss, heading towards the door. I want to say sorry for being a shit fucking friend. For being an even shitter friend for walking away right now and proving their point. I mouth *I love you*, in a weak attempt to salvage things from a distance.

They roll their eyes and I pretend not to see it. I pretend this isn't happening. I walk out and grab my phone from my back pocket, desperate to reach for something familiar.

Something comforting.

Something numbing.

Whether it feels good or not.

I plug into Wonderland, reading through people's adoration, obsession and hatred, letting it pump though my body, drowning out the reality of what has taken place. It's the ultimate escape vehicle from life, allowing me to move outside of the uncomfortable, out-grown human form of my body. The names and places and comments are all-encompassing. I drink in what people are saying about me with an imaginary straw.

Ping

> *Text message from Mum to Eartha*
> 15.13
> Love, I know we're not talking and we're being moody with each other, but I saw the article today on my Wonderland feed. Telling everyone how proud I am of you ...<3

I want so badly to tell her everything. But I don't have the energy. I can't tell her what happened.

> *Text message from Eartha to Mum*
> 15.15
> Hey Mum, There's soooo much going on at the moment! I'M AMAZINGGG! Thanks for the love on the article! How are you?

CHAPTER 25

DIRTY KNICKERS

Time spent on Wonderland: 15 hours a day
Wonderland followers: 300,706

> *Eartha uploads a caption to Wonderland:*
> Whenever the glorious sensation of the sun sinks into my pores, self-doubt and anxiety fill my mind: *What will my body look like in a bikini this summer?*
> If I am about to have sex with someone new, I become aware of my arsehole. *When was the last time I shaved it?* I become aware of my toes. *Should I book a pedicure for ultimate toe confidence?* I become aware of the state of my bed. *Is that period stain still on my mattress cover?* I become aware of the smell of my apartment. *I need to take the bins out more!*
> The insecurities I have prevent me from experiencing joy. That's why, in a way, it's easier for me to live alone and to be alone. *I never have to inspect the basement.*
> #WhatsInYourBasement

The next morning.

I scare myself awake. My vibrator is rotating around my bed

sheets. I turn it off and look down to discover I'm not wearing any knickers. I sit upright and look around, afraid anyone could have witnessed such a horrifically shameful sight. I must have fallen asleep mid-attempt last night. I thought I'd give it another go touching myself – it was not a success. I adjust to the stark daylight and eventually lift myself out of bed, tossing the sex toy at my desk but it flops clumsily onto the floor. I plug my barely awake eyes into Wonderland to check the response to my post.

Wonderland notifications:

@GurlInWonderland Anyone else worried about what's going on here ...

@AaronSamuelsIsGay The girl needs a fucking shower, lol. Greasy ass!

@FatQueen Yeeeeeah, Eartha. Not everyone feels that way about their bodies. Also a lot of us are bigger than you, so you might want to check your thin privilege here, babe. You already have a bikini body.

@JessicasTwoCents What razors do you use! And who does your pedicures!

@BigGirlsCry Ooooof, hard relate. This made me feel so much better. Thank you for showing that feminists don't have it all figured out ...

@FemaleDemon Is this your way of distracting everyone again and avoiding being accountable for causing harm? Trying to make us feel sorry for you?

A wave of shame crashes through my body. I check the damage: 300,706 followers. I lost 10,000+ overnight.

I feel as though I need to wash away the shame pouring in from all my followers. I walk to the bathroom and turn on the shower. While the water heats up I make my bed so that I can't crawl back into it. The sheer weight of shame overloads my muscles and pins me down to the ground. I let myself be consumed by it and lie down on the floor. I look towards the bathroom to check the shower and spot a pair of dirty knickers by my ear. I sit up and go to pick them up, but there's another pair underneath the desk with period stains all over them. I then see that there is a community of knickers littered across my bedroom floor. I walk around collecting the multiple pairs I've left abandoned over the last few weeks, examining the crotch for discharge marks and if nothing's visible, sniffing them to see if they need cleaning. It's a treasure hunt of unwanted souvenirs from the times I've felt too defeated to take care of myself. I find a pair tossed off a week ago during an attempt to masturbate that ended in tears. I scoop them all up and throw them into the washing machine without turning it on.

Above the washing machine is a pile of dirty dishes crusting up, the windowsill is covered in the plants that everyone keeps kindly pointing out are dying in my care and I realise I can barely see through the window pane any more as it's clouded with dirt, both from outside and from within the flat.

I have an urge to just delete last night's post. Remove any trace of it and get rid of the task of a 'public response'. I realise now why so few women speak out or have opinions. It's safer and more comfortable to just shut up. I haven't even texted Rose since I saw them in the café. Or checked in on Mona. Or picked up the phone to Mum. All of this shit I have to do while the weight of expectation crushes and compounds the sides of me together, making any task impossible. I don't know how to escape the endless scroll that my life has become.

It's not as though I am an active participant these days.

I mostly lurk in the shadows and watch, witness and wait on Wonderland. I'm a voyeur of the other people who are black-ticked Wonderlanders, gawking at the profiles of women who look like they're not lying to themselves about being happy the way I do. Their smiles seem more genuine, whole and, dare I say, candid. But did Sam really have a 'beautiful and special' time with her partner on holiday, or did they spend the whole time arguing between the perfectly posed pictures? Did it actually take Priya a hundred attempts before she got that perfect picture of her ass, contorting herself into hundreds of different positions and angles before she got 'the one' with the highest engagement I have ever seen on a butt selfie? Is everyone also living a little bit of a lie? Or is my own tendency to curate the truth distorting my perception of others' genuinely happy and fulfilled relationships and belfies? Perhaps I am projecting my own self-hatred onto both.

In the absolute depths of these comparison spirals, I find myself called to the mirror at the end of my bed, summoned to pick myself apart, to find the things I dislike about myself that I wasn't previously aware of. *A woman must live in a constant state of self-improvement!* My copy of *The Beauty Myth* glares at me from my bookshelf, so I turn it around while I analyse myself in search of imperfections to fix. Things that, once resolved, might make this all go away. Suddenly I'm angling a hand-held mirror around my face to see what I look like from the side. Have I always had a double chin when I tilt my head like this? *That wasn't there yesterday.*

KNOCK-KNOCK-KNOCK

I drop the mirror on the floor; all that fills my big mirror is a dry, ugly potato with my face for a head. I put on my robe and tiptoe over to the door. The only people I've seen for weeks are postmen and delivery drivers. I can afford a takeaway-based diet now that my invoices have dropped. But the money has only enhanced my isolation. I don't even need to leave for groceries any more. And human connection? Well, I have Wonderland for that. There's no reason to leave at all.

But I haven't ordered food.

And I'm not expecting any packages.

I open the door with the chain still on and peer through the slit.

'Eartha! Let me in, won't you? Some guy downstairs let me up.'

It's E.V. I turn around to look at my flat, lifeless and grey with the blinds drawn. Mould growing on a half-eaten loaf of bread that is sitting on its plastic sheeting. I turn back to face her.

'Now's not really a good time.' I find the words come out my mouth stickily. *Am I already out of practice of talking to a real person?*

'I don't care about … what's going on in there. I just need to talk to you. You have turned down the last three invites I sent to you for meetings to discuss the next steps for brand deals. I have the contract here for you to sign for the next job you agreed to do with SkinMeal.'

'Who?'

'The edible skincare brand, darling.'

I sigh and close the door. I quickly open the blinds and place a plate over the bundle of dishes to make it look less cluttered. I unlatch the chain and reluctantly let her in. She pretends not to see the mess surrounding me and politely steps over the folded cardboard I'm yet to put out in the recycling bins.

'I know you're going through it right now, with the embarrassment of what happened at the party. But we've managed to control the situation.' She pauses. Then, 'However, we're not making any money at the moment because you're not posting your normal content ...'

Of course. Because I'm the product. And the product is decaying with the food in her fridge and her plants ...

'It's seriously starting to impact the influx of opportunities we were having come in for you. Your engagement has gone down because you've not been interacting with your audience. Without the styling videos, no fashion brands want to work with you. Without the content about dates and how your queer dating is going, there's no chance of us extending the contract with FIRE. We need you to get back out there, starting up arguments with men ... You know, darling ... calling out the bad guys like you used to. Your post last night was a bit dismal, to say the least. You lost thirteen thousand followers.'

DIRECTOR'S NOTE
Eartha starts screaming, her face is so close to the camera that you can see her tonsils.
She runs around her flat destroying everything she can while E.V sits implacably still.
First, the plants are upturned and smashed up. Then she tears down her desk, ripping her old collages off the walls and starts hurling the contents of her fridge around the kitchen. The window breaks and then she begins to rip the duvet. Feathers erupt across the camera screen.
ENDS

I stare blankly at the mound of dishes.

'I have something to propose to you.' E.V pinches the edge

of the chair at my table and pulls it out to sit on, like she's afraid this lifestyle she once praised as 'authentic' might rub off on her.

'So ... Just like I've taken over your dating apps and relieved you of *that* task you're struggling with, why don't I also go back to posting for you on Wonderland too? It would appear you're—'

'Like when I almost got dropped? When I wrote them and then you posted them for me?'

'Yes, but this time I'll write the posts for you as I know all the things people want to hear from you, while you,' she looks around the flat and continues, 'get your life back on track. You've become one of the most up-and-coming voices on Wonderland; I can just keep on building that side of your life for you!'

'But I'm more than a voice.'

'I *know*. But Wonderland doesn't like things stuck in the middle, it likes things to be binary. Polarised. Like cat or dog. Healthy food or junk food, right wing or left wing, straight or gay. You see? Gay people don't want to hear about your straight dates and vice versa. And contractually you can't even do that anyway. So why don't I take over on your socials, just for now? I know what the world wants to see from you! I have the charts and data! I can write your posts for you and send them over for your approval. This is something we can delegate while you get you back up on your feet. You need to rest and relax and do some thinking after what happened ... I just want what's best for you. What's best for you is best for us. We can't make any money together if you're depressed, can we? And I want you to get out of this flat ...'

Depressed.

Am I depressed?

'It's the truth, isn't it? You're depressed and I am concerned about you. I don't want this to break you. I want you to stay whole in this brutal world. You are my bright shiny thing. Let me help you.'

This hasn't occurred to me until now.

'I think I'm just in a bit of a slump, after being dropped and then the situation I got myself into … I've just felt as though the Eartha I knew and was starting to become has been shaken out of me. I feel hurt. And confused. I'm waiting to find out who the fuck I am. Other people are telling me I'm this and that and I don't know what to believe any more.' I whisper, but I want to scream.

'Nothing *terrible* happened, darling.'

'I think something *really terrible* happened, E.V.'

'Well … you almost got dropped.'

'It's not about being dropped? It's about …' I stare into the floor.

I don't even want to talk about it.

'These young girls look up to me and I feel like I'm lying to them if I can't be my actual self. You want me to do styling content but, really, I haven't worn a proper outfit for days, it's embarrassing for me to even get dressed. I stare at my wardrobe and I just start to cry. It's so overwhelming, I can't believe I ever thought I could help people find their true selves and "lead the fucking way".'

'You're not lying to them, you're inspiring them. You're providing a role model, an example of who they could be.'

'But it's unattainable. No one, not even I ca—'

'EARTHA. Please. Give me your password now. Let me take this load for you. I don't want the world to forget about you. What will you do then? Remember what I told you about Quinnley? DROPPED!' She slashes her hand against her throat as though gesturing an execution. 'This is just a temporary solution until you're feeling more like yourself.'

I look down at the floor again.

'Come on, darling, what will you do if everyone moves on from you? Send me your password now. I know you've changed it since you last gave it to me.'

I sigh and rub my eyes but she won't give in.

'Email it to me now. I'm trying to help you. I'm the only one who is – please trust me. We need to post what people *want* until they are ready to hear what you want to *actually* say. We need to turn the key in the ignition and get the Eartha engine back up and running.'

'I guess it would give me more time to do the boring stuff, maybe go to therapy, try and patch things up with my family— '

'Of course. Of course. Send me your password. Look, I know what's best for you.'

I send us both the log-in code to my Wonderland account while we're sitting at the table and her phone pings off in front of me.

'Please, do go to view some of the apartments I sent you, darling. You can afford to leave here now. I think it's time, don't you?' Her brow scrunches as she stands up from my table and heads for the door.

'What kind of stuff are you going to post?'

'I'll run it all past you first, darling, don't worry . . .' She opens the door and stands in the dimly lit landing. I ask her for another hug. If last week repeats itself, it might be the last one I'll have all week.

'Talk later, okay? Focus on trying to find somewhere else to bloody live, won't you? This just won't do. Not for Wonderland's bright new star.'

Maybe this is all going to work out now. Maybe the solution to finally getting through this wreckage is to delegate the act of 'performing' to someone else for a while. In the meantime, I can finally discover who I am outside of Wonderland. Maybe it's all going to become a lot easier now. I can hear the shower still running in the background. I sprint up from the edge of my bed to turn it off.

Ping

Wonderland notification:

*@Becky53_* has commented on your new post

I plug in to see that E.V has already posted something:

I'll be saying something publicly on the arena, I want you to join me in my sharing of shame! See you in 10 ;)

A swooping feeling shoots through my stomach and my arms start to feel floppy. I sit on the bathroom floor waiting – ten minutes feels like ten years to watch something come out of my own mouth. I am so separated. Like I'm witnessing myself being witnessed. I refresh over and over and over.

Hi EARTHALINGS,

EMOTIONAL CONTENT ALERRRRT: I know how much I have let you super-squad down: when you needed me most, I went silent. I am a WORK IN PROGRESS. And I messed up. I let you down and most of all I let myself down. To all the people who voted for me to be dropped from Wonderland, THANK YOU. I needed to be held accountable. You were right. I know the work you all do every day to make WONDERLAND a better place for us all to live. Policing the right and wrong because you dream like me that WONDERLAND could one day be the multi-universe it was created to be and that we need to STOP BAD BEHAVIOUR and LOCK UP accounts which promote hypocrisy. I let myself down in the real world with the vegan incident and that led to me letting you down on here. THAT'S WRONG. I'M SORRY. The personal should never affect the work we do on here. I am sorry for my actions. I am sorry for downing my share of the load. I am sorry, Earthalings! Will you ever FORGIVE me? This has all been so overwhelming. You are the fuel that feeds me. Together we need to spend more time online than offline to make this a safer place for us all. I want to be a person who belongs on Wonderland. Who is still learning but hoping you will come and learn with me #MoreTimeOnline

I'm about to ring E.V and ask her what the hell she's done when ...

@BeastieBabex We're so glad you did the right thing.

The first nice comments I've seen for a whole week.

@TransBarbie Knew you'd apologise eventually, love you.

@Luv_Girlsss Thanks for modelling REAL accountability Eartha.

@Rose69s Babe are you okay?

I scroll through the rest of the comments.

@FuckTillYouDrop You centred your feelings in this apology 'so overwhelming' – pffft you blatantly don't care, but at least this is a start.

I receive another comment.

@Yazmilledra So glad to have you back, we missed you.

Already the tide is turning. How have these people changed their minds about me so quickly? I refresh again.

A new post appears on my feed, posted by me:

#AD I'm OBSESSSSSSSSSED with the dating app FIRE, YASSSSSS! I haven't been able to stop hooking up with girls. Honestly. It's thrilling. THOUUUUUUGH I should probably stop, it's ADDDDDICTINGGGGGG getting to have your pick of the bunch ... Download FIRE, maybe you can even match with me ;) #Pride

CHAPTER 26

#MORETIMEONLINE

Wonderland followers: 696,038

All night I watch as my followers surge upwards. Since the cumming-out video, nothing has blown up as much as the #MoreTimeOnline post and it's not slowing down. People are sharing my posts and then video recording their hot take on it as though they're news readers.

But they're not even my words.

I am at the centre of the public debate that's spiralling and getting louder and louder both online and offline, people are calling me out for being 'too online', but I'm inundated with messages from Wonderlanders who have stepped more into Wonderland than anyone else. Sometimes racking up twenty-hour-long stints at a time. They call themselves the 'Deep Wonderlanders' and they now believe I too am promoting this way of life over 'reality'.

I plug in and watch as another new version of me becomes bigger than the version I created, I'm once again a point of debate. By 10 p.m., when Wonderland is at its peak usage, I see that *Eartha* has posted again:

WHYYYYY OH WHY DO THE DAYS HAVE TO BE 24 HOURS LONG? Why not 25? Or better yet 40? Was it a MAN that decided this? Why must I be forced to suffer longer in this prison, this skinsuit of OPPRESSION? #MoreTimeOnline

Again, within seconds the comment section is on fire and Eartha is rupturing opinion and debate, polarising those who are pro #MoreTimeOnline with a group who have set up their own reactionary hashtag #MoreTimeOffline. There are teachers who think I'm extremely online and damaging the boundaries that need to be maintained for their pupils' mental health because of the influence I have over young women. There are scientists messaging me asking if they can do CAT scans of my brain to compare and contrast whether my neurological composition has changed as a result of plugging in too much.

All while I sit at home lifeless and as though my life is being written and directed by E.V.

Text message from Rose to Eartha

16.09

Hey love, what's all this stuff you're saying on social media promoting a more plugged-in way of life? Are you doing okay? ☹

16.11

Do let me know if you can make my birthday, we're going Slinky's! WE ALL MISS YOU. Even if you prefer being online ;(

17.12

I don't care if you're being a dick. I just wanna know that you're okay. You can smell my cigarette-sodden jacket all bloody evening if you want!

In all honesty, I'm afraid of setting foot in Slinky's. I type out a response to Rose – *Won't everyone there hate me though?* I stare at it and delete it, knowing they'll accuse me of making it all about me again. I read through some of the posts that E.V has been making and click 'edit'. I start to get rid of a few exclamation marks here and there, to make it sound as 'me' as possible. Removing the grossly hyperbolic language.

Buzz

Buzz

E.V calling.

'Hello?'

'Darling, what are you doing?'

'Nothing.'

'You're editing your posts. I can see you doing it now.'

'How can you see that?' I turn around and look over my shoulder. 'I am changing the posts to sound more like me.'

'I knew you'd try to get back in and start stressing yourself out. We need this, Eartha. And it's working.'

I'm silent.

'*Yes.* You're so predictable, see. I knew this would happen. I want you to step outside of Wonderland and get yourself better, for both our sakes.'

'Rose texted me to ask if I was okay. I think they're sensing that something's up and I wanted to edit some of the posts so I sound more nuanced and less extreme. I don't want to tell people to be more online, I think there's a balance and—'

'Of course *they'd* say that. Have you seen the engagement, though, darling?'

'E ...' I swallow, preparing to assert myself. 'I think we should remove some of the posts. Or at least change how they sound;

they don't sound like me any more. Rose is catching on, which means it won't be long until other people figure it out. My "Earthalings" can be quite ... obsessive! Also, can we not actually call them that? It's a bit embarrassing. I think they'll start to pick up on the fact that this isn't me. We didn't talk about the apology, either. I didn't know we were going to be apologising and I'm not up to speed with any of these new brand deals, like with FIRE and that caption about dating women.'

'Before you complain further, consider that this might be exactly what needed to happen; check your inbox, now.'

An email with the subject 'Latest Engagement Report' lands in my inbox. I open it up on my laptop to see similar coloured graphs to the ones she showed to me at her apartment, along with a breakdown report of the last week of my Wonderland statistics.

Eartha engagement report:

Over 1-week period

Likeability: 110% increase (compared to week prior)

Engagement: 25% on average per post, peak engagement at 50% on most recent post

New followers: 395,332

'Eartha, we're going to need to arrange a photoshoot so we can take some pictures of you. You're running out of content, the old ones of you are getting a bit dried up. We need to shoot you in some new looks and visiting some cafés, or some pictures of you with friends so it feels more authentic. Maybe you can even take some selfies from home and send them over to me?'

I knew exactly what I was signing up for, didn't I?

Maybe I'm better off being more like the online Eartha? I think back to our initial meeting, when E.V said, 'We'll make you into a star. We'll make *you* become the central character in your story.'

I saw the money and didn't think twice about what it would cost me in integrity. I bought into the Wonderland version of Eartha that everyone admired and I bought into how much I was helping others see 'their truth', I believed in the praise and then I believed in the damnation.

Which version of me is me?

I feel like I'm falling.

'Okay, whatever, can I just have my passwords back for my FIRE account? I want to start dating again IRL.'

'Tell me who you want to date and I'll find them for you.'

'I want to look for myself, though.'

'You know how that went down last time …'

A sharp bolt of shock shoots its way from the top to the bottom of my spine as an image of Jaz, wait, Veronica, pulling up her trousers and leaving my flat flashes through my mind.

'What about that girl? The one with the pink hair? Can't you just call her?'

'She kind of just … disappeared. I want to take my mind off her, to be honest, with someone else.'

'I'll screen some appropriate candidates and send them over to you. Don't forget to send some selfies over in the meantime. Oh, and some pictures of your apartment, just things! Bits! Nothing too revealing. We need to keep people involved! But the great news is that people are falling in love with you again, like they did at the start. Once I've fully recovered your reputation, we can reassess.'

Perhaps she's right, but I need to feel I have some semblance of control over something, anything. I want my dating apps back before I can try to assert myself again. But then she trills, 'I'll talk to you later, darling, ciao!'

And the line goes dead.

I get into bed and look at the books I bought a few months ago to read. I pick one up and wipe the dust off the cover, flicking through to where I have turned down a page. I can't remember reading up to chapter six. This chapter is titled 'My Body, My Rules'. I read half a sentence: 'When someone questions your body as if it were the same as …'

Ping

> *Wonderland notification:*
> *@Shirley-Peyton* has commented on your post

I click on the link of the post, a new one, uploaded by me:

> Well, the only thing that can get me off when I'm in a slump is the Suction Conch Shell. Shiny, pearly, adorable and sexy. You can buy at the link on my arena with the discount code 'WANK30'. You don't have to depressed AND have a low libido!

CHAPTER 27

TAINTED LOVE

Wonderland followers: 1,098,223

I feel clearer today because my phone has been turned off all night. I switched it off from exhaustion after reading 'my' latest post:

> *If I even think about a man my pussy recoils like a Venus FLY TRAP.*

Turning it on again feels like coming home to an abusive partner after sneaking off for a night of fun with your friends, knowing it's going to cost you.

I want to creep around it.

I don't want to wake it up.

I don't want to know what E.V has been posting on my behalf.

Logging in feels like I'm attaching the leash onto my own collar.

What have I done wrong this time?

What will I be shamed for?

Or praised for?

I've stopped talking out loud in my flat. I don't remember when I decided it's not safe but it's been a few days now. I have a theory the place has been tapped, or someone's listening in on the conversations I'm having with myself in the mirror.

I plug my phone into the charging cable on my bedside table, the loading screen lights up and I walk into the kitchen to make myself a cup of green tea, savouring the moments before my mind is aflame with my screen's content. I fill the yellow kettle up slowly in the sink and place it on the base, flicking the switch to turn it on. I tap my finger on the counter and watch as the water begins to boil through the glass strip on the side.

What's going to happen when my phone turns on? Has E.V sent me an angry text? The kettle starts to wobble, rocking side to side with water spluttering out of the top. I push the lid down.

I should search my name online to check the latest gossip and rumours. I tear a bag of green tea from its twin and plop it into the cup.

You're incapable of doing anything. I lift the kettle and see just *how* slowly I can pour into it.

You can't trust yourself, Eartha. I watch the water rise higher and higher in my cup.

I can take your career away from you.

Ping!

It's awake.

I flinch my wrist and spill boiling water into the saucer of the teacup. I walk over to my phone obediently, a mother tending to her crying baby. The guilt switch has flicked and I'm back into over-compensation mode. I place the tea down next to my phone.

Ping

It goes off again. I pick it up. My hands are shaking. I unlock it. I have a text from Mona asking to hang out again for Rose's birthday.

And a chorus from Rose.

Text message from Rose to Eartha

21.34

Right, you have left me no choice, I am coming to get you.

4 missed calls from Rose

22.02

You could have at least buzzed me in!

22.11

You won't even unplug from Wonderland to speak to me when I am outside your door. Jeez Eartha.

Shit. I slept through Rose's texts? *And the doorbell?*

But nothing from E.V.

And nothing from Phaedra, whose name never appears nowadays.

Wonderland's silence is even more frightening. It means I'm still waiting for something to happen. The inevitable downfall. I can't bear the unanswered questions of when my next demise will strike. Instead I find comfort in the bad news; it takes me out of the state of anticipation. I open a browser tab on my phone and hashtag search myself. I find a new story – *GENERATION'S 'HERO' EARTHA OPENS UP ABOUT HER 'DOUBLE LIFE'.* There's a link embedded in a blogger's article to a Wonderland post alongside the pictures of myself I sent to E.V this week.

Eartha posted 10 hrs ago on Wonderland:

I need to open up to you all and I want to be honest about the situation I caused. I've been going through something lately that's been really hard to discuss and I want to know if anyone can relate ...

I immediately stop reading and lock my phone. The familiar

sinking feeling returns to my chest and swoops down my stomach. My body feels as though it's about to buckle under me. I can barely move.

THE SITUATION I CAUSED? I unlock and return to the phone.

> ... Does everyone feel burned or is it just ME? The Eartha you've come to love is changing and I've been living a double life but I don't want to any more. I can't trust myself or anyone. Who are we really to one another? STRANGERS. Stranger danger, baby ... I don't want you to feel sorry for me. I want to make sure I am as online as possible, living and breathing this with you. I've lost people I love because of what I am trying to do in this space. SHAKING the ground with my PASSION. Not everyone can handle it. And I am also losing some of you and it feels like a heart-wrenching pain, but then I wonder – are you as dedicated as me? The real me is coming back ... watch this space.

A double life? This is everything that I've wanted to tell people since the night of that party. Is E.V going to give me back my account? Can I finally speak out about what happened?

I need to speak to E.V. The phone keeps ringing. She's not answering.

'Helloooo, darling ...'

'Oh, E! I've seen th—'

'You have reached my voicemail. HOW WONDERFUL FOR YOU! Please leave a message after the tone, byeee.'

I hang up the phone and voice note her instead.

> *Voice note from Eartha to E.V (34 seconds)*
> 07.43

Hey, E! Haven't heard from you for a little while ... I wish you'd texted me about that post going out last night, I'm really worried. How do you think it was received by everyone? Is it true what you said with the 'real' Eartha coming back? Do you really think I'm ready? Do you think we can finally speak? I feel concerned about all this extremism we're promoting and I want to find the balance again.

I lock my phone and sit, waiting, tapping my nails on the bedside table. They're long enough to make a little noise now, their length a measure of how long it's been since my fingers have penetrated anyone. I make a clicking noise with my tongue against the roof of my mouth. I find myself slipping into the cool-girl role I've played many times before while I waited for a text back from Matt, pretending to myself and to the imagined audience of glaring feminists in my head that I'm *not* anxiously awaiting a man's response. I'm a cool girl! I can totally wait for the text back before calling again! I suppress and squash the anxiety deep into my body. But I do need to find something to do with my hands. If only to prevent myself from picking my skin till it bleeds. I reach for my tea on the side table and wrap my fingers around the handle.

Ping

An email comes through to my phone and I spill the hot tea all over my inner thigh. My flesh prickles with red pain.

I notice how this sensation is effective in distracting me. The war in my mind quietening as it focuses on a sore it can see. I sit and watch as my wet upper thigh glistens, turning a new colour.

I open the email on my phone: it's from E.V.

From: E.V (E.V@talentenhancement.com)

To: Eartha (eartha_17@gmail.com)
Subject: Latest Invoice
Hi Eartha,
RE your voice note and your concerns, my assistant is forwarding over the graphs detailing the results from the work I've been doing on your behalf over the last week.
You've gained over 300,000 new followers.
Your overall likeability ratio has increased from 60/40 in favour of hate comments to now 10/90, in favour of positive comments.
You've gained 20 black-ticked user accounts following you, important people are starting to respect you again, not just the sycophants who have no clue who they are. Because of my work, you're building a respectable audience and one that will gain you more opportunities.
So, no, I won't be returning your posting duties over to you. I think you'll agree that your account is safer in my hands after these results. Please stay off Wonderland as much as possible. You don't need to worry about it for a while ...
See the invoice – I've cc'ed in Paula who will attach for our latest brand endorsement.
E.V
From: Paula (assistant@talentenhancement.com)
To: Eartha (eartha_17@gmail.com)
Subject: FWD: Eartha Latest Stats
Hi Eartha,
Nice to e-meet you! E.V has told me lots about you. I hope we get to meet IRL soon.
She's asked me to send you over some of the latest

reports on your engagement since the takeover of the account, so I've just forwarded you the email chain below. Let me know if you have any questions or need any help interpreting them, but they should all be relatively straightforward ☺

Paula

See forwarded message below:

From: E.V (E.V@wonderland.com)

To: Team (BoardOfSocials@wonderland.com)

Subject: Eartha Latest Stats

See attached Eartha's latest engagement statistics, the #MoreTimeOnline hashtag went viral, I am sure you saw it. Perhaps you saw people's time spent online going up too ... Would be interested to know Eartha's effect. Can you send some graphs over?

Good things take time, planning and strategy. I've been able to turn this all around since posting for her, but we need to have space for it to build.

I'll wait for you to let me know you're happy with everything. Then we'll launch the next phase. Everything is in its right place.

(Graph attachment)

(Graph attachment)

Next phase? I thought it was just E.V and me? Maybe she's talking to her assistant?

I press 'reply' and start to type my response to Paula. I keep it professional.

From: Eartha (eartha_17@gmail.com)

To: Paula (assistant@talentenhancement.com)

Subject: RE: FWD: Eartha Latest Stats

Hi Paula,

Nice to e-meet you too.

Thank you so much for these, I'll let her know I've received them.

Speak soon,

Eartha

The email leaves my outbox.

I open up my contacts to call E.V immediately. 'Sorry, I saw on the email that Paula forwarded over, at the end—' I say before she can stop me.

'What do you mean forwarded? She didn't just send you the graphs?!'

'No, she forwarded over an email you sent to someone with the graphs attached to them. I just had a quick question … what's the *next phase??* I didn't realise we—'

Beeeeeeeeeeeeeeeep.

I hold the phone out in front of my face to check the screen.

The phone cut off.

I call her again, it goes straight to answerphone. Maybe her phone died?

I open up our chat and start to type a message. Within seconds a new email from Paula comes through on my phone.

From: Paula (assistant@talentenhancement.com)

To: Eartha (eartha_17@gmail.com)

Subject: FWD: Eartha Latest Stats

Hi Eartha,

Apologies, please ignore my last email – that was sent by mistake.

Here are the relevant graphs below.

(Graph attached)

(Graph attached)

Best,

Paula

My thigh now has a little heartbeat in it. It's flashing red with pain. I open up Wonderland on my phone to check the comments from the latest post where E.V exposed my double life. There's a pop-up message in a green box that I'm not familiar with. It says, 'Please re-enter your password'. It probably logged me out when I turned my phone off last night. I enter my log-in details.

password: *********

INCORRECT PASSWORD

I enter the details again; maybe I forgot to put on caps lock.

INCORRECT PASSWORD, 2 OUT OF 3 ATTEMPTS USED.

YOU HAVE ONE ATTEMPT LEFT.

I enter the password again, this time typing out each character one by one, lifting my index finger slowly and intentionally for each one, to make sure I'm not slipping.

INCORRECT PASSWORD. YOU HAVE BEEN TEMPORARILY BLOCKED FROM ACCESSING THIS ACCOUNT FOR 30 MINUTES.

What the fuck? I typed the password correctly. E.V is the only other person with my password. I lift my phone so quickly to call her it falls out of my hands and onto the floor. I pick it back up and call her.

Brr-brr …

Sent to voicemail.

I call her again.

Brr-brr …

Voicemail. Again.

I call her over and over, eventually it goes straight to voicemail without even ringing.

Text message from Eartha to E.V

19.34

Hey, E! I can't get into my Wonderland account, have you changed my password?

Text message from Eartha to E.V

20.37

I'm really starting to get worried, has something happened? Have I done something wrong?

Text message from Eartha to E.V

21.53

I hate texting you so much like this, I'm so sorry, I just feel so lost?! I don't know what to do.

Hours have now passed and I still haven't heard from her. I'm dotting around my flat, moving from area to area. I wrote my password down, I just can't remember where. It's got to be here, somewhere. Maybe I'm still tired, did I get enough sleep? Maybe I did forget my password. Perhaps I typed it incorrectly? I've overturned every book, looked under every surface and searched all my drawers. I lift up my bed. *I wonder, what are people saying under the post?* I look in the pockets of my blazers. *What if people are saying things about me right now and I can't defend myself?* I turn my trousers inside out. I open every cupboard. *Am I going crazy or has E.V changed my password?* I check the washing machine. I scroll obsessively through the notes on my phone. *She wouldn't do this to me, am I going crazy?* Still, nothing. I send another text.

Text message from Eartha to E.V

22.09

I'm worried, E. Please tell me what's going on. Please get

in touch. I feel so lost. What's happening?
22.20
I might have forgotten my password. I'm searching my apartment for it, but I can't find it anywhere. Can you please help me? I FEEL CRAZY. I'M GOING TO RIP MY HAIR OUT! Lol, LAUGHING EMOJI
22.23
Sorry, I didn't mean to get angry in that text. Can you call me back please, as soon as possible?
22.24
Have you changed the password? I've tried the one I emailed you.
22.26
If this is about me seeing that email, I can delete it if you want me to! It's nothing, really! I didn't even understand it anyway!
Voice note from Eartha to E.V (27 seconds)
22.32
Oh, I guess you are out at a party with your other Wonderlanders! I wish you had asked me. I know it didn't go well last time, but I am feeling so much better and am so grateful for all the support and work you are doing for me, I just feel like I am dead sometimes. But now I don't, I feel like I can do this again! I want to continue making money with you and would love to show you I can still do this work. Do you want to send a driver like before and I can be ready in twenty? Remember, I can get ready in a flash! I promise I won't drink or act badly. I just ... I guess ... I just miss you. I want you to feel that same way about me.

She never turns off her phone, ever. Something's up. I am somewhere beyond panic. I feel a bead of sweat drip down the back of my neck. I collapse onto my bed, staring up at the brown patch on the leaking ceiling. I want to scream. I grab the pillow next to me to clench onto, when I hear music playing next door.

'Dun-dun'

Oh, no.

Not now.

'Sometimes I feel, I've got to DUN-DUN run away, I've got to DUN-DUN…'

The bass throbs through my bedroom wall from next door. I catapult myself up from the bed and land on my feet. I run over to the window and lift it up, leaning my bare torso out to purge years' worth of collected resentment onto my unsuspecting neighbours.

'TUUUUUURN IT THE FUUUUUCK DOOOOOOWN!' I howl.

A dog from someone's garden barks at me in response. I resist the urge to bark back. The music stops shortly after and I hear the screech of their window opening. My neighbour sticks out his head and is shocked to discover that the bellowing neighbour was me.

'Eartha?! Was that you?! You could just ask nicely—'

'YES! IT WAS ME!' I shout.

The dog barks at me again. That's it.

'GRRR!' I bark back.

'HAHAHAHAHA, JOE LOOK, EARTHA'S GONE CRAZY!' They both laugh at me.

'I'M NOT FUCKING CRAZY!' I shout, before slamming the window shut and returning to my lair of misery, like a hideous troll retreating under the bridge after the shame of exposing its raw, bitter, ugly truth to the light.

I pick up my phone from the charging socket and sit with my back to the wall under the window, clutching my legs tightly to my chest. I take a deep breath.

Ring-ring

Ring-ring

Oh my God. It's E.V. Finally. My face lights up with relief.

'E.V, I'm locked out of my Wonderland account, I can't get in …' I start to cry. 'I've tried so many times, I feel like I'm going crazy. I've flipped everything over in my flat and I just barked at the fucking dog outside, I really need you right now.'

'Darling, what is all this crazy nonsense? I turn my phone off for a work evening, which, by the way, I *did* invite you to, and return to find these hideous accusations from you over text?'

'I'm sorry, I can't log in to my ac—'

'Eartha, why would I do such a thing?'

'I thought maybe you changed it fo—'

'Are you sure you entered the password correctly? You sound drunk or delirious.'

'I promise, I typed it in exactly as it is. I even pressed the button that lets you see the password as you type it,' I say, slowly, enunciating the words, like I'm even trying to convince myself at this point.

'Eartha, try it again.'

I remember that I have one more attempt after half an hour had passed; it's been hours. 'I'm going to put you on speaker; the timer should be up by now. It locked me out.'

'Go on then, type it in.'

'Okay.'

I put her on speaker and shakily enter the letters of my password into the box and read them out loud as I type '*StevieNicksKissMyTits!*'

'Capital S, small T, small E, small V … exclamation mark—'

'Eartha,' she interrupts me as I'm about to press enter.

'What?' I ask.

She sighs. 'There's no exclamation mark.'

'Wha—'

'There's no exclamation mark in the password.'

'Isn't there?'

'No, you got your password wrong.'

'Okay, let me try it without.' I erase the exclamation mark and hover my finger over the enter button, too afraid to press it.

'Have you done it?'

'Yes, just loading!' I lie.

Because this is it. This determines everything.

Am I crazy?

I take a deep breath. I press enter.

How could I have forgotten my own password?

The circle loads in the centre of the screen. Configuring, deciding my fate.

Fuck. It worked.

I take a second to swallow and hold back the tears. 'Silly me!' The words roll so instinctively off my tongue that I don't know where they came from. Somewhere deep within me.

'I got the password wrong.' My voice trembles. There's silence. 'E.V, are you still there?' My hands are shaking. 'I, I don't even have the words.'

'Eartha …' she sighs. 'I'm really starting to worry. What's going on with you?'

'I ... I don't know.'

'After tonight I don't think we can trust you with your socials any more. You're one step away from a nervous breakdown. I think it's for the best if I officially lock you out of your account, at least for now. It's the best thing for you, while you get some more rest. You sound like an absolute mess ... Darling, let me take it from here?'

'Uh, I think I'll be okay!' I say, grabbing the curtain to wipe the tears from my face, forcing a cheerful tone.

'No, darling, I'm making an executive decision here. You need to take this break seriously. What's that you said about barking at a dog?! Tearing your hair out?!'

I look around my room and see the mess I've made. Pillows on the floor. Every drawer opened. Clothes spewed everywhere. I look down at myself and my trembling hands. And the large, scarlet scold on my thigh. *Am I crazy?*

CHAPTER 28

IT'S LIKE THERE ARE TWO SIDES OF YOU

Wonderland followers: 1,349,998

I don't know how much to tell Rose or where to start or end, or whether I should tell them what's been happening in my head and in my life at all. How can you open up about something when you're not sure what it is that you're trying to articulate? Or whether it's even real?

It's warm out and I'm wearing trousers. I don't want Rose to see the red blemishes on my thigh. It's the first time I've left my flat for a while and, walking on the street, I feel as though my skin suit has been turned inside out, sticky and vulnerable flesh facing the world. I've covered my entire body. Blacked-out sunglasses and a long-sleeved top. I don't want anyone to know that whatever used to exist of me is currently floating around in the online ether, as though my actual soul has been uploaded into cloud storage space.

All Rose knows is what I've been posting online. Today's post has even divided and conquered the more extreme Wonderlanders. It's the worst yet, I think:

Lately I've been feeling like I can't really trust anyone. This fame crap really gets to you. It's HARD out here being influential.

Which version of myself should I show Rose?

Hi Rose, I am amazing, thanks! As you are probably aware from Wonderland my account has been soaring! I have 1,300,000 followers now and my likeability is 93% so, yeah, I'm obviously very happy!

Or

Hey Rose, yeah, long time since we last hung out! Last week I almost barked at the neighbour's dog with my tits out.

Or

Here's a funny story you are going to LAP UP, it's the one where I forget my password and then I turn my flat upside down into the physical representation of how my mind has been operating lately.

Or

Oh, did I tell you that my account is now run by E.V and I have no clue who I am, who owns me or where I belong?

Or

Did I mention I think I'm split in two? That the person who is talking online somehow knows the deepest, darkest thoughts I have been having in my flat, which, by the way I haven't left for weeks?

Or

Someone is putting it all up online, but the funny thing is, it's not me writing it, Rose … HOW weird is that? Do you think I am actually writing the posts and don't realise it? Am I doing it in my sleep or just in a different conscience?

*

'Roooooose!' I say with a forced smile, trying to convince them that their best friend still resides behind the dead eyes of the automaton in front of them.

'You look …' Their eyes widen, searching for the words.

'Crazy? My lips are dry, my hair's messy, do you think I look like a crazy person?'

'That's not what I was going to say. You just look … different …'

I laugh as we walk into the local pub.

'Why are you talking about yourself like that?' They place an arm around me as we walk to a table at the side of the pub. It's a place that we have often haunted. It's all green tiles, a rejuvenated working-men's pub which used to play sports and sell salted peanuts in a tube; now they charge £14 for a pint and sell fancy crisps in flavours like prosecco and ham, or cheddar and pulled pork.

'Well, that's what I am, right? Crazy, sleeping through your visit to me last week?'

'Of course not, I …' They sigh in exasperation. 'I get the feeling that anything I say is going to land me in it … so I'm going to politely decline answering that question.'

I roll my eyes. Today, not even Rose's charming voice can guide me out of my foggy fatigue. A tall figure shuffles into the pub and I look behind Rose to see who it is. It's not him. This man is in his late sixties and looks like an old soak. Rose senses my panic.

'Sorry, let me get you a pint!' I say, standing up from the chair. They look at me and laugh.

'Is that my birthday treat?'

'What do you mean?'

'That's why we're here? Right? You couldn't make it to Slinky's later?'

'Uh, of course this isn't your birthday treat! I've got something too big at home to bring to the pub for you, obviously.'

Holy shit. Are they playing with me? How did I forget their birthday? I would never. I have never.

I laugh at the evident lack of joke and pat them on the shoulder before heading straight to the bar. I look at the calendar hanging on a nail out of the wall: 1 September. I'm no longer anxious. I feel nothing. I deserve nothing. I order two IPAs and bring them back to the table.

'Here you go, your birthday booze.'

God, I'd literally never say that. Ever. They're going to know.

They smirk at me, knowingly, lift the pint and taste a sip. I can see the disappointment in their face, and the fact they're trying to mask it for me makes it worse. 'Mmmmm! Which hipster family do we have to thank for moving nearby to make this place so expensive! I actually preferred the taste when it was cheap, ya know,' they say cheerfully, looking around the pub and back at me. I realise I've not reacted, so force a quick laugh.

'How have you been, love?' They scrunch their inner brow and lean forward, right into the unspoken tension that lingers between two best friends who have left so much unsaid: *This friendship is not the same as it once was.*

'Well, I've been great!'

'No, Eartha, how have you been really?'

'*How have you been really*?'

I mimic the words but in a whiney voice, as though they said it in a condescending way. Rose nods their head without saying a word and places their pint onto one of the cork coasters.

'You know what? I *am* going to say it.'

They cross their arms.

Shit.

'You've been a right prick lately. All I've done since you came out is try to help you, I've introduced you to people, places, taken you to gay events; I've been there to support you, even with all of this fame shit. But you're just pushing me away and now you're being plain mean. I've given up on you ever asking me about my life. Both of yours seem to have taken up every part of you, it's like you can't even see the world around you. No fucking surprise Phaedra hasn't texted you, why would she?'

I take a deep inhalation of breath at the very mention of her name. This is the first time Rose has ever used my vulnerabilities against me in an argument, which means I've hurt them, badly.

'Well well well, someone's been bottling THAT up for a while. How did you know about Phaedra? Been messaging her, have you?'

'It's true. I'm sick of it!' They throw their hands up. 'And no, OF COURSE I haven't. You're losing your mind. Sometimes it's like there are two sides to you. There's no room for anyone else.'

'I'm sorry. I'm sorry about ... all of the Earthas I'm being right now,' I apologise, looking down at my fingers as they writhe around and scratch their tips. I can't even defend myself. The online version of me is promoting life-changing glittery sex toys while the offline version is crying any time anything comes near her vagina. The two versions of me are pulling in different directions.

Rose shrugs. 'Ahh, whatever.'

'Here we fucking go ...' I say, throwing my hands up in the air.

'You're being controlled,' they say, pointing their index finger into the centre of the table. 'You'll do anything it fucking says. Mark my words, soon it'll be running your Wonderland account for you. You won't even be making your own content. That woman is bad vibes through and through … She overwhelms the real you.'

I scrunch my sleeve over my wrist, looking down at my lap. I feel my upper lip twitch.

'Oh, *fuck,*' Rose says, observing me.

'What?' I can't even look at them.

'You're hiding something.'

'How would you know?'

'Your upper lip twitched. I know you inside out. What's going on?'

I place my hand on my lip, punishing it for revealing me.

'Has she already started running your account for you?'

'No.'

'YOUR LIP TWITCHED AGAIN!'

Rose points at my lip, and I grab their finger. 'Rose, *darling,* stop.'

They yank their finger from my grasp and recline back into the chair. 'You sound so …'

'Chaotic, unhinged, obsessive …? Just a few suggestions!' I smile sarcastically.

'No, you sound different. Take these off …' they say, reaching for my sunglasses. I swat their hand away from my face.

'IT'S ME, DICKHEAD. YOU CAN TRUST ME! Why are you looking at me like I'm some kind of monster right now?' Rose lets out.

'I don't know what to say, Rose. Yeah! I'm all over the place! I don't know what to do or what to tell you. I've gone a bit fucking crazy. I'm making awful choices. I look like shit. It's hard for me to keep up with my own social media presence. I don't know who to trust any more. Everything feels like it's slipping away from me. I can't wank without crying. I take ten naps a day …'

I swallow as they put their head in their hands. 'This is my situation, Rose, not yours, so don't worry about it.'

'*My situation.* You really are so fucking narcissistic, aren't you?'

'What?'

'Today is my fucking birthday and yes, I know you fucking forgot.' They purse their lips tightly. *Oh, God. Please. Don't cry. Do not cry. Rose, do not cry*. They close their eyes before speaking again.

'You think the world revolves around you. I'm trying to help you, Eartha, and I am trying to tell you that this is taking over your life.'

'Rose, listen to me—'

'It's true. You have become EXACTLY the kind of person we used to laugh at. We used to laugh at all these people on their phones, with their heads lost down the rabbit hole of Wonderland obsessed with how they look online.' They throw their hands around, gesturing at the people on their phones.

'Darling, you have no idea what I'm going through because you have no social media presence …'

'Because I don't give a fuck about all of that crap, and neither did you. If you want me to help, you'll have to tell me … "darling".' She air-quotes 'darling'.

'I CAN'T!' I yell.

'You're a frantic mess. Doing all this stuff with your wrists …' They reach over towards me and I flinch. 'Whatever it is you can't tell me – the secret you're keeping from me – it's eating you up and it's splitting us apart. You can't deal with it on your own.

Who else do you have to talk to about it? How's Susie?'

'I dunno …'

'What do you mean you don't know?! You've not even told your own mum what's going on?'

'Me and Mum are still being moody with each other,' I try to explain, while also trying to remember the last interaction I had with her. I conceal my wrists and bury my face into the palm of my hands. I can't take the interrogation.

'You're a lost cause,' they say with no emotion. Those words kick my chest so hard I'm left winded and have to count in my breaths before I am able to speak again. They continue to speak to me with my face in my hands.

'I have tried to pull you out of this shit from day one. It's caused nothing but chaos since you've entered this new fucking world and it's driving a wedge between us. What about my life?' They look over to the corner of the pub. 'Or what about his life?' They point to a man who is looking into the froth of his beer much like someone would look into a crystal ball to discover their future.

'Or does he not matter because he's a "man" and that's bad for your brand now? Because men don't exist unless they are terrible humans. Incels. Monsters. Cheaters. 2D characters who are all inherently bad. You are one person – there are lots of people in this world who are struggling with their life, in real life, not some phantom half-existence through your phone.'

I think the floor's collapsing, or I am.

I'm losing everything.

My mind.

My best friend.

My mum.

My grip on what's real and what isn't.

I push my feet slightly harder into the soles of my shoes, just to check the floor is still there. I am so light-headed that I can't feel my feet. Or maybe I can.

I look up at Rose. My lip starts to quiver and I try to regain control of myself.

'Save the tears.' Rose shrugs. I look for a sign that they believe me in their eyes. A flicker of recognition. Anything. But they look back at me blankly, like a stranger. 'I don't even recognise you any more.'

My hand starts to shake, as I search for something steady to hold onto. I look at the pint in front of me but it's too heavy. I need to find something I know is real. Something to ground me. I can't pick up my phone. I don't trust anything that it tells me.

My hands are trembling. I put them onto my head, to touch my hair. *I'm still real.* I pull a single hair out of my head. And I bring it down to look at. *I can feel this. This is real.*

What day is it? Sunday? I manage to tap the screen of my phone. *Sunday.*

Rose pushes away from the table and stands up from the chair.

'ROSE!' I shout, as they're downing their pint in gulps that must be painful. They get up to leave. 'Can I ask you one question?' I say. They turn around, but only halfway, shunning me in profile. 'You've met E.V? Right?'

Rose has met E.V, I am sure of it. They met in the café. A month ago.

'What the—? What are you doing? Is this some kind of mind game or something?'

'No, I just, I just need to know what's real.'

'Eartha.'

'Tell me. Please. You have seen her, haven't you?'

They shake their head firmly and so finally. I stand up and throw myself across the table. 'JUST TELL ME, HAVE YOU EVER MET E.V?'

The whole pub has stopped talking. Rose turns to face me properly and puts their hands into their pockets. 'I was wrong, earlier,' they moan.

I shake my head in confusion. 'About wha—'

'You are fucking crazy.'

CHAPTER 29

CRAWLING OUT OF MY SKIN

Wonderland followers: 1,417,035

My chewed-up fingernail hovers over Phaedra's picture of her with her friends. If I unfollow her back then it's really over. I look around my flat, at the sombre, dirty space that was once full of life.

Love.

Sex.

Conversations.

Sunsets.

Laughter.

Dancing.

Possibility.

What happened to that Eartha? Clit throbbing in the back of a taxi on her way to a hot date? When I woke up excited to taste the delights of my new life, grateful to be here, to be simply feeling the floor beneath my feet. The Eartha who believed that hating mornings was akin to hating life itself.

And now, I can't stand being awake.

I look at the curtains in my bedroom which are drawn,

holding the sunlight back from me, soaked with my tears from the occasions when I've run out of loo roll. I tug them back so I can look down at the windowsill I shared with Phaedra, now coated in a layer of dust. There are still two faint grease prints in the middle from where our sweaty soles had embraced, a ghost of a good time. I still find the occasional strand of pink hair in my brush, on my carpet or somehow lodged in parts of my existence. Each time it's a break-up exorcism all over again. What's the point in ever getting feelings for someone if this is how it feels when they're taken away from you? Their presence felt in every crevice of your apartment, the woodgrain of your soul and the sentiment in every song? The grief pours out of me from places I didn't know were possible. I'm grieving so much I don't know where to start or who and what to grieve first. In the shower, in certain smells, in the corners of my phone screen, in the skin between my toes.

My life feels like a haunted horror house, tortured by reminders and flashes of the woman I was on my way to becoming. The only things still alive, thriving and flourishing in this flat, are the bacteria cultures growing in my sink and the mould in the corner of my kitchen. I can afford to move out. I just cannot physically bring myself to do it.

The Wonderland Eartha is growing increasingly erratic. The posts are so scarily reflective of the depths of my mind, I've started to consider that maybe I am writing them myself. I'm scrunching my sleeves over my wrists, trying to stop them from shaking. I feel intensely outside of my body, it's become such an unbearable place to inhabit. I wake up with scratch marks on my arms from trying to crawl out of my own skin in my sleep. I've already prepared the list of excuses to tell people. It was the neighbours' cat, or I fell into a bush while I was cycling. Then I realise I have no one to make excuses to.

I wish I could climb out of Wonderland, pulling all these people with me for five minutes: Jaz, Phaedra, the people harassing me, the person who videoed me, all the people who are saying that I need to die. Make them a cup of coffee in my bedsit and ask them what it is that's wrong. Why they're targeting me. Why they're ignoring me. I want to hold their hands, for them to feel my warmth and remind them that I am a whole person. I want to pull them into the real world, where humans exist and no one is shouting at each other, ignoring each other, unfollowing each other or being held to impossible moral standards. I wish I could crawl out of my own skin and live free from the Eartha I'm now a prisoner of. I reach down to wipe the dust with my hand and clear the prints, closing the curtains.

Is the world conspiring to do this to me? Am I living in some sort of simulation designed to make my life confusing? Now that *does* sound crazy ... and narcissistic. I could never say any of this out loud. I sound like a conspiracy theorist.

I wonder what people are saying about me online right now.

I should google my name.

My hands move quicker than my thoughts and before I've fully registered what I am doing, I've googled myself. It's a reflex now, like breathing or blinking. I order the search results to see the latest news. Nothing new. Though I did check only an hour ago.

I erase my name from the search bar and start to type something else into Google.

'Am I bonkers?'

No ... Too vague.

'How do I know if I'm going crazy?'

I press enter.

A whole host of articles pop up.

I click on the first link titled 'What are the first signs that you're going crazy?'

- Sex drive changes (loss of sex drive, high-risk behaviour)
- Episodes of crying
- Excessive hostility or violent impulses
- Suicidal ideation
- Isolating yourself from loved ones
- Extreme mood swings
- Inability to perceive what's real and what's not
- Withdrawal from friends and activities that once brought you joy

The only time I've ever hit full criteria is on a checklist that determines whether you're going insane. I look up at myself over the top of my laptop in the mirror, staring at my reflection.

'This is my right hand,' I say out loud, raising my right hand. 'This is my left hand,' I say out loud, raising my left hand. Good to know that's working. Before I turn to look away, I see E.V in the mirror, not Eartha.

I can't help but feel there's some greater force doing this. Global warming? Misogyny? Astrology? What can I blame? What on earth is happening? I'm starting to morph into my online persona. How the fuck did I forget my Wonderland password? Which way is the traffic flowing? I can't be sure. I look at myself in the mirror. *Am I capable of writing these awful things online? Am I always online nowadays, do I ever turn off? What's more real to me, Wonderland or this flat?*

Wonderland.

Perhaps I can't be trusted with so much power, I'll eventually abuse it. It would appear that everyone around me is leaving me, abandoning me, feeling agitated in my presence. Rose's words ring in my ear. *It's like there are two sides to you.* I start to scratch my arms again. *You think the world revolves around you.* I want to get out of my body. *I don't even recognise you any more.* I scratch harder. When I look through my photos all the pictures I now see are pictures of me – me taking selfies, videos of me, self-timers of me, my life, my lips, my meltdowns, my dating life. Who is more me? The person I have captured and captioned over and over again, or the person who takes the pictures and writes the comments?

I quickly open my emails. I need to test my theory. I need to find something to hold onto. A piece of reality that I know is mine. Something I know is real. I need to test what I can recall that definitely happened and what definitely did not. I type 'E.V' into the search bar to find our first email exchange dated months back.

E.V definitely reached out to me. She told me she'd make me into a star. Then we arranged to meet at The Firestone the next morning. I reach for my phone and search 'firestone' into my text messages. There's a text from Rose and one from Mum.

Text message from Rose to Eartha

11/06/2030 14.04

Good luck at firestone today. I'm proud of you.

Text message from Mum to Eartha

12/06/2030 10.17

Love, let me know about that firestone place! I wanna know if I can get their hand soaps :P

I have a good-luck text from Rose. I read it again. *I'm proud of you.* I want to cry.

At least these texts are proof that I met E.V. That she's even real. But there's something I'm missing …

I click on my junk mail and scroll through. Nothing but third-party newsletters from brands I signed up to for 10 per cent off my first purchase, food-delivery discounts, solicitors who want to help me write my will, updates from podcast hosts I've never heard of.

I can't find anything from E.V.

Nothing.

Has she erased her emails from my laptop? Is that even possible?

A lost intention resurfaces in my mind: who was Velma Quinnley? E.V referenced her once as an old client and I wanted to look into her, but fear or my short attention span got in the way. I open a new tab and type in her name.

A list of articles appears:

> *DROPPED! How Velma Quinnley Lost Herself down the Rabbit Hole*
>
> *Quinnley: Wonderland's Darling Admitted to Psych Ward*
>
> *Velma Quinnley: The Star that Shined too Bright*
>
> *What Women Like Velma Teach Us About Drop Culture*

I go to check her Wonderland page and see that she has been dropped. Her page has been left up, like a graveyard of the person she once was. It's got the transparent grey filter that those who are dropped have. A funeral shroud pulled over her page. I wonder what got to her, or who. I wonder what drove her to this place. Where did it all go wrong? It's all pictures of her doing PR for festivals and posing with DJs on stage, street-style outfit pictures. She had a small gap in posting. Around a few weeks over a year ago. She'd cut her hair and uploaded a selfie from an awkward angle above, with the caption 'New ME, I'm baaaaaack! #Dolus'.

Dolus? I've heard that before. Was it in an email?

I hop back into my email inbox and type it in my search bar. *Nothing.* I click back on my junk email. Before today, I don't think I've actually checked it in five months.

I scroll through to see if anything catches my eye. I spot an actual human name in my junk mail instead of a brand.

From: *Maria Ziltsche (Mziltsche@brownpr.com)*

To: Eartha (eartha_17@gmail.com)

Subject: EXCLUSIVE invite-only PRESS EVENT for Eartha this Thursday

Hello Eartha,

I've sent this through to the email on your Wonderland page but we haven't received a response, so I thought I'd try my luck and give this address a go. I found it on your old website!

My name's Maria Ziltsche, I'm the owner of Browns PR Ltd and we worked on the PR for your FIRE campaign! I'm reaching out on behalf of Good Vybrations, they're a brand-new sex-toy company championing self-pleasure for vulva owners in a way that's never been done before. They're launching the world's first pulsating dildo called 'Woman Propeller' that you can stick to any surface. They'd love you to join them for the launch of Woman Propeller this Thursday at 7 p.m. at Miltron House.

Please RSVP to this email if you'd like to come. I'm very excited about what you're building. I'd love to meet you and thank you personally for helping me find the courage to leave my ex-boyfriend. He was a piece of shit.

Best,

Maria Ziltsche

A dick you can stick on the wall that pulsates and you don't have to experience the smell? The taste? The frightening prospect of emotional dependency you get with fucking actual men? This sounds unbelievable. When did she send me this email? Two days ago? Shit, this Thursday … it's tonight. Can I go?

I instinctively pick up my phone to text E.V and ask her. But then I stop myself. Do I need to ask her permission? She didn't send me this email and she's definitely seen it. I have a feeling that if I ask her, she'll say no. But if this Maria person wants to talk to me about a future collaboration with this brand, perhaps I can prove to E.V that I am still capable of being a businesswoman after all. Maybe this is my chance to make it up with E.V. She might give me my account back. I want to make her feel good about working with me again. Remind her of the Eartha she once met with a fire in her belly. The Eartha she believed could light thousands of candles with her flame.

I close the laptop and look at myself in the mirror. *Does the woman looking back deserve a little party and a free sex toy before she admits herself to a facility for her blatant narcissistic personality disorder?*

I look around my room, I look for a sign, something to tell me what to do. I get up from my bed and walk over to my door to rummage through the contents of my bag that hangs off the handle. I plunge in and dig deep. Receipts, hairbands, tampons … my purse. I pull it out and look inside. I find a penny and remove it.

Which of the coin's two faces will determine who I become for the night? My mum always said that the way to really know how you feel about something is whether you feel disappointed or relieved after flipping the coin.

Heads I go, tails I stay home. I throw it up into the air and catch it between my hands.

Tails.

CHAPTER 30

THE FUTURE IS ~~FEMINIST~~ PHALLIC

Wonderland followers: 1,496,880

I'm handed a glass of blast freezer-chilled champagne from a waiter in a pair of red leather chaps as soon as I enter the party. Waiters of all genders circulate the room. Some of the waitresses have their tits out, some wear coordinating leather bras. I don't know where to look. I wonder how any of us are supposed to feel comfortable. I walk into the centre of the blood-red-draped room and get offered a cupcake with edible metal baubles and the word 'SEX' piped on top. A tray of a dildo-shaped glittery glasses with something creamy inside is offered up to me. If this is the future of feminism, it's strikingly phallic. I'm comforted at the sight of a woman standing by the bar who necks her dildo drink, turns it upside down, shakes it dry and shoves the erect glass into her tote bag. She catches me looking and grimaces, laughing at herself.

I register a woman wearing a pink lanyard, black business suit and clipboard racing towards me. She flares her nostrils and exhales with an entire sentence in her mouth, 'EARTHA-oh-my-didn't-think-you-would-make-it-do-you-like-the-vagina?'

It takes me a second to comprehend anything she has said. I reply slowly, 'You must be Maria and yes I love vaginas, but whose?'

'THIS VAGINA!!' she says, gesturing towards the red room. She goes on without pausing for breath, 'Oh I'm so, so, so, so THRILLED you got the email … mwah.' She goes in for the air kiss and I remain motionless for fear of obstructing her mouth. Is this an industry thing? Close up she really does look thrilled and, on second glance, a little high too.

Rose is right: I am becoming the kind of person we hate.

'So, the step and repeat board is over there …' she says, pointing to a short queue in front of a wall with 'Good Vybrations' logos printed all over it.

'The … step and repeat what?'

She looks at me, like I have told her that the rats have been at my bins again, then looks down at her clipboard. 'We've got you down here to have your picture taken for our socials, the picture will be uploaded to Getty Images so we can use them for the press release for the launch of Woman Propeller,' she says, flicking her wrist as if a mosquito is circling her.

She scrunches her face up with the discomfort of having to say something revolting out loud to this unseasoned influencer – *We give you free shit so we can use your image.*

'This is my first ever solo … event.'

'I had no clue – how very strange.' Her nostrils swell at the strangeness of it all. 'Okay, babes, let's walk you over to the photoboard and then you can enjoy the rest of the night!' I realise her line about her breaking up with her boyfriend at the bottom of her email was likely a ploy to get me to attend the event. She probably doesn't have a boyfriend at all.

'So, I've given the photographer your name, he's waiting for you, you can just skip the queue ...' She walks me over to the photoboard, I can see the repeated logos on the board a lot clearer now: Good Vybrations X FIRE.

'Oh, I didn't know FIRE worked with sex-toy companies!' I exclaim with way more excitement than I feel.

'Yes, they're the sponsor for the event! Some of the people from the campaign you worked on will be here tonight, I need to introduce you later ...' She lifts the red rope in front of the mini red carpet which has tiny, glittery cock confetti all over it. A queue of influencers glare at me like they want to wrap their selfie-preened knuckles on me for skipping the queue.

'People are queueing ... I'll just go to the back! I don't need to skip.'

'No, Eartha, you don't have to do *all* that, your likeability is almost one hundred per cent ...' she scoffs, all white porcelain veneers, like I should just 'know' that I deserve to be prioritised over the other guests. As though hierarchy is a self-evident thing. There is nothing self-evident about acting just like the merchandise she's trying to sell. I hesitate before I move forward, as though by cutting in front of the other girls, I'm co-signing this awful woman's opinion that I am better and worthy of special treatment.

'That's David, he knows you.' She points to the man knelt in front of the board behind the rope with a camera in his hands, looking up at us eagerly. His name tag reads 'Rick'. 'Then we'll upload them straight onto Getty and you can use them for your Wonderland page tonight, as soon as possible, or immediately ...'

I wave sheepishly back at the man. I'm still not sure what the

Getty pedigree means. But it seems to mean a lot to other people. So, I guess it must be important. That's how most of this fame stuff goes. Reach vaguely notable benchmarks of success that are recognised by your peers, even if it's something that means very little to you. Maria is standing back with her clipboard tucked under her arm, her phone poised to film the moment as I go to stand in front of her brand's name. Her mind is already puzzling out the Wonderland caption. I'm about to suggest 'Eartha of Wonderland, the face that launched a thousand pricks' when I realise I can't be seen out. E.V doesn't know I'm here.

'Maria, will my name be attached to the pictures?'

'Of course!' she laughs with total insincerity. The subtext is very clear this time. *That's the whole point!*

I'm 99.99 per cent sure that E.V has a Google alert on my name. If I'm pictured at this event she'll know that I went behind her back.

'I can't have my picture taken, then.' I step aside and apologise to Rick for holding up the queue. I pull a devastated Maria back with me. 'My face belongs exclusively to Wonderland . . .' Which may as well be true.

'Really, is that a new clause?' She looks at me as if I just shat on her shoe.

'But I'll review the Woman Propeller after I've had a few goes with your prick . . .'

'OH, EXCELLENT!' She flares her nostrils and flashes her veneers again. Subtext: *Thank God! I didn't invite the unhinged feminist woman to my event for nothing!*

'My followers will love it, it's very on-brand for me!' I beam back. Subtext: *I don't even have access to the people I've built a digital community with.*

'Well, you can collect your goody bag on your way out at the end of the night. The performance is just about to start!'

'The what?'

The overhead lights in the room start to dim and the waiters walk in unison, forming a line at the back of the room in front of the bar. A red neon light turns on, revealing a stripper's pole on a square plinth about four feet from the ground. I didn't notice in the blood-red gloom, but there's a runway lined with pink velvet sofas and chaise longues. Everyone's rushing to grab a spot in the vagina tunnel. The guests look like they've been waiting for this performance all night. I swoop another glass of now room-temperature champagne from a tray and seat myself in front of the stripper's pole. The lights go down and are replaced with the glow of phone screens ready to record whatever is about to happen. I'd whack mine out too, if I wasn't here secretly – I'm forced to live in the moment. I can hear the shushing of guests and then a haunting jingly guitar riff starts playing on speakers all around the room. It's so loud, I feel like I'm inside the song. The song's familiar, but I can't place it. A figure emerges from within the red light. All the phones now swivel and point towards the silhouette of a woman with long dark hair and stripper heels who is descending the runway, moving her hips in a slow, choreographed way. *Day of the Lords.* Holy shit, is this woman about to pole dance to Joy Division? Just before the guitar kicks in, she runs up to the end of the runway and in one swoop reaches up to grab the pole and spins her entire body around it. Her hair whips the air and her body cascades down the pole. I can hear phone clicks as people start filming the performance. My body flares up and heat rushes to my face. Everything and everyone around her vanishes. I can only see her, glowing underneath the red light above the pole. I'm no longer concerned about what I'm doing with my face, my hands or my body as I have been for weeks now. I cease to exist. This woman is art. She holds the pole with her hands between her legs, wide open in the shape of a V as she slowly descends it. With every lash of her hair that strikes the air, I'm reminded of how truly gay I am. Outside of Wonderland, outside of algorithms, outside of E.V and all the jobs I've been told to do. Outside of all these industry people using my sexuality to make themselves look better.

The song fades out and the lights dim as her body spins, until she reaches the bottom and the room goes pitch black once more. The overhead lights come back on and the room is silent. The woman is gone. Was there a trapdoor? Was she even there at all, or had my deepest desires manifested themselves on stage? The room bursts into clapping and people are spinning their phones onto themselves to look amazed at the end of their videos. I look around with my mouth open – where did she go? How did she exit? Who is she? That was the most mesmerising performance I've ever seen. I'm still sat in my seat, unable to move, my knickers soaked.

The thumbing melodic party music comes back on and I watch as everyone gets up from their seats to continue with their networking and posting. How is everyone carrying on with their lives? Wasn't that the most transcendent thing they have ever witnessed? I haven't felt desire like this for weeks. Like part of the tethered soul that lingers above my body in Wonderland has started to come back into me. I'm reminded of the beauty of desire and of the experiences I have yet to come and I have this urge to talk to someone about it immediately. I walk back over towards the bar, scouring the room, half hoping I'll run into the dancer so I can tell her how alive she has made me feel. I spot the dildo-glass-stealer and head over to her.

'Wasn't that fucking incredible?' I shout, to make myself heard.

'Yes! Right?!'

I neck the rest of my champagne. 'I think that performance just made me realise that I want to continue living after all,' I exclaim, slamming the glass down. She looks at me like I just delivered some awful news about her pet.

Oh. I forgot. Oversharing to strangers doesn't go down as well offline …

She looks down at me with pity and her eyes land on my forearms. She's noticed the scratches. She smiles at me uncomfortably and slowly backs away.

'I have a cat, a cat did it!' I shout. But it's too late. She's buggered off. I shrug my shoulders and look to the waiter next to me, with a fully replenished tray of champagne.

'Can I have another one?' I ask with my hand out.

'Have you never heard of an open bar?' the waiter laughs at me. I abruptly laugh back. I snatch another glass, throwing back my first sip. *Wait, wasn't excessive alcohol consumption on the checklist for being crazy?*

I try to drown out the voice in my head. I raise my glass for another sip and feel a tap on my shoulder. I turn around to see a woman: low bun, low black vest top, not sure if it's a bottle tan or if she's just got back from holiday.

'Eartha! Wow, it's so good to meet you in person. Maria told me you were here.' There's such familiarity in her tone that I don't feel at all.

'Do we know each other?' I smile, placing my empty glass

down on the bar. My eyes widen. *Christ, did I finish that one already?*

'OH! Apologies, we never actually got to meet. I'm Emma, I work at FIRE. I was the one who put you up for your campaign for us. And we're sponsoring the event tonight ...' She raises her hands, pointing to the multiple FIRE logos around the room.

'Oh, Emma!' I say, as though E.V has mentioned her name to me and I stupidly forgot this pivotal main character in my rise to fame. Time to make her feel important. 'Thank you so much. That was one of my first big jobs, you know ... I've not been doing this for a long time,' I say, already reaching for another glass. My forearm comes out of my sleeve as it extends to grab the champagne and I catch her looking, she opens her mouth to speak.

'CATS!' I gesture, making a claw with my fingers.

Was that a strange or normal thing to do? I redirect the conversation. 'So, how's your evening been?'

'Oh, it's been wonderful, thank you! Just closed a few deals before the weekend with a few new Wonderland up-and-comings. We love working with fresh talent. People who care about things, people who are current, colourful, fabulous, diverse ...' She's talking about queer people like we're little collectible tokens. She's one descriptor away from an actual slur.

I swig my drink back. 'Emma, can I ask you a question?'

'Sure, what?' She straightens her back.

'Do you make all of your bisexual talent sign contracts that say they can't date men? Feels a little outdated, doesn't it? And it's actually caused me a few problems, I kissed this guy and ...'

Oh God, I'm so drunk. Shut the fuck up. Why are you still speaking?

E.V would kill you if she knew you were doing this right

now...*EARTHA, DARLING, you're drunk and half crazy. STOP, DARLING!*

But I don't stop: 'Well, I loved working with you, but it felt reaaaaaaaaaaaaaally controlling. I felt really suffocated by it.' I place my hands around my throat and stick my tongue out, faking a choke.

'No, that clause was just for you. The boss fought prrrrrretty hard on that one!' She nods her head before she sips her flute.

'What d'ya mean? I was the only one who had that clause in their contract ... just me?' I say more scrappily.

With a mouthful of champagne, she nods her head.

'SCUSE me?!' I laugh. 'Does your boss have it in for me? Did I fuck his wife or something?' I roll back my eyes and lean myself onto the bar. With another mouthful of champagne, she starts waving her hand in front of my face to suggest I've misunderstood her. She swallows.

'No! Eartha ...' She laughs at me. '*Your* boss fought to put it in.'

'My boss?'

'I know it's something they were insistent about and we managed to get it signed off at FIRE to be able to work with you. It's not something we'd ever done before, the ...' she snaps her fingers, trying to conjure the words between her fingertips,'... the ban, on dating men. But they insisted that it be put into your contract as part of the terms as Wonderland really felt it chimed with their more ...diverse portfolio. We did think it was odd, but we love what you do and ...' *They?* Who is she referring to?

Something catches her attention and she looks off to the side. I throw my head back and erupt sharply into a loud cackle.

'What's ... what's funny?' she asks, looking at me self-consciously as though I've seen something in her teeth.

'It's just … oh my God. This is …fuck. I thought FIRE put the clause in there … I'm sorry, can you say that again?' I laugh.

'Say what?'

'The thing you just said … I need to know this is real. Lately I've been feeling like I'm going crazy and I just need to make sure you absolutely just said what I think you did. It might just be the missing part to everything I've been confused about …' I reach into my bag to grab my phone and open up the voice notes, putting it in front of her mouth.

She looks at me with a face full of pity and pushes my phone away from her face. 'Look, Eartha …' she says condescendingly. I drop my face of excitement.

'What? Why do people keep looking at me like that?'

'I know you're going through a hard time lately.'

'You … do?'

'Yeah, you've been talking all about it on Wonderland, haven't you?'

'Have I?' I ask curiously, leaning in.

I don't know what I want to do more, disintegrate into a million tiny pieces and cease to exist or actually try to google myself to catch up with the persona being created of me online.

'Eartha, have you had a lobotomy or something?' she scoffs. 'Oh sorry, that's probably an insensitive use of language, isn't it? I know you're having a hard time with your depression and the …' she tries to pluck the most comfortable words to use, 'mental illness, stuff, at the moment …'

'It … it just seems you think you know so much about it …' I stutter.

'It's your ENTIRE Wonderland account at the moment, though, isn't it? You're online ALL the time. Also, I keep an eye on all our partners … So yes, I suppose I feel I do know a lot about it. Well, only what you've shared anyway.'

'Yes, yes, all the … stuff I've been posting. But what is that exactly?' I tilt my head, searching her face for the answers. I haven't checked it all day. She purses her lips and gives me another look of pity.

'Oh, bless you. It will get better. I promise. This industry is tough. So many people can't handle it, the fame, the attention … not to mention how fast-moving it all is. Velma, poor girl, she started accusing Wonderland of controlling her, and … It was really uncomfortable for so many of us involved.' She looks at me. 'Oh, but of course, you're nothing like her! I think it all just got to her head, the fame stuff … It's some people's dream come true but it's someone else's hell hole. Did you always want that? You know, to be famous?'

I don't answer her question because the truth is, I don't know the answer. Being a known person wasn't a reality I ever considered for my life. It's not something I ever would have dreamed up for myself. It was E.V's dream. I just wanted to earn some money, get the hell out of that flat and become a respected artist. I decide to dig for more about Velma. 'What was her name again?'

'Velma Quinnley, darling? She was dropped from Wonderland, so they have her profile up behind a grey screen now. You've probably seen her portrait at The Firestone, hanging up on the wall above the bar, where they put all the big "Wonderland women".' She gestures at the nearest wall with her hand. 'Perhaps … you'll be up there soon.' She nods but I can tell she doesn't mean a word of it. In these heels I'm taller than her but still she finds a way to look down at me. I remember the portraits of women, all looking out onto the vibrant and bustling floor of businessmen.

'Oh, God, yeah, she sounds a bit weird, this Velma girl!' I reply in cool-girl-industry-party talk.

'She just had to take a break for a while to recover from it all. She had gone fully online … she basically lived there.' She looks away as though this whole conversation has become toxic. She beams at me, but her eyes look panicked, as though she's revealed too much, or maybe she's just completely run dry of things to say to me. I wait it out while my mind scrambles together all of this new information. And then relief pours through her stiff eyes as she notices something behind me, like she's finally spotted her knickers on the floor so she can get up and exit a regrettable one-night stand. I think of all the funny and tortured things that are about to come out of her mouth …

'Oh, look who it is?'

She looks at me and back at the people behind.

I smell him before I see him. My senses recoil from the scent that has been haunting me. I follow her eyeline and turn around.

In walks E.V, arm in arm with …

Him.

And for the first time in a long time, my heart is not in my phone, but in my throat.

CHAPTER 31

STRANGE YOUNG WOMAN

Wonderland followers: 2,500,004
Likeability: 98%

What's scary is how human he suddenly appears. He has pores. Teeth. Shoelaces. My eyes zoom in with laser focus on the mass of hairs that cover his forearms like thorns. I register him now as a person rather than the deep shame lodged to my side.

My feet move towards *them.*

'IT WAS YOU!' I scream at him.

The music stops. Everyone turns. My words are all slurry outbursts and half-formed realisations. We lock eyes. He's talking but no words are coming out, or perhaps I can't hear them. My mouth flickers maniacally. My head begins to sway as I stare at *them.* My vision starts swimming; I look at everyone, looking at me. I witness myself in the third person. It's all blurry lights, phone cameras pointed at me with the flashes piercing through their pinholes, waiters with their tits out and open mouths gaping.

'Who are you talking to?' a voice – E.V, I think – says.

My body jolts backwards as though dodging a punch. It

happened. It did. *He* did. He locked me in the room at the party.

He's stood now, metres from me, but I can feel his grip on my wrists and the weight of his body on mine and I want to run.

My fingernails move instinctively to scratch my arms, but I stop myself, remembering that everyone here is recording me. I am viral content, once more an unintentional spectacle, a mess of a woman being uploaded for other people to witness in live time.

If only they knew the truth. Would they believe me then?

I hear the sniggers of people behind their phones. I feel the life drain from me into their phones, bolstering their popularity in the process as they livestream my meltdown. I hear the *pings* as comments flood in on their screens.

I look at his face.

From the soles of my feet I feel something rise up through my body. Something pulsating and hot flares into my knee joints, it surges up into my stomach and burns my organs with its acid; it's a poison, an anger I didn't know existed within me. It flows up into my chest, wrapping itself around my lungs until they are enveloped by it. It finally ricochets up, piercing my mind in a single bullet of truth.

This entire time, the night of the party, E.V convincing me to remain silent, my password changing, the extreme posts on Wonderland, being drawn closer and closer to insanity, all of this ...to protect *him.*

It was never my secret she wanted to protect, it was his.

It wasn't about protecting my career, it was about protecting his.

I'm so drunk, but I can still just about make out the corner of his mouth mocking me, working overtime to reflect a different version of reality. One where I'm crazy and he's not a predator.

He doesn't even seem frightened of the truth. Or being exposed. He's eerily calm in his power.

'Can someone escort this strange young woman out of here, please?' his voice says.

'YOU *RUINED* ME!' I scream at him and then, spinning around, I scream it again to all the camera lenses trailing me. 'YOU ALL RUINED ME!'

The flashes all point in my direction. I'm at the epicentre of this public shaming ritual. I'm the hunted. I realise Wonderland is just a modern version of a witch trial with its baying online mob. I stand before their eyes and their phones as the next digital sacrifice.

I feel E.V's fingertips brush the back of my neck up and down, trying to soothe me.

I hate her.

I love her.

I am her.

'You've ...' I stammer, '*you've* done this to me, you work for *him?*'

I see a security guard's arm reach for me and I move backwards away from them. He grabs my arm and I fling it up to release myself. There are gasps all around me. I spin round, ducking from his reach, and crash my body against the staff doors near the vagina tunnel. I push through into a startled kitchen where a woman is leaning over a silver catering trolley piping 'SEX' on top of more cupcakes. There is a tray of glacé cherries prepped ready for a waiter to pick them up; on the tray are cards with 'pop your #GoodVybrations cherry' on them. I run through, find the fire-exit door and yank it open. I'm in an alleyway covered in bin bags. I stick my head as near to the bins as I can before I throw up the sex cupcakes and champagne. I heave and heave. Purging it all out of my system: Dylan's cologne, E.V's lies, the stupid white fucking VENEERS, the expensive hand soap, all of it. As I stand upright the memory of my ritual with Mum on the porch resurfaces: Mum pulling me outside away from the chaos of Dad.

I hear someone laughing and shoot my eyes sideways in the direction of the sound. There are two women who followed me through the kitchen, filming me on their phones. One of them turns around and switches her camera to selfie-mode. 'Here you have it, Wonderland, your "voice of a generation" hurling up in the garbage to which she belongs.'

I shield myself from their lenses and am forced to turn to face the bins once more. I spot little silver baubles in my gentrified, glittery cow pat of puke. My whole body is trembling, but my instinct tells me I need to get out of this alleyway and find safety.

Before they know that I know.

But where is safe for me now? My flat feels like it doesn't belong to me. I can't go to Rose's and risk involving them. I think I'll call Mum. I need her, I can't do this on my own. My phone is lodged in my trouser pocket, I quickly jam my fingers in to tweezer it out but I can't get a steady grip. The phone falls out and smashes face down on the tarmac. There's a cracking sound that tells me the screen is broken and shot into a thousand tiny fractures.

I pick it up and turn it over. I catch a glimpse of myself in its refracted screen, all severed onto different pieces. I look like E.V. And I realise then that E.V is the woman I will become, E.V is who I will be in a few years, picking off the scraps of other women to gain more power in a world that was built for neither of us. As much as I desired the wisdom that comes with her age, she too desired the beauty of my youth. We both extracted one from the other. We're two sides of the same coin, feeling as though the other's quality is superior to her own by the sheer fact that we are not in possession of it. We've both been made to feel as though we are works in progress in different areas – so that we remain in a constant state of improvement and living in fear and mistrust of one another. Does she know that? That she too is stuck chasing something that will never be enough?

I throw my phone onto the floor, stamp the heel of my shoe into it and run.

I just run.

Even when I am out of breath and my lungs can't keep up and my abdomen is riddled with stitches, I run until the streets are unfamiliar. I don't know how long I've been running. I just need to get far enough away from everything and everyone that has invaded my life over the last few months. I take roads I've never seen and run past people I'll never meet. I spot groups of people sat on benches drinking tinnies and people fondling in the dark. For a second I think I see a ghost, but it is just my reflection.

I run through a canal pathway and past people having candlelit, al fresco dinners with what they consider to be the loves of their life. The more I run, the more I merge into one. For the first time in my life, I screw up my face and cry in public without wondering if I look pretty while I do it. Ugly, pounding sobs pour out of me with each thump of my foot on the ground, pedalling myself further and further into the night.

Everything is coming back. All the repressed pain. I begin to relive everything my body was trying to protect me from feeling: the night of the party. The shock, the hurt, the sensation of his aggressive touch. I need something to drown it all out.

A corner shop catches my eye, lit up with e-cigarette neon signs and mobile-phone branding. It glistens at me through the shine of my tears. I turn around to make sure no one's been following me. It feels a long way away from where I was. I feel safer. I slow my pace and compose myself as I enter the quiet, fluorescently lit shop. A ginger cat greets me and grazes its soft head against my ankle. I make my way through a gallery of shelves stocked with brightly coloured tropical juices, fizzy sweets and miscellaneous charging cables. Lodged between synthetic ham sweating in its plastic packet and pre-made samosas, my hand yanks a chilled bottle of prosecco by the neck from the cooler: it's the last in its column, revealing the mirrored back of the fridge. I see the state of myself reflected in it and decide this time I'll make no effort to wipe the mess of streaming make-up from my face. It's time Eartha started to look how she feels on the inside. Broken, imperfect. A woman finally in touch with her pain, her rage, her hurt, her anger. A body that is alive and has been lived in. I take the bottle to the till. I ask for a packet of cigarettes. I'm not sure how I pay.

I walk past houses and look into their windows: I see a couple sat watching TV with their arms affectionately around one another, another couple arguing and pointing their fingers at each other, a group of women sat on the pavement with their heads drooped and their phones turned upright in their palms as they wait for their cabs to take them home. I step over the guts of an upturned burger box and think to myself, *Me too*.

I walk until I find a park, the trees stand tall and grand above me, forming neat columns along each side of the path ahead, hardly moving in the stillness of the night. I unlatch the creaky cast-iron gate and walk onto the concrete path, stopping to sit at the first bench I find, and open the prosecco between my legs.

I think back to the evening of the party. I swig the prosecco and think of the portraits of women at The Firestone and the ones hanging up in his house – the faces of women dead behind the eyes, imprisoned in their frames, paralysed from engaging with the world as they look on at the action. I think of their symmetry with women's selfies and images trapped in the screens of their phones. We are all trophies to these men, things which are theirs to commission and objectify. Where are these women now? Are their souls tethered like mine to the metaverse while someone else runs their account for them? Are they rotting away in their bedrooms, decomposing alongside their plants?

There is something else here, something I didn't want to acknowledge. The root of what a lot of these online avatars and Wonderland users were telling me is true. I am privileged. Even if my dad treated me and Mum like shit growing up. Even if I am a woman and men have played with my body and emotions as though I'm a doll. While, yes, there are many elements working to drag me down, there are many more that are working to propel me up.

As my thoughts slow down and begin to settle, more sensations start to surface. I throw back another swig of prosecco, planning to drink the entire bottle with the aim of self-obliterating. Being in this body and feeling the things that have happened to it are what I've been running from and now it's all catching up with me. I've broken my best friend's heart, my relationship with my mum is dislocated and Phaedra…fucking Phaedra doesn't fucking care.

But above everything I know that what he did to me was violent.

And I'm finally feeling it.

I realise without any emotional reaction that Dylan is E.V's ex-husband, the one who broke her but she couldn't remove herself from. *It's him.* How long had I suspected this? Or is this a new revelation? The man who took everything because he had everything, including her own income stream. How many women have E.V and he done this to? Built up only to be torn down? Women they have manufactured to counter the culture they have created and fuel users' addictions to Wonderland?

I was their queer clean-up woman who hates men so much she won't even date them contractually, the woman who created the perfect progressive storm for their algorithm – until he tried to take too much. Until he blurred the line between using a woman's image and using a woman's body. Dylan felt too powerful and E.V was *his* clean-up woman. They created a mess out of me instead of addressing the poison they had allowed to fester and grow at the root. I was just another Velma in a long line of women used and abused for social media's gain.

Does she know he's assaulted me? My mind can't compute or relate these two versions of her as the same person. The woman who felt like the mother I never had, with the woman who's tried to cover up sexual assault by damaging my reputation. The woman who admired me for my openness about my bisexuality, with the woman who placed a clause in my contract to stop me from dating men. The woman who looked at me as though I was the child she never had, with the woman who failed to protect me when I needed her. *She was supposed to protect me.*

I've completely lost track of time but the sky is beginning to lighten and I can hear the birds chirping awake in the trees. The air is cold, not enough to make me shiver but enough to spray goosebumps across my bare skin. There's dew forming on the grassy hill in front of me, framing the bottom of the city ahead. My eyes are full of tears. The sky starts to turn pink as the sun rises, bracing herself to grace Olympia and wake us all up. Where the first thing we will turn to is not the sky, not the person lying next to us, but our phone screens.

And, in this moment, I feel beautifully insignificant.

DIRECTOR'S NOTE

Camera A: Shot of Eartha in profile, sat on the park bench with the sun rising in front of her; a soft peachy glow graces her face. Her legs are spread as she gazes into the sunrise with her camisole, flared jeans and heels on. Her make-up is smudged and she has a sheen of sweat across her forehead. Her face is awash with sadness but, as she looks out, a flicker of hope surfaces.

Camera A pans around to the front of Eartha. A shrouded Velma Quinnley takes a seat next to her and looks directly at the camera. Then, first in tens and then finally in their hundreds, women move out of the darkness into the frame. Those who have been dropped from Wonderland, hurt by men like Dylan. They stand, all looking out with Eartha.

1st dropped woman: Someone, somewhere in the world, just told a stranger to kill themselves from an anonymous account and the person on the receiving end will, at the very least, contemplate why they should do it.

2nd dropped woman: Someone, somewhere in the world,

just sent a sext to the person they're dating that will cause the person on the receiving end to be turned on.

3rd dropped woman: Someone, somewhere in the world, just told a woman she needs to lose weight and she will make herself sick tonight because of it.

4th dropped woman: Someone, somewhere in the world, just sent a text of hope to someone who didn't think they wanted to carry on living any more, and they'll live another day because of it.

FADE TO BLACK

ENDS

Wonderland Followers: 1,981,912 and declining in the hundreds every millisecond
Likeability: 0%

CHAPTER 32

ALL THAT I WAS BECAME YOURS

Eartha's viral video transcript:

Hi, Wonderland.

It's Eartha on a burner account.

The 'real' Eartha.

I am here to tell you all that I'm not insane. That I'm not a liar. But that I have been abused by the powerful. And that I want to raze Wonderland to the ground.

How am I going to do that? you must be asking yourself. With the only shred of power I have left: the truth.

The internet has no face, you can't reach out your hand to touch it or read its expression. If you look away from your phone screen it ceases to be in your presence, it doesn't sit alongside you or take up too much leg space. Yet, it continues to influence and penetrate every single facet of your life. Even if you shut yourself off from it, the consequences of the online world in our 'real world' are intensifying day by day. Wars, love affairs, ideologies, all exchanged, viewed and experienced on invisible frequencies through the airwaves.

It gives us closer and more intimate access to everyone; those we want to be close to us and those who live in realms beyond our own existence. It makes us feel that we understand them, their lives and their mindsets. We are all intimately engaged with one another. You think you know me, don't you? But you don't, just as I don't know you.

For years there's been a voice inside my head telling me 'you deserve more', so much so that it had begun to feel like a threat. When I met E.V, my social media manager and Wonderland guide after going viral, it finally felt as though this inner voice had found a human form. She told me that she was going to make me the bright shiny thing of Wonderland. I'd been waiting for a woman like her my entire life. Someone who could help me find my purpose. I felt chosen. She promised me everything I wanted. I signed a contract with her to manage me into a version you would fall in love with.

The 'Eartha' *you* know was created on that day.

My persona was manufactured for your public consumption. I became the human representation of your optimised keyword search. Any qualities that were mine or had previously belonged to me were all used to market me as a product of your desire. You owned me because I was a reflection of you. Every moment you have interacted with anyone online – any purchase, any search term, any hashtag on the privacy of your phone – helped to create and build me. I was made in your image and that's why you fell in love with me.

I really wanted you all to like me. I saw you all as my friends. As my lifelines. You provided me with something I'd never felt: a belonging, a community. Where my voice had been downtrodden in my life, you all made me feel finally heard and I started to do anything to keep your attention ... As much as *you used me*, told me what to do, who to be, what to eat, who to fuck

– *I used you, too.* I imagine many of your nervous systems have been fried due to my incessant posting and constant demands for seeking 'justice'. I was encouraged to polarise you against each other, to keep you all 'enraged and engaged'.

I woke up every day to discover *you*: how many of you had followed me, commented on me and liked me. It helped me to modify myself into a better prototype. E.V and I created a living algorithm out of my page. I didn't recognise the person I was becoming because I was becoming a program, a data-gathering source for everyone's needs.

But this psychic split widened, and I could no longer remain whole. I couldn't live up to how much you needed me to be *everything* for *everyone* and still remain Eartha. I was too human. I made human errors. I kissed the wrong people, I was an animal murderer, I had sex with a woman who ran out of my flat to upload pictures of my life while her side of the bed was still warm next to me. I couldn't keep my feelings out of it. There was too much flesh on me and blood in me for you to like me for long. Because I reminded you *of you*.

All that was left of me was a tiny pleading voice: tell me you love me, that I've changed your fucking life! Publicly humiliate me next, I don't mind! Make-up routine, I'll do it! Tell me I'm the best! Tell me I'm not doing enough! Flat tour, I'll try! You think I am being too performative? I'll change! Be more queer? I'll try! You want me to die? I'll go low profile! Love me! Hate me! See me! Be me!

One day I was the voice of a generation and the next I was the voice of a generational problem. I wasn't, and am still not, a binary algorithm. I'm something that exists in a space in between.

Invited by my manager, I went to a Wonderland party to

meet the men behind the machine. Something happened to me that night that changed everything. I met one of the founders of Wonderland, D. B. Firestone. You'll know him from the front cover of *TIME*. He even has a Netflix documentary about his genius. A lot of them do. He owns more global wealth than Olympia's entire economy. He bought the dating app FIRE. He owns a chain of hotels and restaurants including The Firestone. It's harder to find out what he doesn't own or have majority shares in, than what he does. Dylan *is* the industry. He controls so much of your life, and you don't even know it. He has deep pockets and deep power. It's hard to know where his power stops. The videos you have been watching and sharing of me on Wonderland, screaming at an unseen man, called 'EARTHA BECUMS CRAZY'? Well, that unknown man is D. B. Firestone. I am screaming at him because he assaulted me at the Wonderland party. I tried to leave the room but he'd locked me in it. I can already hear the comments flooding in from outraged people asking why I walked into the room in the first place. I can already hear people blaming me, checking my Wonderland profile to see what I might have been wearing that evening. But this is a man who knew his power over me, more than I knew it myself.

I don't remember how I got home that night. I was told not to speak about it. Who would believe me? You didn't even like me any more, having almost dropped me. E.V told me to stay quiet, she employed others to tell me to lie low and I lived in fear of what this man could do to me if I was to speak out. She sought to control me more deeply. You and she were all I had left. You both drew me further and further apart from my friends, my mum … and myself. And so I stayed locked inside my flat and inside Wonderland. My body hurt, I wanted to crawl out of my skin and I often gave in for days to the stillness of sleep. I didn't want to be here.

Did you know in some cultures they call victims of assault 'walking corpses'? This kind of shame has led some women to douse themselves in petrol and set themselves on fire because they didn't want to live with their body any more. I've felt outside of my real and online skin for months.

E.V offered to take over my Wonderland. And she did. The 'me' you've been witnessing online for the last month was written and directed by E.V and you all loved me even more than the first time round. She turned me into an extreme Wonderland voicebox, an untrustworthy woman on the verge of a public mental breakdown and you all followed in your hundreds of thousands for front-row seats. She assassinated my character to fix a man's abuse of power. She was owned by him and in return she destroyed me for him.

My likeability is at 0% and my reputation continues to be run into the ground by a team of people ensuring their representation of the truth is what you see. The tape has been placed over my mouth for long enough and I feel a responsibility to make sure no woman is ever hurt by them again. I know it's highly likely there are other girls out there like me who have been hurt by him and by the world he has created. If I am to truly be the best, most optimised version of myself, I have to expose what's really going on and what you are being controlled by, what he has done and what he continues to do.

The thing is, as much as our Wonderland arenas feel like ours, they aren't. They were built and are run by powerful men. Women are used as puppets to generate more engagement on Wonderland, whether that's our rise or our fall. We sit passively in our screens like we have sat within frames of artworks for centuries. They choose when we are lifted and when we are dropped. We still want our pound of digital flesh, our modern-day sacrifice and our witch hunt – and they create a space for it to take place.

I was made out to be crazy. So have millions of other women. But we do it to each other too. We call each other names, we leave one another out of things, we withhold connection from one another because we believe that everything is so fucking scarce, as if we're begging for a fold-up seat at some bullshit table with these bullshit men. Wonderland is just a reflection of this history playing out before our very eyes, disguised as something empowering. It's coordinated misogyny wrapped in a dazzling bow, using us as its mouthpiece to trick us all into thinking it's validating.

I've led these campaigns against people myself – for things they didn't even do, for things I perceived as 'offensive'. I've done it too and I believe for that I deserve what I have been delivered. I saw avatars, not human beings. I didn't see the people I was doing this to … I also realise now that many of the things you were saying about me were true. Not only that my lens on the world is limited, but that I am privileged and was too clouded by what was going on in my life to acknowledge that both can be true. I can be societally privileged and still suffer. I'm not the voice of a generation and I never believed I was, but the label was stuck onto me and I didn't question it. My privilege, access and education are what encouraged people to hail me as such a person in the first place, despite being so new to Wonderland. I was accepted into its elite entourage a lot faster than others. And again, I never questioned it. I've now been on the other side of my own shadow, the receiving end of bitterness, of moral righteousness, and I've been forced to face how ugly I can be. I speak now because I can. And I'm doing it with the anger of all the women whose stories were told incorrectly. This is for them.

I don't hate you. *I am you.* I see myself in every single one of you. There's an invisible world that exists within the one we all see, a wavelength where you can hear the haunting cries and screams of women who've been placed on a hidden frequency. Like a secret number on the radio that no one knows about until it happens to you too. I've tuned into all these women and I'm pouring out their cries. I offer my digital flesh to you all, to expose the truth.

DIRECTOR'S NOTE
Eartha walks over the cables, towards the camera and the crew, de-mics and asks, 'Did we get it?'
The post goes viral under the username:
E.V in Wonderland
#Girlcrush
ENDS

Wonderland existed 2018–2030

EPILOGUE

THE ONLY THING THAT WAS REAL

My feet carry me quickly to her flat before I allow any doubt to overpower my instincts. I almost don't recognise her front door as she's painted it pink. I stand in front of it and mourn the life that could have been: the two of us finding the right pink by looking through colour wheels together and cosplaying a married suburban couple in the homeware store. The beauty of the mundane experiences we could have had and not even thought to romanticise until later on. I wonder if I would romanticise the experiences as much if we were together, or if they're only so rosy because she's something I can no longer taste, feel or touch. I'm jealous of everyone that has seen her since she disappeared from my life. Every person that has looked into her eyes as they served her coffee, every small dog she has stroked, every customer at her job. I am jealous of them all. I wonder if the mirrors she looks into know how lucky they are to be graced by her reflection.

'Eartha?'

Fuck!

I jump back from the door and turn around. She's standing at the bottom of her stoop wearing an oversized blazer with a hoodie underneath, carrying a tote bag on each shoulder. I don't think I've ever seen her hair this bright before. I've also never seen her dress this casually before. She's out of breath and looks as though she's been in a rush. A sheen of sweat glistens across her upper lip, mirroring the morning dew in the patch of grass beside her.

'What are you doing . . . staring at my flat?' she asks in a slightly accusing tone.

Her *voice,* it's been so long. I've forgotten everything. Including what I came here for.

'I was walking past and saw you painted your door!' I say, yanking at a knot in the back of my hair.

She raises an eyebrow. I release my tight shoulders and drop down in the entrance of her doorway.

'Actually, I was wondering if we could talk, maybe?' I ask, not meeting her gaze.

There's a tense pause as she seems to be trying to understand what I am saying. The strap of the tote on her left shoulder falls and she scoops it back up with annoyance. Her eyes focus on me once more, as though she is trying to place my face. It's like she's looking at a ghost, as though she can't believe I'm still alive.

'I need to talk to you about . . . us, and . . . everything you've probably read about me everywhere,' I carry on.

She seems to deflate a little as she climbs up to the top step of the stoop, letting her tote bags puddle around her feet.

'Go on then,' she says evenly, taking a seat next to me.

A silence drifts between us, interrupted by the chirping birds.

'So—'

'Wha—'

There's a pause.

'Your hair looks nice,' I say meekly.

'Thanks,' she says, accepting my basic and awkward compliment.

We both gaze down at the moss-covered step.

'Phaedra, I have so much to tell you.'

'Me too.'

'Really?!'

'I stopped texting you. It was a dick move.'

'Wait, you think *you're* the dick?'

'No, I never said that . . . it was a dick . . . *reaction.*'

She looks back at the floor.

'It's so fucking embarrassing to say out loud.'

She crosses her arms, scratches her forearms with her fingernails.

'You probably didn't notice, but I unfollowed you on Wonderland a couple of weeks ago.'

'Didn't notice!' I exclaim.

'Well, yeah, your life has been hectic . . .'

'Despite the craziness of my life, that was actually the worst fucking thing to happen,' I reply.

'Really?'

'Yes.'

'But you've been through hell.'

It's oddly comforting to know that she's been paying attention to my life. I want to open up to her and tell her everything – the exact kind of hell that I've been through – but I don't know whether I can trust her. What if she's going to write something about me online after this, like the rest did? What if this is all just salacious intel to her?

'Oh, you noticed?' I blurt out defensively.

'Yeah. I mean, you've been kind of hard to avoid; I can overhear customers discussing you at work like you're some celebrity or whatever and it's so . . . annoying . . . Well, no, it's actually hard. I was trying to forget about you, to be honest . . . but, did you really mean that?'

'Mean what?'

'Us not working out, you regret it?'

'Everything else that I have lost – my reputation, my connections, my platform, whatever – none of it was ever real. So yes, you cutting me out like that was absolutely the hardest thing of all, because you were the only thing that I wanted. Because *we* were the only thing that was real.'

Her face relaxes and starts to soften.

'I wouldn't call it cutting you out . . .'

'Well, what do you call it then, if not "cutting out"?' I snap back at her.

'A soft . . . ghosting?'

'Like that's any better?'

'Eartha, I've tried to stop thinking about you. Those pictures that went round of your room, with that . . . girl. I felt rejected and so . . . humiliated. I kind of suspected you might be dating other people, I get that we're in our twenties, we're single, I don't own you . . .' Her voice wanders off.

'I know all that stuff, but part of me wanted to believe that you couldn't possibly be how *we* were together . . . with anyone else . . .'

'Well, I—'

'Let me finish, I've rehearsed this in my head quite a few times,' she says abruptly. She's been *rehearsing*? My heart shoots into my stomach as my mind flicks through worst-case scenarios. I so badly want to interrupt her and set her straight but I don't want to drive her further away.

'Anyway, I felt stupid for being so upset because we'd only had a handful of dates . . . maybe you just didn't feel the same way and I got invested too soon. Everywhere I look, there you are. It's annoying. I can't even take my fucking socks off without looking at my toes and remembering how they fit between yours . . .'

I try to soak in her words so I can process them. Have we both been feeling the exact same way this whole time? Right down to the same intimate fucking details? Are these words actually coming out of her mouth or am I imagining them? Is this just what I want to hear? I resist the urge to scream. Surprisingly, I feel rage, not peace. I can feel the anger rising up faster and faster inside me, as though the lost time we could have spent together is the worst of all my recent injustices. I feel annoyed at her, but also horrified at the self-pity I've been wallowing in, now that I know she felt the same this whole time. I don't know what to do with my bitterness. All of those weeks spent moping about my flat, when she was doing the same? I need someone to blame.

She's still talking.

Explaining.

I can see she's becoming more and more desperate. But all I can focus on is the new knowledge that Phaedra – the girl who has haunted my life since she left it – still cares about me. She *really* fucking cares. I feel an urge to lunge forward and defend myself in anger but also to make her stop talking so I can tell her how desperately I have wanted her too. I'm not sure if she wants to be heard or reassured.

'I just . . . you probably mean a lot to me since I can't stop thinking about you and yeah . . . anyway, I'm rambling . . .'

I can see the anxious thought process whirling behind every word and I want to rescue her, put out the fire of her doubts. She looks off to the side, her gaze avoiding mine.

But I'm suddenly reminded of her cool detachment. The complete abandonment. The ignored messages. Her unfollowing me when I needed her most. She did all of this while knowing the rumours circling about me. How could she do that? How could she believe them? If she cared, why would she do that?

'Did you not think for a second to ask me how I'm doing?' I quip.

'Is that all you care about?' she asks, laughing with shock.

'I have had the world talking about me for the past few weeks . . .'

'The world?' she laughs again, incredulous.

'You know what I fucking mean, I've had what felt like the world talking about me, the girl I am obsessed with ignoring me and having no clue where I stand with her. I've been slowly losing my sanity and my friends; how do I know if I can even trust you?'

'Eartha, how the fuck was I supposed to read your mind? How was I supposed to know you've been . . . struggling? With anything? Please, try to see it from my point of view, or tell me what's been going on.'

She looks at the floor.

'What does Rose have to say about it all?' she asks me, and my stomach does a little flip at the sound of their name.

'I haven't spoke to them in a while.'

'Why? Rose loves you; what happened?'

We hear the screech of a window opening above our heads and look up. It's one of her flatmates, sticking her head out of the window.

'Phaedra, can you—' She pauses and puckers her face when she recognises me.

'Eartha? Is that fucking . . . *Eartha*? Phaedra, what the hell is she doing here?'

She won't even look at me or address me; I feel like the same non-person I did hours before. The ghost stuck in the machine. Not a physical being at all.

'Can you ask her to leave, please?'

'Sal, what the fuck? Be cool,' Phaedra pleads.

An adjoining window now opens and a much older woman appears in her dressing gown and a sleeping mask and screeches, 'KEEP IT DOWN!'

I look around at the chaos caused by my presence. It appears that all I seem to do these days is wreak havoc. I have so much to do, so much to clear up, to resolve. I feel the weight of it pressing down on me. It takes up all the available air. Phaedra whispers an apology to her neighbour with a warm smile before glaring back up at Sal. They both close their windows and Phaedra puts her hand softly over my shaking one.

'You know, I still have your Velvet Underground shirt,' she says, as though nothing just happened, or perhaps there is a searing-hot rage just one millimetre below the surface.

'Oh, yeah?'

'It's inside . . .'

She releases my hand and gestures to the front door behind her. I take a breath. Close my eyes and feel the space between us. I lock out everything else around us. Everything that has come before and everything that might come next.

My voice falters as it tries to formulate the words that I want to land in the right place, to the right woman, at the right time.

'Phaedra, I came here to apologise to you and explain what's been happening. Yes, I'm being defensive and it's all become so . . . messy. But let me be clear . . .'

I swallow before continuing.

'I like every single thing about you. Every inch, every bit of mess, every beautiful thought and every troubling one that races around your mind,' I say.

Our eyes meet and hers are as wet as mine.

'Truth be told, it's sort of embarrassing, Eartha . . . I've been wearing your T-shirt online, hoping you might see it,' she says, laughing with warmth this time. I try to silence my ego, annoyed she hasn't responded directly to my vulnerable outpouring. I crack a smile and we both erupt into laughter. The walls of caution around me melt. I feel closer to her again.

'Do you know the extremes I've gone to, trying to get your attention?'

'Doing everything except actually messaging me and telling me how you feel?' I snap.

'Eartha . . .' she laughs.

'I don't know why I'm being like this, I'm just . . .'

I start tapping my foot.

'I'm just hurt and frustrated that we've both been feeling the same way and neither of us did anything.'

'Exactly, neither of us. Please put yourself in my position! You felt . . . unapproachable. I thought you'd moved on.' She continues, telling me how humiliating it was that everyone she had told about us, her friends and family, saw me with someone else. That she too felt publicly embarrassed in her own way. I can't believe I'd been so absorbed by my own world that I hadn't considered Phaedra's humiliation. She stops to look up at me. 'But now . . . having seen the chaos of the last few days, I've started to feel like a dick. I kept seeing people saying all of this crazy stuff about you . . . I felt like I should have been there for you or at least asked how you were doing. It was pretty convenient for me to just believe it all. But then I saw that video, last night, the one of you at that party . . .'

She points to her bag, I assume her phone is inside it.

'It's become a bit of a witch hunt, hasn't it?'

She looks at me and squints her eyes. 'As painful as this is to admit, Eartha, I do still want you.'

I wanted to be the one to say it first. How is it possible that she is saying everything I want her to say and yet I still see her as one of *them*? My anger surprises me and I'm not sure which emotion to endorse. I want to be on the other side of my anger. To believe her. But something is stopping me from absorbing it all. It feels like I'm encased in the barbed wire of my emotions; whichever way I twist causes me pain.

'Phaedra, I d—'

She grabs my face with both of her hands and looks at me deeply.

She pinches my cheeks playfully and for a second I float.

'I like all of you, too. And I want you. All of you.'

We hold each other's gaze. She hadn't swept my words under a rug. They weren't insignificant. She just wanted hers to have their own moment, too. I think she's about to kiss me but her gaze lowers down into her lap as she releases my face and then turns to look out at the road, with a smile. My mouth is still open and I close my eyes, relishing the warmth lingering on my puckered cheeks from her hands. Is that the sun? I open my eyes, squinting slowly just to check. Her eyes are closed; she's still facing the road, basking in the sunlight. With her eyes closed, I have the luxury of watching her. I look closer and see that small droplets of dew have formed on the tips of each of her eyelashes. In this moment I have never wanted to kiss her more. My anger dissolves, transmuted through the power of the sun. A voice inside of me tells me that this is the most heavenly moment of my life. I reach out to touch her hand to bring her attention to me, she turns around, squinting in the rays of the sun, and I pull her in closer. She strokes my cheek and I hers. I take a deep breath.

'Phaedra . . .'

'Yes.'

'Can I tell you what I came to say now? Everything?'

She smiles, cheek to cheek.

'God, please do.'

ACKNOWLEDGEMENTS

My literary agent and friend Abigail Bergstrom for believing I have what it takes to write a book in the first place and for holding me up when I needed it the most. Neither of my books would exist without your belief, tough love and persistence that I have something to offer the world.

My ridiculously talented editor Romilly Morgan, who's so smart it's intimidating – I don't know where this book would be without your support and guidance. I've never worked with someone so fiercely devoted to making sure she gets the best out of her authors. I've grown so much as a writer from working with you and I'm eternally grateful.

My parents for always being so fucking supportive of a career that they don't understand. My mum for listening to me describe every slight plot change over FaceTime and my dad for his sage advice and annoyingly accurate analogies for trusting the process when I'm feeling overwhelmed by stress. You both remind me I was built for bigger things and that the lid on my potential is uncapped.

My managers Justin and Kim for being much more than a management team to me. For caring about my happiness above all else while ensuring I make the right decisions for my career. Your belief in me has carried me over the years and I am so grateful to you both.

My assistant Courtney for every single small consideration you took to make writing this book easier. I've never been so glad to welcome a person into my life and onto my team.

The marketing team at Octopus for making sure everything runs smoothly behind the scenes, for the weekly zoom calls and for working with someone who loathes self-promotion. Also to Mel and Jaz at Octopus for working with my editor's genius idea that came to her on the bus, to create the cover. And to Pauline for the weekend editing.

To my friends who have encouraged me to see my vision for the novel through, and also tempted me to join them on nights out to live deliciously right before my deadlines.

Finally, to readers of *Women Don't Owe You Pretty* for the support and encouragement. I am eternally grateful you think I'm someone worth listening to and I promise to never take that responsibility lightly.

ABOUT THE AUTHOR

Florence Given is an international bestselling author based in London. Her work confronts oppressive attitudes towards women and their bodies. An artist and illustrator, she also uses her platform to raise awareness of issues surrounding sexuality, consent and gender. Her debut book *Women Don't Owe You Pretty* was a record-breaking bestseller and has sold half a million copies across all formats. *Girl Crush* is her first novel and became an instant *Sunday Times* bestseller.

This **brazen** book was created by

Publishing Director: Romilly Morgan
Senior Editor: Pauline Bache
Art Directors: Jaz Bahra and Mel Four
Typesetter: Jeremy Tilston
Production Controller: Lisa Pinnell
Sales: Kevin Hawkins, Marianne Laidlaw,
Isabel Tinkler
Rights: Ros Webber
Publicity: Megan Brown
Marketing: Matthew Grindon
Legal: Nicola Thatcher